Cold Steel . . .

Bloody Sword's large, sun-darkened fist slammed the factor's table so fiercely that the mate nearly dropped his cargo manifest.

The factor, on the other hand, neither blinked nor stood. "My father cheats no one," he answered. "He digs a certain kind of rock from deep in the earth, which takes much labor, and turns it into steel, which takes more. He makes swords for your tribe—more work—and has it carried to you on a trip of many days across stormy water. Then he trades it to you for trees which we cut down and take away without effort of your people."

Abruptly the warrior drew his sword and pointed it at the factor's chest. "Your father cheats us," he snarled. "My brother demands to be shown how to make our own steel!"

The factor leaned back, folding his arms across his stomach. Very carefully, very deliberately he answered, "Bloody Sword, leave this dwelling and do not come back. Tell your brother to send some—"

Seeming to take even Bloody Sword by surprise, the thirty-inch blade darted through the base of the factor's throat. Blood spurted as he crashed over backward in his chair. The mate screamed. For just a moment, Bloody Sword stared chagrined at his weapon, as if it had played him false. . . .

THE LANTERN OF GOD

JOHN DALMAS

THE LANTERN OF GOD

A Baen Books Original

Baen Publishing Enterprises
260 Fifth Avenue
New York, N.Y. 10001

First printing, May 1989

ISBN: 0-671-69821-4

Cover art by Larry Elmore

Distributed by
SIMON & SCHUSTER
1230 Avenue of the Americas
New York, N.Y. 10020

This story is dedicated to
Jim Baen
for his years of encouragement

And while I'm at it, I'd like to acknowledge three persons who've influenced this and other stories of mine:

Rod Martin (with whom I co-authored THE PLAYMASTERS) for his interesting ideas and work in metaphysics and metapsychology.

Bill Baillie for access to his personal library, his advice on matters technical, and his manuscript critiques.

And **Gail** for her manuscript critiques and her understanding tolerance of, for example, my strange working hours (like all night when I'm on a roll). It's interesting how many SF writers share life with a truly outstanding spouse.

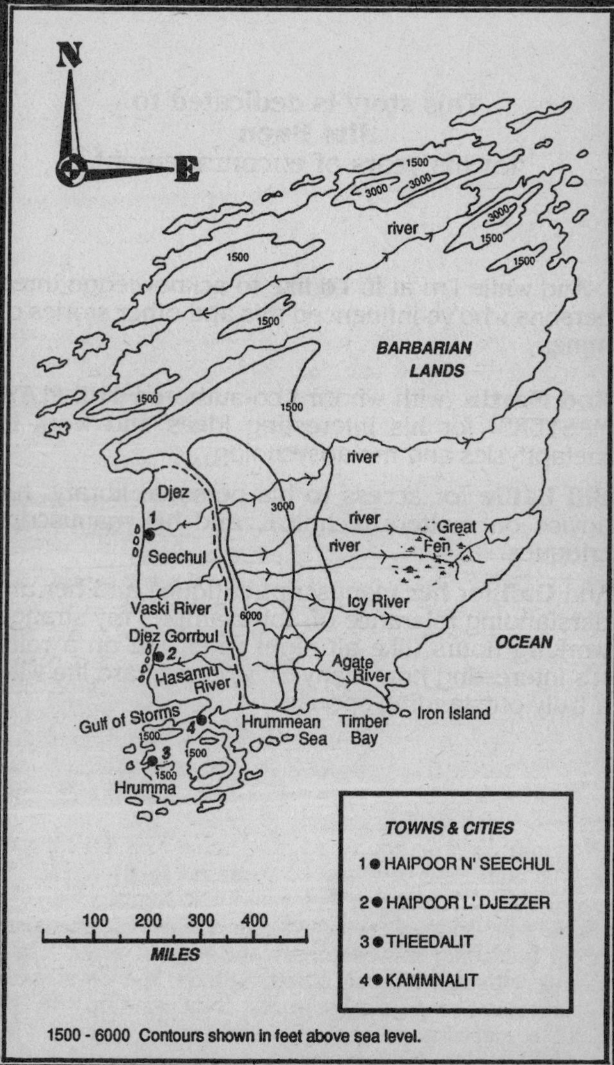
N
E
1500
3000
3000
3000
1500
river
1500
1500
1500
1500
BARBARIAN
LANDS
1500
1500
river
Djez
3000
river
1
Great
Fen
Seechul
river
Icy River
Vaski River
6000
Djez Gorrbul
2
OCEAN
Agate
River
Hasannu
River
Iron Island
Gulf of Storms
4
Hrummean
Sea
Timber
Bay
1500
3
1500
1500
Hrumma
TOWNS & CITIES
1 HAIPOOR N' SEECHUL
2 HAIPOOR L' DJEZZER
3 THEEDALIT
4 KAMMNALIT
100
200
300
400
MILES
1500 - 6000 Contours shown in feet above sea level.

FOREWORD

Writers don't want glitches in their stories, so we're likely to ask friends to read and comment on a prefinal draft, to uncover possible problems. Two friends suggested that a list of characters be provided with this story; you'll find it at the end. One also pointed out that some readers might have trouble because of a common cultural mindset. (I suspect that rather few would who are frequent science fiction readers, but some readers may who are new to SF or read it infrequently.) So I'm going to talk about it up front.

In the United States, our sense of the rates and synchronicity of changes tends to reflect how things developed in North America and western Europe. These things are not hard-wired into either the physical universe or the human species. Some cultures have changed very slowly. Many remained in the stone age till the last century, and some till this century, emerging from it only through contact with technically advanced cultures. Although their people demonstrated innate intelligence comparable to that of the Europeans and Americans who broke their isolation.

Writings from antiquity reflect minds and thinking not basically unlike our own, and certainly not inferior. They just worked with different data bases and viewpoints.

Some past cultures developed considerable technologies in certain fields and missed others entirely. In some oriental cultures, although millenia passed without the development of comprehensive physical sciences, they came up with considerable empirical technologies and highly cultivated arts and philosophies. It's interesting to contemplate what those cultures would eventually have come to be if they hadn't been impacted by aggressive western nations with their growing experimental sciences.

It's also interesting to consider what sort of civilizations might develop in the absence of fossil fuels, for example, or in the absence of iron ore. They'd be different from ours, beyond a doubt.

The exploration of ideas and unfamiliar permutations are things that science fiction does very well. It's a specialty of the field.

Finally, some readers might wonder about two languages (Hrummean and Djezian, in the story) being similar enough that, knowing one, you could rather quickly become competent in the other, yet different enough that at first one could be utterly unable to understand it. As a merchant seaman, I once sailed with a guy newly from Aberdeen, Scotland, and at first encounter I truly had no idea it was English he was speaking! Also, with a modest competence in Swedish, I found I could *read* Danish without too much difficulty, but not understand a word when it was spoken to me.

And with that, let's roll the story. I hope you have as good a time with it as I did.

Prolog

Heskil Brant pressed the security plate. Inside, the bridge lights came on, and the door slid open with a faint hiss. She went in, limped to the contoured captain's chair, and heavily, tiredly, lowered herself onto it. The wrap-around window she left opaqued, its default state; she wanted the sense of solitude—had earned it these past days.

The door she left open, the last valve in a series that would let in outside air.

Brant hadn't always been captain, or even a licensed officer. She'd hired on the WS *Adanik Larvest* as G-4 Life Support Technician (biologist), and for that final trip, acting supercargo. That had been long ago. For the last eight years she'd been the ranking survivor. And throughout their twenty-nine years stranded here, she'd been one of the most important, because like small cargo ships in general, the *Larvest* carried no physician. In the merchant service, biologists were cross-trained to treat the ill and injured.

With the computerized clinic, that treatment would ordinarily have been entirely adequate; on the rare occasions when it wasn't, you could put the patient in a stasis chamber till you got to port somewhere, to a doctor. But here, unknown viruses and bacteria had adapted to the crew, over the years, and the clinic wasn't programmed for unknown diseases. The best it could do, with her help, was treat the symptoms and ease the discomfort, which by itself had repeatedly saved lives. The stasis equipment hadn't been used because they weren't going anywhere—this was the end of the road—and the engineer had been against using the backup power system to run it.

Thus she'd presided over too many deaths, including four of the six children she herself had borne on this world, and two of her four grandchildren. But she was tough. Only the tough—a few of the tough—were still alive.

She touched the key that powered the vocator, and spoke instructions to the computer, then sat silent for a moment, gathering her thoughts. Since Captain Terlenter had died, two others had been captain, but neither had extended Terlenter's side project: He'd dictated a brief history, or most of one, of the sector of space they'd come from. For the generations to come, who would know only this world, who would never even know anyone that remembered. Then the great puking fever had visited, and Terlenter had been the first adult to die. Briskom and Walter hadn't followed through on it. There was always so much else to do, more immediate, more survival-oriented. And writing, even by vocator, was a difficult—an unnatural—activity for some. For many. It was as if they retained no subroutine for it; had to program it anew each time.

Terlenter had gotten as far as the beginning of their own voyage. It had started innocuously enough—a small cargo ship with a crew of nine men and six women, and a cargo of 600 pleasure droids in stasis. Then the war had begun, the sector-wide megawar that everyone had feared and been telling each other could never happen. A war with planet busters. So Terlenter had sent them hurtling outward. That much was already on "paper."

Heskil had taken the story from there, reciting slowly and reflectively to the computer, which extruded a slow succession of printed sheets as she talked. The *Adanik Larvest* hadn't stopped fleeing till they were well outside human-occupied space. Then, as they hunted for a new home, a patrol had challenged them, three tall, asymmetric ships like neo-baroque sculptures of scrap metal, rods, and wire. The holo plate had shown beings horned and leathery, who'd called themselves something like "Garth." Quickly enough, their computers had learned to talk with each other, and the garths had ordered the humans to leave their sector, then gave them boundary coordinates and let them continue.

Outside garthid space, this had been only the third system they'd explored—a type-G bachelor sun with twelve planets, not an uncommon assemblage. One of the planets had displayed habitable parameters in terms of gravity, mass, and solar constant. Optically they could see blue ocean, white clouds, thirteen percent land surface. . . . Probes told them the chemistry was right, including the biochemistry, as mankind had learned to expect of worlds where the physics was right.

From there, she'd told how they'd selected a homesite, on the major island of a large archipelago where the life forms suggested there'd be little or no predator trouble. How they'd unloaded the droids on a continent a third of a planetary circumference away because they'd had no way to program them, then returned to the selected colony site. And how the matric tap had blown on landing, leaving them with only the emergency power system. That had been enough to power the computer, and some ship's accessories including the clinic and lab, but not the complete life support system. They were lucky the local fauna was edible and initially trusting.

The last time she'd dictated, she'd started on the history of the colony itself. They'd named it Almeon, after a mythical island. It would have been a happier history if they'd been trained and equipped for colonization. Instead it had been a matter of cope, struggle, and innovate. The standard ship's library tank, so often ridiculed by spacemen, had proven a lifesaver.

And they, from a planet that had long controlled birth privileges, had reinstituted an ancient imperative: "Be fruitful and multiply!" But their gene pool, tiny to start with, had shrunk from illness and accident. Thus rigid breeding rules had been laid down and enforced, to restrict as much as possible the homozygosity of any lethal and sublethal genes.

Today she continued the history with the first birth on the new world, took it through the first plague, then went on to the first successful forging of local iron, while the silent printer filled sheets with her words, depositing them on the stack in the receiver.

While she'd dictated, her aging muscles had grown tight and sore, and getting up from the seat, she rotated her shoulders to loosen them. It occurred to her then that there was only one copy of the history. True it was nonflammable, the paper-like material extremely durable, the printing integral within it. But she decided that before she left that day, she'd instruct the computer to produce additional copies of the story, one for each family in the colony.

Already the children, and to a degree the adults born on this world, lacked a strong sense of their roots. Even within sight of the 285-foot hull-metal cylinder of the *Larvest*, the problems of primitive colonization coerced the attention, capturing and narrowing one's sense of what was real and important. Even, mostly, her own. It was time for the handful of surviving crew, those whose eyes were still good enough, to start reading the history aloud to the children and grandchildren. Or the native-born adults could read them, those who read well enough, and the elders could explain, clarify, elaborate.

Then, as she was sitting back down, the wall luminosity went out. The codes disappeared from the suddenly unseeable computer screen—and the door hissed shut behind her. She knew instantly what had happened, felt her skin crawl cold and pebbly, and got up again, groping her way through the utter dark toward the bulkhead and doors behind her.

The doors would not budge, and for a moment bile rose in her throat. She fought it down. They'd assumed that someday the emergency power would fail, perhaps in a century or so when the fuel slug was exhausted, perhaps sooner when some other element in the system failed. But it had never occurred to her that the doors, this door, were held open by some mechanism and would close if the power went off.

Again she groped in blackness, looking for something to pry with. All she found was a stylus at the command console, and tried futilely to insert it in the thread-thin space between the doors. That failing, somehow the incipient panic died, leaving her mind clearer than it had been for decades, perhaps ever. She conjured in it the layout of the bridge, looking for a way out—something, anything. If only she had light! She felt for the rocker switch that so many times before had de-opaqued the windows, but when she pressed it, nothing happened.

There should, it seemed to her, be a way out of the ship, a manual override. Otherwise, a ship without power in space couldn't even open its lifeboat ports. But she was no engineer—they hadn't had one for eight years—and nothing came to her.

Still, she would miss no bets. Idly she felt over keypads, knowing from memory what most of the keys did, had done.

Now they did nothing. The console was lifeless. Dead. The whole ship was dead. And if there was a way out of the corpse, she didn't know of it.

In her mind she computed the approximate air volume of the bridge, allowing for equipment, multiplying by twenty-four percent to get the oxygen content. But she couldn't take her computations further because she didn't know the rate her breathing would remove it. She supposed she had an hour or more. Perhaps several.

Mentally she shrugged. She'd lived sixty-four standard years. On this world, that was old. And it would be an easier death than most. Easier than her husband's had been, her children's. It was time, she told herself, for a well-deserved rest.

A little later it occurred to her to wonder if, in a millenium or ten, one of their descendants would reinvent the electric generator. And if, sometime after that, someone would couple a cable to an external service jack, open the ship and find "the book." It seemed almost bound to happen, in time, if the colony survived.

What would she look like then? A skeleton, its fat flesh long gone. More important, what would *they* look like then? With a gene pool no larger than theirs, there'd be genetic drift. Would they still know Interspeak? Hardly. Their language would evolve. But if they retained writing, it might not change too much for the book to be deciphered.

Meanwhile they'd get along without knowing their cultural roots, their history. They'd grow, setting new roots wide and deep. It was what this planet required of them.

She reclined her chair a bit—interesting that that was manually controlled—and let her eyes close, let her thoughts idle, almost as if rehearsing death. After a little while she went to sleep, perhaps to work out old dreams.

One

The *Emperor Dard XII* was fifty-five days east of Larvis Harbor, and Elver Brokols was fifty-four days past his time of seasickness. The morning was fair, as most had been, and a brisk breeze out of the southwest drove them smartly eastward, canvas straining, ropes creaking in blocks and deadeyes.

Now and then a pack of water people swam briefly alongside, keeping pace easily, their sleek, dark-furred bodies forming something akin to sine curves, breaking the surface and often clearing it. Their arms lay snug along their sides, their broad planing fins veed back, powerful tails and flukes driving. Brokols wondered what it would be like to be one of them, to swim like that and seem so carefree. He felt guilty at the thought. Because the water people neither toiled nor laid away for the future—at least not that anyone knew of.

But they were said to be intelligent, supposedly approaching man in that highest of attributes.

And a bit ago, just after breakfast, Brokols had glimpsed a sea serpent raise its head briefly above water to peer at the ship from a hundred yards off. Interesting, those serpents. They weren't native to the ocean around Almeon, nor had the first expedition, in its time, reported them from these eastern waters. Nor had this expedition seen one until the previous day, when suddenly they'd been numerous. Some large ones had made bold to swim close alongside, raising their heads higher than the rail, as if curious, and it had seemed to Brokols that the eyes which met his had been intelligent.

But they'd made him nervous. Their long, toothed jaws had made everyone nervous, and the captain had ordered the gunners to shoot one, some fifty or sixty feet off the starboard bow, with one of the ship's two swivel guns. The four-pound explosive round had struck what he thought of as the shoulders just below the serpentine neck, and a great gout of blood and flesh had erupted. Soon after, another serpent had swum close alongside, barely awash, a hump-like wave rising over its back. Three marines had thrown grenades as it drew alongside, so that it sank from sight in a great cloud of blood, food for the sarrkas now. Unless its own kind ate it first; he saw no sign of that.

Since then no serpent had come near, nor raised its head for a more distant look for longer than brief seconds, as if somehow they'd communicated the danger, passed it on ahead. For a time, even the water people had kept their distance. And it occurred to Elver Brokols that the captain, in his nervousness, may have made an enemy for Almeon.

The thought was absurd, of course.

Comfortable reclining chairs had been set out for Brokols and the several other official passengers; each had his own. He went now to his, took a book from his pocket and sat down. He'd barely opened it to the marker when the lookout on the masthead cried: "Land ho!"

Brokols looked up; the man was pointing almost dead ahead. Two other men, including the bosun, started up the ratlines to see for themselves. "Describe it!" the captain shouted.

" 'Tis a headland showing! A hill or mountaintop! About two points off the port bow!"

Brokols got quickly to his feet and hurried to tell the other mission personnel, tucking the book in his coat pocket without regret. He'd read it several times before. A short companionway led one deck down to a passageway, and he ducked to enter it, the tallest man aboard. At Lord Kryger's door he could hear the chief of mission drilling droid irregular verbs with his aide. Brokols knocked respectfully at the door, and when Kryger's sour voice answered, told him what the seaman had called down. Kryger, who'd been seasick since they'd left Almeon, growled acknowledgement.

Brokols went on to knock at Dixen's door and tell him. Then, after pausing at his own cabin to get his telescope, he went back on deck, Dixen a moment behind with book in hand, a finger holding his place. Moments later, Kryger's aide, a quiet and efficient commoner named Argant, followed, no doubt to keep Kryger informed.

There was nothing further yet to tell. Brokols considered climbing the rigging to see for himself, then thought better of it. He was only twenty-eight, active for his size, and as a youth had been considered remarkably strong. But it wouldn't do to seem impulsive. Or common. He'd learned both lessons long ago, more than once, and this was no place to forget them. Lord Kryger was not a tolerant man.

Captain Stedmer ordered the boiler fired; among much else, mission orders said they would approach the coast under steam to impress the droids. The mate who doubled as engineer, and one of the seamen who'd been trained to assist him, went aft to kindle fires in the fireboxes. The *Dard* had large bunkers in both sides, filled with charcoal, expensive but much more efficient of storage space than wood.

The headland grew till they could see it from the foredeck—a promontory, the culmination of a ridge. Brokols' telescope clearly showed a tower on the headland's highest point, which surely meant a town nearby. Probably the *Dard* had been sighted well before now. Across from that was another headland, lower, and between the two no doubt a harbor. By that time, a long thin train of black smoke trailed from the slender stack aft; in the boiler, the water would be hot, perhaps boiling by now. Argant went below to update Kryger, then came back on deck again.

Far to the south, white clouds were building vertically as if to rain. Soon they saw a sail, then a second and a third, fishing smacks perhaps, or small coastal haulers. According to the first expedition, the people on this continent had no large ships. A fifty-footer with a single thirty-foot mast was regarded here as large. The *Dard*, by contrast, measured 150 feet, bark-rigged with three tall masts.

Kryger came on deck, weak and pale, shrunken from his long near-fast, but no one to sneer at even covertly. Try as he had, Brokols could not like the chief of mission. Kryger was invariably cold and unpleasant toward him. The man's eyes had spoken disapproval at their first meeting, just after they'd been selected for this mission.

Brokols had wondered if perhaps Kryger's dislike was jealousy, a matter of family. The Brokols family was prominent, Kryger's of the lesser nobility. But then, Kryger didn't like Dixen either, and Dixen's family was no higher than Kryger's. Perhaps relative height accounted for some of it; Kryger didn't stand as high as Brokols' chin. Brokols and Dixen both were exceptionally tall, although Dixen's height was gangly. The first expedition had found that droids were considerably larger than humans, thus height had been a factor in appointing ambassadors.

But clearly not the principal factor. The chief of mission was undoubtedly qualified. He'd been on the army general staff for several years, and his dominating presence more than made up for less than normal height.

And Kryger's unadapting, unforgiving stomach had actually strengthened his image of indomitability. Brokols remembered how he'd felt himself, those first few hours at sea; Kryger had felt that way and worse for fifty-five days. Worse, because while Brokols had never been quite sick enough to vomit, Kryger could be heard puking and retching whenever the ship's motion worsened even a little. But whenever the chief of mission had appeared briefly, his flinty eyes, his clamped and lipless mouth, his gray, ever-bonier face had been hard and unrelenting. As it was now.

The three ambassadors—Kryger, Dixen, and Brokols—their aides in tow, gathered with Captain Stedmer. The captain knew the old expedition report as well as they, including the lengthy interviews with the learned slaves the King of Djez Gorrbul had given the first expedition as gifts, fifty-two years earlier.

Costly gifts it turned out, because of the plague they'd carried. In the three droids it had seemed a light cold, too mild to be the same illness that struck and decimated the crew a few days out. It would reap a terrible harvest across all the islands of Almeon. But the slaves had provided much information about the lands of the new continent, information far beyond what the expedition could ever have gained directly. And of course, the slaves had taught them the droid language, so different from Almaeic.

Now there was a vaccine. The ambassador's chests, like everyone's in Almeon, bore the scars of it, and of vaccines for older plagues.

There might, of course, be other droid plagues. The possibility had influenced the emperor's plan. This small mission would spend half a year in the droid lands, likelier a full year, before the army landed. If, during that time, any was infected by some serious disease, word would be wirelessed home, and the invasion postponed. But it seemed to Brokols that the history of his own land included almost every plague imaginable.

The headland grew bolder. Kryger agreed with the captain that this must be the coast of Hrumma, because of the tall hills. The Djezian coast, where the previous expedition had visited, was low and flat. Which meant that Brokols would be the first ashore, for he was to be the ambassador to Hrumma.

The captain ordered the electric generator activated, a small hydraulic turbine built against the hull, then ordered the sails furled; steam pressure was fast approaching the requisite 140 pounds per square inch. As seamen scrambled aloft, Kryger went forward to wireless the emperor's office and let him know they'd sighted the continent at last.

Brokols went to his cabin to secure his gear. It wouldn't take long; much of it had never been unpacked since they'd left Almeon.

Two

From *The Captain's Book*

You need to remember that droids are not human beings. Not that any of us were experts, but we'd all seen droids, and I'd read articles and watched study cubes on them in Genetic Engineering 415. Droids are close to human. They look human. But if you'd ever been around droids, you'd know the difference.

Droids have no parents. They don't grow from the fertilization of an ovum by a sperm. They are, or were, manufactured under imperial license, and develop in vats from raw, synthesized genetic material engineered to the legal specifications of the purchaser.

And a droid learns differently. It doesn't grow up over a period of years, learning in life and in child academies. Like a real person, the droid starts out with basic biological parameters programmed into their DNA. But that's just a small start. Then, in little more than two years, with exact electro-chemical stimulation, it develops to adult size still unconscious in the vats, and gets "primary nurture programming" imprinted into its unconscious mind during the last days before its removal. This imprinting includes basic Interspeak. So when it's taken from the vat, it is physically mature, but mentally it's more like a small child.

With one big difference. Unlike little children, droids have no personality; they are not persons. And under usual procedures they are still unconscious at that stage. Normally they get shipped to the purchaser in stasis. The purchaser gives them their function programming after delivery and immediately before removal from their stasis cocoons. Then, when wakened from their cocoons, they're already trained adults. Ordinarily.

Aboard the Larvest we had 600 of them in stasis, pleasure droids engineered to amuse: 500 females and 100 males designed and built to order for Hedone, a resort world. They looked very much like beautiful human beings, very aesthetic and guaranteed very healthy. But the ones we had only had primary nurture programming; in most respects they were mentally like sleeping three-year-olds who could understand basic speech. And we didn't have the equipment to give them function programming. If we had, it would have been an entirely different situation. But as it was, fifteen crew members would have had to bring up and educate what would amount to 600 less-than-human three-year-olds with fully-grown adult bodies and little social sense.

It would have been impossible. And it would have left us no time or energy to produce a livable environment on a raw new world. There wasn't even any way we could feed them for longer than a day or so.

So we offloaded them on the lesser continent. We wanted them to survive if they could, though that wasn't a high-priority consideration. The climate there was livable, and there seemed to be no life forms at all comparable in danger to the savage packs of predatory sauroids on the major continent. The AG dollies still worked then, the antigravity cargo handlers, and with them we unloaded the droids onto a large grassy meadow. Then we set the cocoon controls on wake.

One of the crew, a biotech named Lori Maloi, had asked to stay with them awhile and try to teach them enough to survive. Sweet, impractical Lori. And Captain Terlenter let her; I suppose he felt uncomfortable about dumping them. I helped her put together a survival chest, with a side arm for protection, and the captain said he'd send someone in a week to see *how things were, and to pick her up if she wanted. He couldn't know that, within three hours, we'd lose our flight capacity, including the ability to launch small craft.*

None of us, perhaps not even Lori, expected her to accomplish much with the droids. What we did expect was that they'd gobble up their emergency wafers the first day and then sit around, or maybe have an orgy, until they got hungry. After that they'd probably wander off and starve, or get killed by predators. And that's almost certainly what did happen. After all, they were pleasure droids, pleasure droids with the minds of little children.

And if some of them did survive for long, which is conceivable, the chances are they had no viable offspring. They were designed to perform sex, but engineering fertility into droids is somewhat tricky and very expensive; otherwise lethal flaws during the embryogenesis of prospective offspring are usual. And assuming these droids didn't come from a bootleg plant, or maybe even if they did, they were probably engineered to be sterile, to avoid the mental trauma of miscarriages, still-births, and defective infants. Most design approvals require it. After all, droids may not be human, but they are living, feeling creatures.

It was Festival in Hrumma, the Festival of the Serpents Returning, and the weather was beautiful, as always in that season. The city of Theedalit was ready, and lovely in the sun. The white walls of its buildings had been scrubbed, many whitewashed anew, their trim fresh-painted in gold or orange-red, blue or green or scarlet. The red and maroon tiles of cisterns, roof skirts and parapets gleamed in the sun. Fruit trees on roof tops glinted glossy green. Above windows and balconies, the colorful awnings had been scrubbed and often re-dyed, while below them, bunting draped white and red and blue. Above it all, vivid banners and pennants waved and fluttered proudly in the usual onshore wind of day, while around the perimeters, tall windmills, pride of the city, whirled long and colorful vanes in the same brisk breeze that made the pennants snap.

Country people, flocking to Theedalit afoot and on saddle

kaabors, in shays and carriages, stopped where the road overlooked the city, to absorb the vista, eyes watering at the glare from distant walls and windows.

The sidewalks too had been scrubbed, like most of the townspeople who walked them that day. Those who could afford it wore new clothes; most of the rest wore clean. Even the kaabors drawing ordinary carts wore collars of flowers, while those that drew the hansoms, carriages, and shays of the well-to-do most often wore embroidered caparisons, and feathers on their short-cropped horns. The rikksha men, glistening with sweat, wore their most vivid loinclothes, and long plumes of the riiki thrust into bright, knitted bands that kept the sweat from their eyes. At stands and racks in every alcove and on the very streets and sidewalks, artisans hawked jewelry, sometimes of silver, now and then of gold, though more often of simple copper or bronze, hammered, twisted, etched and polished, inset with semi-precious stones. People, mostly young to elderly couples, strolled and looked, dickered in good humor, and occasionally bought.

And there was much laughter, for though it was too early for the sale of wine and spirits, there was a sense of relaxed anticipation. On the opening evening of Festival, the amirr and the House of Nobles would stage a feast; the fire pits had been burning for a day already, while barrels waited in the deepest, coolest cellars of the Fortress to be brought up when the heat of day was past. And after the feast, there would be parties in gardens and courtyards, on terraces and rooftops. Few would sleep alone except by preference or incapacity.

The crowds could be heard from the balcony where the naamir sat with her son and youngest daughter. The youth, eighteen, lolled against cushions on a shaded couch. He was tall like his father, the amirr, and had his father's curly auburn hair. But he was still slender, and there was a catlike languor about him.

The girl, on the other hand, was somewhat small for a Hrummean, newly-turned sixteen and only now maturing physically. Standing by an easel, brush in hand, she frowned at an effect. Her subject was the lower reach of town, and the harbor; her treatment was impressionistic, a style she was just learning.

Her brother eyed it from where he reclined. "Don't ask me what I think of it," he drawled.

"I won't," she snapped.

He felt his mother's disapproving glance, and sniggered just short of audibility. Harassing his sister was a sport he'd enjoyed most of his life, not because he particularly disliked her but because she was available and usually reacted. He could no longer reduce her to tears, nor tried. His father's heavy hand had ended that years earlier. But he'd sensitized her enough that he could often anger or introvert her with little more than a word, occasionally a look.

The naamir laid down her embroidery and went over to examine the painting. "It seems to me you're making progress," she said.

The girl shook her head. "I can't get the effect I want—the sun sparkling on the water. And Allfon won't be back till after Festival."

Her brother brayed derisively. "Allfon! At least we don't need to worry that his hands will stray when he's working with you. He's likelier to make a try at me."

His mother's lips thinned. "Tirros Hanorissio," she said, "one more snide remark and your father will hear of it."

He lowered his eyes, neither sniggering nor smirking now. He knew his mother well: Normally her tolerance was greater than this, but she left little margin between threat and act. He remembered the last time she'd complained to his father, a year earlier. In angry exasperation, the amirr had grasped Tirros's narrow nose between strong thumb and forefinger and forced him to his knees. The next day, at weapons drill, Master Gorrik's wooden training sword had left the young mirj welted and discolored, and later in his suite, examining the bruises and abrasions in his dressing mirror, Tirros had wept with frustrated anger.

Remembering it, he lay imagining what he would do, someday, to Gorrik, avoiding for now thoughts of what he'd enjoy doing to his sister. Then faintly he heard a trumpet call from the main tower at the Fortress, seat of government in Hrumma. His immediate thought was that the first serpents had been seen entering the harbor, for this was the date it would happen, invariably did happen. But the Fortress bells did not begin the festive clamor that would proclaim their entry. Nor the measured resonant tolling of impending attack, a sound he'd heard at the biannual drills. This was a signal to alert the harbor defense flotilla, and the battalion of troops domiciled near the Fortress.

But an alert to what? Tirros got smoothly to his feet and went to the balustrade, his sharp eyes finding the watchtower on the hill above the harbor entrance. Three of its flagstaffs flew large flags, and even at this distance his sharp young eyes made out their colors. The first told him a foreign ship was coming, the second that it was a warship, and the third that only one had been seen. Without excusing himself, he turned and left the balcony. He'd stop for his sword, have a groom saddle his kaabor, then ride to the Fortress. Even now, someone at the watchtower would be fastening a message to the leg of a kiruu, to send it winging. More than one, in case a hawk should spy and catch the first enroute.

Something exciting, interesting at least, might finally be about to happen here. One could hope. At least it was more promising than the arrival of the sea serpents. That happened every year.

The great bells exulted in the Fortress's clock tower, bonging and clanging in an orgy of bronze sonority. The serpents had entered the harbor! Now the rains would begin, and the weather turn truly warm; the crops would grow, the orchards flower, and the nation continue to prosper.

In the great gate house, the Chamber of Ministers had wide, strong doors, hinged to move at a touch, giving onto the broad top of the Fortress wall. The amirr's personal secretary went over and pushed them to, then closed window shutters and drew their weather curtains, somewhat dulling the din. In the resulting semi-dark, conversation became practical again, but no one spoke.

His expression patient, the amirr waited for the clangor to still. At his back, a bit removed, stood guards, their presence a matter of protocol more than protection. Around the oval table sat the amirr's chief ministers and a few others. Most were dressed in ceremonial togas—all but the guards and the young Tirros—togas for official celebration. They'd gathered unexpectedly because of the strange ship approaching their shore.

Just before the bells had interrupted, old Viravvo had recalled from his youth, some five decades earlier, a story from Djez Gorrbul of such a ship landing there, with strange men whose speech no one understood. They had harmed no one or any thing, had presented gifts and received gifts in return, then departed westward, never to be seen again.

Their visit had been brief, the exchanges and impacts minor. Communication had been by simple gestures with simple content, and the whole affair had soon been forgotten.

After a long minute the bells stopped, leaving heads still ringing and hearing momentarily dimmed. The secretary drew back curtains, respread shutters and opened doors. Welcome yellow sunlight poured in. When the man was seated again, the amirr spoke.

"So. Seemingly such strangers will be entering our harbor, and on the same day as the serpents." He looked at his privy counselor. "Allbarin, could this be an omen?"

"I believe 'a beginning' comes closer than 'an omen,' " Allbarin answered.

"Perhaps," said a minister, "it has come from Djez Gorrbul, intending ill for us."

"Doubtful," said a third. "Gameliiu is an avaricious king but not a bold one. Certainly he has no ship of his own like that."

"If it's as large as it's said to be," put in another, "it could be full of hidden soldiers, intending to catch the city in Festival and the Fortress open."

The amirr turned to the guard captain in charge of the shift—Eltrienn Cadriio, a centurion in rank. Cadriio wore working uniform, legs bare and muscular between greaves and kilt, his bronze breastplate polished, the plume on his helmet fresh and bright. "Centurion," said the amirr, "how long ago was it that you left Haipoor l'Djezzer?"

"Four weeks, Your Lordship, and—two days."

"And you smelled no hint of war or other action against us, or of any such ship landing on their coast?"

"Correct, Your Eminence. The palace guard there hears and repeats many rumors. It would be astonishing if such plans or events went unremarked. My major problem as a spy was not acquiring information but sorting the true from the false. Their attention is currently on Djez Seechul and their disputed territory on the upper Vaski River."

The amirr turned to his privy counselor. "And Hrum has not whispered anything to you of their intentions?"

The counselor shook his head. "Nothing, Your Eminence."

"Well then." His gaze moved to an older man, robed but also helmeted. "General," he said, "the ship will surely enter our harbor. Why else would it be approaching? See that you have troops ready and visible, but not prominent and certainly not threatening. Commodore, have your flotilla manned, oars in place. Let the marines be ashore, at hand but out of sight, ready to board instantly should the trumpet signal." He looked around. "Allbarin has not divined an attack, and Eltrienn has not overheard of one, so we will not stand truculent. But neither will we ignore common caution.

"Does anyone have anything to add? Comments? Questions? Allbarin?"

The privy counselor nodded. "Your Eminence, from its course, if the vessel lands here—*when* the vessel lands here—a scanner should be gotten aboard it. Perhaps in the guise of a shipbuilder wishing to examine its construction."

"Of course." The amirr scanned the ministers. "Anything else? No? Then you may go, all but Trenno and Allbarin. I have things for you two to do." As in afterthought, he turned to his son, who stood behind him to his left. "Tirros, you stay too. I expect the foreigners will send a person of rank ashore, and I'll want you by me then. The experience may be valuable to you."

On the headland, some six hundred feet above the water, a crowd of half a thousand sat or stood in clusters, watching the great, tall ship as it neared the harbor's mouth. The grass beneath them was tawny dry, and the ground puffed underfoot wherever anyone walked. Yet the crowd was so intent on the vessel that few paid any attention at all to the rain-bringing serpents sporting in the harbor.

From time unremembered, the sea serpents had arrived at the summer solstice to give birth to their young. It was about the time when the tropical current, in its annual northward shift, filled the onshore airflow with warmth and moisture, destabilizing it. And the summer rains began.

One of the people watching was a man with dark stubble on his skull, and a thin beard streaked white. In general, the distant descendants of the droids had little facial hair, too little for an attractive beard. Thus in Hrumma, beards were exceedingly rare, and in general, reserved for sages or any who was called a sage. Those near the man kept glancing at him, as if hoping he'd speak, for when Panni Vempravvo said something, beyond a minimum of transactional communication, it could easily be valuable.

He spoke infrequently though, in public, and seldom went far from his cave. Just now he sat on the drought-crisped bunchgrass with his legs folded under him, his eyes calm and steady on the ship.

It had approached rapidly, without even a patch of sail, and seemed scarcely to slow as it entered the half-mile-wide Firth of Theed. A thin, mile-long streamer of black smoke trailed from a tall object near the stern, seemingly a kind of slender chimney, jutting up from a deckhouse. It was as if some great stove lay within, for some unfathomable purpose.

"Perhaps the ship is a giant crematorium," someone said.

"What purpose could there be in bringing a giant crematorium here?" asked another. Faces turned sober at the question. Someone suggested that Hrum, in his aspect of death-bringer, could be driving the ship; it could be coming to harvest the people of Theedalit. A third began to argue that the people of Theedalit and all of Hrumma followed the Way of Hrum better than any other people. A fourth interrupted to insist that it was exactly the self-righteous that deserved it most.

Panni Vempravvo's mouth opened and laughter pealed forth, a startling bell-like sound. Those who'd been arguing fell uncomfortably silent, reminded that argument had nothing to do with truth.

Near an edge of the crowd, standing instead of sitting, was another with a beard. His hair was blond, his thin beard curly and unabashedly red, his face unlined. He was surrounded by a small group of followers, country people by their traveling garb, all looking to have come a long way. Their faces bore smears of mud, a product of road dust and the wiping of sweat.

Occasionally a would-be sage, a "country sage," arose in the hinterland, and usually, city folk paid them only the respect of tolerance unless they proved themselves. Which happened seldom, especially away from the sea, for the sea was where Hrum's principal attention resided. In this one's entourage, though, were two who wore master's robes, which surely commended his claim.

Now, looking at no one, his eyes on the ship as it steamed up the firth, he spoke as if to himself, though his voice was loud and clear. The sentences were spaced apart, as if stating separate cognitions.

"The foreign vessel is no crematorium."

Faces turned to the country sage.

"Fire drives the ship, fire contained within an iron belly, and men cast charcoal into it."

Fire drives the ship? It seemed unlikely. And what kind of ship would be driven by fire?

"It has come from a land far west over the ocean, a land of which we've never heard."

A few faces looked openly dubious at this. The general view was that the ocean went on unbroken till it had gone full circle and met their own, opposite, eastern coast. Some of his listeners found questions rising, but they kept their peace for now. One did not interrupt a sage, or someone who might be a sage.

More than a few eyes had sought Panni Vempravvo, to see how he was receiving all this. Panni was watching the country sage, and his wide mouth smiled through the scant and drooping white-streaked mustache.

"The ship will leave an ambassador at the city," the country sage went on, "an ambassador from a great and distant king. And the great king intends ill for Hrumma."

Faces showed concern now, and alarm, and for the first time some showed clear rejection. No one wanted to believe this; historically kings had meant trouble. Hrumma had had kings itself, a long time ago, and after a period of turbulence, had discontinued the office. Also, for a few generations, more than a millenium past—an era storied for its oppressions—she'd been ruled by a series of foreign kings, of Djez Gorrbul.

"The ship will leave gifts, as well as an ambassador," the country sage continued. "And trouble will follow it here.

"And a bad sign will accompany its arrival."

Eyes went to the ship again, as if looking for the bad sign.

"Look!" someone shouted, pointing. Beneath the water, shadowy shapes showed suddenly, speeding seaward through the harbor mouth—long necks, oval bodies, tapering tails—perhaps two dozen of them. The sea serpents were leaving the firth!

There was no outcry, no jabbering, only momentary silence. Then Panni Vempravvo chuckled, nodding. The country sage turned his quiet, serious eyes to Panni without smiling, then bowed. Panni unwound his long thin legs, rising, and left with his followers. After a minute, the country sage and his people also left, in the tracks of the elder.

THREE

Seven hundred miles east-northeast of Theedalit, a more prosaic ship had docked, a lumber schooner. Ashore, in an office of a small residence, the sunlight through the door cut off, and Sallvis Venettsio looked up from the manifest the ship's mate had given him two minutes earlier. There'd been no sound of boots on the wooden porch, and now he saw why: It was a moccasined barbarian that stood looking in at him, one he didn't like but had to put up with.

"What brings you down the river, Bloody Sword?" Venettsio asked.

The broad, strong-framed warrior stepped inside and across to Venettsio's table, eyes and mouth hard, hostile. Two other warriors followed him. "Factor, another boat has come from your country. My brother demands to know what word your father has sent about teaching men to make steel."

"The news won't please Killed Many. My father sends word that he will send more swords and tools for your people, but he will not sell them the secret of making steel."

A large sun-darkened fist slammed down on the factor's table, making the mate jump. The factor, on the other hand, didn't blink. "Your father cheats us," the warrior snarled. "He knows we need swords, and would force us to buy from him!"

The factor did not get up. "Bloody Sword," he said calmly, "my father cheats no one. He takes rock from deep in the earth, which requires much labor, turns it into steel, which takes more. He makes swords for your tribe—more work—and sends them to you on a trip of many days across often stormy water. And trades them to you for trees which we cut down and take away without effort of your people. And charcoal made from trees, which we also make without effort of yours."

The warrior scowled. "Your father cheats us," he repeated. "We do not need to give you anything, or have anything to do with your womanly race. My brother demands to know how steel is made!"

The factor leaned back in his chair and spoke calmly. "Bloody Sword, you are a man of ugly words. I will be glad to speak with your brother, but I will no longer speak with you."

Their eyes locked, blue on blue. Then abruptly the warrior's sword was in his hand, pointed at the factor's chest. "You will speak with whoever my brother chooses to send, or you will speak no more. And my brother has sent me!"

The factor's arms were folded across his stomach. Very carefully, very deliberately he answered: "Bloody Sword, leave this dwelling and do not come back. Tell your brother to send some . . ."

With a thrust that seemed to take even Bloody Sword by surprise, the thirty-inch blade darted at the factor, stabbing him through the base of the throat. Blood spurted as the factor crashed over backward in his chair. The mate screamed. For just a moment, Bloody Sword stared chagrined at his weapon, as if it had played him false. Then he snapped a brief order to the two warriors with him, and turning, they left. The mate stared bulge-eyed after them, till after a long half minute he left too, hurrying to find the deputy factor.

Four

Sea lokkras wheeled and swooped on pointed wings, their high-pitched piping seeming too thin for so large a bird. *A different species than at home,* thought Elver Brokols. *White instead of gray, and larger*. He was expecting the differences to be bigger, eight thousand miles from home.

He stood at the rail a little aft of the bow, a place where he supposed he'd be out of the way. Glembro Dixen stood a pace or two aft of him. The ship's engine had stopped, its vibration stilled, and they continued on momentum, slowing gradually.

Both men gazed up the firth toward the town that climbed the sloping valley at its head. A sizeable town, but Brokols didn't think of it as a city, never imagined it to be much the largest in Hrumma. A town. In Almeon, Larvis Royal, Larvis Harbor, and numerous others were many times larger, with buildings much taller, far more massive, decorated with statuary, elaborate filigree, gold plate. This town, whatever its name was, looked nothing like any of them.

But to Elver Brokols it was very beautiful. It seemed to him he'd like it here.

He looked around him. Dixen, and those seamen who were not actively engaged in some duty of the moment, were also gazing at it, some impressed, some simply curious. Kryger too was on deck to watch, as if already taking new life, here where the water was smooth. His expression was calculating.

The captain broke Brokols' mood. "Look lively, you loafers!" Stedmer shouted. "Look lively!" Crewmen who'd been standing, gazing, quickly found something to do, needful or not. For a moment Brokols felt a pang of guilt at his own inaction, then resentment at having felt guilty, and turned his gaze once more toward the town ahead.

The taller buildings—here they no doubt thought of them as towers—were unlike any he'd seen before. Several, the tallest, were simply spires, slender and graceful and invariably white, none reaching even a hundred feet. Mostly, though, the taller buildings were somewhat steplike, the ground story larger, the second stepped back at one end or both to make a terrace, and subsequent stories each smaller than the one below, terraced at both ends or all the way around. And every terrace seemed a garden. The walls were mostly white—a vivid white with flashes of color. At many places among the buildings, and frequent on their terraces, were the barbered crowns of trees, glossy green in the late morning sun.

Overarching it all was a high blue vault of sky accented by puffs of white.

Then Brokols realized he'd overlooked the most impressive building of them all, at the foot of town to one side of the wharves. Not tall but massive. Water lapped the lower courses of its wall. Being whitewashed like the other buildings, it failed at first to register as a fortress. A belltower stood well above its north wall, sunlight flashing bronze off polished bells.

Even recognized, its white walls strong and massive, it seemed somehow unfortresslike, intensifying a sense of unreality and heightened awareness that Brokols felt. At points upon its walls bright awnings clustered, as if to shield loungers from the glare. Irregularly among them, small trees stood brightly verdant—umbrella-like, columnar, or pyramidal. And doubtless there were flowerbeds, Brokols thought.

At the corners though, erasing any doubt, were overhanging turrets. Their slots were undoubtedly for archery instead of guns, for half a century ago the droids seemed not to have explosives. While here and there, sharing the wall with trees and awnings, stood machines for hurling blocks of stone. And even these war machines were painted white, sky blue, or gold.

The deck began to vibrate hard beneath Brokols' feet; the engineer had reversed the engine to stop the ship.

Kryger's voice spoke almost at Brokols' shoulder, taking him unawares. "Primitive," Kryger said, and seemed to find satisfaction in the word. "Windmills. Not a smokestack anywhere."

Brokols nodded. From a pocket, Kryger drew a globe fruit, dried and wrinkled now, popped it into his mouth, chewed for a minute, then expelled the pit into the water. Brokols wondered how much capacity Kryger's stomach might have after weeks of little but broth.

They dropped anchor five hundred yards from the long low wharf, chain rumbling out the hawse pipe. A crowd had gathered along the waterfront, several hundred at least, brightly dressed as if for the occasion, and innumerable others watched from roofs. A floating dock extended out from the wharf, apparently for small boats, with steps to the wharf top. It was clear of people, and at its head, uniformed police or soldiers kept a small area free of onlookers.

It was time. Brokols straightened.

Beside him Kryger chuckled, a sound that surprised Brokols, for one of the things that irritated Kryger, and more than just Kryger, was Brokols' occasional laughter. The younger man looked around to see what might have brought even this low-keyed laughter from Kryger. The crew of the forward swivel gun was cranking its muzzle somewhat skyward; one man held its lanyard. Brokols stared. Stedmer shouted sharply, and both fore and aft guns roared together. Flame shot from their bores—flame, smoke, carbonized particles of powder—but no projectiles. They had fired blank. Explosion rolled across the water, met the steep slopes that walled it, and rolled back with booming, overlapping echoes.

Brokols turned to the wharf again. There was no screaming, no yammering that he could hear, no apparent commotion at all. Too stunned to react, he decided. The crews reloaded the guns, and once more the captain shouted. Again the doubled roar, and when the echoes died, they fired a third time. Then the captain gave a further order, and the crews began to swab the carbon from the rifled bores.

Kryger chuckled again. "That made an impression."

Now the captain's gig was swung outboard on its davits, and men at a windlass lowered it to the water. Brokols walked to the gangway. This would be the first time he'd spoken the droid tongue with a native speaker, the first time he'd even seen anyone not of his own people. His stomach and bowels were nervous; he told himself the problem was mental, and would pass once he was ashore.

A bosun went down the ladder, followed by six oarsmen. After them came Brokols, followed by the ship's master-at-arms, and finally Argant, Kryger's aide, who would carry back to Kryger what was said ashore. Assuming Brokols stayed ashore, which was the sole reason for his being there at all. Argant, with his trained memory, could recite back entire conversations virtually verbatim, though it seemed to Brokols that the man lacked somewhat in intelligence and volition.

Brokols sat in the bow on the captain's seat. As they drew up to the floating dock, he could see the waiting droids more clearly. Three of them, wearing rich cloaks loosely draped, stepped into the open space at the dock ahead, escorted by troops in marvelously quaint gear—a kind of short skirt, harness, breast plate and plumed helmet, each wearing a sword at his belt. None of the three seemed to be the king; people made way for them, but no one even bowed, let alone prostrated themselves in the manner described by the first expedition. They must simply be high officials.

The oarsmen shipped their oars. Two grasped the dock's edge; two others clinched lines around cleats and made fast. *Cleats*, Brokols thought. Considering what *The Captain's Book* told of the droids, they must have invented cleats here independently; invented everything independently. Now one of the seamen stepped onto the dock and helped first Brokols, then Argant from the boat, and finally the master-at-arms. Straightening his waistcoat, Brokols marched up the dock, preceded by the uniformed master-at-arms, with Argant a step to the rear.

Briefly, as he walked, he wondered what the droids made of his clothing. It could hardly be more different than theirs: light-gray velvet knee breeches and pearl-gray blouse; velvet waistcoat matching the breeches; wide-lapelled open jacket, slate-gray, extending almost to mid-thigh; expensive shoes, their silver buckles and glossy leather highly polished; and a hat of lustrous stiffened fur, rithgar, the brim pinned up on one side by a jade and silver brooch. Such garments were affordable only by men of means, and even the droids would no doubt appreciate it, unconsciously comparing it with Argant's less splendid garb and the uniforms of the sailors.

He stopped ten feet from the men who awaited him. Tall as he was, and considered handsome, Brokols had been prepared for men larger than himself and better looking. But face to face, the droids were more impressive than he'd expected.

The three met him soberly, but they failed to bow, so he simply nodded civilly. They duplicated the gesture. Gathering himself, Brokols spoke.

"I bring you greetings from the emperor, Dard of Almeon." He said it in the language he thought of as droid. But droid, so far as he knew, had no term for "emperor," so he used the Almaeic. Their eyebrows lifted. "I wish to speak with your king," he finished.

One of them, the one in the middle, spoke back then, and to Brokols' chagrin, he didn't understand a word of it. All he could do was stare. The man paused, assessing his reaction, then turned and spoke to a guard who stood near. The guard came forward, and facing Brokols, spoke.

"Sir," he said, "I speak your language. We have no king here. In Hrumma, the amirr rules, with the acquiescence of the Two Estates." He gestured at the other man who'd spoken. "His Eminence can understand some of what you say. Djezian and Hrummean are much alike; the differences are in large part matters of idiom and pronunciation. But it seems appropriate to speak through me and let me interpret."

Even some of this Brokols missed, but he understood the essentials of it. *A ruler not born to the throne. A strange way to operate.* For a moment he wondered how to deport himself toward him. *Watch how the others act,* he decided, *and when in doubt, treat him as royalty.* "Thank you," he answered. "The emperor has sent me to serve as his ambassador to your—your amirr, that their two realms may be friends and enjoy commerce and profit with one another."

The guard, surely an officer, repeated it to his ruler, then translated the ruler's reply, obviously paraphrasing. "The amirr would like to know more about your"—he paused over the unfamiliar word—"your emperor. And your nation, and what commerce you have in mind." The amirr spoke again. "He suggests we retire to a more comfortable place, where you may sit in relative privacy and quiet."

Brokols agreed; and with Argant and the master-at-arms, went with the amirr and his retinue into the Fortress, passing through a massive gate and up open stone stairs. It didn't seem as strong or sophisticated as some of the old fortresses in Almeon, preserved as museums from the two centuries of bitter warfare before Kaitmar III had successfully reunited the Islands twelve centuries earlier.

This fortress was more aesthetic—less grim, lighter, brighter. It seemed to Brokols that this was more than a fortress, perhaps the seat of government, though it did seem small for that. Inside, the corridors were richly carpeted, the walls panelled. The third-level room which they entered, opened onto the inner court through wide glass doors, and a balcony with chairs and planters. *Those doors*, Brokols told himself, *required technology as well as art*. The inner court itself, what he could see of it, was a stone-paved mustering ground, but with spreading trees at intervals around the perimeter.

The furnishings in the room were handsome too: polished oval table; richly patterned carpet; small and elegant statuary, mostly geometric forms; and a tapestry and paintings on the walls.

The droids, Brokols decided, were definitely sophisticated when it came to aesthetics. The people of Almeon, having read *The Captain's Book*, had assumed that "pleasure droids" meant engineered for sexual prowess, and perhaps for singing and dancing. Nor had the report of the first expedition disabused them of it. Now it occurred to Brokols that the ancients who'd designed the droids may have included engineering for a broad aesthetic orientation.

The amirr motioned for the others to take seats, then sat down himself. Only his six guards and three aides remained on their feet. He rested his eyes on the foreign ambassador.

An interesting face, the amirr told himself. The nose was well-formed, if a bit long, hair nearly black and a riot of close-cut curls, the chin unusually narrow, and most peculiar of all, large eyes slightly slanted. *Interesting and aesthetic*. "Tell me," the amirr said, "how have you come to know the Djezian speech, if you are not from either Djez?"

Brokols had concentrated on the amirr's words, but the only ones he'd recognized, from his knowledge of Djezian, were *come*, and *speech*, and *Djez* itself. To know what had been said, he'd needed the guard officer's translation. Still, it felt to him as if some other words were almost familiar.

"Fifty-five years ago," Brokols began, "a ship much like the one I came on arrived at the city of Haipoor l'Djezzer, in the kingdom of Djez Gorrbul. The people on the ship knew nothing of the language there, or the name of the kingdom, but the ship's commander and some of his officers met with the king, and they spoke as best they could with their hands. They were shown the city, and some of the plantations around it. Then the commander gave the king a gift, and the king in turn gave him three of his people as gifts.

"And while the ship was traveling the long distance back to Almeon, these gift people, who were slaves, teachers in the king's palace, taught some of the ship people their language—how to speak it and how to write it—and much about the world on this side of the ocean. Thus we knew there was a kingdom, or nation, called Hrumma, though no one from Almeon had ever been here."

Brokols smiled ruefully. "But they did not tell us you spoke a different language."

The amirr smiled back. "Perhaps they didn't consider it important. Tell me, how far is it to—Almeon?"

"From here it's about one-third the distance around the world. Our voyage required fifty-five days, with the wind behind us most of the time."

The amirr raised his eyebrows. "Ah! And you arrived without sails, though your masts wore them when you were first seen. How do you travel, using neither sails nor oars?"

"We have fire inside the ship to drive it. Perhaps we might show you how fire can be used that way, when we know one another better. In trade for something you have that we would like from you."

Brokols' eyes had watched the amirr carefully as he said it. He was reasonably sure the man understood even before the guard officer repeated it. The amirr simply nodded.

"And the thunders you made when you arrived—how was that accomplished?" the amirr asked.

Brokols answered with deliberate nonchalence: "The thunders were from mighty weapons we carry. When we wish, they can destroy like lightning bolts, but of course we would not use weapons here. You have not threatened us in any way."

Again the eyebrows lifted, not in anger—there was no trace of that—but simply as if the amirr was impressed. "And what," he asked, "was the purpose of releasing those thunders when you did?"

"It was a salute. The Empire of Almeon is composed of numerous separate kingdoms banded together in mutual friendship and commerce. And when officials of the emperor visit a kingdom, or when a king visits the emperor, such thunders are made in honor of the visit."

The amirr nodded thoughtfully. "How long will you be in our land? If I accept your embassy."

"I would like to remain here to represent the emperor continuously."

"And how would you know your emperor's will, at so great a remove?"

"I have been well trained."

The amirr gazed calmly and long at Brokols, and it seemed to the Almite that there was a distinct danger of being refused, not in hostility but for some other reason. Nevertheless he kept quiet; attempting to bolster his case unasked might do more harm than good.

"And would your emperor accept an embassy from me in your land?"

"If you wish to send one, Your Highness, the emperor would make him welcome. You may be sure of it."

"Would your emperor be offended if I did not send one to him?"

"Not at all. You may not wish to until you know more about us and what we have to offer in commerce. Which I will discuss over time, when I have come to know your country better.

"But excuse me, sire. I'm forgetting something." Brokols hadn't forgotten; he'd been waiting for what seemed an appropriate moment. Rising, he reached into a pocket, brought out and opened a folded handkerchief, beautiful in itself, and removed something from it. "A small gift from the emperor, if it pleases you." He reached out a hand, and the amirr, curious, received the object from it, a gold ring set with a flawless thirty-carat stone, a brilliant. "We call the stone 'diamond'; they are quite rare in Almeon. The ring may not fit your finger as it is, but it can be enlarged or made smaller of course."

The amirr studied it, impressed, turning it about, watching its facets scintillate, and with seeming ingenuousness blew silent admiration through pursed lips.

"It is very beautiful. I accept with thanks." His hands were large; he fitted it on a little finger, then looked up. "I must give thought to a gift for your emperor."

Brokols looked down at his own hands, palms pressed together before his chest. "The emperor would consider your friendship more than gift enough. It is his wish to be friends with all nations."

Again the amirr nodded. "And how long will your ship stay in our harbor?"

"It is intended that it leave tomorrow, to take ambassadors to the two djezes. But it will be back in a few weeks. Perhaps by then, in council with yourself or with men in your government, I can arrange to buy a cargo for it to take to Almeon."

"And will these others"—the amirr gestured at Argant and the master-at-arms—"will they remain here with you?"

Brokols hoped his relief didn't show on his face. If the translation was accurate, the amirr had used the future tense this time, not the conditional, which seemed to mean that his embassy was accepted.

"No," he answered. "I have an assistant who will come ashore, but these gentlemen will leave with the ship. They are to tell the emperor what is said in each court—yours and in each of the Djezes—and give him their impressions."

"Well then, I'll be glad to have you here." The amirr turned to his captain of guards. "Eltrienn, please show the ambassador and his companions to the courtyard and wait with them there while I discuss his accommodations." He smiled and nodded to Brokols in dismissal.

When the Almites had left, the amirr looked around at the others, then at his privy counselor. "What did you read, Allbarin? What do you make of them?"

Allbarin shrugged. "Only that his emperor has designs embracing much more than commerce. He intends to rule us. As for the ambassador, he is no evil man, but he has the capacity to be devious. As you'd expect."

The amirr's lips tightened. "And the distance he told us; was that the truth?"

"I have no doubt of it. I got no sense of lying when he said it."

"Indeed!"

It seemed to the amirr that this situation required careful handling. And protocol for dealing with embassies was not well defined. Hrumma had not exchanged ambassadors with Djez Gorrbul for almost two centuries. An amirr forty years past had sent an envoy to Haipoor l'Djezzer to propose an exchange of embassies. Only the envoy's head had returned, in a sack. Djez Seechul had an occasional envoy in Hrumma, but these served little function beyond occasional attempts, half-hearted, to obtain Hrumma's alliance in an attack on Djez Gorrbul, which lay between them. A syndicate of Hrummean merchants had a commercial agent, Sechuuli born, to arrange business connections between themselves and Djezian merchants.

Allbarin continued. "And there is something more. He will have among his affects . . ." The privy counselor paused, in hesitation, not for emphasis. "He has a means . . . a physical means of communicating with his superior at a great distance. I don't know what it is—what to call it or how it functions—and I realize the reading is hard to credit, but he has such a means. And that superior will be located in Haipoor l'Djezzer."

The amirr contemplated the new ring on his finger thoughtfully, moving his hand about, admiring the flash. "This physical means of communicating at a distance: does it involve adepts?"

Allbarin shook his head. "I'm sure it does not, Your Eminence. But it brings me to what may be our biggest advantage. I can tell you with certainty that not only is the ambassador no adept, *but he has no screen whatever for his mind!* Nor do the two who came in here with him. I have never encountered such mental transparency before, except in infants. It seems to indicate a complete unawareness that anyone might read their thoughts or see their pictures. In children, the mind screen forms automatically when the child becomes aware that others can read his mind. I believe we can assume the same of these people."

The amirr pursed his lips. "Then—we must take care that he doesn't find out."

"Exactly, sir. In Hrumma he is almost certain to find out sooner or later, but we should take steps to delay it as long as is practical.

"Also, with your approval and perhaps your assistance, I will try to visit their ship, to speak with its master and the ambassador's superior. I may learn things from them that will help us."

"Look into it."

The amirr paused, looking at a thought of his own and frowning slightly. "Allbarin, I may not be an adept, as you well know, but sometimes I perceive things, whether from Hrum or from my own imaginings and prejudice. And I like this ambassador, regardless of his purposes."

The counselor nodded. "And I, Your Eminence, though I will still beware of him."

"Exactly, Allbarin, exactly."

The amirr looked around at his staff then. "Gannet, arrange suitable quarters for this ambassador. Perhaps Arnello Bostelli has something satisfactory. Trello, go down and tell Eltrienn that he is to serve as companion to the ambassador, to be the ambassador's ears and tongue and to tutor him in our speech. I'll have him replaced on the guard for now." He paused, a hand raised to stay his aide. "Better yet, remain with the ambassador briefly and send Eltrienn up to speak with me. I need to warn him that the ambassador must not hear of mind reading. Then, when Eltrienn gets back down, you will guide the other foreigners to their boat."

Trello hesitated. "Your Eminence, rather than Eltrienn, might it be better to have an adept with the ambassador?"

The amirr examined the suggestion, then shook it off. "It must be someone who speaks Djezian fluently, and Eltrienn is my choice. Others can read him when we wish it."

Trello bobbed an abbreviated bow and hurried out.

"And now, gentlemen," said the amirr, "we still have everything to do that we had before this unusual visit. This is Festival, and there are final plans to look at and approve. Let's get started."

Five

Vessto Cadriio, the country sage, had felt no impulse to mix with the crowds in any of the parks. He had followed Panni Vempravvo from the headland, not because he intended to speak with him, but simply because their path was the same. Then, walking into the city, Panni had met a merchant, Mellvis Rantrelli, and his sons, who'd been watching the district semifinals at the archery field. Rantrelli, with a cry of joy, had ordered his driver to stop the carriage, and asked Panni and his followers to his home for supper. Panni had smiled broadly and nodded, then turned and beckoned to Vessto. Vessto, with his own small retinue, had accompanied him. The old sage had declined to ride while his followers walked, and they'd all trailed behind the carriage, which had gone slowly, not to lose them.

The merchant had been startled at Panni's inviting the other group of holy men, but decided it was good fortune, not bad. This unknown country sage must have more than presumption, might even be a sage indeed, if Panni Vempravvo invited his company. And who could boast having had two sages at his table for the same meal?

The sages had likely eaten nothing since breakfast, if then. So as soon as he got home, the merchant ordered fruit and loaves and juices brought for them and their followers. Afterward, the two sages shared the large hot tub with the merchant while the lesser devotees napped or meditated in the garden, in the shade of fruit trees.

Old Panni was scrawny; far too thin, the merchant thought. But then, sages seemed to live long and in health with little more than the company of Hrum to sustain them. The country sage was lean and wiry but appeared strong nonetheless. The merchant looked unself-consciously at his own ample abdomen. He was more than content to let others be holy clergy, and himself to buy and sell and transport crops to the city.

He'd have been happier though if they'd talked, there in his hot tub. It would have been nice to hear some cognition that might well have helped to light his way through life, and perhaps to oneness with Hrum.

Afterward the sages thanked him for his goodness, and joined their followers in naps, to sleep almost till supper. At supper he'd had food enough spread for a crew of wagoners, for while the sages, the older one at least, wouldn't eat much, who knew how much the disciples might consume? But to his surprise, old Panni smiled at him, took a serving of nearly everything, and ate almost heartily, his disciples following suit. The younger sage ate less than the elder, though he too did not seriously stint his appetite.

But alas, it was the quietest supper at that table for a long time, for the merchant and his family felt constrained to say no more than their guests, who said almost nothing at all.

After dark, which came late in that season, the two sages went apart from most of their followers, accompanied each by his principal men, who were masters. Leaving the rest to murmur quietly in the evening, they climbed together a little way up the slope behind the villa, to sit looking silently out across the lower part of town, at the stars and the dark and quiet water of the harbor. They could hear the sounds of celebration in the distance.

After a bit, Vessto spoke quietly. "The foreigners are here for ill."

Panni smiled. "True," he said.

"The serpents know them for what they are."

Still smiling, Panni nodded. "That too is true."

"But the rains will come regardless, and the serpents will come back. Many people will forget that they ever fled." The country sage fell silent then for half a minute before adding: "Our days of innocence are numbered."

This time Panni chuckled. "There are roles. And scenes. And acts. And the stage of life is broad and richly furnished, its scripts subtle and ever changing, full of surprises."

His eyes watched the younger man shrewdly, but Vessto

Cadriio said nothing more, simply looked quietly out at the water. The thought drifted through Vessto's consciousness that what Panni said was true. And it was also true that right and wrong were no more than considerations, polarizations, to shed if one could. But pain and joy, suffering and happiness, felt very real upon that stage. And he had no doubt that, by his nature, he'd continue to equate wrong with that which caused suffering, and right with that which brought the most happiness to the stage.

He would not go home to Kammenak, as he'd considered doing. He'd stay in Theedalit and see what he could do about the foreigners.

Elver Brokols had hardly started on his second goblet of wine, but felt nonetheless mesmerized, as if he were in some magic universe. He never even wondered if he'd been drugged; the sights and sounds themselves had transported him.

The park was lit by round lanterns of colored glass, their bright flames remarkably steady. It rollicked with flute, drum, dulcimer and chant, was adrone with the voices of thousands talking, eating, drinking. The fire pits had been refilled with earth, that no one having drunk would fall in and be burned. Dance sites—ovals of hard-packed clay—were alive with movement, ranks of men and women stepping, spinning, cavorting through traditional evolutions, while singles and couples, half naked and agleam with sweat, performed virtuosic, usually graceful, and often acrobatic dances of their own. Here and there a couple would slip away into the darkness.

And somehow Elver Brokols wasn't offended, though by Almaeic mores the dances were immodest or even wanton, and fornication a crime. Nor did he think to blame it on their being droids; they seemed entirely human to him, only different. The evening seemed like some fantastic, yet very real dream which, in a sort of déjà vu, he could almost remember having dreamt before.

And the people! He'd seen no one who was homely; simply, some were more attractive than others.

"It is—marvelous," he said to Eltrienn Cadriio. "Like nothing of this world."

"You don't have festivals in Almeon?"

"Not like this."

Among the things he'd never seen before was the degree of public undress among the more gymnastic dancers—"dancers before Hrum" they were called. The men wore nothing at all above the waist, while the women, mostly well-endowed, wore pantaloons, and above that, little more than a harness to support their breasts through the leaping, twirling, and general acrobatics! But tonight, outside himself as he was, it was too aesthetic to offend him.

Just now he stood beside Eltrienn Cadriio at the rib-high balustrade of a landscaped terrace, five feet above the general level, a terrace to which the aristocracy could retire if they wished, to drink without being jostled, and talk quietly. Mostly though—and to Brokols this was as remarkable as the half-naked dancers—mostly the aristocracy mixed with the commoners; greasy-fingered, eating roast meat and hot buttered rolls elbow to elbow with tanners, laborers, fishermen, drinking with them, joining in their dances. Brokols himself, when he'd finished eating, had yielded to an astonishing impulse and tried one of the group dances, one that began simply. Soon though, he'd gotten sweaty and confused, and withdrew.

"Eltrienn," he said, "you told me this festival is in honor of the serpents returning. What did you mean by that?"

Cadriio answered without taking his eyes from the celebration below. "Each year on the summer solstice, the serpents return to our harbor, swimming down from the north. They bear their young in firths and inlets all along our shores, and nowhere else. So far as we know. Perhaps so the young can be born and develop in the warm water that's just starting to reach here from the south. And the firths and inlets being nearly enclosed, they can defend their young more easily from sarrkas and other creatures that might harm them.

"And invariably, within a few days of their return, the season of rains begins. The land freshens, the streams swell, reservoirs fill, crops grow . . ." Cadriio turned to him, spreading his hands expressively. "It's an important event for us, so we celebrate. The Festival of the Serpents Returning is our biggest celebration—bigger even than the Harvest Festival."

"We saw serpents," Brokols said. "Yesterday, near the ship. They looked dangerous. Do they ever attack sailors or fishermen?"

"I've never heard of it, not even a rumor. Like the sullsi, the people of the waves, they are intelligent. We never molest them, and they don't trouble us. Indeed, they make the harbor safer, for when serpents are in the harbor, sarrkas are never seen there."

"Hmm. We saw no serpents when we steamed in; we saw them only in the open sea."

Cadriio nodded, sobering. "They arrived this morning, somewhat before you. Then, people on the headland, watching your arrival, saw them hurry out while you were sailing up the firth. The report of it spread widely. Allbarin—he's the amirr's privy counselor—says it's enough that the serpents arrived, and they'll be back when the ship leaves. It's his opinion that the serpents were alarmed by so large a ship in the confines of the harbor, and we've taken pains to make it publicly known that your ship will depart tomorrow.

"If the serpents don't return, we may find your presence here a serious embarrassment. We call them 'the Messengers of Hrum,' and hold them sacred. There is even a long poem telling how they once saved the daughter of Hrum."

Gazing out over the noisy crowd, Brokols blew silently through pursed lips. He was lucky not to have mentioned the marines killing two of them.

"The daughter of Hrum?" he asked.

"The daughter of Hrum, Lormalia; she's the foster mother of the people. Our ancestors arrived as spirits, in chrysalises from which humans emerged instead of fairy flies. And Hrum sent Lormalia to foster us and teach us how to live.

"One day she showed some of the people how to make a raft, and how to net fish, and in so doing, she fell into the sea. A sarrka was about to take her, but she was saved by a serpent, who drove the sarrka away, then lifted her gently with its jaws and laid her on the raft again, unharmed."

Brokols said nothing at this, simply nodded acknowledgement. The story shook him. Not that he believed the business about the serpent, but he'd read *The Captain's Book*, in translation of course, and the name of Hrum's daughter could hardly be coincidence. Lormalia had to be the biotech, Lori Maloi. Clearly there'd been at least one heroine in the ancient world besides the *Adanik Larvest*'s last captain.

Cadriio eyed the silent ambassador. "I presume you worship Hrum in Almeon."

Brokols shook his head; it seemed best to be truthful when he reasonably could. "We know very little about Hrum," he answered. It occurred to the Almite that with the droid religion, Hrummlis, as central as it seemed to be in Hrumma, he'd do well to know something of it, if only for political reasons. So he added: "I'd appreciate your helping me learn."

"I will. Perhaps tomorrow I can take you to a teacher, one who instructs in Hrummlis. Or . . ." He paused as if considering something. "I have a younger brother who is regarded by many as a sage, a man who knows Hrum directly and speaks his truth. He may be in Theedalit for the Festival. If I can locate him, you might find him interesting.

"Meanwhile though, shall we go down and have more wine? Or meat?"

"No," said Brokols. "It's been a long day for me. I'd like to go to my apartment now and get some sleep."

"Another good idea," Cadriio answered, and turning from the balustrade, they left.

Tirros Hanorissio, the mirj, was intensely interested in the foreigner, wanted to meet and talk with him. Finally he'd spotted him on the terrace with Cadriio, but by the time he'd worked his way there, the man was gone. Tirros swore under his breath. He sensed opportunities there, and was eager to explore them.

For now though . . . he vaulted lightly over the balustrade and entered the crowd again. He would find some pretty girl who'd be impressed with his status, and they could go to a place he knew.

Six

The next day, in fact the next two days, Brokols and Eltrienn Cadriio did not visit a teacher of Hrummlis, for it had occurred to Eltrienn that most teachers would be engaged in the festivities. Also, Brokols needed to move from the first-floor apartment that Eltrienn had arranged, to a top-floor apartment. He supervised it personally. He had a small but heavy casket of gold and a little leather bag of diamonds to finance his activities. He'd had to sign for them of course, and he'd have to account for them when this was over, so he had no intention of letting them out of his sight when anyone besides he and Stilfos, his assistant, had access to them.

The move accomplished, he had his antenna installed on his roof, along with his wind generator, explaining them as religious instruments. It had been decided, in planning the mission, that the ambassadors would explain as religious anything whose meaning or function they wanted to conceal.

That night in his apartment, in the oil-lit privacy of an inner room, Elver Brokols used his wireless telegraph, the pride of Almaeic technology, to tap out in code a resume of his day for Kryger aboard the *Dard*, which had left Theedalit and was sailing northward toward the Djezian coast. Then Brokols went to bed, letting the small, breeze-powered generator recharge his storage battery.

It was important that he become competent in the Hrummean language as soon as possible. Therefore, much of the third day was spent in his roof garden, working on it with Eltrienn. They went over the basic differences in sounds—in Djezian the stress was almost always on the penultimate syllable; in Hrummean it was more variable, differing with the word and even shifting with the rhythm and stress of the sentence.* Djezian pronunciations tended to be glottal, Hrummean palatal, and Djezian vowels tended to be shortened and homogenized, even, to a degree, in stressed syllables. The alphabets were almost identical, and differences in the sounds assigned to the letters were fairly consistent.

Most of the time, Brokols' servant, Stilfos, sat out of the way listening, repeating their drills more or less to himself. He needed Hrummean too.

They drilled pronunciation of representative words that were similar in the two languages, which was most of their vocabularies; the sounds differed much more than the spellings. They also drilled some of the words and idioms that were unique to Hrummean. Already, when Eltrienn spoke slowly and simply in Hrummean, Brokols understood much of what he said. It seemed to both of them that a few more days should find him conversing rather freely, with only occasional stops for clarification.

During a morning break, looking out at the harbor, they'd seen serpents. And later, thunderheads were visible, a line of them moving coastward to the south. It seemed to Brokols that the death of the two serpents would have no ill effects after all.

**Hrummean writing indicates the syllable with major stress by doubling the final letter in the syllable, most often a consonant. And because in Hrummean the stress sometimes shifts in different sentences, a word may be spelled slightly differently in different contexts. This contributes to the flow of Hrummean poetry in a major way, permitting techniques that are unavailable in most languages.*

SEVEN

The namirrna, Juliassa Hanorissia, drew lightly on the rein, and her kaabor stopped at the cliff's edge. A cloud had cut off the sun, and the ocean below had turned steel gray. A few sea lokkras soared, watching for fish. The major moon, Great Liilia, was out of sight, but she was full, and the tide would be strong. Just now, Juliassa knew, it would be ebbing. There'd be more than ample time to ride the beach if she wished, before the high water returned.

Jonkka, her bodyguard, had stopped when she had, a couple of hundred feet behind her as she'd prescribed with her father's approval. She waved cheerily back at him, then touched the kaabor's flanks with her heels, starting it down the trail that angled precariously across the cliff face to the beach.

In brief minutes she arrived at the strip of damp sand, now thirty to a hundred feet wide below the cliff. The sharp smell of stranded floatweed and other beach life stung her nostrils, and swinging down from the saddle, she led the kaabor along the strand, pausing at intervals to examine a shell, a figured, wave-polished stone, a stranded seine-fish dissolving in the sunlight like some poisonous illusion.

She'd gone only a little way, a quarter mile, when she saw the sellsu and cried out inadvertently, for at first she thought it was dead. Since she'd been a child, she'd loved to watch them sporting in the sea, sometimes body surfing, and had tried unsuccessfully to catch the spirit of them on canvas with her paints. But approaching it, where it lay just past a dark rock, she saw the movement of its shallow breathing, and her own eased.

With a word to the kaabor, Juliassa dropped the rein and went to the sellsu, half-knelt, half-bent, and cautiously touched a smooth-furred flank, ready to jump back. A sellsu's tail and flukes were powerful, its arms long and muscular, its teeth sharp for tearing fish. And if she startled it . . .

It made no response to her touch, none at all.

She stepped back, pondering, then knelt and stroked its head and neck, crooning to it. Nothing. After half a minute she turned and waved for her bodyguard. He rode up, expression curious, until he saw the sellsu. His face turned wary then; he'd grown up far from the sea.

"Yes, namirrna?"

"It's alive, but something's wrong with it. It's sick or badly hurt. Help me turn it over."

The guard dismounted, a tall heavy-shouldered man hiding his hesitancy, and the two of them rolled the four-hundred-pound body over. There was no visible wound.

"Jonkka," she said, "ride back to the house quickly, and have the men bring the boat. We'll take it home and I'll nurse it back to health."

Distress flashed briefly behind the soldierly eyes. "Miss, I can't do that. My post is to keep you in my sight, lest harm come to you."

She turned face on then, fists on hips, expression severe, though the top of her head came no higher than his chin. "Then help me drag it into the surf. We'll take it home swimming, holding its head above water. You and I together, because you have to stay with me. Or me alone, if you cannot swim."

His face too turned severe at that. "You do me ill, Juliassa Hanorissia. You know I can scarcely swim; I'm from the Eastern Dale, where water is for drinking and we bathe in a basin. And you know as well that I am charged with your safety."

Her cheeks darkened, and her fierceness faded. "I do know, Jonkka, and I'm sorry. But somehow I must save this sellsu, and I know no other way. I'd ask for your help to load it on Sannshi, but it seems to me it would surely die, riding across a kaabor's back so far. And anyway, how would we tie it on?"

She turned back to the sellsu, the child of the waves, and kneeling again, grabbed the flukes. "Here. At least help me pull it into the shade of this rock. It's said they do not tolerate the sun well for any length of time."

He'd never heard that. He'd heard they raised their young on the beaches. But he bent to it, and with his strength they readily dragged it out of the sun. "Now lend me your helmet," Juliassa said. "Then gather wet floatweed at the water's edge and cover the sellsu with it. To help keep it damp."

His expression was both hesitant and puzzled, but he handed her his helmet and trotted off. As he filled his arms with the long and pungent strands, he paused once to see what the namirrna was doing. She was carrying seawater in his helmet, pouring it on the sellsu. He muttered a prayer and continued to gather. It was the will of Hrum that they do what they properly could.

When they'd spread the weeds over the unmoving body, she looked it over. "Another load should do it," she said, and trotting, he returned to the water's edge. This time he didn't look back until he'd gotten most of a load. When he did, he dropped the weeds and shouted angrily. The namirrna was a hundred yards away, riding *his* kaabor back along the beach, leading her own by the reins. He strode toward them, calling his mount to come to him, but when it tried, she dug heels in its flanks, using the reins and bit harshly. It yielded to her, and she rode on.

"You do me ill indeed, Juliassa Hanorissia," Jonkka called after her, and she stopped.

"I know," she cried back, "and it grieves me. But this way it's out of your hands, and you can scarcely be blamed for my treachery. It's me that'll be punished. I'll be back as soon as I can, with a boat." Her tone changed then from apology to command. "Meanwhile stay by him."

With that she urged her mount into a trot, and moments later Jonkka watched her start up the cliff trail. With an oath he turned and kicked his helmet some fifteen feet, hurting his toes despite his boots, which brought another curse. After retrieving the helmet, he looked at the second load of floatweed, lying where he'd dropped it. Probably its only purpose had been to occupy his attention while she sneaked off, he told himself. Taking no chance though, he picked it up and strewed it over the sellsu, leaving only head and neck exposed.

She's willful, that namirrna, he thought. *And all this for a sellsu that's as good as dead already*. *As for punishment . . .*

By his observation, the amirr's idea of punishment for headstrong children was nothing compared to his own father's. Now there was a man who knew how to punish! Although in all truth, the whippings had been few, if memorable, dealt only on severe provocation. And when they were over, that had been the end of the matter.

He stroked the sellsu's sleek head. "You are a good-lookin' lad," Jonkka murmured. "And who knows? Maybe you'll come through this after all." Did this fellow truly have the intelligence of a human, he wondered? Or, as some insisted, the soul of a human, resting for a cycle from humanity's labors and responsibilities? He'd even heard from fishermen that the sullsi talked to one another, though their words were strange, beyond human comprehension.

Jonkka chuckled. Maybe the sellsu'd been a soldier, once upon a time. "How'd you like a soldiers' song?" he asked, "to let you know you're among friends. Maybe you'll even wake up and join me." Then, still stroking, he began to sing, but instead of a soldier's song, it was one he'd heard his mother and grandmother sing the younger children to sleep with, and no doubt himself as well, farther back than his memory reached.

It had many verses, and as he was finishing, something caught and drew his eye. Two sullsi lay at the tide's edge, not more than fifty feet from him, where the light surf hissed softly up the sand. They were not moving, not even their heads, but they watched intently. And in his present mood, Jonkka called softly to them.

"Peace, lads, your buddy's sick; either that or hurt inside. My lady's gone to fetch help; she means to nurse him through it."

They neither bolted at his voice nor showed any sign of attacking. Maybe they *were* smart, Jonkka told himself, for he had his sword still at his belt, and ashore he was much nimbler than they. Cloud blocked the sun again, and he looked up. Cloud indeed! A curving wall of thunderheads now, from that angle seeming vast, hid the sky to south and west, near enough that he could not see their heads, but only their flanks and blue-black undersides. The rains were at hand, he told himself, despite the foreign ship and the serpent's brief flight.

Again he stroked the sellsu's head. "It looks as if I'll not have to fetch more water to keep you wet," he muttered, and wondered where the namirrna was by now. Halfway to the villa or farther, he guessed. She'd not hesitate to run the kaabors hard. The slower part by far would be rowing here around the curve of shore. Men would have to leave other duties to be her boatmen, and they had several miles to come.

Soon enough the rain arrived, with Borrsio's hammer banging and booming, his lightning spears stabbing sea and earth. Like all children of Hrumma, Jonkka'd been raised to love wild storms, but not out in the open like this! He huddled in the lee of the great rock, grateful for even that little shelter, listening between thunders to the cold hard sheets of rain hiss on the sea and slash the streaming stone. When next he peered out toward the two sullsi, they were gone. *Back into the sea to keep dry,* he thought wryly.

He was shivering by then, skin blue and pebbled. Once he felt the spirit of Borrsio, making him tingle and his hair stand on end. A moment later, the god cast down a great and blinding spear that struck somewhere very close, and the thunder with it burst the air so that Jonkka was knocked flat and for a long moment forgot to breathe. Finally, after further booming and rumbling, the wind changed, and he shifted round the rock, grateful again because, to an ex-herd boy, it meant that the storm had passed half over. When next he thought to look at the sellsu, its eyes were open, looking at him, although it seemed not to have moved. Perhaps the thunders had wakened it, Jonkka thought, or the spirit of Borrsio when it had caused his hair to bristle.

Finally the rain became fitful. The wind stopped, and shortly the sun came forth to raise steams from the sand and rocks. The tide was rising now, had been awhile, and Jonkka began to wonder which would arrive soonest, the surf or the boat. The surf would take some hours yet, he supposed, but he wasn't sure how many; he wasn't that familiar with the sea. Meanwhile, here the high tide mark was on the base of the cliff itself, and perhaps the boatmen had delayed starting till the storm was over, on grounds of safety.

The tide was still twenty feet away when they hallooed him. His clothes were dry by then, even somewhat his boots, which he'd set out on a rock, and twice more he'd poured water over the sellsu, whose eyes had long since closed again, though it still breathed. They loaded it into the boat, which rode perilously low with all the added weight, water splashing over the bow as they launched out through the mild surf. They were hardly two hundred feet from shore when two sullsi came alongside; the same two, Jonkka supposed, that had watched him on the beach. The boatmen eyed them watchfully, and called assurances that only good was meant for their kinsman.

Juliassa left that to the men. Her attention was on the sellsu in the boat, stroking it and crooning, and every little while she poured another helmetful of water on it, till the bottom was three inches awash. Jonkka hoped the sellsu wouldn't wake up in the boat. A four-hundred-pound bull trying to get over the side would surely overturn them, maybe breaking someone's bones in the process.

But quickly enough he forgot about that. The motion of the boat, up, down, sideways, introduced him to seasickness.

At least the boatmen made haste, pulling the oars till the sweat ran, and at length Jonkka could see the villa, well back from the water. What, he wondered, would the namirrna do with the sellsu when they got it there? She had something being prepared for it, he was sure.

EIGHT

At noon on Elver Brokols' fourth day in Hrumma, Eltrienn Cadriio took him to a school where children were given knowledge of Hrummlis. By neighborhoods and ages, they attended twice a week for four hours, to recite with the teachers and ask and answer questions. And, when they were old enough, they were taught to meditate.

And no, Eltrienn said, they did not learn to read and write and reckon there; those skills they learned at home, from a grandparent, or lacking that, their mother or an aunt.

Without actually giving it any thought, Brokols had expected a stone box of a building, like the city schools in Almeon. Instead he found a small building of whitewashed bricks, unstuccoed—a residence for the bachelor teachers, Eltrienn said. With a courtyard behind it, and shelters—roofs without walls—for the classes to crowd into when a rainstorm struck. Even in the rainy season, summer, rains were mainly a midday phenomenon, and should a day begin with hard rain, classes might be cancelled.

They'd arrived minutes before the morning class left. There were no seats, no tables. The children wore short dresses of light colors—blue, pink, yellow, pale pure green. Brokols realized then that they wore nothing underneath. Inexcusably indecent, he thought. It fell short of obscenity only because the wearers were children.

Sitting cross-legged on the grass, the children's voices piped in rhythmic unison with the teacher who chanted before them. The individual words had meaning for Brokols now, most of them, but what was being said seemed gibberish.

The concepts, and the events and persons alluded to, were unfamiliar, and he felt twitchy listening. With Eltrienn, he waited near the gate till it was over. Shortly, as if at some signal, the children leaped to their feet, and with a chorus of squealing, poured as a swift stream of color past the watchers into the alleyway outside the courtyard and were gone.

Then Eltrienn led Brokols over and introduced him to the senior teacher, requesting that the man speak slowly for his guest. Brokols felt ill at ease with him. The teacher had shaved his head, leaving it bare and shiny, and worse, he wore only a sort of diaper. Convenient, presumably, for the strange, cross-legged posture he'd used in leading the chant, and it did cover his genitals, but it was far from decent attire for an adult. His belly was bare to the navel, his legs to the groin; in Almeon he'd have been jailed. And there was no sense of nobility about him; he looked nothing at all like a repository of knowledge and wisdom.

Brokols' mood of the Festival evening was definitely gone, replaced by proper Almaeic disapproval.

The teacher looked at him. "Why have you come to see me?" he asked.

"In my country," Brokols answered carefully, "we know nothing of Hrum, or of Hrummlis. I hoped you could tell me something about them."

The teacher's eyes were calm and steady, and Brokols adjusted his evaluation upward a little. "Ah," the man said. "In your country, do you know something of the world? The universe?"

More than you do, teacher, Brokols thought to himself. "Yes, we do. Quite a lot."

"Good. Then you know somewhat about Hrum. And do you know much about mankind?"

Brokols suspected what was coming, but answered anyway. "Yes, of course."

"Excellent. Then you have already made much progress in the study of Hrum. For the universe and the people in it are reflections of Hrum." His eyes seemed to search inside Brokols. "And who do you worship in your land?"

Religions had sprung up in Almeon in more primitive times, and even become prominent on some of the islands before the islands had been unified. But they'd been suppressed by the empire, and had all but died out after the

Larvest had been opened and *The Captains' Book* found and finally deciphered, giving them the facts of their origin.

"We worship no one," Brokols answered. At that, with a pang of chagrin, he remembered that he'd used religion to explain his antenna and generator, and hurried to cover the slip. "We worship *The Book of Forbiddances* and *The Book of Right Comportment*," he said. Which was true in a manner of speaking, he realized, though he'd never looked at it that way before.

"Ah," said the teacher. "It is not feasible to teach you what I know about Hrum while we stand here in the courtyard. However, you are welcome to attend classes with the children if you wish. With your maturity, you might prove to be one of our best pupils." He paused. "Meanwhile, perhaps I can answer a question for you. Is there one you'd care to ask?"

Not really, Brokols thought. "Yes. Describe Hrum for me."

"Hrum is—" The teacher paused, gray eyes evaluating Brokols, then went on.

"Hrum is not our father but our foster father, for you and I came from very far away in an earlier life. Hrum is the builder of the theater, the carpenter who created the stage. Hrum-In-Thee, who is not Hrum, who is yourself in the audience, names the play and chooses your role, then allows you to play it as you will.

"Hrum has provided you the spindle and the wheel, has given you the loom. You must ret the limma yourself. The pattern is your own, and you weave your own tapestry."

He paused, his eyes still on Brokols' eyes.

"What I have told you is the truth, and each word of it is a lie."

He paused. "That should suffice for now. Are we done for this time?"

Brokols nodded curtly without speaking. He felt . . . angry, cheated, insulted. He could not have said what, subconsciously, he'd anticipated, but certainly not this nonsense.

"Very well. Should you come here again, you will be welcome." The teacher nodded dismissal, then turned away and walked toward the house.

Come here again? Not likely, Brokols told himself as he left with Cadriio.

He was sweating in his suit and hat. With the rainy season had come heat and humidity, and they were walking uphill now. Eltrienn had said the dry season was cooler, sometimes even cold, but it would be hot and humid like this for more than a quarter of the year. At home it was seldom this hot, and he almost envied Eltrienn his short immodest skirt, bare legs, nearly sleeveless tunic.

But not his religion. He'd never cared for riddling games, and certainly not for fraud or pathological stupidity. While for something like this to be presented as a central and serious aspect of life . . .

Walking, he wiped his forehead with his handkerchief. "What now?" he asked.

Eltrienn had sensed his guest's annoyance and had been waiting for Brokals to initiate conversation. His answer was cheerful: "We're going to a monastery, where I hope you may talk with a master. A monastery is where masters live in celibacy, and lead would-be teachers and would-be masters to the wisdom of Hrum."

"I thought the children were taught the wisdom of Hrum. I thought that's what we were listening to back there."

Eltrienn shook his head, still cheerful despite Brokols' surliness. "The children are *exposed* to the wisdom of Hrum. They learn enough to help guide their behavior. But wisdom is not like knowledge; it cannot be taught. Wisdom comes from within; from Hrum that is in each of us.

"It is something that most of us gain only small pieces of. Enough, hopefully, to make our lives happier and more pleasing."

Brokols thought he'd be happier and more pleased with a cold drink, and for a dismayed moment realized that there'd be none here. Not even in winter, as he understood the Hrummean climate. These people hadn't developed ice factories where one could send a servant to fetch a supply.

And he was committed to spend years here if necessary!

"But there are those," Eltrienn went on, "who after much meditation achieve in a sudden rush the full wisdom of Hrum. It doesn't remain on them, but once it has struck, they thenceforth look at the world through different eyes. It is these who are called masters."

"And was that a master we talked with back there?"

"No. That was a man who has learned very much of the Books of Knowledge and memorized parts of them. Whose mind and behavior have been greatly influenced by them. But knowledge and wisdom aren't the same. A teacher will also have gained numerous pieces of Hrum's wisdom, but only pieces. His knowledge and wisdom are enough that his master certified him to teach and to meditate disputes."

"Umh," Brokols grunted, and found himself warily hopeful that a master might at least show less idiocy than the teacher had. "How far is it to this"—he paused, groping for the word—"this monastery?"

"Less than three miles. Just outside the city."

Three miles. Brokols looked around as if to conjure up transportation. "That's farther than I want to walk on a hot day like this," he said. Thinking he wouldn't have minded so much if it hadn't been for the woolen suit he wore.

"Fine," said Eltrienn, "we'll take this way then," and turned right down a cross-street. The next street over was a thoroughfare, and he whistled shrilly, once, twice, loud blasts that startled Brokols. At home, no citizen would make a noise like that where people were. Within seconds two rikkshas appeared, their runners loping easily, sweat gleaming on corded limbs and torsos, one's loincloth scarlet, the other's vivid indigo.

Brokols hadn't seen a rikksha runner up close before, and was awed by their bodies. He was already used to the size of the Hrummeans and their frequently fine musculature. The acrobatic dancers had impressed him deeply, as had Eltrienn's muscular arms. But these rikksha runners were unlike any men he'd seen before, their chests deep and broad, thighs and calves corded, torsos sinewy. Even their arms looked strong. They stood grinning at him, dripping.

Somehow bodies like theirs didn't offend him.

Following Eltrienn's example, and while the centurion gave directions to the runners, Brokols seated himself in one of the two rikkshas. The two runners began to lope. At first Brokols, leaning back and holding his hat, found the ride exhilarating. But within a block his runner began to fall behind the other, and the man called something which Brokols didn't get.

"Elver," shouted Eltrienn, "don't lean back! It's uphill, and your runner needs more traction."

At that, Brokols leaned forward, forearms on thighs, and now his runner kept pace. In about twenty minutes the city street became a country road, almost abruptly. Minutes later they pulled up outside a high courtyard wall, stopped and dismounted. Eltrienn paid the runners, who grinned, then loped toward a huge, broad-crowned tree, presumably to park their rikkshas and rest.

Here Eltrienn did not simply open the heavy gate; perhaps it was locked, Brokols decided, or it might be a matter of protocol. Instead he raised the bronze knocker and dropped it twice, while Brokols wondered what they'd find inside. The wait was brief. An old man opened for them, bald and wrinkled, spidery within a sacklike sleeveless shift that showed thin shanks and knobby knees, gaunt shoulders, loose-skinned long and wasted arms. Eltrienn nodded nonetheless respectfully to the man, and Brokols swallowed his annoyance. Surely such aged, unaesthetic bodies should be better covered.

Eltrienn spoke quietly, and they were ushered in. Now Brokols could hear a low bass resonance, a sort of thrumming. After closing the gate again, the old man led them toward a long wooden shed, open-sided, with four long, low, raised platforms, like broad benches, each with a row of men sitting straightbacked on folded legs. The sonorous thrumming was from them, and Brokols realized that the sound was the name of *Hrum*, resonated, protracted, and repeated. As he approached, he realized with a shock that, like the children, these men wore nothing beneath their short, coarse, unbleached shirts.

Stopping near one end of the shed, Brokols and Eltrienn watched. Two robed men, shave-headed like their students, quietly walked the aisles between the benches, each carrying a slender five-foot rod with a small knob on the end. Now and then one of them reached and tapped, or sometimes sharply rapped, the head of some student. After several minutes of watching, Eltrienn nodded to the old man, who led them to an adjacent building. There they stopped, and seeing Eltrienn remove his boots, Brokols bent and took off his shoes, leaving them beside the entrance.

They went down a hall then, and stopped again while the old man spoke through a door. A voice inside said "come in," and they did, the old man closing the door behind them without entering.

The man who'd answered met them standing, a man of less than medium height for a Hrummean, a bit shorter than Brokols. But he had presence! Brokols felt it at once. It was more than the way he stood, more than the calm eyes that seemed to perceive beyond light and form and color. To

Brokols, even in that first moment, this seemed a different sort of entity than the teacher.

"Master Jerrsio," Eltrienn said, "I've brought a guest of the amirr's to see your initiates in training, and to meet you. You may have heard of him. He is Elver Brokols, the ambassador from beyond the ocean."

"From Almeon," Brokols heard himself say. It occurred to him that part of what he felt was subordinacy, and subordinacy was inappropriate here to a representative of His Imperial Majesty. But he let the matter stand; he didn't know how else to feel, although he added, "I represent His Majesty the Emperor."

Master Jerrsio's shaved head nodded polite acknowledgement, and he gestured to a low, padded bench. When they were seated, the master, folding his legs, sat down on a small rug and spoke. "Will you have satta?"

Brokols nodded; no words came to him. "If you please," Eltrienn said. He sounded entirely casual.

The master struck a small gong, and they waited without talking. After about a minute a youth arrived, perhaps fifteen years old. He half bowed, and the master told him to bring satta. The youth left, and Master Jerrsio's gaze returned to Brokols.

Again they waited silently. Shortly the youth returned with a tray containing a pot and three delicate porcelain cups. Setting the tray on a low stand, he served them, cup by cup, his movements precise. When the youth had served all three, Jerrsio sipped and nodded approval. The youth left. Brokols, following the master's example, was sure he'd blistered his upper lip.

"How may I help you?" Jerrsio asked.

It struck Brokols that this man, this master, could be courteous and even common without losing presence. "In my country," Brokols said, "we know nothing about Hrum. I hoped you could tell me something about him."

"*About* Hrum I can tell you. Be informed though that knowing *about* Hrum and knowing Hrum are not the same. One can ride a kaabor, but one cannot ride a description of a kaabor. Still, knowing about Hrum may be useful to you, and it may also be sufficient to your purposes." Jerrsio paused. "Would you care to ask a specific question?"

Brokols cast back to the little, unintegrated and meaningless, that had been written down of what the slaves had said about Hrum, decades earlier. Perhaps they hadn't volunteered much on the subject.

"What use it is to know Hrum?" he asked.

"Ah! To the individual, Awakening to Hrum gives much greater neutrality, and hence more stability in life, greater appreciation of life, greater pleasures of life. As for nations— a nation whose leaders know even certain aspects of Hrum, and whose people respect Hrum, can enjoy greater justice and more happiness than if they did not."

He paused and smiled slightly at Brokols. "Nothing I can tell you here will much enlighten you. But let me suggest that when you have come to know our country better, you will know somewhat about Hrum."

Brokols looked intently at Jerrsio; he was an easy man to look directly at. "One more question, if you please," Brokols said. "My people first heard of Hrum from slaves given to them by the King of Djez Gorrbul, and according to them, Hrum is worshiped there. Yet in Djez Gorrbul they hold human beings as disposable property for life. What can you say about this?"

Again Jerrsio smiled slightly. "You are right. In Djez Gorrbul they *worship* Hrum. And one can find a certain satisfaction in worship. A certain peace, a certain ease. But knowing Hrum, one cannot worship him. And until one ceases to worship Hrum, one cannot know him. Worship gets in the way."

He struck the gong again, then rose from his platform smoothly and without effort, despite the need to unfold his legs. "I am glad you visited me," he said to Brokols. And to Eltrienn, "Thank you for bringing us together."

The visitors too stood up. This time it was the old man who answered the gong, and after they'd put their shoes back on, he led them back to the gate. The rikkshas were gone, but it was downhill from there, and Brokols and Eltrienn walked back, not talking very much. A lot of questions lurked just out of sight in Brokols mind, and he let them be, somehow knowing that this was not the time to dredge for them.

It occurred to him that the master's answers hadn't been much more informative than the teacher's, but the way the two men affected him had been altogether different. Partly a matter of courtesy perhaps, but more of— something else. Charisma. Magnetism. Something.

And it seemed to him he hadn't been ready to talk to either

of them, master or teacher. He'd continue to question Eltrienn from time to time, and perhaps visit the master again.

They ate lunch at an inn in the lower part of town. "Eltrienn," said Brokols thoughtfully, "your religion is really basic to your nation, isn't it? You're drilled in it from childhood. What further elements should I see? You mentioned having a brother who's a sage."

"That's right. Vessto's his name. I haven't been able to locate him. He was in town for Festival, that much I've learned, but I suspect he's left by now for Kammenak, our home district. That's the isthmus that connects Hrumma with Djez Gorrbul. In ancient times, 'Kammenak' meant 'Neck of Mountains'; the isthmus is only six miles wide, a series of parallel ridges, very rugged. We raise vehatto there."

Brokols knew that *vehatto* was some kind of domestic animal, presumably a grazer or browser; beyond that he knew nothing about it. "I need a map of your country," he said. "I've got very little idea of the geography here.

"Now about Hrummlis: One thing the slaves from Djez Gorrbul told us is that the worship of Hrum, in their country, was ruled by what they termed a *priesthood;* is that what you call the teachers and masters? And the sages? A priesthood?"

Eltrienn considered the question thoughtfully. "Here Hrum is much more influential than in the Djezes. In the Djezes, the priests are appointed by their high priests, and their high priests by the king. In Hrumma, instead of priests we have sages and masters and teachers, which we call 'the holy clergy.' "

He almost went on to mention the 'secular clergy'—the adepts—but it seemed best not to. If the ambassador asked what the secular clergy did, he'd have to lie, so he skipped them, continuing with the holy clergy.

"And the amirr names none of them; they are appointed by Hrum, so to speak. While on the other hand, sages have much to say about who is elected amirr, and amirrs have been ousted by the Two Estates—the Lords and the People—led by the holy clergy."

Brokols' eyebrows lifted. He'd assumed that an amirr had the powers of a king. Just now he was overloaded with unfamiliar concepts, and groped for something further to relate them to. "How do you know when a person has been appointed by Hrum?" he asked.

"Hrum appoints someone as clergy by giving them some degree of wisdom."

"Umh. And how do you recognize wisdom when you see it?"

"Masters recognize it in initiates, and give them the title of master or some lesser title such as teacher. As for sages—a sage is usually a master whose wisdom impresses people enough that they agree he's a sage."

"You said your brother is a sage."

"He is widely considered one, in Kammenak and the districts around it. But to become fully recognized as a sage, one must be considered a sage in Theedalit."

Eltrienn looked questioningly at Brokols. "Would you care to visit a sage? We have two in Theedalit, or nearby. Tassi Vermaatio is said not to talk though, at all, while Panni Vempravvo may be meditating at any hour. Or he might simply give you a riddle to contemplate."

Inwardly, Brokols grunted. What kind of wisdom was that? "No," he said, "I'll wait awhile before visiting a sage. I need to sleep on what I've experienced today. And I need to visit more of your country."

"Good. I'll hire a shay for the rest of this afternoon, and we can drive about the city—visit some businesses. Tomorrow perhaps we'll look at some upriver farms."

NINE

On the private rooftop garden outside his apartment, Brokols ate a quiet, solitary supper, a late meal, watching the fading bands of silver and old rose in the western sky, beneath the brilliant bit that was Little Firtollio in his first quarter. Something in bloom perfumed the evening with a fragrance he hadn't noticed during the day.

He was in a strange mood, random detached thoughts drifting idly through his consciousness. *Jerrsio*. The man had impressed him, but from a perspective of eight hours there seemed to have been no cause for it. In anything the man had said or done. Maybe the initiates droning *Hrum* had had some psychological effect, rendering him susceptible.

Interesting that the frequent bare torsos and even limbs in Hrumma weren't usually offensive. Perhaps subconsciously he knew that droids weren't truly human and human rules didn't fully apply. He looked at the thought and rejected it. And anyway the monks really should wear something, some undergarment, or else sit differently to better conceal their genitals while they intoned the name of their god. And the aged should definitely not be allowed to expose their unsightly wrinkled limbs.

In general though, the Hrummean physique tended to be quite superior. As one might expect of the progeny of pleasure droids. His own physique should get back into shape here. There were five long flights of stairs to climb from the street, each time he came home; he took them fast and hard, and his thighs had burned from it. And Hrummean food promised to be less fattening. He'd had Stilfos downstairs at the kitchen of their landlord part of the day, learning Hrummean cookery.

Stilfos was important to him, someone he needn't hide things from. Any servant Eltrienn might have procured for him would be a spy. Of course, Eltrienn was too, in a manner of speaking, but Eltrienn didn't have the run of the apartment, access to the wireless room or arms chest.

Feet sounded softly on the deck behind him, followed by quiet words in still-awkward Hrummean. "Milord, there's a gentleman at the door. A Tirros . . ." Stilfos hesitated over the unfamiliar polysyllable. "A Tirros Han-o-riss-i-o. And a male companion. Mr. Tirros appears to be noble, and he'd like to speak with you. He gave me this."

Stilfos handed Brokols a folded sheet of paper, or something like paper, its wax seal impressed with a sigil he couldn't make out in the thickening twilight. Not, he thought, that he'd recognize it in any light.

But *Hanorissio*. That seemed to mean his visitor was a member of the amirrial family. "Thank you, Stilfos." Brokols said it without rising, without turning. "Tell him I'll be with him in a moment."

As the footsteps receded, Brokols sat staring not at the paper but down the harbor, through its entrance at the ocean beyond. *Serpents*. How much intelligence could something have, use, without hands to go with it? The water people had hands, even if they used them for little besides catching fish.

He got to his feet, feeling the slight soreness in his thighs as he did so, and turned to the terrace door. Soft fluttering light shone from the glass globes of oil lamps. He entered, then waited standing till Stilfos ushered the visitors into the sitting room. The smaller, less well-dressed of them stopped a pace behind the other, as if perhaps a servant. Brokols recognized the first, a slender youth, inches taller than himself, who'd stood behind the amirr's shoulder that first day. They shook hands, the strength in Tirros's long slender fingers surprising the Almite.

"I'm Tirros Hanorissio," the young man said. "The amirr is my father." He gestured at his companion. "This is Karrlis Billbis, a friend of mine."

Brokols nodded. "Pray be seated," he said, gesturing at chairs. "A cup of satta perhaps?"

As Tirros Hanorissio sat down, his eyes took in the room.

Its furnishings were Hrummean, of quality. "We prefer wine," he answered. "At your pleasure."

Brokols nodded, then instructed Stilfos. When the servant left, Brokols sat.

"I've never talked with a foreigner before," Tirros told him. "This is a nice apartment, though I'm surprised that Eltrienn took an upper floor for you. For someone of your position, that makes a lot of steps to climb. Are you satisfied with it?"

"Entirely satisfied. I specifically asked for an upper floor. The view, you know."

"Ah. And is Eltrienn a satisfactory representative of my father?"

"Entirely satisfactory."

"Good." Tirros paused, his gaze frankly calculating. "Eltrienn's a herdboy from the Neck, you know—intelligent enough, but common. And provincial. He's ignorant about our level of society—yours and mine."

He paused again, as if watching for a reaction, then changed the subject. "My father has instructed me to arrange a reception for you. On Fiveday night."

A reception, Brokols thought, would allow him to meet and evaluate a lot of important people. And Fiveday was only two days off.

Stilfos came in carrying a small tray with three glasses and a decanter. He poured for them and left, and they drank.

"There'll be young women of quality at the reception," Tirros added smirking. "They're all interested in the ambassador from across the ocean. Very interested. Your social life can be highly enjoyable here, if you'd like."

"Indeed?" Brokols wasn't sure what Tirros meant by 'social life'; the smirk had triggered suspicion.

The mirj's eyes gleamed darkly, lizard-like and watchful beneath half-closed lids. "But of course, you needn't wait till Fiveday if you'd like to meet young ladies. As I said, Mr. Ambassador, you're interesting, and I know some who'd like very much to meet you. At your convenience. Some very accomplished young ladies. I know at least one who'd happily meet you this evening; a charming girl."

Brokols felt his loins stir. *The pup is deliberately tempting me*, he thought. *Or testing me*. "Indeed!" he answered stiffly. "In The Empire we are cautious about young ladies."

The smile returned, a grin this time. "None of these has

committed herself to anyone. They prefer their freedom yet awhile. Is there anything else I can do for you? Any entertainment you'd prefer at the reception? Dancing? Music? Anyone you'd particularly like to have attend? Or *not* attend? Food or drink you like especially well? That we might have in Hrumma?"

Brokols felt angry annoyance. He could think of one person he'd prefer not to be there, but he wasn't in Hrumma to make enemies gratuitously, certainly not in the amirrial family. "I'm sure that whatever you provide will be satisfactory. After all, the amirr is your father."

The curly head bobbed, a miniature bow. "Indeed, Your Excellency."

"And where is this reception to be held?"

"At the Palace. It is written in the invitation. Eltrienn knows the place. Or I can have someone else bring you, if you'd like a change of companionship."

"Not at all. I consider Eltrienn a friend, as well as guide and tutor." Brokols got to his feet. "Well. I'm sure you have—more interesting things to do this evening than talk with me. While I have things that I must attend to."

For a long moment, Tirros Hanorissio made no move to get up, and Brokols wondered if the youth would have the insolence just to sit there when his host had indicated the conversation was over. Or—perhaps it was inappropriate in this country to send someone on their way on such short notice.

But then the mirj unfolded his long body from the chair and stood. "Thank you, Your Excellency, for your hospitality. I may call on you again before the reception. If I don't, I'll see you there. And don't hesitate to call on me if there is, um, any favor I can do for you."

After leaving Karrlis Billbis, a grinning Tirros Hanorissio strode alone down a dark street. Except for the amirr himself, male aristocrats seldom had bodyguards in Hrumma, and Tirros would have felt restricted by one.

Karrlis's reading of the foreigner had been more than promising. If there proved to be no profit in him, at least this ambassador could provide amusement; he'd even blushed a little.

Elver Brokols read till his eyes felt red and tired. Oil lamps were no substitute for electricity. He set aside one of the books Eltrienn had given him, a history of Hrumma. It was interesting, if perhaps a bit imaginative. As he read though, his mind kept slipping off to the impudent mirj and his offer of girls.

He'd have trouble going to sleep tonight, he knew. Since Valda had died in childbirth, almost two years past, he'd had a woman only once, a comely wench in a place of illicit sex. Being there had been risky, a felony, and he'd found no pleasure in it, only brief excitement and subsequent self-disgust.

Somehow he felt sure that Hrummean girls would be far beyond anything he'd known with sweet but proper Valda. Or with the prostitute. He shivered. Pleasure droids! He'd avoid this Tirros at all costs, he decided.

But beneath the surface of his decision, he felt fantasies lurking to distract him from sleep.

TEN

The next day Eltrienn and Brokols drove up the valley in a light shay, visiting farms above the city. In the fields, some of the men wore only a sort of cloth band to contain their genitals, though most of them wore a short skirt as well. The women's skirts were longer, but hardly or not at all below the knees, and Brokols wondered if there was even an undergarment beneath; he hoped so. While above the waist—like the acrobatic dancers, some wore only a sort of supporting harness for their breasts, and a few of the younger none at all. Many children ran completely naked.

Mostly the adults and older children were hoeing. The rains had brought germination indiscriminately to crops and weeds, and there was a lot of field work to do.

In Hrumma, according to Eltrienn, the land was held quite differently than in Almeon. Except for grazing lands in some plateau districts where surface water was infrequent, there were no great ownerships. Each family held its own land, subject to eviction only in the case of land abuse. In the valleys, most of them banded together in cooperatives, paying one or more of their number to market for all the members, arranging transport, dealing with buyers or for space in the markets, collecting money, keeping records.

They bought their midday meal at one of the larger farmsteads and had gone inside to eat when the usual daily shower came, brief but hard. It was over by the time they'd finished, leaving the air steamy but somehow not oppressive.

The hills bordering the valley were mostly in orchards, where they weren't too steep, while occasional heavy-bodied gleebors, their upright horns cut short to stubs, grazed among the fruit trees. The steeper slopes were covered with coppice growth, with horizontal strips cut for fuel.

Most of the dwellings were of unbaked bricks, plastered over with the same kind of dried mud, and whitewashed. Most roofs were sodded or thatched. A few of the larger, finer homes were built of baked bricks, and had tile roofs. Native wood, whether as fuelwood or charcoal, had long been too scarce to fuel brick kilns with, Eltrienn explained. Charcoal for making tile and brick was mostly imported now from a small Hrummean settlement on the wild east coast of the mainland, operating at the sufferance of the barbarians there. Even much lumber came from there.

It was a long haul, Eltrienn said, a thousand-mile round trip by boat.

After he'd said it, he seemed to introvert, falling silent.

Barbarian tribes. The teaching slaves had told about the barbarians who occasionally raided the eastern and northern duchies of the Djezes, duchies that bordered wild and forested mountains. "How is it," Brokols asked, "that the barbarians allow your people to operate there?"

"We trade with them," Eltrienn answered.

"Trade what?"

The Hrummean lagged a moment before answering. "Gemstones. Silver. Occasionally gold. They're fond of jewelry."

Jewelry? Brokols wondered. "Have you considered selling them steel? Tools? Weapons?" He watched the centurion's face as he asked; it told him nothing.

"They make their own."

"Their own steel?"

"Not steel. Hardly. But their own iron."

"What do they mine with?"

"They don't mine. The use bog iron; they collect the scums in certain ponds and springs."

"Huh! I've never heard of that. How is it done?"

Eltrienn shrugged. "I don't know. It's nothing I've ever seen done. But their trade has eased the pressure on our fuel supplies. And much of our larger timber is brought from there."

Brokols got home earlier than he'd expected. Stilfos was out of the apartment and didn't get in for another half hour.

"Where were you?" Brokols asked when the man returned.

Stilfos colored slightly. "I was downstairs getting a lesson in baking. Bread, with a flour made of a ground tuber."

"Hmm. Well. I look forward to eating some."

After a bit, Brokols went downstairs to see the landlord, and asked to meet the cook, to thank her for her help. She was perhaps twenty-five years old, handsome and strong-looking.

"Married?" Brokols asked the landlord afterward.

The man chuckled. "She'd like to be. Her husband was a sailor, lost in a storm last winter. I believe she's taken a liking to your man, though he's somewhat smaller than her."

That evening after supper, Stilfos asked if he could leave for a while. Brokols was inclined to deny him, but a contented servant was preferable to a resentful one, and the man was not replaceable here.

"I presume you've tidied the kitchen?"

"Yes, sir."

"Where would you go? And for how long?"

"I'd . . . like to go for a walk with Gerrla. Mr. Bostelli's cook. Not for very long. There's a park near here we can stroll in."

Brokols frowned thoughtfully, then looked at the Hrummean clock on the mantle. They'd somehow come up with a twenty-hour clock here, but he was getting used to it.

"Be back by eighteen hours then," he said. "Meanwhile I'll have used the radio, so when you get in, see to recharging the battery."

Brokols was not pleased with the situation, but sometimes it was necessary to view these things philosophically: Stilfos *was* a commoner, and though rather intelligent, more susceptible to biological urges than Brokols would be. Thus Brokols set the matter aside and returned his attention to the history.

At seventeen hours and a quarter, he put aside his book to radio Kryger. There wasn't much to report, but it was important to maintain regular communication. When he was done, it was nearly seventeen and a half—17.46. He wondered what Stilfos was doing just then, with Gerrla. Gerrla. A female descendant of pleasure droids.

He shivered, took a deep breath and let it out slowly, bleakly. He was twenty-eight years old, approaching twenty-nine, and he'd very likely be here for two years or more, perhaps five or ten.

But his father was an earl, and his older brother would be

in his time. He himself had been knighted on acceptance into the university. He would spurn Tirros's offer and behave like an Almite noble. Like a Brokols.

He returned to his book, and at 17.96 heard Stilfos come in. A few minutes later he heard him on the roof, putting the generator in gear to recharge the battery. It would kick out after a preset number of revolutions. Shortly afterward, Stilfos knocked and asked if Brokols would like a pot of satta, and Brokols said yes. A few minutes later, Stilfos delivered it steaming hot, with a cup and a small pot of sugar cubes. Then, with Brokols' permission, he went to bed.

Brokols went to bed at 19:00 feeling grim. Damn it but the man had looked happy! He closed his eyes, and within seconds there was an image behind the lids, of Stilfos coupling with Gerrla in a shadowed grove. *Double damn!* he thought, sitting abruptly up. For a moment he glared in darkness, then lay back down to deliberately start a non-erotic thought chain, a distraction from the erotic.

He'd been offended by the semi-nudity of the teacher, but not by the rikksha runners. Why? The runners' loincloths were skimpier than the teacher's. Something else must underlie his feeling. Aesthetics? The teacher's body hadn't been unsightly, but neither was it handsome. And what was his basis for allowing aesthetics to justify indecent dress?

Brokols got up and went to the pantry, poured himself a glass of wine and walked back to the sitting room, his mind still busy.

As he sipped, it seemed to him that perhaps he'd disliked the teacher at first sight, disliked the look of him sitting in his diaper before his pupils. But he couldn't actually remember feeling like that.

Or had his dislike come later—grown out of their conversation? He had no doubt that the teacher had treated him superciliously—been condescending, almost insulting. He tried to remember just what had been said, but the words refused recall.

So did Master Jerrsio's. But there was no doubt that Jerrsio too had spoken as a superior to an inferior. Or no, that wasn't it. As an expert to the uniformed, appropriate enough to the circumstances. Not as an adult to a dim-witted child though; he hadn't felt demeaned by it.

And the subordinacy he'd felt before Master Jerrsio was different than his subordinacy to Kryger. Kryger was his superior in status and experience, no doubt in toughness, and probably in single-mindedness. But Brokols recognized his own relative strengths—empathy, balance, and quite probably intelligence. By contrast, Master Jerrsio seemed almost a different kind of entity, with different defining parameters.

And what about the scrawny old man who'd ushered them in and out of the monastery? What parameters defined him as a person? How, Brokols asked himself, did he feel about the man? Even without speaking or acting markedly perculiar, he'd seemed—perhaps not bright and surely not quite sane.

Brokols shook his head. He was giving these matters more attention than they deserved. His problem was, he'd been thinking of these people as fully human. So. Should he forbid Stilfos to consort with Gerrla? He shook his head, rejecting the thought, then stood and drank the last swallow of wine. Stilfos was, after all, common, and eight thousand miles from home and any proper woman.

He, on the other hand, was a knight, son of one of the best families, a graduate of the university, reserve army officer, a representative of the emperor. And in a few years, still young, he'd be back in Almeon, would marry a pretty woman of good family, one who played the scintar and sang nicely, who wouldn't die while losing her first child, who'd raise a family he could be proud of.

Elver Brokols went back to bed then and was soon asleep.

ELEVEN

It was early evening, still daylight, when Elver Brokols and Eltrienn Cadriio arrived by hansom at the amirr's palace. Brokols hadn't been there before. It was large but not huge, not in the sense that the imperial palace was, in Larvis Royal. Slightly smaller than the Brokols family seat in the Falmar Valley.

And different; the architecture and landscaping were much simpler. But the simplicity was elegant, its beauty deriving from a harmony of proportions and relationships, not relying on, or even much using, ornamentation. Like almost all of Theedalit's buildings, it was white, but the white of native marble, not whitewash. There were roundnesses and angles never clashing, many large and awninged windows, mostly open now, and double doors giving onto terraces, promenades, balconies.

The doormen were well covered, uniformed in chalk white hose and tunics, with soft boots and stiff-shouldered vests of golden velvet. Swords in gold-plated scabbards were worn thrust into sashes of scarlet or cobalt blue. The overall purpose was clearly aesthetics, but Brokols felt sure the swords were entirely functional, and no doubt the men who carried them. The amirr and naamir were waiting in a foyer, and to Brokols' brief confusion, both embraced him.

They led him to the reception then, in a spacious suite obviously intended and furnished for galas. Although he'd arrived almost exactly at the time prescribed, there already was a crowd. Apparently the other guests had been assigned an earlier arrival time, to be there when the guest of honor appeared.

And apparently there was to be no banquet in the usual sense, though the assortment of food and drink, still being set out on several long serving tables, seemed equal to a banquet. A sort of casual half cheer, half called-out greeting met Brokols when he walked in—or was it for his host and hostess they cheered?—and as waiters circulated with trays of drinks, people began to drift toward Brokols.

The drinks too were visually aesthetic, and the one he took seemed only weakly, if at all, alcoholic.

There was no formal reception line nor any swarm of greeters. They came up to him singly, for the most part, introduced themselves, said something polite, then gave way to someone else. Brokols was grateful for his gift of remembering faces and the names that went with them—a gift that had already helped his career in government service and may well have been a factor in his selection as ambassador.

After ten minutes or so a gong sounded, and a steward announced that food was now being served. There were plates of several sizes and kinds, to suit individual wants, and numerous tall tables, some small, some not, at which one stood to eat. Talk continued, though more slowly.

Some of the conversation was trivial, but he was asked many questions, and given a number of suggestions dealing with his functions as ambassador. Meetings were offered. After a bit, Eltrienn suggested to Brokols that he might wish to circulate, then left him on his own.

Among the affluent, dressing was obviously an art form. Variety was considerable, though white was the basic color. There was no semi-nudity to perturb him except for the almost invariable, though not monotonous decolletage. He couldn't entirely keep his eyes from straying to female breasts exposed halfway to the nipples, and the sight, so close, made him slightly uncomfortable, though not actually unhappy.

Mostly, though, he managed to ignore the display, and being asked so many questions helped a lot. Hrummeans were especially interested in Almeon, its culture and government. Part of what he told them was truth, and part was lies well-rehearsed before he'd left home, with the Minister of State and with Kryger.

Eventually he had moments when no one was talking with him. It was one of these that Tirros Hanorissio interrupted.

Brokols was standing beside a double garden door when there they were—Tirros and two lovely girls of about the mirj's age.

"Elver Brokols!" said Tirros, sounding delighted. "I'd hoped we might talk. My father told me I could if I'd behave myself and not intrude when others wanted to talk with you. I've been waiting to find you unoccupied."

Brokols nodded, concealing his annoyance.

"This," Tirros said, indicating the girl on his right, "is Marinnia. And this"—he nodded to the smaller of the two—"is Lerrlia. Twins, though they don't look it. Ladies, this is His Excellency, Ambassador Lord Elver Brokols of Almeon."

Both girls smiled, showing white and even teeth, and for the first time that evening, Brokols felt out of place in his Almeaic dress suit. And for the first time that evening he found himself truly distracted by decolletage, for theirs was dangerously lower. "I'm charmed," he said, somewhat short of convincingly.

"I've hoped I'd have a chance to meet you," Lerrlia answered. Her hair was straight and shiny black. Her eyes were sapphire blue, and they fastened on his. "It's intriguing to think of an entire nation, an entire people, that we'd never imagined existed. How long will you be in Hrumma?"

"I'm not sure. Presumably several years. I'm to learn all I can about you—about your country. The better to see the possibilities and potential problems for trade, you know, and develop proposals."

"I saw the ship you arrived on," she said. "What a marvelous vessel! And for more reasons than its size. There was the way it entered the harbor with neither sails nor oars!" She paused, an eyebrow raised. "I've heard it's driven by fires inside."

"True," Brokols said, "it is. Driven by fires inside." When he'd said it he felt his cheeks warm, and knew he was blushing. *This is ridiculous,* he thought.

She smiled again. "Perhaps you'll show it to me. When it comes back."

"Perhaps. Unfortunately though, it's not my ship. That would be up to its master."

Tirros had turned to a passing waiter, and when the man had gone on, the mirj had a glass in his hand. He held it out to Brokols. "I saw this and wondered if you'd tried one yet," he said. "It's called claerrmed. Very warming. Here."

Brokols had had one that looked like it earlier, but before he could say so, Lerrlia spoke again. "Try it," she said. "I think you'll be surprised."

He took it and sipped. It *was* different. There was a distinct bitterness, and a slow warmth began diffusing through his chest.

Her eyes were bright, expectant. "Did you like it?"

"I'm—not quite sure. It's a little bitter."

She laughed. All three laughed. "Here," she said, extending her hand. "Let me taste it."

He gave it to her, almost twitching when their fingers touched, and she raised it to her lips, then licked them with a pointed and delicate tongue. "Nice," she said, and gave the drink back.

Again their hands touched, and he felt it all the way to his chest. "Where will you go after the two or three years are over?" she asked him.

"I'm sure it hasn't been decided, or probably even thought about. Quite possibly I'll continue here, if I want to."

"Elver," said Tirros, "I have a boat, a pleasure boat. We'd planned to take a turn around the bay, in the moonlight, and hoped you'd come with us. We'll be glad to wait, if you'll be available after a bit."

Brokols raised his glass again and took a larger drink. *Claerrmed*. By then the warmth had diffused throughout his body, and colors seemed brighter, sounds clearer.

Pleasure boat. Pleasure droids. "I think I'd like that," he heard himself say. "Definitely I would like that."

Tirros grinned. "We'll wait. When you're ready to leave, go out in the garden." He motioned toward a pair of open doors. "We'll watch for you."

Brokols shook hands with all three of them, and watched them leave through the garden door. Then he sought out the amirr.

"Your Excellency," he said, "I've had a busy day, and with the food and drink, I've become rather sleepy. Does protocol allow me to leave soon?"

The amirr's brows lifted. "Of course, of course. Whenever you'd like. The reception is first of all for your pleasure, and surely no one can say that you've been other than approachable and affable." He looked around. "I'll have someone fetch Eltrienn for you."

"No no," Brokols said, "don't bother. He needs a vacation

from me, or deserves one at any rate. I'll take a brief stroll around your grounds and walk home." He grinned, surprising the amirr as well as himself. "I drank more than I'm used to. It's less than a mile, your streets are safe, and the walk will do me good."

They shook hands, Brokols thinking how much more amiable the amirr was than the emperor; then he sauntered to an open garden door and out into the night. His eyes found no one else there just then. With a delicious sense of conspiracy such as he hadn't felt since he was twelve, he walked to a hedge that formed a shadowed alcove. There was a bench there, and he'd have sat down, but Tirros and the two girls were already coming, from a different door than he had. Recklessly Brokols waved an arm at them.

As they approached, he could feel his grin stretching his cheeks, and they grinned back. "I've had a carriage waiting," Tirros said. "This way."

The mirj led down a flagstone path to a marble balustrade, and he and Brokols let themselves over it to a lawn a bit lower than the garden. The girls had swung their legs over, too, and reaching up, Tirros grasped Marinnia by the waist and helped her down. A grinning Brokols followed his example, and when Lerrlia's feet touched down, he held her against him for a moment, looking into the eyes that sparkled at him. Then they ran, actually ran!, across the lawn to a waiting carriage, keeping to the shadows of a row of trees, arriving with low giggles, soft male chuckles, a vibrant sense of anticipation.

Tirros and Marinnia had gotten there first, and when he'd given an instruction to the coachman on top, Tirros opened the front door and helped her in, then got in behind her. Brokols and Lerrlia got in back. When they were seated, Tirros tugged a little cord and the carriage began to move, the hooves of the two kaabors clopping on the flagstoned street.

There was something in the drink, Brokols told himself as he reached for the girl beside him, and the realization didn't bother him at all. She was as eager as he, their hands groping, lips finding lips in the darkness.

He wasn't immediately sure whether to be glad when the carriage stopped. Straightening their clothes, they got out. They were near one end of the city's wharf, at a place where several pleasure boats were tied. Tirros gave their coachman instructions, and the man drove off into the darkness.

The boat they boarded had a sort of cabin forward, curtained with thick rich material that could be rolled up. Amidships and aft were eight deserted rowing stools, and in the stern a tiller. The oars lay in the bottom. Brokols chuckled. There were no oarsmen; of course not. Tirros had never intended an excursion. The front of the "cabin" was open, and they went inside. On either side was a broad couch, and Tirros and Marinnia lowered themselves onto one of them to take up where they'd stopped when the carriage arrived.

For just a moment, Brokols had a brief, faint unwillingness. There was no privacy here! But Lerrlia's quick fingers had moved to his buttons, and his reluctance evaporated.

He'd never imagined, truly never imagined, a night like that, nor anyone like she was. Nor a performance like his own! It was the drink, he knew, something in the drink, and she was a pleasure droid, beautiful beyond his dreams. When finally Tirros dropped him off in front of his apartment house, it seemed to Brokols he could detect the first hint of dawn in the east. His head was starting to ache, and it was becoming difficult to stay awake.

TWELVE

Although it was approaching full daylight, the morning sun would not clear the hills behind the city for an hour or more, and the stone-paved sidestreet was silent except for the chirp and flutter and occasional song of birds. That and, just now, the soft thud of leather-booted hooves as Eltrienn Cadriio jogged his kaabor through the cool down-alley breeze, all that was left of night. He'd seen almost no one since the sentries had saluted him out of the army compound, more than a mile away on the other side of the Fortress.

He was approaching the north side of the valley. The ground began to slope more strongly upward, and the street, which had been rather straight, started curving west to avoid the steepening, leaving behind first the almost solid ranks of buildings, then the paving blocks, and finally the last city dwelling. From there it was little more than a footpath across the firth's steep lower slope. Eltrienn stopped, dismounted, and removed the thick bullhide boots from his mount before riding on.

Gray dust was a thing of the season past; now the trail was moist and tan. Shrubs walled the path, their pungent leaves small and waxy, their blossoms just now opening to the morning. The sky was a high blue bowl, and sun touched the hilltop across the firth.

Rounding a curve, he saw the hut just ahead, on a small bench cleared of scrub. Its tile roof was faded, but its walls of chinked stone were newly whitewashed. Thin smoke hazed from a stone and mud chimney to dissipate seaward in the breeze. A man, having heard the quiet thud of hooves, peered out the open door, then stepped out of sight.

Eltrienn stopped at the edge of the clearing and dismounted, tying his reins to a stout bush. His kaabor could browse the twig ends. While he tied the reins, another man had come out of the cottage, recognized the centurion, and called quietly to him.

"Eltrienn! Brother!"

"Vessto!" Grinning, they strode toward one another and embraced, then at arms length looked each other over, the sage thin-bearded and now shave-headed, the soldier smooth-faced, with curly hair like a close-fitting cap.

"It's been quite a while," said Eltrienn.

Vessto nodded, beaming. "You look good, big brother. Stronger than ever. Hrum has been good to you."

"And you." Eltrienn cocked an eye at the lean body. "I wouldn't want to race you any longer."

Vessto laughed. "Which first: questions or breakfast?"

"Questions. I don't have time for both; I'm supposed to be somewhere else shortly."

"Then come." His brother led him to a steep and narrow footpath up which they scrambled, stiff twigs plucking at them, to a rock outcrop. There they sat down, Vessto on folded legs as if to meditate.

"So. Ask away," he said.

"Master Ganycll told me where to find you. He's heard you plan to stay at Theedalit and not go back to the Neck. Is that right?"

"For now at least."

"I've also heard that Panni Vempravvo recognizes you as a sage."

Smiling, Vessto shook his head. "You'd have to ask Panni. But I doubt it, although he treats me as a peer. I never became a master, never had the Awakening, so I can't see things from Panni's point of view. Or old Tassi's." He shrugged. "I have my talents though; in that, Hrum has gifted me beyond all but a rare few. I do what I do, say what I say. Others can make of it as they wish; that's not important to me."

Eltrienn nodded. He could feel the change in his brother. The adolescent Vessto had striven to seem special, sometimes flaunting his clairvoyance, and had resented the occasional gibes of other youths. That had been years ago, of course. Since then he'd spent years—four? five?—in the monastery at Liscotti's Vale. And most of a year as a mendicant; that might change a person too.

He wondered if Vessto knew his thoughts, here on this rock, could see without using questions to probe through the veil around his mind.

"I have a friend," Eltrienn said. "The foreigner, the ambassador from across the ocean. You've heard of him."

Vessto nodded.

"I've been assigned by the amirr as his guide and tutor. They know nothing of Hrum where he comes from, and he wants to learn. I've taken him to the central school, to talk with the senior teacher there, and then to the monastery, to Master Jerrsio. The answers he got didn't help him much. Actually, at this point, what he's really looking for is knowledge about Hrum and Hrummlis, not for the Wisdom of Hrum.

"And I wondered if you'd talk with him."

Vessto didn't answer at once, his gaze across the firth. Finally he looked at Eltrienn again. "You are my brother," he said. "If you ask me to talk to this foreigner, I will. But don't expect him to go away satisfied. One does not go to a sage for knowledge *about*, or to an adept. In his knowledge of Hrummlis and Hrum, he is like a little child. It would be better to show him the library at the Fortress, and let the librarian give him a children's book to start with."

Eltrienn had already asked the librarian to find one that said nothing about adept powers. The man had promised to see what he could come up with.

Vessto's face turned out across the firth again, his eyes losing focus. The brothers sat in silence for a minute or so before he looked once more at Eltrienn. "Yes, I will meet with your foreigner. I believe I'm supposed to. Bring him to me this evening, and I'll talk with him then."

It was his bladder that awakened Brokols. He was sprawled across his bed with shirt and underclothes still on, also a sock. His head hurt so badly, he knew better than to lift it suddenly. Even his eyes hurt. *The drink,* he thought, *something in the drink*.

With an inhaled hiss of pain, he rolled carefully onto his

stomach, then off the bed onto his knees. He stood up more carefully yet, almost vomiting from headache, and wobbled to the toilet. His member was sore. The nightsoil man had emptied and limed the dump-trough below, of course, but still the smell threatened to sicken him.

Stilfos had heard him moving about, and peering round a doorjamb, saw him reenter the hall. Brokols avoided his eyes, and Stilfos decided not to mention breakfast. He'd heard when Brokols came in, and later, by daylight, had peeked in to see him sleeping partly dressed across the bed, shoes, pants, and hat on the floor. He assumed that his master had been drunk.

"Milord," he said quietly, "I've heated the tub, in case you're interested."

Brokols didn't pause or answer, barely nodded and went into his room. A few minutes later he shuffled back out in a bathrobe, and along the hall to the bathroom, which was separate from the toilet. There he stepped down gingerly into the water, hissing at the heat, seated himself neck-deep on the bench and stared blankly at the wall.

He had not been drunk; it had been nothing at all like drunkenness. There'd been something in the drink. And the girl—the pleasure droid—had been incredible. Truly incredible. But . . . he'd been manipulated, tricked, made a fool of. Tirros had added something to the drink, and the girl had known. He was sure of that. Probably she hadn't drank any herself, had only pretended.

Why had they done it to him? What purpose could Tirros have had? A practical joke? In Almeon it would have been a serious felony. And as a result, he'd exposed himself, fully naked, committed fornication and unnatural acts, witnessed others fornicating and allowed them to witness him.

No, worse! he told himself. He'd committed bestiality, because Lerrlia wasn't human!

As soon as he'd thought it, he rejected the thought. But the other crimes were severe enough. He stared bleary-eyed and unseeing. People in Almeon were not sinless. They offended against the *Book of Forbiddances* more than one heard or read about. Even members of the nobility did; he knew that. But he wondered if anyone, short of an utter criminal or lunatic, had ever committed such a battery of gross sexual sins in one night, even rejecting bestiality. And any Almaeic court of law would . . . well, they wouldn't reject the bestiality charge; it'd be the one they'd make the most of.

Yet somehow he didn't feel conscious-stricken at what he'd done. Nor fear that he'd be found out. What he did feel was that he had alienated himself from his own culture, and wondered how he'd ever feel comfortable at home again, withholding what he'd done.

It also seemed to him that no woman in Almeon could ever attract him now, after the pleasure droid.

The amirr, Leonessto Hanorissio, was reading his mail. His eyes moved quickly, and at the end of each letter or report, sometimes sooner, he dictated comments or a reply. Then his secretary's pen moved with astonishing speed, the sound of its furious scratching broken only for a dart at the inkwell, a quick touch on the blotter.

When he'd read the last piece, the amirr sat back and stretched. "Any questions?" he asked.

"I think not, Your Eminence."

"Good." Both men got up. "I'll be out in the garden. Have Allbarin informed that I'm ready to hear him about the ambassador. With anyone he cares to bring with him."

The amirr strolled out open garden doors into morning sunshine. The day was heating up, and clouds were stacking toward the midday shower. The acallchia had begun to flower, visually so beautiful that one could hardly fault their lack of fragrance.

The amirr wore no robe, simply hose and short tunic. And slippers that in another place and time would have been called *poulaines*. A powerful man, middle age had thickened his waist. Dropping to close-trimmed lawn, he did thirty quick pushups on his fingertips, stopping short of sweat. He'd always been vain about his strength, and made efforts to maintain it. Allbarin and another man were just entering the garden as the amirr got to his feet. He waited for them; then the three of them strolled while they talked.

"What did you learn?" he asked.

"I had Gestriivo talk with the ambassador at some length." Allbarin indicated his companion. "He'd have been less relaxed with me. I kept my distance, and read what I could of anyone besides Gestriivo who talked with him." He turned to the man who'd accompanied him into the garden. "Tell His Eminence what you learned."

The man bobbed his head. "He's remarkably easy to get into, as you know. Any question I asked accessed a whole sequence of more or less related subliminal concepts and images. He has a most interesting store of prejudices and inhibitions."

Allbarin interrupted. "Gestriivo's recited it all to my secretary, in detail. You can review it at your convenience." He handed a sheaf of papers to the amirr, then nodded to Gestriivo to continue.

"The most important parts are these," Gestriivo went on. "His emperor plans an invasion. No date has been set, but it's likeliest to be about a year from now. I'm not sure whether of Hrumma or one of the Djezes or all three of us. A very large fleet is being built; apparently much of it is built already. Two hundred ships like the one that brought him here."

The amirr's expression changed from strong interest to abrupt concern little short of dismay.

"They have weapons that I don't understand," Gestriivo continued, "but there's a sense of noise about them, like the thunder noises their ship made at anchor. And of great killing. Interestingly, a feeling of distaste, tinged with guilt, seems to be associated with this in his subconscious.

"Also, the ship has left or will leave an ambassador at each of the Djezes. The one at Djez Gorrbul is senior, the one to whom the others report, and he has authority over them. I also received a clear sense that Djez Gorrbul is to attack us in connection with that, but no real indication why.

"The ambassador here reports to the one at Djez Gorrbul at night, by an instrument he has in his apartment. Apparently it has to do with the wires strung above his roof, and the little windmill." Gestriivo shrugged. "I have no idea how it works, but I received an impression of him sitting at a table, tapping on some contrivance with a finger, in an irregular cadence that suggests a code."

"Hmm." The amirr pursed his wide mouth. "If he can communicate to Haipoor l'Djezzer with that instrument, then perhaps he can communicate with his emperor across the ocean."

"Perhaps. But I got no sense of his doing so." Gestriivo stopped talking then, stood waiting.

"Is that it?" the amirr asked.

"Yes, sir. That's all that seems to relate to our security."

"Very good. You may leave now. I appreciate your good services."

Gestriivo bowed half a bow, turned and left the garden. When he was gone, the amirr sat down on a marble bench, Allbarin on another across from him.

"Comments?" said the amirr.

"Gestriivo is very good. He tends to see more deeply than I, and I have never known him to imagine what isn't there. His perceptions have always proved out, where we've had an opportunity to check.

"As for my own readings last night—there were two free-lance adepts there who questioned our good Brokols. They were well screened of course; I got no sense of who'd employed them."

"Hmm. We should have foreseen the possibility. They must have come in with invited guests. Of sufficient status to be allowed a guest of their own. See what you can find out."

Allbarin nodded. "There was also an untrained talent of rather good ability," he added, "eavesdropping like myself on the questioners and the ambassador."

He paused, waiting for the question he knew would come. The amirr frowned. Untrained talents, when they arose, were required to register and be trained, for reasons of simple ethics.

"Do you know him?"

"Neither personally nor by name. He was dressed as one of the waiters brought in to back up palace staff. Though I didn't notice him fetching drinks or food. He stood in a corner as if watching for shortages."

"And you didn't have him arrested?"

"No, Your Excellency. I had him followed."

"Ah! Better yet! Who did he report to?"

"I don't know. His follower lost him."

"Umh!" The amirr frowned. "Is that it then?"

Allbarin lagged for three or four seconds before answering. "Tirros was at the reception last night. Nothing wrong with that, of course. But the Vencurrio sisters were with him, both of them, which is something of a surprise. Considering."

The amirr's frown deepened to a scowl. The Vencurrios

were a noble family fallen on hard times of their own making—the kind of people Tirros was attracted to. Various members had been in trouble with the law, for matters ranging from malicious mischief and simple theft to extortion.

He shook his head. "Why didn't I see them?" he asked.

"They were staying on the fringes of things. They seem to have remained mostly in the garden—didn't even visit the buffet. I saw them together once, very early; after that I only glimpsed them twice, one or two at a time, peering in through one of the garden doors. Watching the ambassador."

What, thought the amirr, *could this mean?*

Allbarin wasn't done yet. "I left for a few minutes, later in the evening, heeding the insistence of nature, and after I came back, I didn't see them anymore." He paused. "I didn't see the ambassador anymore, either."

The amirr's face darkened. "Are you implying . . . was there any evidence of—connection?"

"Nothing clear; nothing certain. I do not read residuals particularly well you know, and there were a lot of people, moving around a good deal."

"Did you sense anything from them when you saw them? Tirros and the Vencurrio girls, I mean."

"Only a sense of secrecy."

Leonessto Hanorissio exhaled gustily. "This troubles me greatly. As amirr and as a father. Do not let any of these matters go uninvestigated, and let me know whatever is learned."

Tirros had slept till after noon, then left home on foot. Walking, he was less conspicuous then when riding his kaabor. He met Karrlis Billbis at a little satta shop, where they sat in a private corner, screened by curtains. In murmured undertones, Karrlis told him what he'd learned about Brokols. He'd monitored him throughout the reception.

They didn't stay long at the satta shop. When they'd finished their second cups, Tirros paid Karrlis for his services and they went separate ways, Tirros retracing the streets to the palace.

Karrlis Billbis was useful, Tirros told himself. Some thought of Karrlis as lacking wits, but that was because he usually didn't say much. Among his few confidants he talked freely enough, if not brilliantly, and the talent—the talent he had in abundance. His biggest lack was of self-direction, and that suited Tirros perfectly.

As for the foreigner—now there was a strange one. Strange and vulnerable, and the road to wealth and power. When his emperor conquered Hrumma, they'd have need for a regent to rule for them here. And Tirros would be that regent; all he had to do was figure out how.

Mellvis Rantrelli stopped at the top of the stairs, wheezing hoarsely, and mopped his forehead with a sleeve. It was dark, but early enough that it hadn't cooled off much.

He was not so unfit as he appeared, but this was one of the tallest apartment buildings in the city, and even the man with him was breathing heavily. While catching his breath, Rantrelli looked across the roof garden; if Tassi Vermaatio wanted to discourage visitors without retreating to the hills, he thought, living in a tiny seventh-floor penthouse would do it. The penthouse door was open. A scarecrow figure sat just outside it on folded legs, facing them but seeming not to notice.

If that is a watchman—the merchant said wryly to himself. But he didn't really doubt that the fellow was aware of them, and very likely knew who they were. And had probably notified his master without moving or speaking, if notification was needed.

Rantrelli had a high opinion of the abilities of holy men.

He hitched the belt of his robe over a generous belly and started toward the penthouse, his companion following. The "watchman" didn't even look up as they passed him to peer in through the open door.

The single room was thick with incense and charcoal smoke, none of which seemed to reach outside the door. There was no stove, only a small fireplace with the remains of a charcoal fire in a brazier. A kettle sat next to it, and a single large bowl hung on a wall, flanked by numerous smaller bowls. Two men slept on grass mats on the floor, and three others, like the "watchman," sat straight-spined on folded legs, their eyes open but seeming not to see.

One of the three was very old, and hairless except for long wisps like old cobwebs that hung from chin and upper lip. Tassi. He was said to be almost a hundred. His face seemed small, as if his skull had shrunk, and even in the smoke and feeble light, displayed a fine and intricate network of lines.

As a strange incongruity, his hands, palms cupped loosely upward on his knees, were remarkably large, and looked still strong. It occurred to Rantrelli that this had not always been a holy man. In his youth he had labored hard.

It also occurred to Rantrelli that Zivas Linforrio had been right: There'd been nothing to gain by coming here. True, if the old sage would deign to advise them . . . but Tassi Vermaatio, while still in this world, was no longer of it.

Rantrelli turned away to leave, hoping that a voice from the room would stop him. None did, and he recrossed the roof garden, Linforrio a step behind, and went back down the stairs and onto the street. Raising a foot to the step of his carriage, the fat merchant hoisted himself in, with no hand from Linforrio. Which irritated him slightly, considering Linforrio's fee. But an adept was an adept. They didn't hire out as footmen.

"Can you find the cave of Panni Vempravvo?" he asked his coachman.

"I know where it is, sir. But we can't drive the last little distance. There'll be a walk."

Uphill no doubt, Rantrelli thought. "Take us there," he said.

By evening, Brokols' headache had passed, though he still looked rather drawn, and he'd started off on a long walk with Cadriio.

Or so he said, Stilfos thought. He hoped Brokols wasn't turning into a drunk. He looked in on the wireless telegraph. Kryger's private instructions had been to let him know any time Brokols had difficulties. Without Brokols finding out, of course, and Brokols hadn't a clue that Stilfos knew code.

Kryger didn't trust Brokols; he'd told Stilfos that—a remarkable thing for a nobleman to say to a commoner about another nobleman. Brokols was too young, unproven, inexperienced, had gotten his post through family influence; and there was a softness about him. So said Kryger. Maybe he was right. Stilfos was nonetheless glad to be stationed with Brokols instead of Kryger, and he hoped his master wasn't going bad.

Meanwhile he wouldn't send a message now. One bad night did not a drunkard make.

He wished he knew for sure, though, who Brokols had

been with last night—Cadriio, probably—and whether he was loose-mouthed while drunk.

It was past midnight, but overcast, which kept it from cooling off. Rantrelli's robe was wet with sweat, and he was limping badly as they walked up to the hut. He'd had to leave the carriage behind again, half a mile behind, and the path had been uphill. Of course.

He'd found Panni's cave earlier, and Panni. It had been a cruel uphill walk; harder than this one. And all Panni had given him was a smile, saying that the country sage was the one he should talk to. Panni hadn't called him a country sage though; he'd simply referred to him by name: Vessto Cadriio, the man who'd visited Rantrelli's home with him. He told him where he lived.

This door too was open. Several men were sleeping inside on mats, and one was meditating—one of the masters, by his robe. Vessto didn't seem to be there. Hesitantly, reluctantly, Rantrelli walked in, approached the master, and spoke softly.

"Master."

The eyes, which had been open all along, shifted focus from infinity to Rantrelli's face, unaccompanied by words.

"Master, I have walked my feet sore, coming to see the sage. Can you tell me where he is?"

The master turned his gaze to one of the sleeping men, a disciple; the disciple stirred, groaned, sat up and looked around. The master's focus returned to wherever it had been before. Rantrelli felt the short hairs crawl on nape, arms, legs. He looked at Linforrio, who went to the disciple.

"We've come to consult with the sage," Linforrio told the man. "Take us to him."

The disciple looked at the silent master, then nodded, got up, and led them back out into darkness. He took them half a dozen yards to the edge of the dense and bristly scrub, where a path led upward. "Up there, meditating," he muttered. "You can't miss him. The path ends where he is." Then the man went back into the hut.

Rantrelli sighed. If he'd known ahead of time . . . but he hadn't.

He'd never get up the narrow path with his robe on, so he shrugged out of it, left it on the ground, and started. All he had on now were sandles and loin cloth; the stiff twigs scratched almost like thorns. The way was nearly as steep as old Tassi's stairs, and the footing far poorer. Even without the robe, he was sweating like a rikksha runner when the path ended at a rock outcrop.

This sage too sat upright on folded legs. Rantrelli stood for a moment, not quite knowing what to do, then took the bull by the horns and spoke.

"Master," he said.

"Yes?" The country sage answered without moving, without turning his face to them.

"We have come for your advice."

Rantrelli felt foolish saying it. To come for advice in the middle of the night, on a matter which could have been addressed the next day. But he'd been shunted from one sage to another, and hadn't expected to be *here* by either night or day. And it was his way to persist on a course until he'd finished, if at all practical.

"Ask," said Cadriio.

Rantrelli turned to Linforrio, who took it from there.

"It's about the foreign ambassador," Linforrio said, "the one from across the ocean."

Cadriio said nothing.

"I am an adept, employed by this gentleman, Mellvis Rantrelli. I spoke with the foreigner last evening, at a reception in the amirr's palace, casually asking questions about his homeland and what he hoped to accomplish here. His answers were innocuous, but beneath them I perceived his pictures, and more . . . his great king, his 'emperor,' intends to conquer here—the Djezes and Hrumma, all three. He is building a great fleet. And there is more to it than fleet and army—subterfuge is part of it—but the rest was not clear to me."

He gestured at the merchant. "Mellvis Rantrelli is a man who loves Hrum and Hrumma. A man also of considerable resources. You have been to his home, on the first day of Festival; you know him. He would like you to advise him on what to do to forestall the foreign emperor's plan."

Vessto's reply came without a lag. "I have been meditating on it, while I awaited you. I will send a man to Mellvis Rantrelli in the morning or go to him myself, and talk with him."

It was clear that he would say no more, and Linforrio in

the lead this time, the two visitors went back down through the scrub, then down the path to the carriage more than half a mile farther. Rantrelli's limp had become a hobble, and he carried his robe on his arm for whatever cooling might be gained, sure that at least a few of his scratches must be bleeding.

If he knew we were coming, if he was waiting for us, why didn't he wait at the hut? Rantrelli thought. *Or better yet at the end of the road?* But when the merchant had settled himself on the carriage seat, it was with satisfaction as well as physical relief. For it seemed to him that the country sage would not only advise, but in some way would act. Meanwhile he, Mellvis Rantrelli, would soak in the hot tub when he got home, have a servant put ointment on the scratches, and then sleep late.

THIRTEEN

Brokols' "long walk with Cadriio," the evening before, had taken him to the steep north wall of the firth, where he'd met Eltrienn's brother Vessto. Vessto lived in a hut with half a dozen followers. And no furniture except a low table and some grass mats; apparently they sat on the floor to eat. Brokols had gotten the impression that none of them worked, or at least not Vessto and the two whom Eltrienn afterward told him were masters.

Vessto had led him and Eltrienn scrambling up a steep path, close-walled by bristly shrubs, to a rocky outcrop where they'd sat for what must have been close to an hour. Brokols had asked Vessto questions about Hrum and Hrummlis. Vessto had actually given answers, too, more or less, and in turn had asked him questions about Almeon and life there, his childhood and his function in Hrumma, and the *Book of Forbiddances*. And the ship.

While they'd walked back into town, it had occurred to Brokols to wonder how Vessto knew about the book; he was quite sure he hadn't mentioned it to him. Probably he'd mentioned it to the teacher in front of Eltrienn, and Eltrienn had said something about it to Vessto at an earlier meeting.

His meeting with Vessto Cadriio was the most successful he'd had with a clergyman of Hrummlis, despite the way the sage lived, and he'd arrived back at his apartment clear-headed, though physically tired. What he had in mind was a peaceful night's sleep, because the next day he'd begin a weeks-long trip around Hrum with Eltrienn, to become familiar with the rest of the country.

* * *

After Vessto Cadriio had bid his brother and the foreigner good evening, he'd stayed seated on the rock outcrop far into the night, meditating. It was not pure meditation. It had another objective than contemplating Hrum-In-Him, or losing himself; he was looking for something, an answer. But none came to him.

Brokols' sleep that night was a frenetic sequence of dreams, largely sexual, more or less outrageously so. Lerrlia was prominent in them, but there were also Valda, and other women recognized or seemingly new to him. In one dream, the prostitute he'd visited, back in Almeon, had found him on the roof coupling with a sea woman, a sellsu, but with legs. The prostitute had turned and fled, calling back that she was going to tell. Which, Brokols knew, meant tell Kryger. By that time the child of the waves was no longer a sellsu, but a lovely young girl, or more likely a pleasure droid, who laughed joyously with him as they walked along a beach. He'd wakened to darkness then, certain he'd been laughing aloud in his sleep.

And remarkably, throughout his dreams it seemed that what he did was not vile but quite all right, albeit amazingly virile.

When he woke up, he felt rested and alert, though the dreams stayed somewhat on his mind through breakfast. If Kryger ever found out what he'd actually done . . . but there was no reason that Kryger should ever know, and Brokols felt no anxiety over it.

Vessto Cadriio had never seen the trail to Panni Vempravvo's cave or heard anything about where it was. Nonetheless, after finishing his dawn porridge, he'd bidden his people stay, then walked the five miles alone, finding his way by knowingness.

The last half mile was away from the rough road, on a trail that angled up to a ridgeline, then along its top. From the crest, he could see across a lesser ridge to hazy-blue sea, and on the slope below the path, several men seated singly in the sun, half hidden by grass and wildflowers that were higher than his knees.

The last hundred feet of the path was downhill again. The shallow cave at its end had been modified at some past time.

The wide opening had been mostly walled over with squared, dry-set stone; coarse blankets had been hung on the inside. At one end of the wall a fireplace had been built; an opening had been left at the other as a door.

Neat piles of bedstraw vine were lined along the back wall, each with a sleeping mat folded on top. A twig broom stood beside a straw broom in one rounded corner, and a disciple squatted near the wooden water cask, eating a late breakfast with his fingers from a clay bowl. His master, he said, was meditating, and went outside with Vessto to point the way.

Going to Panni, Vessto squatted down a few feet away, facing him. That he didn't assume the meditation posture marked how concerned he was with something. Panni's eyes focused and moved to him, waiting for whatever the younger man might say.

"I have come for help," Vessto said.

"The foreigner," Panni answered.

"The foreigner." Vessto told him then what he knew—had read in the man for himself and been told by others, notably Rantrelli's hired adept. "Clearly the great king, the emperor of his land, intends to conquer us, both the Djezes and Hrumma. And has great resources. And it seems to me that I should do something about this, but action of that kind is. . . ." He shrugged. Such action, unless it was precisely correct, would be a resistance, which would make the difficulties more solid.

Panni's mouth curved in the slightest of smiles. "Who are you?" he asked.

"I am myself. But in this life I am being Vessto Cadriio."

"And what world do you live in?"

"My own world. Upon the creation of Hrum." This was from the children's catechism.

"Whence came the wisdoms you are said to have spoken? And the knowledge I myself have heard you voice?"

"From Hrum-In-Me."

"Yet you come to me instead of opening yourself to Hrum-In-Thee?"

"Hrum-In-Me does not answer on this matter."

"Ahh. Are you neutral on the subject?"

"No. I have been unable to be neutral on it."

"Well then—in that case, who writes your script?"

"Me. As Zan, and Naz."

The smile widened. "Would it be all right for you to simply follow it? Doing whatever seems best as you go?"

"That's what I have done. In coming to you."

Panni grinned broadly. "Very well. You may come to me whenever you wish. Perhaps sometime I will have advice to give you that you aren't already following. Meanwhile, in living a role with strong importances, strong preferences, be prepared to feel afraid and anxious and torn. And perhaps angry. Remember that these are on the surface, regardless of how deep they feel.

"And if sometime you need quiet from them and cannot find it, you may wish to meditate in the presence of Tassi Vermaatio. He is the very Is-ness of Hrum, and will undoubtedly allow it."

When Vessto had left, Panni continued briefly to sit in the sun, soaking up its warmth, regarding what the young man had said. He laughed. Things were moving about within the backstage of Hrum's world: Scripts were being altered, props shifted.

After a time he got up and, wrapped in his own world, strode to the trail. It was time to contact other people's worlds again. He could access them from his hill, but not so readily as when he was among them, nor in anything like such numbers.

I am not yet a Tassi Vermaatio, he told himself cheerfully. And did not regret it. He'd almost forgotten what regrets were.

Fourteen

Eltrienn arrived while Brokols was packing his bag. The ambassador would carry two dress suits, carefully folded, for whatever special audiences there might be. On the road he'd wear an ordinary traveling suit and carry another.

Brokols could see problems in travel here that hadn't been foreseen back in Almeon when the mission was being planned. They hadn't appreciated how hot it would be. Hrummean summer clothing was cool and easily cared for. His own clothing, on the other hand, was woolen, from fleece of the *porla*. He was, after all, an Almaeic nobleman. But woolens were hot, and not properly amenable to cleaning while traveling. Here at their lodgings, Stilfos could maintain them nicely, with careful laundering and ironing, but Stilfos would remain in Theedalit to look after the apartment instead of traveling with him. And nothing at all could be done about how hot they were, unless one cut off the legs and sleeves, which was unthinkable.

It was tempting to obtain Hrummean clothing, but Brokols had decided it wouldn't be proper; a representative of the emperor should look the part.

They rode off behind a matched pair of kaabors, in a strong-wheeled shay with the top let back, beneath a dazzling sky that seemed not to have heard of the summer monsoon. And over the next two weeks, toured a broad cross-section of Hrumma.

There were no other cities than Theedalit. The infrequent sizeable towns, with three or four thousand people, might have their main street paved, but otherwise dirt streets were the rule, sometimes graveled and with the softer places cobbled. And invariably their water came untreated from streams, dug wells, and cisterns. Still, their people were civilized. Their buildings were almost always whitewashed, while planted trees, shrubs, and flowers were abundant.

Most of the country was less prosperous than the rural valley above Theedalit. They visited fishing districts where the people lived on tiny subsistence farms along the shores of firth or inlet, people who worked with net and set-line, drying rack and smokehouse and large pickling crocks, to produce fish for local consumption, cartage to other districts, and export to the Djezes.

There were also rough mountainous districts where almost the only economic activities, aside from tending the household's fruit trees and vines and vegetable gardens, was the herding and shearing of *vehato*, an animal rather like the porlo but horned, the spinning of thread from their fleece, and the weaving of textiles. An animal called *kienno* was used to help herd the vehato. The kienno was seldom used for other purposes, the Hrummeans regarding it as a sophont not properly kept subject to humans.

Sausage was also made, highly spiced to prevent spoilage. Much of what was produced from the vehato—cloth, yarn, fleeces, sausage—was consumed in the home district, but cartage to other markets and to harbors for export was an important business.

Less rugged hill districts bore vineyards and orchards, or were grazed by gleebor bred for milk or meat. In thick-walled houses with cool sod roofs, or in caves where there were any, farm wives and daughters made cheeses that would be eaten at home or sold. Here too, meat was smoked, chopped, ground with spices, and stuffed into gut to be shipped as sausage.

In broader valleys, fields of food crops were tended for waiting bins and sheds. And there, a much smaller carnivore than the kienno was common. Slender, short-legged, pointy headed, it seemed invariably present around graneries and storage cellars. Called *chissa*, it too was regarded as a sophont, and as an associate of man was more independent than the kienno. Chissas served the purpose of controlling vermin, and farmers put out milk to encourage their presence.

Almost every rural home had its *lorrchios*, short-furred omnivores kept penned or sometimes tethered, fattened on wastes of the kitchen, the creamery, the orchard and winepress and butchering table. To be butchered themselves in their time. There were two evident varieties, one fairly large and rangy, one small and round, to suit the family and the farm.

Though agriculture and fisheries were by far the largest industries, Brokols saw ships being built, and only half a day's ride from Theedalit, a limestone quarry and cement mill. The mill was an ingenious-looking arrangement of sheds and ramps, and cylinders some twenty feet tall, with carts, barrows, gleebor-driven capstans, and smoke. While one narrow firth they visited was astink with fumes from a factory that cooked down vats of oil fish to provide for Hrummean lamps.

A common element everywhere were the archery butts. Outside every village where the two of them spent their evenings, men and boys would gather after supper to shoot at targets. Their skill was impressive, both in measured fire and rapid. Several times, Brokols and Eltrienn had gone to watch. Eltrienn had shot a set once, very creditably, and with a borrowed bow at that.

And everywhere, Brokols found the people wearing cool summer clothes of plant fibers, the cloth imported from the Djezes, mostly Djez Seechul. And as important as the fabric was the coolness of its cut, the general bareness or partial bareness of limbs. For the people in the countryside were less style-conscious and wore less clothing than in Theedalit. Children commonly ran naked till seemingly age eight or ten. Brokols wondered what games such children played behind the stone fences or in the dense coppice patches. Or what games the adolescents and adults might play, inflamed by the sight of each others' limbs.

He was more comfortable with these thoughts, though, than he might have expected. It was as if that night on Tirros's boat, or whoever's boat it had been, perhaps reinforced by the strange dreams of the following night, had dulled his sense of propriety and morals.

In every district there were coppice woods, with stout stumps scant inches tall, a ring of shoots sprouting from their bases to be cut off for fuel when they'd reached the thickness of a wrist, more or less. Seemingly every farm had its own small coppice stand, for home fuel. Other stands were large, for commercial production. These fed the charcoal kilns that supplied smithies—and towns, for they too needed fuel. And for more than just cookery. Winter would come to Hrumma in its time, winter cool enough for woolens, though mild compared to those in Almeon or inland districts of the continent north of Hrumma.

Winter weather in Hrumma tended to be dry and breezy, he was told, with infrequent days of mists and rain. On winter nights it sometimes froze, especially in the higher interior valleys. Now and then, brief damp weather even brought transient snow, which might persist for two or three days in the interior, or longer on the higher plateaus and hills.

After fourteen days, Brokols had seen much of Hrumma—a representative cross-section, according to Eltrienn—while being rained on only six times. On the fourteenth evening they sat in an inn, eating a late supper and talking.

"You know," said Brokols, "I haven't seen your metal works—the factories or shops where you make steel. Nothing but little local smithies."

Eltrienn nodded. "They're in the deep valleys of the east coast, where most of the ore is. They're too far; it would have taken too long. And in Hrumma, they're a very small part of our economy. All together they employ fewer people than we saw working in the fields that one short afternoon above Theedalit."

He changed the subject then. "Tomorrow we'll cross the Aettlian Plateau. There'll be little to see but gleebor herds—few villages, and the houses are far apart—but the country is mostly near flat, and we'll make good time. The soil is fertile, but too stony to cultivate; it's the greatest pasturage in Hrumma. We'll carry our lunch, and in late afternoon stop at a villa that belongs to the Hanorissios', called Sea Cliff. They own several thousand acres of rangeland there. Zeenia Hanorissia manages it, and if you let her, she'll tell you more than you want to know about the business. We'll spend tomorrow night there and be in Theedalit the next afternoon."

Brokols nodded, staring absently at his glass as he swirled the sour and watered wine. Something else had occurred to him, but he didn't know how to broach the subject. Simply begin, he told himself, but that was difficult. In Almeon, discussion of sex and reproduction would be almost out of the question, but here, he thought, it might well be acceptable. And if he offended his friend and guide, he'd rely on communication and the centurion's good nature to repair any damage.

"Eltrienn—" he began, then stopped. It occurred to him that he didn't know the Hrummean word for sexual intercourse. He'd have to translate the Almaeic euphemism and hope it was understood.

"Yes?"

"Do the Hrummeans—do they, uh, couple a lot?"

"Couple? What do you mean by couple?"

Brokols took a deep breath. "By coupling, I mean—do the men and women . . ."

He stopped, Eltrienn looked quizzically at him. "Make babies," Brokols finished. "A lot, I mean."

Actually it wasn't what he meant. From the way they dressed in Hrumma, and the way Tirros and his two girls had comported themselves, it seemed to him you'd see a lot more children around than he'd actually noticed. The number of children in Hrumma seemed rather low in fact, for the number of adults.

"You mean fuck?" asked Eltrienn.

Brokols blushed. The Hrummean word was unfamiliar to him, but he was pretty sure . . . the very sound was uncouth, suggestive, much like the sound of coupling while sweaty. "I believe so," he said. "Yes."

Eltrienn didn't look at all perturbed at the question; only curious. "Why do you ask?"

With that, a little haltingly, Brokols told him how the partial and juvenile nudity seemed to him, yet there didn't seem to be a great number of children.

Eltrienn's expression was surprised and bemused. "I suppose," he answered slowly, "that we're used to seeing skin. In the right circumstances it can be quite—stimulating of course, but ordinarily it's not."

It occurred to Brokols that pleasure droids might well be engineered to perform sex well but not have strong sexual desire. Or perhaps it was simply as Eltrienn had said—they were used to seeing skin.

"As for the number of children," Eltrienn was saying, "Hrum would have us live in harmony with the land. For a long time now, in Hrumma, our number has not much increased."

"But then . . ." The notion of no increase was utterly foreign to Brokols, and to the *Book of Right Comportment*. "But then, do you stop coupling, once you've had two or three children? Or four?"

Eltrienn misunderstood, or rather, understood only the lesser part of Brokols' reaction. "That's no problem," he said. "There's an herb that grows along brooks; I can show it to you. We call it lamb foil; vehatos sometimes eat it, when they're hungry enough, and if they eat it in breeding season, they don't conceive. They breed, but there aren't any lambs. The flowers of lamb foil, dried and powdered, can be added as a condiment to food and protect a woman from conceiving. Many people raise it in their gardens."

Brokols was thunderstruck. These people, these pleasure droids, not only coupled without intention to conceive, but deliberately prevented conception!

"Is something the matter?" Cadriio asked.

He shook his head in quick denial. "No, no. It's simply that . . . the possibility is new to me." He paused. "Then—how often does one couple here? A—say a typical married man of our age?"

Eltrienn made a face and shrugged. "I never asked anyone. They share the same home and presumably the same bed, so I suppose they might couple very frequently." He tilted his head quizzically. "And in your country?"

The question took Brokols unprepared. "In my country? It, it varies with the person, I'm sure. But it's forbidden, criminal in fact, to couple with other than one's wife. And with one's wife, one couples only with the intent to produce a child."

Eltrienn's eyebrows jumped. "Oh? Interesting. You have large families then?"

Brokols wasn't sure what Cadriio considered large. "I was one of five children. Nine, including those my father sired by his second wife. My mother died in childbirth, and later my stepmother also. In his grief, my father has since declined to marry again."

"Hmm. Nine children. And did your father couple only nine times in his life?"

Brokols could feel the color rise in his face, though he felt no anger. "I—could hardly know. It's very doubtful. One might couple numerous times before successfully conceiving."

Eltrienn nodded, his lips pursed. "Ah! Then they do not know the birthwort in Almeon. Here, if a couple wishes a child and does not get one, the wife takes birthwort. It's an herb with flowers much like those of lamb foil, but the potency resides in the root, or actually in the skin of the root. One digs it up, or the herbalist does, strips and dries the inner bark, powders it, and adds it to food. It's available from any herbalist, and it's fairly reliable."

A thought occurred to Eltrienn then. Large families like Brokols' meant large populations, even if epidemics sometimes decimated them. "How many people are there in Almeon?" he asked.

"Forty million. More than forty-three million at last count."

The number stunned the Hrummean, but Brokols didn't notice because another thought had taken his attention. "Do you have any other herbs that deal with coupling?" he asked.

The question brought Cadriio's attention back. "None," he answered. "Or, there is one other, of the same family, but its use is illegal."

"Illegal? Why so?"

"It causes strong sexual desire. With it, a person can be gotten to 'couple' who otherwise would not. Which is a crime before Hrum. Also it's somewhat poisonous."

"Poisonous?!"

"It makes one ill, and prolonged use can kill. In the Djezes it has been used by nobles for extended orgies, and people have died from it. Though even there, it seems seldom used."

Brokols sat, shocked. Eltrienn nodded. "It is strange, I agree. Apparently if you take a second dose before the sickness strikes, the sickness is forestalled until you stop. But then you get twice as sick. Thus you can take it a number of times, one after the other, continuing the orgy without illness until, after several days, you drop dead." He shrugged. "There are those who otherwise are no longer able to couple, who consider it the best way to die. The reason it's illegal is the temptation to give it to someone other than yourself, someone who might otherwise refuse you."

The centurion's clear gray eyes were intent on Brokols; when the ambassador became aware of it, he shook his head as if to clear it. "This is all . . . all utterly strange to me," Brokols said. "I had not imagined such a thing as these herbs."

Eltrienn nodded. "We seem so much alike in some ways, it's interesting how different our two countries are. Perhaps as we come to know one another better, we will learn from each other."

Elver Brokols' biggest shock had not been the herbs. It had

been a feeling—a feeling that hit him when Eltrienn had mentioned their countries learning from each other: *He didn't want Hrumma to become like Almeon! He preferred it as it was! And that was not consistent with why he was here—with the emperor's plan.*

Eltrienn Cadriio had something on his mind, too: Almeon's population of forty-three million! That was a great number of people, twenty times Hrumma's. Twice that of the two Djezes combined. He wondered how large an army Almeon might field.

A buzzer burped loudly in the luxurious palace apartment in Haipoor l'Djezzer. Lord Vendel Kryger, dressed in silk lounging pajamas, put aside a book and strode briskly to the radio room. Argant was there ahead of him. Kryger sat down and, after positioning a pad of paper, tapped out an acknowledgement, then picked up a pencil and sat ready. A moment later the set began to rattle off a series of letters which Kryger jotted as they came, Argant craning his neck to see.

> STILFOS TO KRYGER STOP RELIGIOUS LEADER HERE SPEAKING AGAINST ALMEON STOP SOME LESSER RELIGIOUS FIGURES HAVE JOINED HIM STOP THIS EVENING I ATTENDED RALLY STOP—SPEAKER KNOWS ALMOST EVERYTHING INCLUDING FLEET OF 200 SHIPS STOP CROWD NOT VERY LARGE ABOUT 500 600 NOT UNRULY STOP REQUEST INSTRUCTIONS STOP STILFOS END

Kryger's mouth twisted into something like a snarl. He began rapidly tapping out his reply without taking time to write it down first, voicing the words as he sent them, so that Argant could jot them down.

"Message received. Stop. What meant by 'knows almost everything.' Question."

Stilfos answered that the Hrummeans knew about the impending imperial invasion. That apparently they thought it would be, or at least would include, an invasion of Hrumma.

Kryger sent again. "Received. Stop. Unless dangerous to you, attend future meetings until B returns. Stop. Keep me informed. Stop. Kryger End."

He waited briefly. The machine began to rattle again:

> MESSAGE RECD STOP STILFOS END COMPLETED

Kryger's finger tapped out a final "Kryger end. Communication over." Then he got up and left the room and Argant. *There's only one way they could have found out our plans,* he told himself grimly. *That ass Brokols has a loose mouth—either that or he's turned traitor.* Which seemed highly unlikely; there'd be nothing in it for him, with an imperial takeover a certainty.

Or was it a certainty now? This security breakdown might cost heavily in Almaeic lives, but could it also change the outcome? He needed to reevaluate.

He threw himself down in his reading chair, but left his book where it lay. *How could Brokols have let so much slip?* Had the man begun drinking? Or gotten mixed up with a droid woman? He'd been investigated thoroughly before the prime minister appointed him. They all had. One might expect that any problems with drink or women would have been found out.

The most serious thing was, the problem went beyond Hrumma. Fortunately, King Gamaliiu had no ambassador in Hrumma, but he might well have spies there, Hrummean traitors perhaps, in which case they'd report all this to him. Which would be bound to alarm him.

If that happened, Gamaliiu would no doubt ask some hard questions. It would be well to have some good answers in advance. Probably the best would be a simple denial—say that the Hrummeans were imagining things. And that according to his informant, it was frightening the people there. Taking the heart out of them.

That just might work. Beneath those waxed curls, Gamaliiu was not an imbecile, but he had an unreasonably low opinion of the Hrummeans. Unreasonable because, if they were as inept as Gamaliiu insisted, they'd have fallen long ago.

Meanwhile, when he sent his weekly report to Larvis Royal, day after tomorrow, he should probably make a case for advancing the timetable. Get this place conquered before too many things went wrong. Of course, he'd have to think of a good reason without telling the truth. It wouldn't do for the emperor to know about the leak. Because he, Kryger, was in charge of this mission, and the blame would be his regardless of where it properly lay.

Meanwhile he'd speed Djez Gorrbul's attack on Hrumma. If Gamaliiu advanced his timetable, the emperor would advance his of necessity.

Fortunately, lacking wireless, word would travel slowly

from Theedalit to Haipoor l'Djezzer. Probably not many Gorrbian ships went to Hrumma. The Gorballis *had* few ships; Djez Gorrbul just wasn't a maritime nation. So most cargoes would go in Hrummean hulls. And the Gorballis felt enough disdain for Hrumma and things Hrummean that probably few, if any, Gorrbian seamen understood the language there anyway. Or would attend a Hrummean religious rally.

As for Brokols—he was a liability now. Stilfos, Kryger decided, would have to become ambassador there. And . . .

That meant getting rid of Brokols. Would Stilfos do it if ordered to?

He should have discussed Brokols with Stilfos while he had him on the wireless, he told himself, but that could wait. Replacing Brokols could wait, as far as that was concerned. The damage was done, and he'd see what the man said when he reported in from his tour. According to his pre-trip plan, he'd be back in Theedalit any day now.

Kryger sat down at his desk and began to diagram the problems and possibilities on paper.

Fifteen

The day's shower had turned out to be twins, bracketing noon. Now, in midafternoon, the sun was out and the shay's top folded back, sacrificing shade for view. The matched kaabors trotted briskly, hooves thudding on the firm, wet soil of the highroad, splashing occasional puddles. The plateau tilted slightly toward the seacliff nearby, its soil thin atop basaltic caprock, its thick stand of bunchgrasses grazed down by scattered roan and white gleebor, dehorned and well-fleshed.

It seemed to Brokols the nicest landscape he'd ever seen for riding in, and he wished he was in a saddle instead of the shay. He was not an avid rider, but a rather skilled one. As a youth and a member of a noble family, he'd ridden a lot, and his military service had been as a junior officer of cavalry.

The day was moderately hot and the humidity high, but with breeze enough to keep Eltrienn comfortable in kilt and sleeveless tunic as he drove the team. Brokols, on the other hand, wore a woolen formal suit in preparation for their stop at the Hanorissio villa, and even with his jacket off, useless sweat ran down his face.

They crossed a slight rise. Before them, a broadly rounded draw breached the caprock and sloped away southwestward, opening on the sea. A slender ribbon of brook glinted along the bottom, and the highroad, crossing it, sent well-worn wheel tracks branching toward the sea.

Eltrienn pointed. "The road to the villa," he said. Minutes later they turned off on it, the brook beside them clattering and splashing downward toward a sea indigo blue beneath the sun. For a few minutes, the view and the brook music took Brokols' attention from the heat and sticky sweat.

Where they rolled out of the draw, the flank of the plateau was steep but less than cliffy, toeing out to broad sandy beach. Brokols shrugged reluctantly into his jacket as they approached a walled compound open toward the sea. A guard motioned them through the gate and, while they dismounted, called a second to take them to the villa and a third to care for their kaabors.

Within the outer wall and forming part of it were stone sheds, a low stone barn, and what seemed to be a smithy; these opened onto an outer bailey. A second wall separated the outer bailey from an inner—the grounds of the villa itself. Entering the grounds, Brokols found them subdivided in turn by screens of hedge and whitewashed sections of low wall. A large fountain splashed; honeysuckers darted gold and scarlet among blossoms; and massive, sprawling-limbed trees shaded much of the villa. Eltrienn and Brokols followed their guide across a patio furnished with movable cushioned chairs, and into the building.

A servant was just now opening doors and windows. The midday heat had gradually penetrated the thick walls, layered roof tiles, double-floored loft, overcoming the lingering coolness of a dawn long past. The two visitors waited briefly in a reception room until a large, black-haired woman came in to them, russet-cheeked, strangely amber-eyed, wearing loose, white trousers and sleeveless shirt.

"Hoo! Eltrienn!" she hooted, and embraced the centurion. "You vagabond! I haven't seen you since Leonessto sent you Hrum-knows-where, years ago. How many? Four? Five? I suppose you've eaten lunch."

"On the road," Eltrienn answered. "Rolls, cheese, and a strawbag of greenberries. What we need more than anything is to move about on our feet a bit; we've been jouncing in a shay for too many hours." He half-turned to Brokols. "Zeenia Hanorissia, this is His Excellency, Elver Brokols, Ambassador to the Court of Hrumma from His Highness Dard, Emperor of Almeon. I'm sure you've heard of His Excellency's arrival. Elver, this is Zeenia Hanorissia, the amirr's sister."

Brokols bowed. The tall woman looked him up and down, her eyes even with his own, taking in his exotic features and foreign garb. "Honored," she said, then gestured toward

Eltrienn with her head. "I'd heard this scoundrel was assigned to be your guide." She motioned them to follow, and led them into a hall. "I hadn't expected to meet you," she told Brokols over her shoulder. "I go to Theedalit no more than I need to, which blessedly is seldom. It bores me silly." She gestured around as if to indicate the house and beyond. "I manage this place for the family, cattle and all. Daratto runs the home plantation, while Leonessto prefers government to managing a livestock operation."

Great Kaitmar! Brokols thought to himself, *have they no protocol here?* He'd never seen an aristocrat so unreserved about family affairs. And with a soldier and a stranger—a foreigner.

A broad door entered a sitting room built on two levels; she ushered them in. "Eltrienn used to be guard captain here," she said to Brokols. "He's a marvelous swordsman; we badgered him into demonstrations now and then. Back before my husband died—a merchant, lost at sea." She went to a desk-like work table where a journal lay open, and turning the chair, sat down facing them. They took seats on a couch opposite. "I'm indisposed today," she went on. "Happens every few weeks; Hrum's way of getting me to stay in and update my records. Otherwise you'd hardly have found me home; I'd have been off in the saddle somewhere. You'll stay the night, of course."

Eltrienn nodded, grinning at her volubility. "That's why we stopped. And to see you, naturally."

"That had better be part of it. I don't make houseguests of just anyone, you rascal. Only my friends, and theirs if I like 'em. Incidentally, Juliassa is here, probably down by the mouth of the brook. She's got a sellsu she spends a lot of time with, learning to talk their language. Found it on the beach, close to dead, and been nursing it back to health. It could have returned to the sea by now I suppose, but they both enjoy her language lessons. She sits by a lamp all evening till after I'm in bed, writing down what she's learned."

Learning to talk with the sea people? Brokols' interest was captured. The possibility had never occurred to him.

"And Tirros," Eltrienn said. "Is he around?"

Her jaw clamped. "I threw the rotten little troublemaker out two weeks ago," she snapped. "Somehow he'd heard about Juliassa's sellsu and came to visit. She caught him down on the beach, tormenting it, jabbing at it with a pitchfork. I heard her screaming clear up here; then she came up and got a bow and quiver. He thought it was funny! I've told Leonessto to keep him away from here or I'd have him thrashed."

She changed the subject then. "Two of the men brought in a pail of fresh skulter a bit ago; a favorite of yours I recall. Cook's making a salad of them. Now if I don't get back at the records, they'll have to wait another five weeks, and I'll have forgotten too much. We'll have supper the same time as always here, and talk later."

"Well then," said Eltrienn, getting up, "we'll go out and see Juliassa's sellsu, and then bathe before we eat."

When Juliassa had brought the sellsu home, she'd had some of the household staff build a weir across the mouth of the brook, curving like a deep *U* around the lower reach. Enough, she thought, to keep a weakened sellsu from escaping. After a few days of enclosure though, she'd had the sides of the *U* removed, making it easy for the sellsu to depart around the weir if he wished. What was left would keep predaceous fish—sarrkas and sea lances—away from him. The sellsu had been content to stay, at least until he'd recovered his strength.

The weir was of saplings tied with rope and anchored to posts driven into beach and stream bottom. Brook water flowed out through it, and the high tides flowed freely in. Here, where the stream gradient was low, the brook was fifteen feet wide, three times its width a hundred yards upstream, and several times deeper. Except when the tide was in, the water was pure brook water, but the sellsu had suffered no ill effects from the freshwater environment. The ocean itself was not very saline, not nearly as much as on planets with two or three times the relative land surface.

As Eltrienn and Brokols strolled along the beach toward the stream, they could see Juliassa sitting in it, head and neck above the water. And shoulders; as they got nearer, Brokols could clearly see her shoulders. With no sign of clothing on them. He'd noticed the sellsu, too, its head, neck, and upper back showing sleek and dark. The girl and the sea mammal were making noises back and forth, noises that didn't sound much alike.

Juliassa, glimpsing her visitors from the corner of an eye, turned and waved.

"Eltrienn!" she called. "It's you!"

"Juliassa! I've brought a visitor! An interesting one."

She looked at the sellsu and briefly exchanged words with it, then stood and waded toward them. Brokols was both aghast and relieved. Here was a princess, in a sense of the word, standing bare-breasted to greet a stranger, but she did have a garment on—short loose breeches that covered her clingingly from just below the navel to the mid thighs.

And she was lovely! Utterly lovely! Tanned despite reddish-blond hair. Startling green eyes. And young, not yet fully matured, with pointed breasts the size of pinkfruit. In Hrumma the breasts of mature women, even as young as Lerrlia, seemed generally more the size of sugar fruit or larger.

But she was simply—lovely!

Juliassa stood looking quizzically at him, and so did Eltrienn. Brokols realized then that Eltrienn had been talking, had introduced them, and that he himself hadn't said a thing in return. "I—it's a pleasure. I'm afraid you're quite the loveliest young lady I've ever seen."

He could hardly believe he'd said that! His face turned hot; he was sure it must be crimson. Perhaps purple. "In my country," he explained, "we're not used to seeing ladies without clothing. I'm sorry if I stared."

For a moment he felt wild-eyed then, horrified that his traitor mouth could have babbled what it had.

"Oh," Juliassa said, and her smile melted him. "Well then . . ." she walked out onto the sand, picked up the shift she'd laid there, and slipped it over her head. Brokols was awed by her poise, her face, her dimples.

Suddenly, the smile was gone, replaced by a frown. "You came on the great ship," she said.

"That's right. I did."

"And you killed two sea serpents." The words were accusatory. There was nothing sweet about the way her eyes pierced him.

Brokols shook his head, dismayed. "Not I! The captain ordered it, and some marines did the . . . how did you know?"

"Sleekit told me." She gestured at the sellsu. "Some sullsi saw it happen—not him but others—and it's known far and wide among the children of the waves. Don't you know that sea serpents are the Children of Hrum? And His Messengers? That they harm no one? And saved Hrum's daughter? Even the Djezians wouldn't kill a sea serpent!"

Brokols realized that Eltrienn too was staring at him, his expression startled, concerned.

"I know that now," Brokols said. "I've learned a lot since I've been in your land. In our waters, there are no serpents, and to our captain, they looked simply like dangerous creatures that might snatch a sailor overboard. They were swimming right alongside us, their heads higher than our rails. And their teeth are quite fearsome, you know. We had no idea . . ."

Her severity lightened, though her expression still was serious, and briefly she exchanged sentences with the sellsu. Then she gave her attention to Brokols again.

"I told Sleekit what you said. He wasn't very impressed. I didn't actually suppose that you killed them yourself, but what one's countrymen do, one's fellows, tends to reflect on one's self. Shall we go to the house? I'm ready for some shade."

They started back. "Your speech and the sellsu's don't sound much alike," Eltrienn observed.

"True. I do the best I can though. I started out repeating him, of course, so he knew what I was trying to say, and got used to the way I copy his sounds. I've even talked to other sullsi a couple of times, when they came up to the weir. After they got over their surprise, they understood me too. And I them, of course." She chuckled. "Sullsi laugh, you know; they couldn't help themselves a time or two, listening to me savage their language."

Back at the villa, she paused to rinse her feet in a garden fountain, then excused herself to clean her hair and put on other clothes. Eltrienn and Brokols sat on a shaded patio to talk.

"So your marines killed two serpents." The centurion's tone, though not indignant, was serious, as at some enormity.

"Not in malice," Brokols answered quietly. "They were so near, near enough to snatch one of us in an instant."

"They never would have," Eltrienn said, then added thoughtfully, "I can see why someone might be frightened though, who didn't know them. I remember the first time I ever went boating on the firth while they were there. One swam not ten feet off our side and raised its head to look us over. I *was* intimidated; I admit it.

"But a Child of Hrum! Only his daughter was closer to him. We're just his foster children, and apparently your people are not even that." He looked intently at Brokols. "I don't know whether Hrum can forgive you."

"I don't know either," Brokols answered, "but it was done without intention to offend." *I won't worry about it though,* he added silently to himself, *as long as you don't mention it to anyone when we get back to Theedalit*. For though Hrum might be myth and superstition, Hrummean belief in him was obviously very real.

SIXTEEN

Juliassa walked to the weir carrying a pail of rockfish and a filet of raw gleebor chuck. The western sky was dark purple hemmed with dusky gold, while overhead stars gleamed between tall dissipating cumuli. The tide had peaked and was ebbing again. She could make out Sleekit's dark form, somewhat seal-like, somewhat dolphin-like, different from either, waiting by the stream's edge below the weir. He'd been fishing in the sea; his body had left a trail on the wet sand.

"Hail, Sleekit," she said. Her approximation of sullsit was practiced but inevitably crude. "How was the fishing?"

"For this season on an open coast, not too bad." He made the low, throaty, warbling sound she'd come to recognize as a sullsit chuckle. "I might have tried harder, but I knew you'd bring supper." He voiced an approximation of the Hrummean word for evening meal; among themselves, the sullsi didn't name their meals, eating when appetite and opportunity coincided.

Juliassa squatted down and dumped the rockfish on the damp sand beside the stream. Sleekit preferred fish to the chuck; eating red meat, he said, was closer to cannibalism than he preferred, though he accepted it cheerfully enough as a supplement.

With his long, rather human-like hands he rinsed the sand from a rockfish, then tucked it headfirst into his mouth, bit it in two, and swallowed it without chewing.

"What did you think of the big-ship man?" she asked curiously.

"Don't know enough to judge him as self-being. But know

big-ship men killed two of the long ones without good cause. No warning, just . . ." he coughed sharply, a resonant sound, a second-hand imitation of a cannon shot. "Two dead. Lord of Ocean cannot be happy at that."

He rinsed and swallowed another rockfish, then another. Juliassa, squatting, watched without comment. She'd liked the foreigner, Elver. He was different, polite, and interesting looking. No, he was interesting, *period,* and handsome in a way. Especially his eyes! If his clothing looked peculiar, it was not uncomely, and he wore it well. They'd talked for a bit in the garden before supper, while Eltrienn and Zeenia, in the sitting room, caught each other up on their lives. Elver had seemed intelligent, thoughtful, and an odd mixture of ignorant and informed.

"What you think about?" Sleekit asked.

"The big-ship man."

The sullsi nodded, then rinsed and ate the last rockfish before speaking again. "Tonight I go from here," he said. "I am strong enough now, and my pack has stayed close by, waiting. They wish to go elsewhere where the fishing is better, and I would not delay them longer."

The heavy body heaved nearer then. The hand that reached and touched her shoulder was pebbly-rough, harsh textured, and smelled of fish. The sullsit eyes glinted obsidian, reflecting the lustrous jewel of Little Firtollio. "You saved me from death," he went on. "Of having to be born and grow up again, or maybe—" he chuckled. "Maybe from being hatched as a clam." His voice softened. "No one cares to die, I think, no sellsu. To lose identity. While there is hope of pleasure, the life one has is dear.

"Also, you became my friend, even learned to speak with me, a strange thing told of only in an old story. Now you have given us a new story to tell. I will tell it always with love, and it will be repeated far and wide as long as there are sullsi, for we travel far with the seasons."

His voice softened further. "I will always remember you."

Hot tears blurred Juliassa's eyes, and she began to sob, softly at first. Then emotion overwhelmed her, and crying hard, she hugged the thick round body. Sleekit said no word. Nor did she; she wasn't able to. And when she'd straightened, quieting somewhat, he silently turned and humped his way into the stream below the weir. For a moment his head was visible, moving down the current to the sea. Then he dived and was gone, but it seemed to her that he'd turned to look at her one last time before disappearing.

That brought another flood of tears, but briefer this time. Then, wet-eyed and distracted, she picked up her pail and the sandy filet and started for the house.

Soon after the sun had disappeared below the horizon, Brokols had walked down to sit on the bench beneath a sprawling, wind-molded evergreen and watch the western sky, vivid at first, its play of colors changing from minute to minute, losing intensity but not, for a time, beauty.

There'd still been considerable light when he'd seen the sellsu waddle from the gentle sea, then flop its way to the weir no more than eighty feet from where he sat. It hadn't noticed him though, apparently, motionless as he was, at least it showed no sign, and after a moment Brokols' attention had returned to the sunset.

The color display had dwindled nearly to nothing, and Brokols had been about to leave, when Juliassa walked by toward the stream, following along the tide's edge. It still was not yet fully night, and he stayed to watch and listen. Their words meant nothing to him, but as they went on, their tone changed, and it seemed to him he was witnessing a farewell. He saw the sellsu touch the girl, which startled Brokols and for a moment alarmed him. He did not recognize the first few sobs; the hiss of even this gentle surf obscured them. But he heard when she began to cry harder, and her grief wrung his heart.

Then the sellsu returned to the sea, and after a minute Brokols saw Juliassa start back along the beach, angling toward the landscaped grounds. He held still, scarcely breathing, not wanting her to see him, to know her grief had been witnessed. But this time her path took her closer. She was fifteen feet away when she noticed him and stopped.

"I'd been watching the sunset when you came by," he said quietly. "I grieve with you in your loss." It wasn't strictly true. What he'd felt was not loss, but heartfelt compassion for her own.

For a long moment she stood without moving or speaking, pale in her chemise. Then she stepped quickly to him, knelt and hugged him for just a second, kissing his cheek, and hurried away, all without speaking.

When she was gone, he remained seated awhile, still feeling the press of a young breast against his shoulder, the wetness of her tears on his temple.

And it seemed to him that no man before could ever have been so totally and suddenly in love as he was with this girl. This stranger. This descendant of pleasure droids.

SEVENTEEN

Thunder still rumbled farther up the Theed Valley, but in the city the sun had reappeared, and steam rose from the pavement as Brokols folded back the top of the shay. Shutters were being thrown open; merchants or their employees were emerging to sweep puddled water off concrete sidewalks into the broad main street; cheery voices called back and forth.

Brokols found himself glad to be back. He was sure that no other sizeable town anywhere was so bright and friendly.

The street they were on, Central Avenue, opened onto Hrumma Square between the Fortress and the Theed River. As the shay rolled into the large open rectangle, Brokols and Eltrienn could see a crowd gathering—perhaps regathering after the rain—in front of the stone speaker's platform at one end. There were six or eight hundred of them, Brokols estimated, tiny compared to the throngs that turned out for the imperial government.

"Let's stop and hear what it's about," he said.

Eltrienn nodded, and when they were close enough, reined in the team. After a moment, they saw two men climb the steps to the platform, one fat, wearing an expensive, intensely white robe, the other lean, his robe unbleached. Brokols recognized the lean one as Vessto, Eltrienn's brother.

That's when it occurred to him that this was not a gathering by decree. In Hrumma, it would be legal to gather outside the seat of government to listen to anyone, perhaps even without approval. Somehow, illogically, a breath of fear touched him.

"People of Theedalit!" the fat one shouted, "I give you the

sage, the Trumpet of Hrum! May you listen closely." And having said it, stepped back, leaving Vessto Cadriio standing alone. Vessto waited a long moment. When he began, his voice had power and reach without seeming loud, in fact while seeming quiet.

"People of Hrumma. Your nation is threatened. The very worship of Hrum is threatened. A distant land across the sea, called Almeon, has sent an ambassador to us, and one to each of the Djezes. In friendship, so they say. To establish commerce between us, so they say."

Vessto glanced at the shay then, just for a moment, not long enough to turn the crowd's heads toward them, then returned his gaze to the Hrummeans who stood listening. Brokols' whole body, his whole being, had tensed when Vessto began his speech, had frozen when the eyes touched him. When they moved on, it was release.

Vessto continued. "But talk of trade is subterfuge. Talk of friendship is lies. Almeon's king over kings, who calls himself *emperor*, intends to rule us. He plans war against us."

Vessto paused, scanning his listeners. "But how can he conquer us from 8,000 miles away?" Again he paused, as if waiting for one of them to tell him, then went on. "You have all heard of the great ship he sent here. Which brought his ambassador. Some of you saw it, and heard the great thunder of its weapons when they shot forth fire. He is preparing 200 such ships. Two hundred! And each of the 200 will come here full of soldiers, with weapons far more powerful than any we have against them."

Again he paused. And it seemed to Brokols that escape was impossible. He sat within thirty feet of the crowd's edge. In a moment the holy man would look at him again, point him out, tell them to turn around and see the enemy. And he'd be torn to pieces.

If only Eltrienn would start up again, drive casually away without drawing attention. But that was impossible. To start away now would draw attention, and there he was in the shay with the top back, wearing clothes that proclaimed him *enemy*.

"Hrum is testing us," Vessto went on. "Testing all of us. As he has tested our nation before. But this will be the hardest test of all. Although Hrum has the power to deliver us from any fleet, any army, any weapons, it is up to us to save ourselves. And we must save ourselves *without transgressing the laws of Hrum!* If we do this—if we act with all our strength to save ourselves, as if there could be no help—then he will help us. He will thresh the enemy, and scatter the chaff like dust in the wind."

Vessto raised his arms now, and his voice swelled. "All we must do is do all that we can, within the strictures of Hrum's words, and we are ensured victory. But to stint will be to lose."

He lowered arms and voice then. "Tell others of this. I will speak here again, two days from now as the sun sets, and at high noon on the next Freeday, for those who would hear me for themselves."

With that he turned and left the platform, and the crowd seemed to relax. The fat man stepped forward as another man, wearing a leather apron, climbed the steps. The fat man too glanced at the shay, but said and did nothing to call attention to it.

"There are people here," he said, "who were on the headland when the enemy ship approached the firth. They heard the Trumpet of Hrum prophesy that the serpents would leave when the ship entered. Though such a thing had never happened before. And . . . but here. Here's someone who was there. Let him tell you himself what he saw. What they all saw!"

He stepped back, turning the crowd over to the aproned man, the witness to Vessto's accurate foretelling. Eltrienn chucked to the kaabors, and they moved briskly off toward the north gate.

"That was the most frightening thing I ever experienced," Brokols murmured as they left the crowd behind. It was as if he'd said it to himself. "I was petrified."

Eltrienn's brows lifted. "Why?"

"Well . . . I'm the ambassador. Of the emperor that Vessto called the enemy. I was afraid Vessto or the heavyset man would point us out and the crowd would attack us."

Eltrienn shook his head. "Nothing like that would happen here. Hrum forbids it."

Brokols looked uncertainly at his guide. "But the things he said . . ."

"That's another thing. They aren't convinced yet; they don't know Vessto. Rantrelli may consider him a sage, but to the crowd he's from a far province, an unknown quantity. Without enough recognition to draw a larger crowd, even today, a Freeday, even though he's spoken before."

They were at a side gate now, and after Eltrienn had given an order to the guards there, got down from the shay. Two of the guards took their bags and put them in the gatehouse for temporary safekeeping. Another mounted the seat and drove away. Brokols was sure they'd looked strangely at him. "He's spoken before? How do you know?"

"Half the crowd were farmers. By their clothes. So he's spoken before, enough that some people, in from the country, have come round to hear what he has to say. But it sounds strange to them."

They walked through the arch-topped gate that penetrated the thick wall.

"The purpose of Vessto speaking to them is to raise wide concern and disapproval among the people," Eltrienn continued, "and force the Two Estates to consider replacing Leonessto Hanorissio as amirr. That's the procedure for removing an amirr. And to get anywhere with it, unless the amirr is criminal or grossly inept, requires the leadership of a sage. The fat man, Mellvis Rantrelli, is a prominent merchant, a noble, a member of the First Estate. Apparently he couldn't talk Panni Vempravvo into supporting him in this; otherwise he would have. And people realize that; it makes them more skeptical. So he turned to my brother. Perhaps in three or four weeks, if things go well here, he'll take it to the provinces. After that, Rantrelli may raise the issue to the First Estate."

"What do you think of what Vessto said?" Brokols asked. "Do you believe it?"

Eltrienn glanced sideways at him. "You're the one who knows whether it's true or not. Maybe I should ask you."

There was no accusation in Eltrienn's voice or eyes as he said it. He was simply making a point.

The amirr was eating lunch with Allbarin in what amounted to his private corner on the wall, and had them brought to him. When they were seated, he looked Brokols over.

"Well, Mr. Ambassador," said the amirr, "what did you think of our country?"

"Quite interesting, Your Eminence," Brokols replied, "and very comely. Perhaps more to the point, I now have information on a number of products that should interest Almaeic merchants, and the names of people and villages who are or might be interested in providing those goods."

The amirr said nothing for a long moment. When he spoke, it was drily. "Interesting enough or comely enough to be worth conquering? Or perhaps rich enough?"

Brokols' lips tightened. "Your Eminence, our own country is quite rich and fertile enough. As to what dreams your neighbors to the north might entertain, I don't know, but I suspect the quality of your archery must give anyone pause who'd care to invade you.

"Considering the distance involved, Almeon's interest in things Hrummean must be restricted to those things more or less unique to Hrumma. For example, your art. And certainly the furs I've seen examples of, that you obtain in trade with the barbarians."

The amirr's hazel eyes probed his own. "In that case, I trust you will excuse my question. There are reports, rumors I should say, to the effect that your nation does intend to invade us." He paused. "These rumors include a fleet of 200 great ships being built to carry Almaeic soldiers. You'll understand that I'm concerned both with the rumors and with their effects on my people."

"Of course, Your Excellency. I might also point out that to build 200 great ships would be an enormous expense." *As the emperor's advisors pointed out,* he added to himself.

Allbarin interrupted. "Mr. Ambassador, is it possible that your emperor has designs on our neighbors to the north? The Djezes?"

Inwardly the question shook Brokols. "I find it highly improbable," he replied. "As I indicated before, eight thousand miles of ocean is a very great distance across which to mount a conquest."

There was another long, sharp-eyed lag by the amirr. "To be sure, Ambassador Brokols," he said at last. "To be sure."

When Brokols left, Eltrienn stayed with him long enough to arrange transport home for the ambassador and his luggage, then excused himself, commenting frankly that he needed to report on their trip. In parting they shook hands, Eltrienn seeming now as friendly and genial as ever.

On the ride home, Brokols asked himself how Vessto had gotten his information about the 200 ships. Could Stilfos have said something to someone? To Gerrla perhaps? But surely Stilfos was smarter than that. And what possible reason could he have had? As far as that was concerned, how would Stilfos have known the size of the fleet? The number hadn't been part of his briefing; Brokols was sure of it, had helped give it. And it wasn't open knowledge. The ships were being built at a number of shipyards on different islands, and hadn't been marshalled—some of them hadn't even had their keels laid—when the *Dard* had left Larvis Harbor.

It *must* have been Stilfos who'd mentioned it though. Who else could it have been? Maybe he'd overheard something on it before they left. He'd question him when he got home.

Interesting that Vessto had gotten the number of ships right, but not the target country.

Stilfos wasn't home when he arrived—not in the kitchen or the roof garden or his room. He could hardly be far though; the stove's tiny auxiliary firebox was hot, and the kettle was on it. Brokols made satta and strolled with it out onto the roof garden where there was a fair and cooling breeze. His meeting with the amirr was on his mind. These *were* strange people. Clearly the amirr had considered what Vessto was saying as at least possibly true. Yet there'd been no sense of hostility, really, from either the amirr or Allbarin. Or from Eltrienn, who after all was Vessto's brother.

As Brokols sat thinking, a sound impinged on his mind until it breached his consciousness and he turned around. The wind vanes of his generator were spinning, as they were more often than not, but the sound . . . hmm. The generator was still engaged! The automatic cutoff hadn't disengaged it! Quickly Brokols climbed the steps to the roof of his penthouse and tripped the manual cutoff, then checked the battery. No damage! Incredible! And he hadn't used the wireless for sixteen days! Surely they hadn't had sixteen days of near calm here.

Frowning thoughtfully, he went back down to the roof garden and into the apartment, then to the wireless room. Dragging his index finger across the table to the left of the sending apparatus left a visible track through dust. To the right, where the notepad would rest while receiving, there was no dust. With his handkerchief he wiped the key itself; no sign of dust soiled the white fabric.

Someone had been using the wireless while he'd been away.

Stilfos chose that moment to return; Brokols heard him enter the apartment and walk down the hall past the open wireless room door. After a moment there was an opening and closing of cabinet doors in the kitchen. Brokols went down the hall after him.

"Shopping?" he asked from the kitchen door.

Stilfos looked around from putting purchases away. "Yes, milord. Nice to have you back, sir. I've been to the greengrocer's. Assumed you'd be back within a day or so." The smaller man's quick smile covered nervousness. He'd seen that the wireless room door was open.

Brokols' voice was mildly sardonic. "I take it there's been an ordinary amount of wind while I was gone?"

Stilfos nodded. "A fair bit, sir. Off and on."

"Then you've used the wireless."

Apologetically: "One time, sir."

"Explain."

"I thought I should inform Lord Kryger of the public meetings, sir, so I put on native things and went to hear the second for myself. Then I let him know."

"Interesting. I attended one myself today. In proper ambassadorial garb, I might add. And heard something that quite surprised me—that the emperor's preparing a fleet of 200 invasion ships. Where do you suppose they got that number? Two hundred?"

"Well, sir . . . I really don't know. Is that number correct?"

Brokols ignored his aide's question. "How many ships do you suppose he's actually got built or building?"

"I have no idea, sir. It'd have to be a great many though, to bring an army big enough. Is the . . . is 200 right?"

Brokols studied Stilfos thoughtfully. "It would seem that one of us leaked to the Hrummeans."

"Yes, sir."

"The idea of us invading them could easily have grown out of human suspicion, but the number . . . two hundred is the actual number, you know."

"No, sir, I didn't know."

Brokols said nothing for a moment, his attention withdrawn. "When did you learn to use the telegraph?"

"During my army service, sir."

"Why wasn't I informed?"

"I suppose it never came up, sir."

Brokols pursed his lips, eyes hooded. "I see." He didn't see though, at all. It should have been on Stilfos's dossier. And Stilfos had wirelessed Kryger about the anti-Almeon rallies, had probably mentioned the figure of 200 ships, too. What had Kryger thought when he heard that? What could he have thought?

Kryger'd never liked him. He'd assigned Stilfos as an informant as well as aide.

But that didn't answer the question about the leak. Stilfos almost had to be lying about not knowing the number of ships. How else could they . . . then Brokols remembered the night of the reception, and something in the drink. But it couldn't have been himself that had told. He hadn't sat around talking that night; he'd been fully occupied with—other things.

It had to have been either Stilfos or himself though. How else could Vessto have found out what he had? Surely not a lucky guess? With an effort Brokols shook off the mystery, the loop of circular questions.

"Well," he said, "I suppose you have things to do."

"Yes, sir." Stilfos scurried off.

Brokols wandered to his room to work on a schedule of possible Hrummean exports and prices. He didn't accomplish a great deal though. His mind was on other things.

"There's no doubt at all, Your Eminence," Allbarin said to the amirr. "Two hundred is the right number, and it's Djez Gorrbul they plan to invade, not ourselves. Gorrbul is to invade us; that was clear this time. Get its army deeply involved down here. Then Almeon will land its army at Haipoor l'Djezzer, presumably take over the government, and after that, pacify the countryside. I suppose they plan to take us afterward, at their leisure.

"But our immediate problem seems to be with Djez Gorrbul. As it has been so many times before."

After Brokols' call that evening, Lord Vendel Kryger sat brooding at his wireless, beside the penciled notebook pages with his record of their exchange. That scoundrel Brokols hadn't so much as offered a speculation, let alone an explanation. Or a confession, though he'd hardly expected one.

He'd already made his weekly report to the emperor's office, and mentioned that Gamaliiu was seriously considering moving up his invasion of Hrumma to late summer. And that that would seem to call for scheduling the departure of the fleet for late summer, if they were to land here while the Gorrbian army was embroiled away from home.

He hadn't mentioned that he'd been working on Gamaliiu to make the change, of course. That wouldn't do at all. First it would make them extremely unhappy with him. Second, they'd demand to know why he'd done such a thing. And third, it would not do to tell them of Brokols' leak. Or perhaps treachery. As mission leader, the responsibility and blame would fall on himself regardless.

Of course, if the fleet did leave in late summer, the Gorrbian army had damned well better be tied up in the south, or there'd be the headsman to pay.

His lips twisted grimly. Brokols had put him in a very touchy situation.

But so far Gamaliiu'd been receptive to every other suggestion. He'd been impressed, of course, with the *Dard*'s artillery salute, and the gunnery demonstration on the island up the coast. And had seemed quite accepting of the argument that the emperor, as a matter of principle, could hardly traffic for long with less than another emperor—with three separate states having three separate rulers.

The idea of conquering Hrumma, and later Djez Seechul, were in line with Gamaliiu's long-held interests anyway. While the promise to help him make his own artillery, along with the idea for a seaborne attack on the Hrummean north coast, had seemed to the king just the edge he needed to ensure success.

Now the deliberately planted worry that the Hrummeans might find out and take new defensive measures would almost surely bring Gamaliiu to move his plans ahead.

At least, according to Brokols, the Hrummeans didn't know that the fleet would strike Djez Gorrbul. And Stilfos's report implied the same.

But if the Hrummeans thought the invasion would strike Hrumma, then why hadn't they arrested Brokols and done away with him? Admittedly the droids were strange, their thinking undisciplined and often illogical, but that was still a bit much. Unless, of course . . . and there was that thought again: that Brokols, for some inconceivable reason, might be a traitor instead of simply loose-mouthed.

Eighteen

Brokols settled down after supper with a history of Hrumma. It had been lying on the librarian's table, and he'd picked it up to browse through while the Hrummean had been off somewhere. The librarian, though always polite, had been surprisingly adamant in denying him access to the shelves, doling out books to him like a teacher to a lower-form pupil. So Brokols had tucked this one in his satchel without asking.

It was an interesting book, mostly seeming quite factual, but with occasional references almost amusingly imaginative and superstitious. The other books he'd read contained nothing like them, and it occurred to Brokols that the librarian might be a rational, nonsuperstitious person who was embarrassed at the thought of the foreign ambassador reading such things.

There were superstitions in Almeon too, Brokols reminded himself, but they were personal, not cultural—minor aberrations, not major institutions. He wondered what Almeon would have been like if Kaitmar III had been superstitious and enforced some religion with as much energy as he'd used, in fact, to suppress them.

He was sipping juice and reading about the last invasion of Hrumma by Djez Gorrbul when Stilfos interrupted.

"Milord, Mirj Tirros Hanorissio to see you." This time he announced the name without effort or awkwardness. "He has a friend with him; the same young gentleman as before."

Tirros! Brokols was surprised that the criminal mirj had the gall to visit, after what he'd done at the reception. There was a table of hard alabaster beside him, a pale figured pink, and marking his place, Brokols laid the book down on it. "I'll see him," he said tersely, getting up. "In the waiting room."

The two youths were slouched on the settee when he entered. Brokols had no intention of sitting: standing gave him altitude and established that the audience would be short. "How may I be of service to you?" he said. It wasn't an offer, but a formal greeting.

"Why, Your Excellency," Tirros drawled, "that's exactly what I came here about. How *I* could be of service to *you*." His tone became confidential. "I've heard what the so-called 'Trumpet of Hrum' has said about your emperor's intentions for us here. And it occurs to me that while he may be just a country sage, he's quite probably right about it. Certainly it makes good sense.

"So I'm offering my services in your emperor's behalf. And in yours, of course. I'm sure you can make good use of my knowledge and advice, and I can connect you with others who could be invaluable to you. For example, I can have the country sage silenced if you'd like. Very thoroughly, very—unobtrusively."

Tirros looked expectantly at Brokols. When the Almite only stared at him, he continued.

"You're wondering what I'll want as recompense. That's simple enough, and it won't cost you anything at all, personally. When your emperor has conquered us, he'll want to rule as profitably as possible. Which means he'll want a native Hrummean, someone who knows Hrummean affairs thoroughly, to be his regent here. To see that taxes get collected and that things are done the way he wants. That sort of thing.

"I'm proposing myself for the position. He'll find me efficient and loyal, quite able to assume his viewpoint and his purposes."

"Hmh!" Brokols had no doubt that the young man was serious and meant what he said, without scruple of patriotism, of loyalty to country or family. He was an utter scoundrel, without redeeming quality.

And dangerous to deal with, that he also knew, capricious and undisciplined. "An interesting offer," Brokols replied. "I'll need to give it some thought and perhaps take it up with my superior."

Tirros's eyebrows raised. "With your superior? How would you do that? Isn't it 8,000 miles to your homeland?"

Chagrin flashed through Brokols. "You people have your kiruus," he answered. "Mine have their methods too. Now if you will excuse me . . ."

Tirros and Karrlis got up, and Tirros reached out a hand to shake with Brokols. Brokols met it, clasped and shook it. When they'd gone, he washed his hands.

Tirros chattered as the two young Hrummeans walked down the stairs and onto the street. Karrlis half listened, his thoughts taking their own course. He decided to keep to himself much of what he'd learned from Brokols' mind. Let Tirros think there was a reasonable prospect of success with his plan. An illicit adept got very few jobs. To advertise was out of the question; even word of mouth was dangerous. He needed to keep this one going for the thin flow of coins it meant.

"What would you say the odds are of his agreeing?" Tirros asked.

Of course, Tirros was not an utter fool. His eyes were sharp enough, and he could add two and two. "Just now it's uncertain," Karrlis improvised. "He doesn't like you, doesn't trust you. But he does see strong advantages in your proposal."

Tirros nodded smugly as they started down the sidestreet, toward its corner with a nearby major street where hansoms and rikkshas would be available. "I won't push him hard. I'll hold off a few days, then come around and ask what he needs taken care of that's a problem for him. Perhaps ask him if he'd like to meet another girl." Tirros laughed, the sound clear and light.

"If he doesn't come around," Karrlis said, "I have an alternate suggestion you might like."

Tirros looked quizzically at him as they strode along. "And what might that be?"

"You can try his man. The little foreigner's more than just a servant. He's the one who'd serve as replacement if anything should happen to the ambassador. If this Brokols proves intransigent, we might, ah, retire him. Then perhaps you could work with the replacement."

Tirros examined the suggestion, then crowed with delight. "A marvelous idea. Well, we'll see what we see. The ambassador is the stronger person, of course, with higher rank. Correct? He can do more for me. But if he closes the door in my face . . . I'll hire someone tomorrow morning; your little brother maybe? Have him watch the ambassador's street entrance and follow him if he goes out. If he goes to the Fortress or seems to be leaving town, we'll catch a coach, you and I, and talk to his man. What's his name again?"

"Stilfos."

"That's it. Stilfos." Tirros seemed to taste the name, trying it on his tongue. "Stilfos. And see what sort of man he might be to work with."

NINETEEN

Stilfos had finished his morning work and settled on a chair in the garden with a cup of satta dosed with sweet wine, to browse the book Brokols had been reading the evening before. He read not with any particular intention of learning from it, but as a diversion, and was probably learning as much from it as Brokols had, when he heard the knocker clack on the entrance door. Frowning, he put the book down and went inside to answer.

Tirros and Karrlis were waiting.

"Yes?" he said. He didn't like either of them, didn't trust them. Nor did it help that he came only to Tirros's throat and to Karrlis's chin; at home his height was average or a bit more.

"We'd like to come in and talk with you, if you please," Tirros replied. "It's about the ambassador."

"We can talk where we are," Stilfos answered. His tone carried suspicion and disapproval. "I'm to let no one in without permission."

Tirros shrugged. "Have you heard of the Trumpet of Hrum?" he asked.

"The man who speaks against Almeon? I've been myself to hear him. What about it?"

"Some of us here in Hrumma think it would be a good idea if your emperor did rule here. Last night the two of us offered to do what we could to help; help your emperor take over here, that is. But speaking frankly, we have doubts that your Lord Brokols is morally fit to serve as your emperor's representative. We thought you'd want to hear about it."

Stilfos's impulse was to order them away. Instead he found himself saying, "It had better be good, or I'm closing this door in your face."

Tirros nodded soberly. "Your ambassador, frankly speaking, is a libertine and sex pervert. He's . . ."

"I don't believe it! Be on your way now, both of you!"

Stilfos moved to shut the door, but Tirros's foot blocked it. "Mr. Stilfos," Tirros said earnestly, "I beg you hear me out. This is too important to leave unsaid."

Stilfos stopped, unsure.

"It may be," Tirros went on, "that his moral depravity does not affect his mental function, his judgement. All I ask is that you watch him, observe, and judge for yourself. Then decide what, if anything, you should do about it. We'd like to see your emperor succeed, if possible, and do what we can to help."

Stilfos still stood, not knowing what to say.

"How do you suppose the Trumpet of Hrum learned of your emperor's plans?" Tirros went on. "And about the fleet. The 200 ships."

Stilfos looked stricken. He remembered his concern at his master's drinking, and the trouble it might cause. "You gentlemen really have to go now," he said. "I've work to do."

This time Karrlis spoke. "Just one thing more, and we'll leave."

Stilfos waited.

"Have you ever seen the ambassador sick with a terrible headache after being out all night?"

"What if I have?"

"It's from a drug he took. To enable him to, uh, couple with different women all night long. And engage in acts other than coupling. A close acquaintance of mine was there and witnessed part of it; he's a servant of the house where it happened." Karrlis shuddered; Tirros looked on, impressed with him. "The things he did!" Karrlis added. "And in front of other people!"

Tirros interrupted. "Enough," he said. "It's not right to burden this man with all that ugliness." He looked at Stilfos. "Unfortunately, these things are true. But I can understand how hard it might be for you to hear them. We'll leave now, but I'll get in touch with you again in a few days. In case you decide we can help."

They backed away then, turned and disappeared down the

stairs. After a moment, Stilfos closed the door and went to the kitchen to wash pots, forgetting all about the book laying on the garden table. Fortunately it didn't rain.

Tirros and Karrlis laughed and giggled most of the way to the satta shop.

The next day at almost the same time, Lerrlia knocked. Stilfos was stunned by her appearance. She wore a light and clinging frock that didn't reach her knees, and she seemed to him lovely beyond belief.

"Is the ambassador at home?" she asked.

"Ah, no ma'am—miss—he's not."

"When do you expect him?"

"I'm not sure. Late afternoon most likely."

She frowned prettily. "Perhaps I'll come back then. I've been invited to a, um—very special party this evening, and I hoped he'd take me. He enjoyed the last one so much, and I've never known anyone who could, ah, party all night the way he did." She shivered. "He's marvelous!"

Stilfos simply stared.

She shrugged. "Oh well. I suppose he's very busy, or perhaps he's spending his free time with one of the other girls he met there. I shouldn't be pursuing him, but . . ."

She turned and left. It was half a minute before Stilfos closed the door and went back to his kitchen. He tried to finish cleaning the stove, the project he'd set for his morning, but it was no use. After a few minutes he went to the wireless room and radioed Kryger.

No one answered the signal at the other end though—no one seemed to be there—and Stilfos gave up on it for the time being.

Maybe, he told himself, none of it was true. Maybe they were lying, even the beautiful young woman. Although it was hard to imagine anyone so lovely being a liar.

Perhaps, he thought, he should wait a few days before telling Lord Kryger what he'd heard. Wait and see how Lord Brokols seemed. The truth was, he liked Lord Brokols much better than he did Lord Kryger. And as for the two young Hrummean gentlemen, there was something about them that seemed positively evil.

TWENTY

Eltrienn Cadriio had spent little time with Brokols since their return. The ambassador had less need of a guide and tutor now, and linguistically he'd made the switch from Djezian to Hrummean pretty thoroughly. His Almaeic-Djezian accent was interesting rather than troublesome, and only occasional words and idioms, relatively little used, caused glitches in communication for him.

The centurion had not been returned to his position on the amirr's guard though. He was to remain available to Brokols for the time being, and was quartered with the "unassigned" officers that formed a pool for miscellaneous temporary details. Mainly, just now, this involved helping the training cadre drill recruits, which were increasing sharply with the concern over possible invasion. Because of Cadriio's reputation as a swordsman, he'd been giving demonstrations and supervising drills with the weapon.

The palace messenger found him at the military compound, in the officers' dining room, and handed him the sealed envelope, then stood waiting. It was not, Eltrienn noted, an official envelope, nor was the seal familiar to him. Opening it, he began to read.

Dear Eltrienn,

It was my pleasure, during your visit at Sea Cliff recently, to talk a little with Ambassador Brokols. I found him to be a nice man and quite interesting. I would like to be better acquainted with him.

It would please me very much if you would arrange for him to meet me tomorrow at the palace after lunch, so that we may talk. I would like to know more about him and his country.

Fondly,
Juliassa

The centurion grimaced slightly, folded the message and tucked it in his belt pouch, then looked at the messenger. "Tell the namirrna," he said, "that I'll deliver her invitation."

When the lad had hurried off, Cadriio shook his head and returned his attention to his food. *From captain of the amirrial guard to messenger boy for the namirrna*. He didn't know where Brokols was today—in the library perhaps, or at home, or maybe visiting some merchant . . . *probably not the latter*, he told himself. *He'd likely have asked me along on anything like that*.

It would be interesting to know what was on Juliassa's mind. She'd been a nice child, and now she seemed a nice young lady. But she'd always been adventurous and impetuous, and a bit spoiled. She'd be better off, he thought, not to develop a romantic interest in Brokols. Not only was his political status somewhat uncertain; personally the ambassador was something of a stick. Quite a likable stick, basically a decent stick, but a bit of a stick nonetheless. The odds are, he wouldn't know how to respond to her.

The lady in waiting led Brokols into the garden, where Juliassa sat beneath a large umbrella, embroidering. She looked up as he came out the door, and smiling, rose to her feet. The lady in waiting turned demurely and went back in, leaving Brokols on his own.

It occurred to him, seeing Juliassa there, that a few evenings back he'd felt hopelessly in love with her. Then he'd arrived in Theedalit to an anti-Almeon rally, and after that there'd been the matter of Stilfos reporting behind his back to Kryger. He'd scarcely thought of Juliassa again till Eltrienn had delivered her message the day before.

As he walked toward her, he found her as lovely as before, as sweet, and the feeling rekindled inside him. But the emotion wasn't the same as it had been on the beach. On the beach there'd been her sense of loss and grief, his own sympathy . . .

Now she was smiling broadly, teeth white and even, and as he stepped up to her, she raised her hands for him to stop.

"You're wearing Hrummean clothes!" she said.

He grinned sheepishly. "They looked so much cooler, I decided it was foolish not to. I'll reserve my ambassadorial garb for ceremonial and official occasions."

She looked him up and down, warming him with her eyes. His suit was cut conservatively, white of course, and lightweight, with sleeves to the elbows. His fitted hose were snug from the knees down, and his lightweight blue calfskin boots ended a little above the ankles. He'd always had very good forearms and calves, and thought them comparable to those of most Hrummean men.

Reaching out, she took his hands, squeezing his fingers lightly, then motioned him to a chair on the other side of the tiny umbrellaed table, and they sat down.

"I'm glad you could come."

"I am too. Things are a bit unsettled, you know."

She nodded, sober now. "I've heard. Mother told me about it—about Eltrienn's brother and some of the nobles being worried about your country attacking ours." She brightened. "I'm not worried though. We're a strong people, a strong country. And if your country does something wrong against ours, I know whose side you'll choose."

Her conclusion, her confidence, her comment jarred Brokols to his heels. He'd been totally unprepared for it, hadn't considered that there might be a choice. She actually seemed to think he'd abandon his country and his emperor over a matter of principle! Of principle as she saw it!

It left his psyche in momentary confusion. For there *were* principles involved, an entire array of principles, and he hadn't looked at them. Now they began to roil within the borders of his consciousness: his senses of morality and propriety, of duty and responsibility and happiness and life and . . . and he wasn't sure where they led, how they fitted together, what they meant.

So he grabbed one of them, duty to emperor, as a stable datum. He was a loyal subject. Beyond that he'd go as far as he could to make things right—as far as he could while remaining loyal.

"I'm glad to have your confidence, Juliassa. This isn't a comfortable situation for me, I'm sure you know."

"I do," she said, nodding. "But now that you're here in a

land where Hrum is listened to, you'll hear him too." Abruptly she smiled again and changed the subject. "Now that you've seen so much of our country, what do you think of it?"

In a minute or two he was out of himself, describing what he'd seen and what he'd made of it, with increasing animation. She added her own comments, asked questions, made faces. There was laughter. When he left, after almost an hour, it was with a promise to have lunch with her and her mother the next day. It seemed to Brokols that he'd never enjoyed any hour in his life as much as this one.

Not even, he realized, during that drug-heightened night on the pleasure boat. He'd forgotten about that, and it brought back the swirl of uncertainties about principle.

Instead of returning to the Fortress and its library, he walked back to his apartment, where the similarly introverted Stilfos was still troubled by his visit from Lerrlia that morning. And read some more on the history of Hrumma.

TWENTY-ONE

The steward ushered Eltrienn into the amirr's office, then backed out and closed the door. Leonessto Hanorissio beckoned the centurion to sit, then sat down himself and regarded the younger man for a moment. Besides the two of them, only Allbarin was there, sitting to one side of the amirr and a little back, a wise and observant shadow.

Eltrienn knew the amirr well, and it was clear to him that something was wrong.

"Perhaps you're aware," the amirr said, "that your Almite is interested in my daughter. Yesterday they visited in the palace garden, and today he's to have lunch with her and her mother."

"Begging your pardon, Your Eminence, but it appears to me that her interest came first. She invited Brokols to yesterday's meeting—had me carry the invitation to him."

The amirr withdrew his gaze, his lips pursing. "Umh. I shouldn't be surprised."

"Also, Your Eminence, if I may say so, he's not *my* Almite. As a matter of fact, it seems to me he doesn't need me anymore. Perhaps I should be given another assignment."

The hazel eyes focused on Eltrienn again, and suddenly the mouth smiled. "Ah! And now you bring us to the reason I sent for you. You're the only person in government, so far as I know, who speaks the barbarian language."

Eltrienn nodded. "Not fluently, but functionally perhaps. It's been several years. There are people on the east coast, some of Ettsio Torillo's people, who should be quite fluent in it. If you need someone who speaks the language, one of them might serve you better."

The amirr shook off the suggestion. "They're part of the problem. Not that they caused it; so far as I know, they didn't. And I need someone I can depend on. Namely, I need you. After all, their great chief knows you."

"An upset with Torillo?"

"Upset isn't quite the word. I received a letter last evening telling me that the great chief's brother murdered Torillo's factor, his son, at Agate Bay. With a sword, supposedly in cold blood, while the factor was unarmed. And before witnesses. So the deputy factor, Torillo's nephew, pulled out the entire operation, loaded everyone on two lumber schooners at the wharf there, and went home. That's the report.

"The lumber and charcoal trade are suddenly gone, and if we don't reestablish them, it will cause us all kinds of problems. And our flow of swords to the barbarians has been cut off at the worst possible time.

"That's what I want you to handle."

The amirr sat back and shook his head, exhaling gustily. "As far as that's concerned, I'm going to need someone there soon anyway. There's no doubt, you know, that Gamaliiu is going to attack us. He undoubtedly would have anyway, within a few years—ten at the most. We haven't been invaded since '23; they're overdue. Now it'll be within a year, almost surely. Almeon's emperor plans to invade not us but Djez Gorrbul, within a year; Allbarin has it clearly from Brokols' mind. And the emperor's plan seems to be to incite Gamaliiu to invade us before that. So that the Gorrbian army will be engaged in Hrumma—preferably deep inside Hrumma, I'm sure—when the Almaeic army lands at Haipoor l'Djezzer.

"The assumption is, apparently, that with Gorrbul in Almaeic hands, Seechul and ourselves will certainly fall. Which, easily or bloodily, we will."

He paused. "Do you see?"

Eltrienn nodded. "So we want the barbarians to attack Djez Gorrbul at about the time the Gorballis intend to attack us, and we want them well-armed and eager. Enough that Gamaliiu will keep his army at home."

"Exactly. And that means barbarians with good steel swords, not crude, heavy, bog-iron clubs. Something light and strong. But just when we need to increase the flow of weapons to them, I find out the channel's been completely cut off."

"A question, Your Eminence."

"Yes?"

"Might it not be simpler to send an envoy to Gamaliiu, telling him what the emperor plans?"

"What was done to the envoy my predecessor sent? And if he decided to receive mine, would he believe? He'll think we act from fear of his invading us."

Again Eltrienn nodded.

"I do intend to send on though—a volunteer. Though it feels to me like sending someone to his death. I will not willingly forego a possibility.

"As to how helpful a barbarian invasion might be to us, in truth I don't know. I doubt that the barbarians are organized for such a campaign, and we know they're not experienced at them. Of course, they might be able to keep the Gorrbian army home, or bring it home. But then what? I've tried to imagine how things might develop, what might happen. And I've come up with several scenarios. And I'll tell you, it's much easier to imagine bad than good, given the circumstances. It's hard to believe that the barbarians might reach Haipoor l'Djezzer, and inconceivable that they'd join with the Gorrbian army to fight the Almites.

"While if the situation seemed uncertain for a landing by the Almaeic army, their ambassador in Haipoor might message his emperor, or their admiral, in the way that they have, and they might decide to invade Djez Seechul instead. Or ourselves!

"We could imagine on forever," he finished heavily. "Right now we do what we can. And all that we can. And hope Hrum is pleased with us."

Eltrienn nodded. He felt as if someone had tightened a band around his chest. "I'll get ready to go to Agate Bay then. I'd like to take . . ."

"Not Agate Bay. Not yet. The letter I got was from Ettsio Torillo himself. Hardly an unprejudiced reporter. He wants me to send a military force to Agate Bay to capture and execute the murderer. If I don't do it, he says he'll send a raiding party himself, to assassinate him."

The amirr leaned back, shaking his head, and exhaled gustily. "I want you to ride to Gardozzi Bay and find out what actually happened. Find out, if you can, what led to the murder, and what problems we might have to solve to reestablish trade. And make it clear to old Torillo that I will not stand for his sending any raiding party. Get his firm agreement.

"Take Lardunno with you, to read him. If Torillo won't agree, or if he says he agrees but secretly thinks he might send one anyway, tell him I'll lock him in the Hole of Shame if he has the murderer killed. And I will. Or if you see fit, you can tell him the Gorballis plan to invade, and we need the barbarians as allies. But if you tell him that, make sure he understands that it must be kept secret.

"Then come back here and report to me as fast as you can. I'll want it in writing. How long will it take you?"

"Hmm. Two hundred and fifty miles—if I can have your written authorization to requisition remounts at postal stations, and I leave by noon today, I can be there late the day after tomorrow. Give me a day there, two at most, to talk to people and write things down while they're fresh—I'll be back in six days. Seven at most."

"Then go."

"Yes, sir. And if you'll have someone inform Lardunno . . ."

The amirr nodded impatiently. "As you leave, tell Friimarti to take care of it. Tell him it's my order."

"Thank you, sir."

The centurion turned and left. The amirr looked at Allbarin. "Comment?"

"About Eltrienn Cadriio, nothing. He is direct, he is clean. He says what he thinks, and he thinks linearly to the point, or as linearly as a situation allows. He'll be back in six days with all the pertinent information. Unless he's struck by lightning."

The amirr raised an eyebrow. "I hope you don't see anything like that in his future."

Allbarin allowed himself a small smile. "A figure of speech, Your Eminence. I'm not much of a seer, but if I had to predict, I'd say that that young man will live long, regardless of wars and any other dangers."

"Umh. I suspect you're right."

"And now, Your Eminence, I'd like to make a suggestion that may seem to intrude into family matters. If I may."

No answer was spoken; there was no nod. The look the amirr directed at his advisor was hard. After a long moment the man continued in his usual calm way.

"I've said I'm not a seer. But I do sense that Ambassador Brokols will prove invaluable to you, to us. And beyond that,

I hope you will not discourage any reasonable interest your daughter may show in him."

"Why?" The word was less question than command.

"It seems to me that she has some role to play in all this, too. Though I have no idea what it is, and things sensed so vaguely . . ."

The amirr's jaw jutted; his mouth was a slash. "You were right; you do intrude." Again he exhaled gustily, then relaxed a bit. "Well, when one appoints an advisor, one must expect advice. And when his advice is as good as yours has invariably been, it's probably well not to reject it out of hand. 'Reasonable interest.' Hmh. I'll go this far: I won't forbid her, for a while at least."

He glanced at the clock ticking loudly on the wall, then got heavily to his feet. "My friend, in less than an hour we'll be listening to people asking favors of me; not my favorite activity. Shall we take a swim in the pool before then?"

TWENTY-TWO

Having been caught robbing his mother's money crock, Karrlis Billbis had been persona non grata at home for more than a year. Since then he'd lived in a small room with an entrance on a six-foot-wide alleyway, with a single window looking out at a featureless brick wall. The sole amenity was an outside stairway to the roof, where in a tub-like pot a tree grew, root-bound and puny, too small to cast meaningful shade. The view of sky and harbor were quite nice however.

Occasionally he had a guest; tonight it was Tirros Hanorissio. They sat on stools on the roof, watching a late thunderstorm pulse with lightning off the mouth of the firth. Tirros emptied his wine glass and Karrlis handed him the bottle.

"She said she didn't have to be an adept to see how shocked the little norp was," Karrlis said. "She was tempted to seduce him on the spot."

Tirros grunted. He was depressed this evening; it seemed to him that things weren't developing well at all.

"I told her it was a good thing she didn't," Karrlis continued. "Your only handle on him is, he considers himself more moral than his master."

Tirros got abruptly to his feet and stood stiff and silent, still facing seaward. Karrlis couldn't see his face, but the smoldering anger in his mind was more unequivocal than any scowl. After a long moment, Tirros spoke. "I don't need a handle on him."

His voice was like a rasp. Karrlis kept quiet.

"We'll kill Brokols," Tirros went on. "Then the little man will have no choice. He'll have to be ambassador. We'll set

Lerrlia on him and he'll do whatever she says. Which'll be whatever we tell her to."

"He's already fucking someone," Karrlis ventured. "A big strong woman."

Tirros shrugged it off. "Let Lerrlia put half a pinch of passion dust in his satta. That'll break him. Or we can get rid of the woman he's already seeing."

Abruptly he turned hissing on Karrlis. "Hrum's name! I don't want to hear about problems! We'll kill Brokols first; then we'll decide what to do next!"

Before he slept that night, Karrlis went and hired a boy for Tirros, to watch Brokols' building next morning. When the ambassador came out, the boy followed him half a block behind, till he saw him cross the square into the Fortress. Then he ran and told Karrlis.

Tirros met Karrlis at noon, at the usual satta shop. The mirj had rented a small, two-wheeled carriage with a luggage box as the seat. After lunch, he drove to the main street above Brokols' building. Their hired boy was playing on the sidewalk near the corner, spinning his top on a chalked matrix of numbers and waiting for Brokols to come past. "No," the boy said, "the foreign lord hasn't come back yet."

Tirros gave him a second silver coin and ran him off. "Can we trust him to keep quiet?" he asked Karrlis. "Or do we need to get rid of him too?"

"He'll keep quiet. I told him we're with a secret group spying on the Almite enemy, and if he tells, we'll kill him."

Tirros grunted, then chucked to the kaabor and turned down the sidestreet to barely past Brokols' place, where they could watch for him in the rearview mirrors without being visible to him. After an hour or so, Tirros got sleepy and told Karrlis to watch, then slouched down and closed his eyes.

Karrlis had no trouble with boredom. His eyes watched the street, but mentally he eavesdropped on Tirros's dreams, which, if uninformative, were interesting. He'd waken Tirros when Brokols turned the corner, and they'd call to him when he arrived. Assuming no one else was in sight. Each of the two had a short, lead-weighted club on the seat beside him. When Brokols came over, they'd cosh him, pull him into the carriage, strangle him, stuff him in the luggage box, and take him to a place Tirros knew, out of town. There they'd tie a rock to him—they had the rope—and sink him out past low tide.

Karrlis had suggested leaving the carriage and waiting in an alleyway between buildings. An attack would have been easier from there. But Tirros hadn't wanted to wait on his feet.

It wasn't necessary to waken Tirros. He woke up on his own, needing to relieve himself. Before he could get out of the carriage though, a rikksha rounded the corner and moved briskly down the sidestreet. They listened as, only a dozen feet behind them, Brokols paid the runner, then went upstairs.

Tirros swore, then chucked again to the kaabor, stopping at a nearby alleyway where he hopped down and ducked out of sight for a minute to urinate.

"What now?" Karrlis asked when he got back.

Tirros didn't answer at once, simply drove around the block and stopped just past Brokols' stairway again. "We wait here till he comes back out. Then we grab him."

Karrlis was skeptical. Tirros was not very good at waiting. Half an hour later Brokols came out. With Stilfos, the two of them talking in their own language. The ambushers watched the Almites walk up the street to the corner, where they separated, going in opposite directions.

As soon as they were out of sight, Tirros jumped from the carriage. Karrlis, after a moment's hesitation, followed. Up the stairs they went, to Brokols' door.

"Open it," Tirros said.

Karrlis tried the handle to no avail, then took a small metal hook from a pocket and, after several tries, got the door open. Once inside, Karrlis looked questioningly at the mirj. Tirros led out onto the roof garden, where they waited around the corner of the garden door.

Tirros took a half-dried sourdrupe from his belt pouch, popped it in his mouth, and a few seconds later spit out the pit. "If the ambassador comes back first," he said, "we take him. If the little man comes first, we'll . . ." Tirros groped mentally, then abandoned the problem. "He won't have to know we're here. He probably won't come out here, and we'll still wait. When the ambassador comes back, we'll tell him—something; it'll come to me—and we go out with him."

Karrlis began to wish they hadn't come here: Tirros wasn't making much sense. After a quarter hour, Tirros decided he wanted a cup of satta, and went inside to make some.

That's when Stilfos came home. Karrlis heard the bolt turn, heard footsteps down the hall, and Stilfos's exclamation when he reached the kitchen door.

"What?! What're you doing here? You've got no business in here!"

Karrlis went in too.

"I'm making a cup of satta," Tirros said. "I talked to your master a few minutes ago, and he told me to come up and wait for him."

"That's not so! I told him you came up and talked with me, and he said I was to have nothing to do with you. So be off now, or I'll report you to the police."

Tirros tried to cosh him but he dodged, and they grappled. Karrlis stepped in to help. To them the Almite was small, but his father had been a stone mason, and Stilfos had worked with him throughout his adolescence; he was a lot stronger than either of the two Hrummeans expected. When the brief struggle was over, Stilfos was unconscious, strangled by a throatlock. Both Hrummean youths had marks where they could be seen—Karrlis a split lip and Tirros a scratch on his forehead.

Neither of them said anything just then. Supporting Stilfos between them like a drunk, they went down the several flights of stairs to the street, then loaded him into the carriage. Not till they had him in the luggage box did they look around. There was no one in sight.

Karrlis jumped back out. "Drive around the block," he said, and disappeared back up the stairs. Tirros stared angrily after him, then did as he'd said. When he got back, Karrlis came out of a nearby alleyway and climbed in.

"There's no blood up there," he said. "I put the rolls and sausage away, and the wine—the things he had in the sack. Then I scanned off the pictures and emotions we left there, him and us. If the police sent a scanner up, he could easily have seen who did it—seen the whole thing. I scanned off what little there was on the roof garden too, and the stairwell."

He'd thought Tirros would be impressed with his foresight, but the mirj said nothing, simply started the kaabor with a slap of the reins. All Karrlis could read in him was bitterness, as if somehow he'd been cheated.

Brokols came home with his new guide and watchdog, Reeno Venreeno. Who was also an adept, though of course Brokols didn't know it. As soon as they came in the door, they smelled scorched metal, and Brokols hurried to the kitchen. The kettle, boiled dry and blackened, sat on the stove.

"Huh! I wonder . . ." He passed his hand close over the stove, which was no longer more than warm, then gingerly touched the kettle. "Strange. Stilfos should be here, but apparently he hasn't been for some while. And it's very unlike him to leave the kettle on when he goes out, except on the sideburner."

By that time Reeno had scanned the kitchen and found nothing. Not even the normal, mixed and blurred residuum of daily life. Nothing. Which told him that someone had scanned the place clean. It also told him that something had happened here which someone didn't want known. And why would anyone do that unless they anticipated an investigation?

While violence was rare in Almeon, there were that anti-Almaeic speeches to consider.

His eyes went to Brokols, who looked troubled, uncertain. *Maybe*, Brokols was thinking, *maybe he's at the Bostelli's downstairs. Maybe he'll be back soon.*

He led Reeno out onto the roof garden, where they sat down to watch the sunset. Reeno felt uneasy. After two or three minutes, Brokols turned to him.

"I have a bad feeling about my man. Stilfos. As if something's happened to him."

"I have the same feeling," Reeno said.

"Do you think we should call in the authorities, with nothing really to tell them? They might very well consider me overwrought. Which in fact I may be. But it occurs to me . . . there's growing sentiment against Almeon, you know."

"I suggest we do bring in the police," Reeno said. "We have some very good men on our force."

"Well then." Brokols got up. "I'll . . ." He stopped and bent over, then straightened. "I stepped on something," he said, and went inside. The adept followed. In the light, Brokols looked at what he'd stepped on. The adept felt a quick pulse of excitement—his own, not Brokols'.

"What is it?" he asked, knowing.

Brokols handed it to him. "It looks like a sourdrupe pit. See the wrinkles on it?"

Reeno nodded. "A sourdrupe, without a doubt." He looked questioningly at Brokols.

"It's not mine; I'd never discard a pit on the floor. Stilfos wouldn't either, and he doesn't like sourdrupes anyway."

"Then someone's been here. Come with me."

Locking the door behind them, Brokols went with the

Hrummean down the stairs and up the street to the thoroughfare, where they soon found rikkshas and rode to the Fortress. There Reeno took him to the central police offices. At his insistence, the duty sergeant sent a man to fetch the inspector of detectives, an adept.

While they waited, Brokols and Venreeno went up on the wall to watch the sunset. They didn't talk much. Surprisingly soon, the inspector came up.

"Ambassador Brokols," Reeno said, "this is Inspector Travvos Disotto. Inspector, Ambassador Brokols."

"I'm very glad to meet you," Brokols said as they shook hands.

"My pleasure." The inspector turned to Reeno. "What have you called me for?"

"Actually," Brokols put in, "the problem is mine," then went on to describe what they'd found and hadn't found. When Brokols was done, Disotto stood looking thoughtful. Actually he was examining the thoughts and mental pictures that Reeno displayed for him.

Brokols' apartment had been scanned off: kitchen, garden, hall, stairwell. Conceivably it could have been done by other than an adept, but hardly so thoroughly. There was also the information that Brokols knew nothing of the adept powers, and was not to learn of them.

Brokols interrupted. "Something just occurred to me. It must have been someone Stilfos knew; he'd never let a stranger in. An emergency could have come up downstairs, at the Bostelli's; he could have gone there. He's—been keeping company with their cook."

Disotto nodded, though not in agreement. "Take me there. I need to examine the site."

Before they left, the inspector belted on a shortsword, which didn't soothe Brokols' nerves. Some minutes later a police carriage let them out across the street from the apartment house. "I'm on the top floor," Brokols said.

They were crossing the narrow stone pavement when the inspector stopped, his attention on something there. On minor streets like this one there were no raised concrete sidewalks, but paving blocks set on end formed a low curb four feet from the buildings, setting off a narrow walkway for pedestrians. Disotto walked a few feet along it, intent, then stood frowning. Reeno relaxed his attention till he picked it up too. A carriage had been parked here. Two . . . two men, youths, had . . . his scalp crawled, and gooseflesh spread over his body.

"Lord Brokols," said Disotto, "have you had any visitors at your apartment lately?"

"Why, yes. Yes, I have."

"Who were they?"

"The mirj. And a friend of his he called Karrlis."

Disotto nodded, a decisive headjerk. "Mr. Venreeno, I have something to check on. I recommend you spend the night with Lord Brokols." He started across the narrow street to the carriage. "Constable, leave your saber with Mr. Venreeno. I want him armed tonight."

Venreeno had followed Disotto, a troubled Brokols a stride behind. The ambassador watched, sober-faced, as Venreeno accepted the constable's weapon. Then Disotto removed his shortsword from his belt and handed it sheathed to Brokols. "You'd best have one too," he said. "And I'll send some men to watch from outside." He climbed into the carriage then and it drove off.

As Brokols and Venreeno went up the stairs, Venreeno was re-examining the impression he'd gotten of two youths carrying/dragging what seemed to be a dead man. The impression was too vague to make identifications from, for him at any rate. No doubt one of them liked sourdrupes though, and very probably one was an adept.

Brokols was thinking that Disotto was certainly decisive, but he wondered about the man's competence. He'd behaved strangely in the street, almost seeming to sniff the air, then seemed to come to some conclusion out of nothing.

Later, while drinking satta with Venreeno on the roof, Brokols found himself listening for Stilfos to come in with a perfectly good reason for having been gone, and outside of the kettle and a little embarrassment, there'd been no harm done. But after a bit he could find no good reason to sit up longer, and went to bed disappointed, to worry for an hour or more before he found a restless sleep.

TWENTY-THREE

In the morning there still was no Stilfos, only a messenger from Inspector Disotto, with a request that Brokols meet with him at police headquarters. When they got there, the inspector was waiting, and after telling Venreeno to wait outside, questioned Brokols in his office over satta.

"You mentioned having been visited at your apartment by the mirj. When was that, and for what purpose?"

Frowning, Brokols thought back. "The first time was within a few days of my arrival here. Supposedly to inform me of the reception to be given in my honor at the palace. Actually, it seemed more a matter of trying to impress me with his importance; he grossly overstated his function in the affair.

"Then, several days ago he—um—came by to ask . . ." Brokols paused for several seconds, set his jaw for a moment, then went on. "Frankly, he believes the rumors that my emperor plans an invasion of Hrumma, and believes that I'm here to somehow assist in it. He offered me his services. He told me that after the conquest, he hoped to serve as the emperor's regent here."

Brokols was prepared for disbelief, but Travvos Disotto merely met his gaze and nodded slightly in acknowledgement; he'd learned a lot from Brokols' words and more from what lay beneath them in his mind. And deeper still, something more moved, something that hadn't quite shown itself.

"Have you had any other traffic with the mirj?"

This time Brokols hesitated long before answering, while Disotto watched what boiled up from underneath.

"Yes. Yes there is."

The words came slowly at first, the story of their meeting at the reception, of what clearly had to have been his drugging, of the night on the pleasure boat and his sickness the next day. When he started, he couldn't have said why he was telling it. In a way, telling it was the most difficult thing he'd ever done, partly because of the content, so utterly criminal in his own culture, and partly because—because he'd *enjoyed* it so! The telling may have been cathartic, a little, but when he was done, he was still tense, muscles twitching in his torso.

Disotto's eyes had never left him, nor shown the faintest censure, amusement, or embarrassment. "Thank you, Your Excellency," he said. "Your frankness has been most helpful. Unless you have something to ask, my business with you is over, at least for now." He paused, giving Brokols a chance to comment or question, then walked him to the door, and Brokols left.

When the door had closed, the inspector went at once into an adjacent room. His secretary looked up. "Corporal," Disotto said, "I want you to prepare an affidavit of arrest for me." He waited while the man laid out paper, took up his pen and dipped it. "The accused is Tirros Hanorissio. The charges . . ."

The accused being who he was, the inspector himself went to make the arrest, accompanied by two officers dressed inconspicuously in plain clothes. Had the amirr been at home, he'd have presented the certificate to him. As it was, he had the doorman call the steward.

"How may I help you, milord?" the steward asked.

"Come aside," Disotto said. "I wish to speak privately." He showed him the certificate. "I've come to arrest the mirj. Please take me to him."

The steward didn't entirely manage to conceal his satisfaction. "Of course. He did not breakfast with the family, so he may not be at home. Or he may simply have slept late. Would you care to be taken to his apartment?"

"If you please."

The steward led the inspector and his men down a sidehall, up a staircase, and along an upper hall. "This is his," he said, gesturing at a door.

"Is there another exit?"

"The next door down."

Disotto turned to one of his men. "Jianni, if you please."

The man nodded and went to it.

"Baarto, you wait here."

Then he struck the door sharply with its knocker. When no one answered, he tried turning the handle; somewhat to his surprise, the door opened. The apartment was empty, the bed either undisturbed or remade.

Next the steward questioned the housekeeper, who queried a maid: Tirros's bed had been used sometime during the night.

The inspector left with both his men. He couldn't stay himself, and arrest by a constable or sergeant would have offended protocol. He'd send a lieutenent to wait for the mirj's return.

Meanwhile he decided not to trouble the amirr with the situation until he was in a position to make the arrest.

Brokols had declined to have Reeno stay with him another night. Police watching the place from outside would do, would *have* to do. Meanwhile he needed to let Kryger know what had happened, and didn't wait till the hour set for reporting. After supper, which tonight he ate with the Bostelli's on the ground floor, he went to the wireless room and sent a signal the 300 miles to Haipoor l'Djezzer, then waited for a response. A response that might not come; no one might hear the signal at that hour.

In less than a minute though, he had one:

KRYGER HERE STOP END

Brokols' middle finger tapped an irregular staccato with the key: "Stilfos kidnapped last night. Stop. Fate unknown. Stop. Kidnappers unknown. Stop. Local police investigating suspects. Stop. End."

He picked up a pencil and waited. After a moment, a reply arrived.

> LOCAL POLICE WILL NOT SOLVE ANYTHING STOP THEY ARE PROBABLY RESPONSIBLE FOR IT STOP IF YOU HAD HAD CONTROL OF YOUR MOUTH IT WOULD NOT HAVE HAPPENED STOP END COMMUNICATION.

Brokols stared dismayed at the neat letters which had formed beneath his pencil. If he had had control of his mouth! What did that mean? His hand went to the key again in protest, but didn't touch it. "End communication!" Kryger wanted to hear no more from him tonight and probably wouldn't acknowledge.

Dismay turned first to hurt, then to the resentment of someone wrongly accused and not allowed to ask why or to argue their case. Why was this being done to him?

He knew though, when he thought about it: Someone had leaked information to the Hrummeans, and from Kryger's point of view he'd be a far more likely candidate than Stilfos, who presumably had had little opportunity to say the wrong thing in front of the wrong people. Or even to know the wrong thing.

But it hadn't been himself. He'd let nothing slip, said nothing about an invasion or any imperial intent to rule. Or 200 ships . . .

He rolled the whole miserable situation over and over in his mind, and the only explanation that presented itself to him was that Stilfos had told Gerrla and that Gerrla had told . . . but somehow Brokols didn't believe it. For one thing, there was the matter of how Stilfos could have known the size of the fleet.

But it had not been himself! He'd let nothing slip, not even drugged on the pleasure boat. Whatever it had done, the drug hadn't curtailed his memory or loosened his tongue. Talking had been the least of his activities that night. But then, Stilfos had hardly . . .

Brokols became aware that he'd been standing in the wireless room for ten minutes or longer, his mind going in circles, stuck in a mystery loop. Leaving, he went to his sitting room and picked up the history again. Reading didn't help though. When his eyes reached the bottom of the page, he realized he knew nothing it said; just beneath the surface, his mind was still turning the question over and over.

So he'd gone back to the top and had just started rereading when someone knocked.

He went to the door assuming it was one of the guards, or possibly Reeno or Inspector Disotto. No one else was likely to have been allowed. "Who is it?" he asked.

"My name is Panni Vempravvo."

It took a moment before the name clicked with him. The sage! He'd never imagined a visit from the man, and doubted it was him. There was a peekhole in the door—he'd forgotten it—and he pushed aside the little cover to peer through. He'd never before seen the person who stood there, but somehow he drew the bolt back and opened the door. Panni waited to be asked in; it took a moment before Brokols got his mind in gear.

"Well. Come in, Mr. Vempravvo." He stepped aside, and when the sage had entered, closed the door behind him, bolting it. Apparently if an acknowledged sage wanted to go somewhere, no one, not even the police, were likely to refuse him. "Uh, I—shall we sit in the roof garden? Would you like wine? Or satta?"

Panni Vempravvo smiled at him. "The roof garden would be fine. And satta."

Brokols took him out into the thin moonlight and offered a chair, then hurried in to make satta from water in the new kettle, hot on the sideburner. When satta steamed in both their cups, Brokols sat down facing his guest.

"To what do I owe the pleasure of your visit?" he asked.

Panni sipped, then grinned at him with teeth surprising in their even whiteness. "Hrum directed me here. Hrum-In-Me." His dark brown eyes looked black in the night. "Are you troubled?"

"If I am, I would hardly discuss it."

"Ah." The eyes did not probe, did not impose in any way. Brokols was scarcely aware of them now, but their attention was total. "There are policemen protecting you," Panni went on.

"Yes. My assistant has disappeared. The police are concerned that someone may try to harm me."

"I see. What does—" Panni paused for just a moment. "What does your superior make of all this?"

To Brokols, the question was like a cup of ice water thrown in his face. If he'd been standing, he might have staggered backward. To his surprise he heard himself saying, "He seems to think it was my fault."

"Ah. How did that make you feel?"

"Hurt. Wronged . . . threatened."

"I see. And was it your fault?"

"Of course not!" *Careful now,* Brokols told himself. It would be too easy to say something that would verify the claims Vessto Cadriio was making.

The calm eyes hadn't left him for a moment. "What could your superior do to you, if he decided to punish you?"

Brokols found himself talking almost without volition. "He—

he could expel me from my position! He could lie about me to Almeon, disgrace me there, ruin my future!"

"All that! And what could you do if he did those things?"

"I could . . ." Brokols stared at the sage. "I could . . . *I could stay here!* I could become a Hrummean! It's all I'd have left to me if I was expelled."

"M-m-m. Would the people of Hrumma accept you, do you suppose?"

"I—I think so, yes."

"Could you be happy as a Hrummean?"

Brokols felt almost dizzy, and for whatever reason, his vision went foggy. "I—I don't know."

"Well." The sage put his hands on the arms of his chair and got up. Smiling. "I, for one, would welcome you. Should you ever make such a decision. As nations go, as humankind goes, we are quite happy in Hrumma.

"But I am here without invitation, and you have things to do. I believe you were reading when I knocked." He went to Brokols' front door, his host trailing behind. "If I can be of assistance in anything . . ."

Brokols shook his head, confused.

"Meanwhile may Hrum be with you."

Then the tall sage opened the door and left, closing it carefully behind him. Brokols stared at it for a moment, then bolted it and walked slowly to his study. And his book; it lay there where he'd left it. He hadn't taken it to the door with him. Gooseflesh crawled.

When the gooseflesh was gone, he sat down and opened the book again. *Unthinkable*, he told himself. *I'm a Brokols. An Almaeic noble. I represent the emperor himself*. And it occurred to him that there could be no lasting refuge for him here. The emperor would own Hrumma soon enough.

His eyes went again to the chapter heading, and he began to read. But it didn't go well, even with the mystery loop banished from his attention. Suddenly he was desperately sleepy; he got undressed and went to bed. His night would be full of dreams.

On his mountain, Panni Vempravvo sat himself down on folded legs in the thin light of Little Firtollio. Insects chirped and chrilled. The still air was rich with the fragrances of grass, meadow flowers, rich moist loam. Silently and very lightly, not insistently at all, he contacted Hrum-In-Him, then slowed his breathing to a regular, measured cadence. His eyes were open but he ceased to see with them. Briefly his attention was on his breathing; then it ceased for a bit to be on anything. His body sat within the reality matrix, but he himself slipped into the boundary layer, to the outside that is at the center, from where, like everyone, he had open channels to the universal data base.

When he aroused, Panni didn't remember in any detail what he'd seen or done, or really where he'd been. By that time the sky was paling, the first meadow birds breaking their nocturnal silence. During his psychic absence, Little Firtollio had calmly sailed over the rim of the ocean, leaving no wake.

The sage got up knowing two new things, two items from the data base that he'd been able to bring back with him. Brokols' assistant was dead, his body beneath the sea. And Hrum was testing his foster children—humankind on this world. Standing, the sage looked out over the ocean, raised both arms, and called/whispered/felt out psychically to any who might wish to join him. Did this very lightly, with perfect willingness to be refused. Those who would hear would hear and know they heard. Those who wished to play a role would play one.

Vessto sat on his outcrop, pondering rather than meditating. It is difficult to attain the necessary calm when one is anxious or troubled. Or strongly polarized. And he was all three. Thus he did not overtly hear. But neither was he totally unaware. Simply, the awareness was at a level he'd lost touch with.

Birds were numerous in the palace grounds. They were beginning to waken and give voice, their sleepy chirpings increasing. One began to sing his morning challenge. He was answered. In a minute or two the combined birdsongs would build to a brief clamor.

Leonessto Hanorissio's body shifted restlessly as he dreamed. What he listened to was not birdsong.

The sellsu surfaced in the shallow trough between two swells, audibly exhaled warm wet breath, and the nictitating membranes slid away from shining pupils. The pack had been traveling north. Now it rested dozing on the surface; he'd been on sentry go. In the west the stars were still bright, thinning and paling toward the zenith. In the east, only the brightest still shown.

Someone had called, someone not a sellsu had beckoned to him in the spirit. For a moment it had seemed like a human, but that wasn't possible. The Lord of the Sea, that's who it had been.

Softly he spoke to the pack in the sullsit air speech, an articulated mouthing, grunting, clucking. Vaguely it resembled human speech, but metallic, exotic.

Two answered. Now Sleekit turned back southward, the two following. The remaining fourteen would continue as they had been. It wasn't unusual for pack members to separate themselves for varying periods. Each always knew where all its packmates were, at whatever distance, and they'd rejoin eventually unless something happened to prevent it.

The faint dawn hadn't yet penetrated the smoky, pungent room. Gripping the wooden spoon, the disciple made swirl marks in the thick porridge. Master Dazzlik had assigned him breakfast duty, no great chore since there was only one dish on the menu. His finger dipped, a cautious tongue tested; almost cool enough.

A cackling laugh startled him, and he looked at the very old man who sat crosslegged on a mat. Tassi Vermattio laughed again, although his eyes were unfocused. A bit awed, the disciple wondered what that was about.

Twenty-Four

Tirros's judgement was always apt to be poor. When he'd been drinking, it got poorer. He'd been buying—the tavern wasn't crowded and as usual he had money—and when he bought a round, he naturally included himself in.

In most respects his ability to hold his liquor—wine, actually—was good. He wasn't given to staggering or slurring or loud singing. But his judgement, or more properly his slyness, deteriorated notably with the third drink. Just now he was on his fourth. His ambitions had been taking a beating lately, and he intended to get drunk.

At the moment though, his attention was on a young woman with quite an ordinary face, as Hrummeans went, but outstanding physical development. He was sure she'd given him the eye. The young fisherman with her hadn't noticed, besides which he was somewhat smaller than Tirros. And anyway people tended to give way to him because he was the mirj, though in law, in a place like the Red Mare, he had no more rights than the next man.

Tirros nudged Karrlis Billbis. "What do you think?" he asked. "Is she interested? How do you read her?"

Karrlis leaned toward Tirros, swinging his torso in an arc to murmur near the mirj's ear. He was on his fourth, too, and more susceptible than his companion. "She knows you've been looking at her," he said, "but she isn't ready to dump her friend yet. He's a good screw."

"Huh! She doesn't know what a good screw is! Want to see me move in?" He'd had to raise his voice a bit; the three musicians had begun to play and sing another song, and several people had started dancing.

Karrlis's head moved from side to side as if he were trying to look around a tree. Tirros told himself his friend was getting drunk. "Sure," Karrlis said. "But be careful; he thinks he's pretty good in a fight."

"Shit! Won't have to fight. And anyway, I could whip his ass in a minute." The mirj got up and walked over to the couple. "Excuse me, sailor," he said. "I'm looking for someone to dance with." He held out a silver coin. "Why don't you take this crown and buy yourself the best drink in the house. And keep the change. I'll bring her back when the music's over."

The fisherman looked at the coin, then at his girl friend. She nodded. "It's 'The Bosun's Slowdance,' " she said. "It's short."

His expression was distrustful, but he nodded, and Tirros led the girl onto the dance floor.

"I'm the mirj," Tirros said.

"That's what I told Tarrni when we came in. That's the mirj, I told him." She smiled up at Tirros. "He wasn't much pleased at it."

"Why not?"

" 'cause you've got a reputation."

Tirros grinned, first at her, then at the watching fisherman whose expression was distinctly surly. "A reputation for what?"

"The girls are supposed to go for you." She looked up at him coyly. "I don't know why."

"How'd you like to find out why?"

"Tarrni wouldn't like that."

Tirros grinned again. "Makes no difference whether Tarrni likes it or not. You'd like it. All we need to do is dance our way over near the back door. Then out we pop and run up the alleyway. There's always a hansom on the block. We'll hop in and be gone before he can decide which way we ran."

She giggled. "Sounds like fun."

In half a minute they'd come even with the door. Abruptly he stopped dancing, and with her hand in his, slipped through it; it should take a few seconds before the fisherman reacted. Still holding hands, they ran across the back utility area and down a dark alleyway to its narrow opening onto the street.

Where Tarrni stood with his hands clenched into knuckly balls. Tirros almost ran into him. The fisherman threw a knobby fist that caught him on the nose and knocked him into the wall, then missed with a followup. Tirros kicked at him, his foot striking the man's shin; an elbow took the mirj in the side of the face. He grabbed wildly, trying to throw Tarrni to the paving stones, but the fisherman had hold of his shirt, which ripped down the back from collar to tail as Tirros himself went down. A stoutly-shod foot struck his hip before onlookers pulled his assailant back.

"Leave be," said one. "You don't want to go to the lockup."

"Right," said another. "Come on in. I'll buy you a drink."

The cluster of men began melting back toward the door and in. The girl hesitated, then followed them. Tirros sat on the concrete holding his nose, from which blood had flowed onto his trousers and ruined shirt.

One of the working men paused and looked back at him. "You gonna be all right?" he asked.

Tirros nodded, and the man followed the others inside. He'd get that sonofabitch Tarrni, Tirros told himself. Feed him to the fish, like he had the little foreigner.

Karrlis had watched from near the door. Now he came over and offered Tirros a hand, hoisting him to his feet. "Let's go down to the wharf," he said. "Take a swim. Sober us up and wash the blood out of your clothes before it sets."

Tirros didn't answer, but followed along, still pinching his nose. He didn't give a damn about his clothes; he had plenty at home. What was worrying him was something his father had said the last time he'd been in a tavern brawl: "If you like to fight so much, the next time I'll take you to the recruiter and we'll see how you like the army. As a common foot soldier!"

After a couple of blocks, the bleeding seemed to have stopped. Shrugging out of his shirt, he threw it into a trash station at a public latrine. His left eye was swelling, but not alarmingly, and his nose didn't seem to be broken. He didn't even have a split lip; the blood he'd been spitting was from a cut inside his cheek. If the eye didn't get too discolored, and if he kept out of his father's way, he might escape without even a tongue-lashing. A little powder on his scratched forehead had gotten him by at supper.

They swam for about half an hour, then sober he walked home, approaching by a back way and scaling the garden wall where he'd be sheltered by a tree from the eyes of house-guards. From there he kept to the shadows of shrubs and trees and climbed a familiar, well-used vine to the balcony outside his room.

All's well that ends well, he told himself.

Next morning his mirror showed him how discolored his eye was—bad enough that his mother would surely mention it to his father. Bad enough that the house servants would talk. It wouldn't do to go down to breakfast.

And the crowd at the tavern would be talking about him, about how someone inches shorter had bloodied him and knocked him down. The man had taken him by surprise, he told himself. Otherwise things would have gone differently. But that's not how they'd tell it. Wait till he was the emperor's regent; he'd see what tune they'd sing then.

That reminded him that the small foreigner was dead, and he hadn't figured out how to get at Brokols, get into the ambassador's favor. Leverage. He needed leverage.

He looked in his purse: not much there, two gold coins and a few silver. The porcelain bowl on his dressing table held miscellaneous coins, including gold.

He donned traveling clothes and belted on his shortsword, then emptied the bowl into his purse. It was time to get away for a few days, out of town into the countryside. Till the swelling in his eye went down and the color faded, and he'd come up with some way to get close to Brokols. It would worry his mother, too.

In the stable, he put bridle and saddle on his kaabor himself, then rode out, headed for the back gate. As he stopped his kaabor before it, the gateman came out of the gatehouse less than ten feet from him, with a sergeant of police and a constable. The police moved quickly, the constable reaching for the bridle as the sergeant opened his mouth to speak. Leaning, Tirros slashed the constable across the face with his crop, and the man let go, covering his stricken eyes, while Tirros turned the kaabor toward the sergeant and reined sharply back, so that the kaabor reared, striking with its forefeet, knocking the sergeant on his back.

Tirros drew his shortsword and shouted at the gateman: "Open for me or I'll cut you down!"

Instead the man ducked back into the gatehouse and slammed its heavy door. Cursing, Tirros jumped from the saddle and struck with his shortsword at the constable who was stepping forward again to grapple with him. His blade caught the man's shielding arm, sending him staggering back to fall with a quavering cry. Tirros turned the gate bar on its pivot, then vaulted into the saddle, and forcing the kaabor against the gate, pushed it open. He crowded through, galloped out into the street and was gone.

Travvos Disotto was with the amirr when an excited guard interrupted to report what had happened at the gate.

"My men," Disotto asked, "how badly hurt are they?"

"One's arm was sliced to the bone," he said, showing on his own forearm where the wound was. "That's the constable. He's lucky it was an angled blow, or it would have been lopped off, but it's an awful wound. The sergeant's up and walking, but I think his arm is broken."

The inspector had more than the man's words to go by; as he'd talked, Disotto had seen the mental images beneath them. "Your Eminence," the inspector said, "I must go to the gate and see what I can scan."

The amirr nodded and went with him. At the gate was a psychic mass of pain, anger, a stink of murderous fear, but he could find nothing to tell him where the mirj planned to go.

"Inspector," said the amirr, "we'll mount no manhunt for my son."

Disotto turned sharply, as if to argue.

"Find the scoundrel who was in this with him," the amirr went on, "and question him. Probably the one the ambassador mentioned to you. Find out who Tirros might run to, to hide, and capture him that way."

"Your Eminence, he is mounted. He could easily leave the city, flee the district."

"If he does . . . but he won't. He has too little self-control to fend for himself. He needs others to take care of him, and he knows it. We'll find him hiding in the home of one of his low-life associates, perhaps the Vencurrio's."

For a moment the inspector seemed unsure, then he nodded. "Yes, milord. By the ambassador's description, we believe your son's associate was a Karrlis Billbis. I'll take some men there at once, and question him." He turned then and strode off.

The amirr blew through rounded lips. The wait was over, the wait he hadn't consciously known he was waiting. Looking back, something like this had been inevitable. Now the suspense was over, though the waiting wasn't.

Twenty-Five

Juliassa Hanorissia came in to lunch from a long morning on a hill, painting, and hung her sun hat on a rack. At first she didn't pick up on her parents' moods.

"Hello, father," she said cheerily. "Hello, mother."

The naamir didn't reply, didn't look at her. The amirr grunted and spooned in another bite of melon.

Umh! Something to do with Tirros, the namirrna decided. She looked the table over, crystal a transparent yellow, with yellow napkins on a snow-white cloth, harmonizing aesthetically with the golden-fleshed melon, ripe greenberries, milk and breadfruit. She reached, not bothering the serving girl to serve her, not bothering her parents with questions. They'd tell her if they wanted to.

She'd mostly finished eating when her father spoke.

"I want you to go back to your aunt in the morning," he said quietly. "For a week or two."

She looked up at him. "Is something the matter?"

"Your brother is in serious trouble. It has to do with the foreigners—and other things. There will be unpleasantness."

This piqued her curiosity. "I can stand unpleasantness."

The amirr shook his head. "And you will no longer see Ambassador Brokols. That is best for both of you. He is a source of serious troubles for Hrumma, and albeit inadvertently, for the family."

She opened her mouth to speak, but her father's gesture and warning look stilled her. "I will brook no argument on this," he said.

Green eyes flashing, Juliassa Hanorissia got stiffly from the table and left the room.

* * *

Leonessto Hanorissio knew the news was bad. Travvos Disotto was a hard man, but just now his face expressed regret. "We arrested Billbis," the inspector said. "And questioned him. He confessed to practicing as an untrained adept. The mirj has employed him on a number of occasions for purposes immoral and sometimes criminal. He confessed to five burglaries in company with the mirj, and to being an accomplice in the kidnapping and murder of the ambassador's assistant."

He paused, avoiding the amirr's eyes. "It was Tirros who actually killed the man. He didn't know what else to do with him, so he stabbed him. Through the eye into the brain, to avoid a large flow of blood. Billbis has offered to show us where they dumped the body—into the sea with a rock tied to his neck and another to his ankles. On Brindossi Cove."

The inspector paused, looked up now at the amirr's gray face, and continued. "He knows of no place except the Vencurrio's where the mirj might hide. We've checked there, but they haven't seen him. I have men watching the approaches, but I don't expect he'll show up."

An evening-warbler sang in the early dusk outside the window, sounding like a trill pipe but purer, more perfect. It was the amirr's eyes that had fallen now, and Disotto turned his mind away. He felt for this man and preferred not to see his pain.

"Have you told the ambassador?" the amirr asked.

"No, milord. I intend to when I leave here."

"Do not. I'll tell him myself. In the morning, when he comes to the Fortress. Or failing that, I'll send a messenger to fetch him. But not tonight." Now their eyes met.

"As you wish, Your Eminence."

The inspector excused himself then and departed. Leonessto Hanorissio stood alone with his thoughts, which perhaps surprisingly turned to his daughter. He'd been unjustly severe to her. But still, it *was* better for her to be away from here now. And it was better if she stayed away from the foreigner, Allbarin's presentiment notwithstanding.

Twenty-Six

Elver Brokols had somehow felt like a criminal being taken before the magistrate.

Which made no sense: It was a messenger who'd come to him, not a constable, while the summons, if it left him no alternative, was courteously written. And a hansom, not a police wagon, had come to fetch him. Yet riding with Reeno through the morning's cheerful sounds and sunshine, he'd felt like someone on his way to be sentenced. Then a guard had met them at the gate and, still courteously, had taken him and Reeno to the amirr's office.

When Leonessto Hanorissio told him of Stilfos's death, Brokols had thought for a moment that that was the reason for his misgiving, though it was hardly a surprise to him. But then the amirr told him all they knew of the emperor's plans—somewhat more than Vessto Cadriio had known. He knew of the Gorrbian invasion, the imperial intention to land at Haipoor l'Djezzer—all of it.

Brokols was stunned. *Stilfos must have talked to his kidnapers before they killed him,* he thought. That was the only explanation he could see. It occurred to him that it may have been the police who'd stolen Stilfos, perhaps torturing the information out of him and then killing him.

"Who is the murderer?" His voice was thick and rough as he asked it. The amirr didn't answer at once. "I think you owe it to me to tell me," Brokols insisted.

"I do not owe it to you!"

Brokols' stomach knotted at the amirr's abrupt vehemence, his blazing eyes, but after a moment the glare died, and the amirr spoke quietly. "I do not *owe* it to you, for you share responsibility in it. As I do. And you are an enemy of Hrumma." He paused a long moment. "But I will tell you nonetheless. The murderer was my son Tirros, and when we catch him, he will be tried for both treason and murder. He and a friend of his."

He stopped with that, unable for the moment to say more. Brokols stood dumbfounded, his mouth open, and after momentary shock felt a surge of spontaneous sympathy for the man in front of him. He didn't speak, wasn't sure he could. It was Allbarin that broke the painful silence, looking at the amirr.

"Your Eminence, may I speak with you privately?"

Leonessto Hanorissio nodded, and had Reeno take Brokols into a side room. "Milord," Allbarin said, "this Brokols is a decent man. He felt with you when you told him of Tirros. Felt deeply. And he knows the enemy as he would a brother. Perhaps he can be subverted to our cause."

"How?"

"Give me leave to speak with him here. To make him an offer, and bargain with him."

Leonessto sighed, a release of spent emotion. "Very well." Allbarin went to the door and spoke to Reeno, who brought Brokols back in. It was Allbarin who addressed the Almite then.

"Ambassador Brokols, you see our position. You *are* an agent of a hostile nation, you know. As such, it is not appropriate that we let you remain free here. Our proper action is to deport you, send you back to Almeon, but as we have no means to do that, we have to settle on an alternative. The most obvious one is to imprison you until your people come for you. Which should not be very long, I believe; your ship plans to stop here on its way back to Almeon. We will put you aboard her, deporting you as an agent of an enemy state." He paused, then added: "With a listing of all that we've learned, to establish, to demonstrate that you are our enemy."

Brokols looked at him, frozen-faced. *They'll never believe I didn't tell,* he thought. *They'll have me before a public tribunal as soon as we get to Larvis Royal. My family will be humiliated and disgraced, my brother's career ruined. They'll make a holiday of my decapitation.*

He'd never attended an execution himself; like his father, he'd never had the stomach for it. But millions did have. Three hundred thousand would pack the square; thousands more would line roofs. Field glasses would rent high.

"Can you think of an alternative for us?" Allbarin asked.

Brokols shook his head. "None." Actually, suicide occurred to him, but he knew he wouldn't do it.

"Tell me, Ambassador Brokols, what do you think will happen to Hrumma when the Gorballis invade us?"

The question surprised Brokols. He hadn't really looked at it before.

Obviously the emperor had had his reasons for placing a member of the general staff in charge of the mission. He didn't want the Gorrbian army tied up near the border; he wanted them deep inside Hrumma when his own army landed. Kryger was no doubt a busy man, much busier than himself, and giving little or none of his attention to trade or the study of Gorrbian culture. He'd have too much else to do.

And as he thought these things, Allbarin had access to what lay beneath those thoughts.

"I suppose," said Brokols quietly, "you'll defend yourselves. Fight back."

"Do you think we can hold them out?"

Brokols shook his head. "I don't know. It seems doubtful."

"Your General Kryger will provide the Gorballis with weapons we're poorly suited to confront, wouldn't you say? Projectile casters? Thunder weapons?"

Great Dard! Was there nothing they hadn't found out? He didn't know for sure himself, had only wondered. "Quite likely," he said.

"Would you like to know what happened to Hrumma the last time the Gorballis conquered us? What was done to people here?"

"I've—read of it."

"It took centuries, with the help of Hrum's holy clergy, before our people lost their hatred. They didn't fully lose it till after the great sage, Kiruu Hemaruuvo, learned to merge the parts of his beingness and began to teach it in the monasteries."

The privy counselor paused. "Of course, the Gorballis won't

occupy us through more than two generations as they did the last time. Wouldn't you say?"

Brokols nodded. Probably they wouldn't.

Allbarin cocked his head slightly as he continued to look at the Almite. "Your emperor will station troops of his own here, won't he?"

It was difficult for Brokols to answer; his throat had gone dry. His conscious mind seemed frozen. "Undoubtedly," he answered. He remembered stories of the occupation of Kelthos, southernmost of Almeon's major islands. Although the history books didn't say that much about it, stories were told. The Kelthians had resisted as an underground, held secret religious services, retained their own dialect, until Kaitmar IV lost patience and loosed the army on them. The result had been futile resistance and massacre; some of the stories had been the kind that boys in early adolescence tell in breathless, bright-eyed whispers.

As for the Hrummeans . . . they *were* human! Droids were made in vats, and programmed, whatever that was, not nurtured. Something to do with electricity, it was thought. Hrummeans had been born of mothers for millenia, twenty millennia, the astronomers estimated, and knew nothing of electricity. But Dard and Kryger would not consider them human. Perhaps—probably—it wouldn't make much difference if they did.

"Ambassador," Allbarin said softly, "I do have an alternative to offer. I'm sure you know what will happen if you're sent home. Under the circumstances. However, if you should agree to help Hrumma repel the Gorballis . . ."

Allbarin bowed his head a moment as if apologizing, then raised it again to look thoughtfully at Brokols with no trace of discomfort. "We do not ask that you directly oppose your own people, only that you help us against the Gorballis. With all that you know."

Brokols stared at him.

"You needn't decide at once. Think about it; sleep on it. Reeno will stay with you, your keeper now as well as guide and liaison. And he is to be with you if you decide to use your communicating machine, your—your 'wireless.' "

They even know about the wireless, Brokols thought numbly. *Is there anything they don't know?*

He couldn't remember afterward whether he'd nodded or

not; presumably he had. He was sure he hadn't answered aloud. But he was aware of walking to the door with Reeno.

And encountering Juliassa entering the antechamber from the hallway, dressed in riding clothes.

"Elver!" she said, surprised and pleased. For the moment she forgot what her father had told her, forgot she'd come, at her mother's entreaty, to say goodbye to him. A cold and unfriendly goodbye it would be. "I'm so glad . . ." Then she saw her father in the doorway behind Brokols, and on impulse put her hands on the Almite's shoulders, kissing him on the mouth. "I'm so glad I got to see you before I left."

Brokols stood with his fingers touching his lips where'd she'd kissed him.

She frowned slightly. "Is something the matter?"

"No. Yes. Stilfos is dead. My aide. Murdered."

At once her face changed, became concerned. "Oh no. I'm sorry."

"It's all right. I mean . . ." He stopped, not sure what to say, knowing that "all right" sounded all wrong. "I mean, it's done."

"I hope they catch whoever did it," Juliassa answered. She looked questioningly at her father, who made no sign, then back at Brokols. "I'm going to stay with my aunt again. At Sea Cliff. But I'll be back." Once more she looked at her father, still saw no scowl, no frown, no disapproval; he only shook his head slightly, as if wanting her to cease.

"I'll send a page when I get back," she added. "To let you know."

"Thank you," Brokols said. Then with Reeno he left the room, the amirr and his daughter watching them go.

The morning sun low on his back, Panni Vempravvo had been walking along a bluff, looking at the ocean across a lower ridge. He had no conscious purpose in walking this morning. Usually when he walked, he noticed everything: stones, flowers, insects, birds, clouds, sensed their beingness, their awarenesses. This morning, though, he noticed only enough to keep from stumbling.

Yet few thoughts drifted through his awareness, which told him that a part of himself was thoroughly engaged at some metaconscious level, occupied so thoroughly that it left little capacity for conscious attention. Absently he chuckled. He didn't know what was going on, but he was sure it was interesting.

On the way home, Reeno stopped at an herbalist's shop. It seemed to him that Brokols' roiling mind needed soothing sleep without waiting for night. He'd make tea when they got home, with an additive for Brokols' cup.

Twenty-Seven

Tirros Hanorissio had ridden north out of Theedalit, then northeast. That way the country was rugged, its hills offering more security than the plateau to the south. He'd decided to ride northeast to the Neck, staying out of sight at all times, then into Djez Gorrbul. He'd tell King Gamaliiu what he knew about the foreigners, and the king would make a prince of him. Gamaliiu would be ready when the Almaeic fleet came, and with Tirros fighting in the van, he'd drive the invaders back into the sea. Then he, Tirros, would ride at Gamaliiu's side when the Gorrbian army marched into Theedalit, and the first person he'd have drawn and quartered would be his father.

By noon of the second day, Tirros looked as if he'd been on the road for a week. He was dirty, hungry, saddle-sore, and he'd hardly gotten started on the long, long ride to Haipoor l'Djezzer. The day before, he'd eaten nothing but some not-yet-ripe mornoles, plucked where the cart trail ran past an orchard, and they'd upset his stomach. That morning he'd killed a vehatto, then realized he had no firemaker, no way to cook it. He'd tried eating a bit of it raw, and managed to swallow a few bites, but decided he couldn't live like that for long. Sleeping on the ground he could get used to, but he'd have to chance stopping at inns to eat.

But to eat at inns cost money, and what he had with him wouldn't take him halfway to Haipoor l'Djezzer. He'd have to steal some. And the only place he could be sure of finding it in any quantity, without exposing himself to serious danger, was the ranch. He knew the place thoroughly, could find his way around the villa in the dark, and rob his Aunt Zeenia without anyone being the wiser.

Glancing at the sun, he turned his kaabor southward. He'd make a big semicircle and head for Sea Cliff. If he pushed really hard, he could be there the next night but one.

Brokols had slept like a baby for four hours, and awoke feeling renewed, without memory of dreams except that there'd been some. For a minute or two he didn't even remember what had happened earlier. When he did, it was like a cloud settling over him, but even so, he was in considerably better shape than he'd been on their ride home.

Reeno was sitting in the entryway when Brokols came out of his bedroom into the hall. The Hrummean looked up, a book open on his lap, then got to his feet. After Brokols had washed his face, they went out and ate a late lunch at a satta shop, took rikkshas to the Fortress and rode kaabors north out of the city, then up out of the valley onto the ridge above the firth.

It was a day without rain, without even a threat of it. The sky was a high vault of blue, with small white clouds. A breeze, cool for the season, moved the lush green of grasses and forbs. Reeno rode a dozen yards behind, saying nothing, leaving Brokols to himself, monitoring the Almite's thoughts and the pictures beneath them.

Brokols was reviewing mentally. His official function here was to keep Kryger informed of what went on in Hrumma, what the conditions and potentials were. And when the time came, to tell the Hrummeans of the Gorrbian intention to invade. And tell the amirr that a friendly Kryger had passed him the word. He was not, of course, to tell him that Kryger had instigated the invasion.

He was also to be sure that Hrummean forces would not collapse too readily.

Really, there was no great conflict between imperial orders and the proposal that Allbarin had made. He could satisfy the amirr without clear and overt treason against the emperor. Whereas, if he refused the amirr, there was deportation and the headsman's axe.

And perhaps something would come up—perhaps there'd be something he could do, as the emperor's agent, to protect Hrumma from occupation. Perhaps Hrumma could exist as an internally autonomous tributary of Almeon. Hrumma was not a rich and fertile land. The emperor might be satisfied with tribute. Admittedly it wasn't likely, but if he could work something . . . if the Hrummeans showed enough military strength, enough ferocity in battle, perhaps occupation would look too costly and troublesome. In that case, tribute might seem a good and intelligent alternative to occupation and direct rule.

At any rate, he'd go along with Allbarin's proposal.

And tonight—tonight he'd definitely have to report to Kryger. He needed to give that some thought. Lying would take more care than telling nothing but the truth.

Reeno watched the ambassador as they rode. He liked the man. He seemed to be into wishful thinking today, but given his circumstances that was just as well. And you couldn't help but hope.

TWENTY-EIGHT

When he'd finished his exchange with Brokols, Lord Vendel Kryger sat frowning at the message pad in front of him. Midshipman Werlingus, Argant's replacement, sat at the key looking at him. Brokols' communications were in the midshipman's simple letters. Kryger's communications alternated with them in crabbed cursive.

Brokols' report held both bad and good. Which was better than the all bad that Kryger'd been prepared for.

> STILFOS MURDERED STOP ONE MURDERER CAUGHT STOP OTHER ONE STILL FREE STOP STATED REASON FOR MURDER WAS ENMITY TOWARD ALMEON STOP HOWEVER PUBLIC MEETINGS HOSTILE TO ALMEON HAVE CEASED STOP I HAVE TOLD AMIRR ABOUT WIRELESS STOP TOLD HIM YOU INFORMED ME OF GORRBIAN INTENTIONS TO INVADE HRUMMA STOP LOCAL SUBJECT IN THE STREETS IS NOW THE GORRBIAN THREAT STOP AMIRR DEFINITELY FRIENDLY TO ME NOW STOP END

"Message received. Stop. Continue your work. Stop. Any further report? Question."

> AS PART OF ONGOING COVER I HAVE TALKED TO AMIRR AND A NUMBER OF MERCHANTS ABOUT TRADE WITH ALMEON STOP THEIR ARTWORK AND FURS IN EXCHANGE FOR STEAM POWERED ORE CRUSHER STOP HRUMMEAN GOVT WILL BROKER STOP END

The rest had been the closings.

Just now it appeared that Brokols might prove satisfactory after all, though the situation there still troubled Kryger.

Making a decision, Kryger picked up a pencil and scribbled some more. For security reasons, the *Dard* was anchored in the harbor rather than being tied to the dock, and it was far more convenient to communicate with her by wireless than to have her captain come ashore for a conference.

"Stedmer," Kryger wrote. "I have changed the procedure you will follow when you arrive at Theedalit. As it stands now, you will land Argant there and stand by while he evaluates Brokols' fitness on the site. Only if he sees fit will you land personally, serve my warrant of arrest on Brokols, and return him to Larvis Harbor. Argant now has alternative, repeat, Argant has alternative, of deciding that Brokols should remain as ambassador in Theedalit. In that event you will bring Argant back to me before steering west to Almeon. End. Kryger."

When he had it written, he motioned Werlingus to send it. Stedmer wasn't going to like the possibility that he might have to turn around and bring Argant back, but he'd have to swallow it. He'd have steam up by dawn, and leave for Theedalit with daylight; he hardly had time to argue. Not that arguing would do him any good. Kryger outranked him militarily, and as Mission Commander he specifically had overriding authority.

That evening after his exchange with Kryger, Brokols felt unaccountably sleepy and went early to bed.

Usually, though by no means always, Panni Vempravvo ended his evening meditation sometime before midnight. This night he continued in trance on the mountain till long after midnight, his open eyes seeing nothing. He was busy creating dreams, or rather helping someone else create their own, something the sage couldn't do in an ordinary conscious state, or as effectively while sleeping. His beingness which he thought of as "Hrum-In-Me" always had more than enough of such matters to attend to, with one and another.

Finally it was enough. It was nearly dawn when the sage went into his cave and lay down on his mat to sleep a few hours.

Twenty-Nine

Leonessto Hanorissio sat reading trial records. In Hrumma, the amirr was the court of final appeals. His secretary interrupted by opening the door and looking in.

"Sir, Ambassador Brokols is here with Mr. Venreeno. They wish audience with you."

"Umh!" He'd hoped he was done with the foreigner for a while. Brokols could have given his acceptance or refusal to Allbarin; surely Venreeno knew that. Perhaps he had something more than a simple yes or no. "Send for Allbarin," he replied. "I'll see them all together."

He returned to his reading then. It was several minutes before his secretary knocked again, and he had the visitors sent in. He did not get up when they entered.

"Sit down," he said. When they had, he looked at Brokols. "What is your decision?"

"Your Eminence, I will do all I know how to help you resist and defeat the Gorballis. I've had specific thoughts on the matter."

The amirr leaned forward a bit at that. "Let's hear them."

"You recall the thunder weapons at the front and rear of the ship. It has others, more powerful, below deck. They're called cannon, and they're powered by something called 'gunpowder'; it was gunpowder made the thunder you heard when the ship fired its salute. I'm not familiar with how cannon are made. My knowledge of weaponry is limited very largely to use; it doesn't include manufacture. So it would take me too long to work out how to make suitable cannon and then see them made. But I believe I can make a primitive form of gunpowder.

"I envision making objects called grenades. They are like—small jars filled with gunpowder. Small enough that soldiers can throw them, or cast them with slings. Grenades can be thrown among the enemy to burst with great force, and each grenade can kill or wound several men. They need not hit a man to kill him. Close—several feet away—is often enough."

"And you believe you can make this gunpowder?"

"I believe so. There are problems involved. I have never made it before, or even seen instructions, but I know something of the ingredients, and with some experimentation . . ." He shrugged.

Leonessto Hanorissio nodded. He supposed he could make a sword of sorts himself, if he had to, but the first would be crude to the point of uselessness except as a club. And even a crude sword would be beyond him if he had to start with raw materials—iron ore, dry wood, and whatever else was necessary. "What do you need?" he asked.

"Just now, I don't know explicitly. In Almeon I could simply ask for the ingredients by name. Here I first need to learn what they're called, and then where to find them. I've discussed it with Reeno, and he can steer me. Later I'll need a place outside the city, to work on the mixture. Eventually you'll need shops to produce grenades in large quantities, assuming that I'm successful in making gunpowder."

Leonessto pulled thoughtfully at his chin and looked at the two adepts, Allbarin and Reeno. Was the foreigner sincere? He asked the question mentally while opening his mind to them. "What have you to say, Reeno?" he asked aloud.

The answer was clear, but obliquely put so that Brokols would never know what the question truly was, or how the answer was obtained.

"If Ambassador Brokols believes he can do it, I consider the prospects good, Your Eminence."

"Allbarin?"

"By all means we should let him try, and see that he gets the necessary help. With your permission sir, when we are done here, I'll prepare a suitable letter of authority for him, for your signature. Granting him the power of acquisition and hiring."

"Good."

They were looking at the amirr as if waiting for dismissal,

but he had more to ask. "Ambassador, your superior is at Haipoor l'Djezzer, and I believe you've mentioned that he is or was a military man, a general. Not so?"

Brokols didn't remember mentioning it, but supposed he must have. The day before perhaps, when being questioned. Or did they know it from the same source they knew so much else from? "Yes, Your Eminence, he is a general."

"Isn't he likely to be providing the Gorballis with these—grenades?"

"It's possible," Brokols said thoughtfully, "but I rather doubt it. As you already know, the emperor will land an army in Djez Gorrbul, probably at or near Haipoor l'Djezzer. He would prefer, I'm sure, that the Gorballis not meet him with grenades.

"If—if Lord Kryger provides them with weapons that are unfamiliar to you, then . . . then I'd expect they'd be heavy cannon not suited to being moved rapidly. Something cumbersome, difficult to transport, that could be emplaced opposite your border fortifications. They could batter down your walls from a mile away, but couldn't readily be moved north to defend Gorrbian cities. Nor through the hills into Hrumma to collapse your resistance there.

"In fact, it might be well for you to prepare defenses in depth, in the Neck, not depending on your border fortresses."

The amirr nodded. "Thank you, Ambassador Brokols," he said. "We'd do that in any case." He looked around. "Unless someone needs to say something, I'm going to adjourn this meeting. No questions? Good. Allbarin, prepare the letter of authority. You gentlemen go with him. Ambassador Brokols, I'll want to hear of your progress or lack of it."

His visitors stood up and left. Leonessto Hanorissio looked down again at the trial record he'd been reading. It wasn't as interesting as the meeting just past, and it was hard to get back to it. But he'd be happy to forego the kind of national emergency that was developing—to have nothing but the routine affairs of a nation at peace with its neighbors—especially the poorly-known "neighbor" some eight thousand miles west.

When they left the Fortress, Brokols and Reeno didn't go back to the apartment. Instead they went to a nearby satta shop to sit quietly in a corner and talk, and to eat the breakfast they hadn't yet had. The shopkeeper gave Brokols dirty looks—Brokols had noticed more and more of those since the rallies had begun—but they were served readily enough, and the food was actually quite good.

The rallies still continued; Brokols had lied to Kryger about that the evening before. He was surprised things hadn't turned ugly—had asked Reeno if safeguards might not be necessary to protect him from violence. The Hrummean had looked surprised. Hrum's people would require truly extreme provocation for that, he'd said. He himself would be protection enough.

Such widespread public moderation remained somewhat unreal to Brokols. True, Eltrienn had explained the purpose of the rallies, and also true, the one he'd heard had not been truly inflammatory. But it seemed to Brokols that some people would still be driven by them to violence. In Almeon to make a public speech without a permit was a felony because of the violence that might result.

This morning though, the Almite paid little attention to the shopkeeper's look. He had things on his mind: the ingredients for black powder. Carbon shouldn't be a problem; not if crushed and powdered charcoal would serve, and surely it would. And sulfur? They were bound to have sulfur here.

"Reeno," he said, "I need a substance that I don't know the name of in your language. It's a yellow powder, a rather pale yellow. Do you have such a substance here?"

"Perhaps. When we've eaten, I'll take you to an herbalist's shop, and you can see what he has."

"What I need isn't a plant substance."

"Herbalists use all kinds of materials besides plants. It's simply that historically, plant materials are what they began with, and I suppose they're still the most important. But an herbalist will have most of the substances known to man."

"Hmm." Brokols relapsed into silent thought. *So probably neither charcoal nor sulfur will be a problem. But saltpeter? I wouldn't know the stuff if I saw it. What was it, really?* He recalled something about saltpeter being obtained from the large deposits of nightbird dung in certain caves on Kelthos, Almeon's southernmost island. Was it unique to nightbird dung, or was it found in other dung? And saltpeter wasn't simply dung; it would be a substance *in* the dung. How would one extract it? He hadn't the slightest notion.

Well, he told himself, *if herbalists use all sorts of substances, they must know how to get them. The question is, do they have saltpeter.*

"Reeno, do you have nightbirds on Hrumma?" He translated the Almaeic name for it, a compound of *night* and *bird*. "They're a bird that stays in caves during the daytime, where it's dark. They come out at night and catch insects."

"Yes, we have birds like that."

"What do you call them?"

"What you did. Nightbirds."

Brokols didn't pursue the matter further just then. It would have been indelicate to discuss dung at a meal.

But *somehow* the ancients had made saltpeter, probably in a form none too pure, and made gunpowder with it. And if they had, presumably he could too. He'd better. The amirr expected it of him.

THIRTY

Neither moon was up; only starlight relieved the darkness, and only distant surf the silence, that and the soft sound of hooves on earth. Tirros made no attempt to sneak up on the compound. He'd nearly used up his kaabor; he'd have to get another here, and he couldn't do that unnoticed.

And they wouldn't know here of the murder, he was sure of it. His father wouldn't have made it public; he was too protective of the family reputation for that.

Still, he was tense when the gate guard held up the lantern, opening the bullseye to see who was coming.

"Mr. Tirros!" there was surprise in the man's voice, but no pleasure. "Just a minute." Climbing down from his platform, the guard opened the gate, and Tirros rode in past him. The man paused to close it. "I'll wake a groom to tend your kaabor, sir," he added.

"No. I'll take care of it myself." Tirros swung stiffly from the saddle and led the animal to the nearby stable, leaving the gateman staring after him. Mister Tirros tending his own mount?

He didn't actually. He took off neither saddle nor bridle, and of course didn't rub the animal down. Didn't even remove the bit from its mouth, fork hay into the manger or give the beast a dipper of grain which, after three days of ill use, it sorely needed.

It was darker inside than out, but he knew the stable. He felt over another animal, found it satisfactory, found tack on pegs, put bridle, blanket, and saddle on it and the bit in its mouth. He'd want to leave quickly when he was done here. Then he left the stable and went to the house, walking softly, raised the latch as silently as he could, and entered on predator's feet.

He knew where his aunt kept her ready cash. As a child he'd sneaked silver pieces from it more than once, only three or four at a time so she'd never notice, or at least never be sure.

It was still there—a small wooden chest half full of loose silver. With a little leather drawstring purse that by its weight held gold; that was new. He didn't think to wonder why he hadn't found it there before. He put the purse in his belt pouch, then closed the chest, put it back, and slipped into the hall, feeling the weight of the gold on his belt. He'd be glad to transfer it to a saddlebag.

He knew which room had been his sister's. If she was there now, he'd begin his real revenge. And she was! Her door was slightly ajar for the breeze, and listening at it, he could hear her breathing. He slipped inside. It was her all right; it wasn't too dark to mistake the slender form. He closed the door behind him, heart thudding now, hardly able to breathe for excitement. He removed his soft boots, unbelted his pants, stripped them off, then kneeling, fumbled a vial from his belt pouch and opened it.

Hasn't moved, he told himself, *but she will soon enough.* She'd even made it easy for him, sleeping nude with the pillow shoved half off the bed. He put the vial on the night table, took the pillow and with sudden violence jammed it over her face, throwing his body atop hers to hold her down. She grabbed at the pillow and, stronger than he'd expected, tried to push it away, struggling violently, twisting, bucking, but he stayed atop her until, after half a minute or so, she went limp.

As quickly as he'd moved before, he put the pillow aside, grabbed her nose, and with the other hand spilled bitter powder from the vial into her open mouth, then as quickly jammed the pillow over her face again to keep her from yelling till the drug had taken effect. Again he kept her smothered for half a minute, then raised it, not wanting her dead yet, thinking half a minute enough.

She spit almost at once, a mouthful of saliva and drug, at the same instant jabbing Tirros hard in one eye with stiff fingers. He cried out, grabbing at his face with both hands, and she shoved, rolled, dumping him onto the floor, stumbled over him and ran gasping and screeching into the hall.

Tirros heard his aunt's voice call, asking what the matter was, and naked below the waist, groped for his pants, then scrambled barefoot across the bed and out the window. Tears flowed copiously from both eyes, and he ran nearly blind across the garden, stumbling into and over things, falling, scrambling, yelping at a stubbed toe, a scraped shin, heading blindly for the sound of surf until he felt sand beneath his feet, then a breaker washing over them. Turning north, he ran limping along the beach, feet slapping on wet sand, carrying his pants, the sounds of shouts from the house spurring him on.

Juliassa had realized what was happening as soon as the smothering pillow and male body had wakened her. She even knew who it was, who it had to be, though her face was covered. She'd stopped her struggles while she still had strength, hoping the pillow would be removed. And she'd known at first bitter taste what her brother had dumped in her mouth, what it had to be.

Somehow, instead of running to her aunt's room for protection, she ran out of the building and across the same garden that Tirros would cross seconds later, ran to the beach and into the water, not looking back, swimming out through and beyond a high-running surf spawned somewhere at sea by a storm. Then she turned south, parallel to the shore, swimming hard. Soon she tired though, and treading water felt an undertow, which frightened her more than her brother did now. She paused to peer at the beach, scanning, seeing no one. Nothing moved. She must be more than a quarter mile from the compound, she thought.

She could feel the drug in her, feel the hungering in her body, her terror feeding on it, exaggerating it, till she was more the effect of her fear than of the drug. If Tirros got near her now! . . . or any man! She swam toward the beach, still slanting away from the compound, and once ashore ran southward, gasping for breath, keeping to where the larger breakers had wetted and kept firm the sand. From time to time she cast a hurried glance back over her shoulder, and occasionally ran through the run-out of the surf.

The tide was coming in, the beach narrowing. Staggering with fatigue, she slowed to a walk, the terror ebbing. She came to a notch in the cliffs, littered with boulders, and scrambling up it, lay down miserable in the blackness. Her exertions had burned off the peak of the drug effect already, but it was still strong in her.

As the heat of her running dissipated, she began to shiver. She almost climbed back down to return to the house, but fought off the temptation. She'd stay where she was till the drug wore off.

Meanwhile it was Brokols she fantasized about, until at last she slipped into a sleep of exhaustion.

Tirros tired more quickly than his sister would, and soon slowed to a walk. A mile north of the compound was a stretch where the beach pinched out. He was caught between cliff and rising tide, each breaker now hissing over his feet, some wetting him to the knees. Not far ahead, waves broke against sheer rock.

He realized then that he should have gone south, but to go back now meant capture, he was sure.

Just ahead was a jumble of boulders, the largest as big as a shed. After pulling on his pants, he went to them and clambered wet and slipping onto one of the smaller. From there, finding toeholds for his bare feet, he scrambled onto the largest, where he hoped he'd be safe from the tide.

Soon he was shivering, and the rock was a hard bed. Tears began to flow. He clutched his badly scraped shin and moaned almost continually. His leg hurt, and his toe. He had no kaabor. He was hungry. And somewhere, probably in the house, the heavily loaded belt had pulled from his pants, leaving him without money or knife. Everyone was against him, even Hrum, and guards were looking for him with swords.

When his grief had spent itself, he began to seek ways out of his trouble. Perhaps, if he gave himself up to his father, begged forgiveness, offered to go to a monastery—perhaps he wouldn't be executed. But unusual for him, exercise of his imagination did not revive his spirits. The rock was too hard, the night too chill, and most of all, too many things had failed him. The surf began to break on his rock, wetting him with spray, and he wondered if the tide might reach him, the waves smash him against the cliff.

He was sure he wouldn't sleep, but after a while he did, fitfully.

THIRTY-ONE

Eltrienn Cadriio rode into the fortress an hour after sunrise, not having slept. Turning his kaabor in, he trotted across the courtyard and up the stairs, and gave his sealed report to the captain of the guard with instructions to have it carried to the amirr. Then he lay down fully clothed on a guard bunk, asleep in seconds but readily available to the amirr, should he want to question him.

The amirr was finishing breakfast when the guardsman arrived with the report. Dismissing the man, he had a second cup of satta poured, then broke the seal, took out the thick sheaf of papers and began to read.

Greetings, Your Eminence.

Some of this you and I already knew of course, and much of it I got from old Torillo's nephew, Ressteto Istroovio, who was deputy factor at Agate Bay for years. Ressteto knows the history and personalities there better than anyone else in Hrumma. I'll review the whole situation for you.

The great chief known as "Killed Many" is the elected chief of the Agate River Tribe. By a year ago he'd extended his authority north to the Great Fen. As nearly as I can estimate it, this is an area three or four times the size of Hrumma, but much less populated.

His intention is to conquer the Djezes.

As an adolescent known as "He Means It," Killed

Many led a small band of others to penetrate a Djezian border district, something apparently unprecedented among the eastern tribes. They planned to steal some things to show their skill and daring in the game of becoming warriors. To do this, they had to travel 500 miles west through the territory of other tribes, a major feat in itself.

Arriving in a Djezian border district and observing a Djezian mounted patrol, they decided to steal some kaabors. But they knew little about kaabors. The fifteen-year-old He Means It was bucked off, and when he woke up, he was in chains. After a severe flogging, he was worked as a slave in a copper mine for nearly two years before escaping.

When he'd made his way home, a warrior teased him for having been caught. He'd always been exceptionally strong, and being none the weaker for having dug ore in the mine, he whipped the warrior, establishing himself as no one to trifle with.

He Means It was the eldest grandson of the clan chieftain. A few years later the old chief was killed in a hunt: A large sarrho was brought to bay, and he claimed the honor of killing it, but this time the honors went to the sarrho.

The clansmen then had to elect a new chieftain, from old chief's son or grandsons, if any were deemed suitable. At the time, the clan had been feuding with two other clans, off and on. He Means It, who'd earned a reputation for integrity and common sense, was also an outstanding raid leader, and he was the one they chose.

He Means It had a younger brother, "Always Fighting," who was generally disliked because he was surly. Always Fighting would one day murder Sallvis Venettsio. He Means It was the only one in the clan who Always Fighting could call a friend. Their father had been killed while He Means It was in captivity, and Always Fighting, with his bad disposition, had been a near outcast. Then He Means It came back, made his own lodge, and took his brother in. Always Fighting, only fourteen at the time, responded by becoming a loyal supporter and sometimes problem to He Means It.

One weakness the tribes have had, relative to the Djezians, is no capacity for a protracted military campaign. Clan raids never lasted more than a few days, the infrequent tribal wars a few weeks at most. If nothing else, there was the problem of carrying a food supply or living off the land during war, if a campaign was to last longer. He Means It, in his dreams of Djezian conquest, recognized this problem.

Another problem was the poor quality of barbarian swords. Bog iron is adequate for arrowheads and spearheads, but it is weaker and more brittle than steel, and swords of it have to be made somewhat heavier to reduce breakage.

Thus the bow, spear, and knife were their main weapons in interclan and intertribal fighting. When they raided the Djezians (which the Agate River clans never had, being so far from the border), most barbarians, besides their bow, carried a spear or a battle axe, neither of which was equal to a sword and shield for close fighting. Against the better armed, helmeted and mail-shirted Djezian soldiers, this had long been a serious disadvantage.

The recent trading activities of the Ettsio Torillo family, of course, began to change this.

Not long ago, a timbering expedition to the barbarian mainland was a hurried and somewhat risky affair. They'd anchor close offshore, land, and put out sentry parties with alarm horns. Then they'd furiously fell and cut up trees, float the logs through the surf, and load them. If discovered, they fled to sea.

On one occasion, He Means It had been leading a small scouting party in the territory of the neighboring Tchook tribe when he spotted such a timber-cutting expedition. Coveting their steel, he went alone to them. Using lots of gestures and the Djezian he'd learned, he offered to protect the logging party while it worked; in return, the loggers would leave their axes and swords on the beach when they sailed.

He also made it known that his clan was the Kinnli Innjakot, *the Agate Bay people, and that their territory was east along the coast about four days on foot.*

The logging crew loaded their boat as deeply as they dared, then left their tools and swords and went home. But the longer voyages to Agate Bay weren't attractive to the boat's skipper-owner. His boat was small and his usual mode of operation wasn't all that dangerous. Their other timber voyages that year were to the usual section of coast.

In Hrumma the story got told around on the east coast, and Ettsio Torillo saw a market for his steel goods. The next year he went to sea with a timbering crew and his second son, Sallvis. They found Agate Bay, and Torillo landed in a small boat. He "talked" with the clan chief, and they were allowed to cut and load a cargo of timber. Then he left young Sallvis with the barbarians to learn their language and customs. The ultimate purpose was a trade agreement.

After a year, an agreement was made. Torillo could build a water-powered sawmill and charcoal kilns on the Agate River, and cut timber along the river and bay, in trade for good steel swords, axes, and knives.

Young Sallvis had also scouted the ridge on the south side of Agate Inlet. He found surface evidence of a workable iron ore deposit but said nothing about it to the barbarians. Deducing that a chain of barren, uninhabited islands beginning some thirty miles offshore was a continuation of the same hills, he suspected there might be a workable deposit there too. Three years later, Torillo was covertly mining iron ore on one of the farther islands, smelting the iron on site and shipping it home as ingots.

The next year, He Means It became chief.

Sallvis was in charge of the lumbering and charcoaling operations. When He Means It became chief, he told Venettsio that he wanted to unite the southern tribes and make war on the Djez (Djez Gorrbul, actually). That he wanted swords much faster, that the Hrummeans could take more timber if they wanted to and he would add furs to the trade. He also wanted Hrummean jewelry to help win loyalty from chieftains of other clans.

The Agate Bay Clan, the Kinnli Innjakot, was already the most powerful clan in the Agate River Tribe, the Innjoka. Having steel swords had made them confident, acquisitive, and dominant.

He Means It was then elected chief of the entire Innjoka tribe, and gathering all its clans, conquered the Tchook in a war unprecedented among the tribes for its drive and relentlessness. You'll recall having heard about this through Torillo before sending me to spend a winter with the Kinnli Innjakot.

He then gained the good opinion of the Tchook clans by honoring the bravery of their warriors. He also promised them that, before many years, they "would sweep together through the Djez like a forest fire." He left the Tchook clans their self-governance, requiring only that they swear allegiance to him as high chief. And that the chieftain of each clan send a young son or, lacking one, some other adolescent male relative, to the main village of the Kinnli Innjakot to be trained in new ways of war. In fact, of course, they were also honored hostages of a sort.

The two united tribes, Innjoka and Tchook, then moved northward, meeting strong resistance from the Aazhmili south of the Icy River. In the past, the Aazhmili had been the fiercest tribe in the south. However, led by warriors with steel swords, and using new strategies and tactics conceived by He Means It, the Innjoka and Tchook warriors beat the Aazhmili. It was in a battle of that war that He Means It earned the name "Killed Many."

He had a bard sing the praises of the Aazhmili then—how brave they'd been, how stalwart and clever. Another sang praises of the Innjoka and Tchook, for their victory. Gifts were also given, and the richest gifts—jewelry traded for from Torillo—went to war chiefs of the Innjoka and Tchook clans. The Aazhmili too swore allegiance to him, and sent sons to his main village.

Always Fighting had proven to be a savage fighter, brave even beyond barbarian standards of recklessness, and was renamed Bloody Sword. But as a field commander he'd been too reckless.

After being acknowledged by the Aazhmili as their great chief, Killed Many returned to his village and sent for Sallvis Venettsio. He wanted the Hrummeans to show him how to make his own steel. But old Ettsio wasn't willing to give up his monopoly; instead he offered to increase the shipments of swords. This, of course, involved increasing the amount of ore mined, the size of the smelting operation, and establishment of more sword-smithies, several of them on the island known as Iron Island. And all this required more charcoal and considerably bigger timbering operations.

This didn't satisfy Killed Many, but it helped. And he was soon occupied with politicking the tribes between the Icy and Great Fen Rivers for their acceptance of his suzerainty. They'd already heard about his great victories, and when their assembled clan chiefs had listened to his plans, they too acknowledged him as high chief, without fighting.

He purposely didn't politick the highland tribes. That would have risked the Djezians learning of his plans, and he wants surprise if possible. He believes that, having all the tribes south of the Great Fen under his command, the highland tribes will join him when he starts his move against Djez Gorrbul, or at least not contest his passage.

When Killed Many returned from the north, he began the serious training of cadres who would in turn train the clans of the several tribes for the invasion. This included bringing home with him three renegades from Djezian ducal armies who'd been living as barbarians with the Icy River Tribe. Men whose experience would help in developing tactics.

According to Ressteto Istroovio, when Venettsio was murdered, Killed Many had been involved with the new training regimen for several weeks. Istroovio had talked with Killed Many only days before the murder, and the high chief had not been hostile. It's Istroovio's theory that Bloody Sword went to Agate Bay on his own initiative, or that he was sent to do something less than deliver an ultimatum. The latter fits mindscans of our only eye witness, a ship's mate, mindscans obtained both by Lardunno and an adept at Gardozzi Bay, and described in the enclosed deposition.

It is my recommendation that I be sent to Agate Bay as Your Eminence's envoy, to straighten things out with Killed Many. *Now more than ever, Killed Many needs weapons, because the energy and altitude of such a newly established authority as his depends on almost continuous victories or other evidence of progress. I believe I can negotiate an agreement for the government not too different from the one he had with Ettsio Torillo. We can then contract with Torillo and others to make and supply the swords and carry them to Agate Bay.*

Considering the need, this should be done as soon as possible. I recommend that you approve the attached commission and authorizations without tendering the matter to the Two Estates, as that could cause prolonged debate and publicity.

Your obedient servant, Eltrienn Cadriio, Centurion unattached.

The amirr stared unseeingly now at the papers. For a few moments he considered adding some restrictive clauses to Eltrienn's proposed authorizations, but decided to have them made up as the centurion had written them.

Thirty-Two

When Juliassa had run from the house, Zeenia had gone to the girl's room, where she'd found a man's boots, and a belt on the floor with a pouch and her gold. It seemed to her that it had to be Tirros. By that time some of the staff, roused by the screaming, were coming in from the staff cottages. Jonkka, sword in hand, was already out searching the garden; she sent others to help him and to search the buildings. Tirros, or whoever, might be hiding in a shed or loft.

Then she'd questioned the gate guard and learned of Tirros's arrival; that settled any question of identity. After a quarter hour, the men who'd searched the grounds and buildings had all reported; they'd found nothing. Meanwhile she'd ordered Jonkka with three other men up the road on kaabor-back with torches. Tirros might not be terribly bright, but he should have enough animal cunning to head for the night-bound plateau to lose himself.

About a half hour after the alarm, one of the searchers came in to mention something he'd noticed that he hadn't thought to mention earlier: There'd been the tracks of two sets of bare feet crossing the beach into the water. Tracks of bare feet were hardly unusual on the beach, but it occurred to him afterward that these had continued out onto sand that had been washed clear by the last high tide. That's what had made them noticeable.

Sword in hand, he'd gone back to look again, and this time it struck him that both sets had been made by *running* feet; the strides had been long, and one set was definitely a man's while the other was probably a woman's. No, one hadn't seemed to be following the other; they'd been parallel about eighty feet apart. No, they hadn't seemed to be converging; only forty or fifty feet of them were apparent, but what there were were parallel.

Her own sword in hand, Zeenia went with him to the beach to see for herself, meanwhile reviewing the situation in her mind. She was short on manpower now. Four men were somewhere up the road on kaabors. She'd posted a man with a lantern on each wall to watch for anyone approaching, and sentries at their beach ends to prevent anyone from sneaking around them. That left her with three men uncommitted.

She looked at the tracks. It certainly didn't look as if one person had been chasing the other. And Juliassa swam like a sellsu; Zeenia doubted that Tirros could catch her in the water. Unless he caught her in the shallows.

As she stood looking, it occurred to her that the man had been limping! And apparently running more slowly than the woman. His strides were shorter: some were five feet long, the alternate strides less than four.

Which was encouraging. That and the fact they'd crossed the beach so far apart.

But then, where in the name of Hrum was Juliassa? If he hadn't caught her?

Zeenia ground her teeth, then went back to the villa and got another man with a sword, and they hunted the beach for a little distance in each direction. There were no tracks, but that wasn't surprising. The tide was coming in; it would have washed out any tracks unless they'd been made well back from the water.

Zeenia stood looking bleakly out to sea. Would the tide wash Juliassa's body up on the beach? Or was she simply hiding off the grounds somewhere, afraid Tirros would find her if she tried to come back?

And what in Hrum's name had possessed the child to run out into the ocean? Why hadn't she come to her?

She ended up sending two men south along the beach, looking. The third she kept on the grounds, armed and watchful, just in case. On an impulse, she lit a lantern then and went to Juliassa's room to examine it. To see if there might be blood she hadn't noticed before; Juliassa might have been hurt. Instead of blood she found the vial, and somehow knew what it held, felt certain. The smell resembled lamb foil a bit, and she wasn't about to taste it.

It seemed certain to her now that if Tirros caught Juliassa, he'd kill her when he was done with her, to keep her quiet.

As big and unpleasant as Tirros was, Zeenia had never been afraid of him before. Now she was. To her, he'd ceased to be a nasty, rather vicious delinquent. He'd become a murderous psychotic. She had all the women gather in the big sitting room of the villa; she didn't want any of them found dead in the morning.

After a bit, the two men came back from the beach to report they'd been pinched out by the rising tide, first to the south and then to the north. And had seen nothing. The four men came back from the plateau to report that they hadn't seen anything either. Jonkka seemed more murderous now than Tirros could ever be. He went out and paced the beach, sword in hand.

It was a nerve-wracking night for Zeenia Hanorissia, waiting for the tide to ebb enough to send three mounted men shouting up the beach in each direction. They wouldn't be looking for Tirros, but for Juliassa.

Juliassa never heard them calling. She was sleeping off the drug. Jonkka's party rode almost two miles south—as far as the sea allowed, wading in places—found nothing, and came back by dawnlight.

Filthy and bedraggled, Juliassa limped home at midday with a horrible headache and legs sore from her wild run. She told her aunt what had happened, then went to bed. Zeenia wrote a brief, inexplicit report on separate slips of delicate paper and sent them north on a pair of kiruu. Tirros, she said, had come to the compound at night, robbed her, done other serious mischief, and fled.

No one at Sea Cliff knew what had actually happened except she and Juliassa, though there may well have been some guessing done. Certainly if Jonkka had found Tirros, the least resistance or effort to flee would have left the mirj dead, amirr's son or not.

The day after that, Juliassa rode to Theedalit, accompanied by Jonkka and another guard, starting after an early breakfast. She'd told her aunt she didn't want to stay at Sea Cliff anymore. It wasn't a matter of fear; somehow the place was spoiled for her now, she said.

That was only part of the truth. The other part was that

she'd gone there under duress, and now she had a reason to leave. She'd actually recovered her normal mood and tone to a surprising degree. Zeenia had assumed she was putting it on. As well as she knew Juliassa, who was one of her favorite people, she didn't realize how strong and resilient the girl was.

Juliassa's mother had heard about Tirros's visit to Sea Cliff. The amirr had referred to it as "Tirros's raid." Both assumed that the "other serious mischief" had been vandalism. When Juliassa arrived, she did not enlighten her mother. She felt, however, that her father needed to know. He needed to know how criminal her brother had become (she wasn't aware of his other crimes), and she needed to give him a reason for having left Sea Cliff.

So she went to the Fortress, hoping to have lunch with him. His Eminence, she was told, was closeted with Eltrienn Cadriio, and no, the amirr had not eaten lunch. She settled herself in the waiting room where Eltrienn would pass; it occurred to her that she had something to say to him too.

She didn't wait long; Eltrienn came out and they went onto the wall together. As they stepped out, a thundershower was just beginning, the first big drops splatting, and they hurried through the quickly-thickening fall to a red and white-striped awning, where they sat down to watch slanting spears of rain shatter on the stone.

"What is it you want, Juliassa?" he asked.

"I wish to continue seeing Ambassador Brokols. I've had only two opportunities to talk with him since he left Sea Cliff. But my father said I wasn't to, and sent me to stay with my aunt Zeenia. I've just come back today."

The centurion's eyebrows raised.

"I was hoping you'd speak to my father for me, and use your influence to change his mind." She took the centurion's large left hand in both of hers. "I know I shouldn't ask you this, but I don't know who else could help."

Eltrienn was frowning now. "And what would you have me say, namirrna?" he answered stiffly. "It would be entirely out of place for me to advise him on family matters, or even bring up such a thing. He would not appreciate it."

Her expression was forlorn. The centurion didn't know if it was genuine or feigned.

"Well then, could you just mention to him that you'd seen me? And that I'd asked you? Please?"

Feigned, he decided. Even as a child, she'd known how to get the staff and the guard detail to do what she wanted. And been smart enough to use her talent sparingly.

The shower had already passed, leaving behind the smell of ozone, and Eltrienn got up to leave. "I'll consider it," he said. "I'm to see him again this afternoon. Whether I mention it or not will depend on his mood at the time. It seems very doubtful that I will."

She nodded soberly. "And Eltrienn . . ."

"Yes?"

Her gaze on the table, she didn't continue at once, then said, "Thank you for considering it. I know it's unfair to have asked. I just didn't know what . . ."

"You're welcome, namirrna," he interrupted. "And you're right; it was unfair."

But when he left, he was considering how he might phrase such a comment to the amirr.

Her father ordered lunch set for his daughter and himself on the wall, where they might eat together undisturbed. He was prepared to be upset with her for leaving Sea Cliff, but would withhold judgement until she'd told him why. And because her explanation might well anger him, he'd postpone asking till they'd finished eating. Meanwhile he'd find out what the "serious mischief" was that Tirros had done.

"So," he said, "Zeenia messaged me that Tirros made trouble at Sea Cliff, but she didn't tell me what. Was there much damage?"

"There was no damage," she answered. "He stole a purse of gold, but he even dropped that when he fled."

"She wrote that he'd done other serious mischief."

"Nothing material. Although he tried to." She looked at her father, caught and held his eyes, then told him what had happened. Before she'd finished, his face had turned nearly white. She'd expected him to be scarlet with rage.

He's shocked by how close I was to being killed, she thought, and the realization affected her. She reached and laid her hand on his.

"So I swam out through the surf, which was high," she went on, "swam south as long as I dared, then went ashore again and ran south along the beach. The tide was rising, and I ran in the edge of the runout so I wouldn't leave tracks. Finally I climbed up a break in the cliff and went to sleep among the rocks. I was deathly sick when I woke up, but after a while I went home. Zeenia gave me a potion and put me to bed.

"Tirros either went up the creek onto the plateau or north up the beach. There weren't any tracks. But he has no kaabor, and he lost his belt with his belt pouch and knife, so he's out there with nothing."

The color had returned to Leonessto's face, and there was cold doom in his eyes. Tirros's other crimes had been bad enough, but this . . .

"Father?"

His eyes focused on her again.

"May I stay at home for a while? Here in Theedalit? After what happened, I—don't like Sea Cliff anymore. I think I will again, after a bit, but right now . . ."

He nodded. "As you wish," he said. "Now if you'll excuse me, I'm going to my office. By myself. To meditate and see if I can find the peace of Hrum again." He got to his feet. "Shall I ask Allbarin to eat lunch with you? Or would you rather eat alone?"

"Send Allbarin," she said, "if he wouldn't mind. We haven't talked much since I was a child."

The amirr turned to the door, thinking he meditated far too seldom anymore. But even the peace of Hrum, he told himself, would not save Tirros now.

Juliassa watched him leave without bringing up the matter of Brokols. Her father didn't need any more unpleasantness.

Brokols had an unusual dream that night. Unusual in its seeming reality. Only the viewpoint was unreal, shifting from place to place, mostly as if he watched from half a hundred feet above the ground.

The invasion force was mustering, its columns clogging the roads to Larvis Harbor. His oldest brother was there, a brigadier of artillery now, giving orders. In the fields near the encampment, farm crews were harvesting *lenn*, stacking the cut vines to dry, piling them loosely on branched poles as high as their pitchforks could reach. It seemed he could even smell the vines.

And the harbor was full of tall ships.

Brokols awoke to morning birdsong, the images persisting. He felt sure that somehow what he'd seen was real. Or would be. Lenn harvest was in late summer. With a voyage of, say, sixty days, it seemed to him the fleet would arrive at the Djezian coast before mid-autumn. And it didn't seem at all that it would be autumn a year removed.

He'd go to the Fortress right after breakfast, he decided, and tell Allbarin.

The next evening after supper, Eltrienn was leaving the officer's messroom, preoccupied with what he planned to do next, when Brokols called to him. He looked around, did a double-take; so far as he knew, the Almite had never visited the military compound before.

"Elver! What are you doing here?" His expression was neutral, concealing a certain exasperation; he had a lot to do and was feeling rushed.

"I've come to see you. Reeno mentioned that you were back." He gestured at Venreeno. "I presume you know each other."

"Right." The two Hrummeans shook hands.

"There was another public meeting in the square when we were leaving for supper," Brokols said. "There must have been fifteen hundred people there. And it seemed to me that . . ." He paused. He knew what he wanted to ask, and why, but he hadn't yet spotted what lay beneath it. "I wondered if you'd be so good as to talk with me about the sages. I mean—Panni once came to my apartment to talk with me, and I must say I felt much better afterward. While Vessto is hostile. I feel that one day I'll need to go see him again, and talk things out with him. But I still know so little about them—Vessto and Panni—and nothing at all about Tassi Vermaatio."

Brokols stopped, feeling suddenly that he'd come there half cocked.

It seemed to the centurion that Brokols' reason was trivial. He put a hand on the Almite's shoulder. "Elver, I'd like to help you, but I just don't have time. I leave tomorrow on a new assignment, and there are things I have to take care of this evening."

I've been imposing, Brokols told himself, and an old discomfort flowed through him. "Of course," he said. "Eltrienn, my apologies. And every success in your new assignment. You've been a world of help to me, and a good friend." He reached out and they shook hands. Then he and Reeno turned and left.

Eltrienn watched them go. He'd been briefed by Allbarin on what Brokols had committed to do, and had some notion of what the Almite might be going through personally. He had to be groping, looking for meanings. *Perhaps I should have taken the time, done as he asked,* he thought. He'd see what time it was when he came back from talking with Vessto.

Thirty-Three

Awakening *is not the Ultimate, it is simply the fulfilled flower from which the seeker of wisdom can mature and fruit. It is the platform from which the Ultimate can be perceived.*

To let the mind be still is the first step toward perceiving the ultimate. To see one's shattras, *those which control the play, is the second step, beginning with the two luminous aspects of one's self; to merge one's shattras is the third; and to merge* with *one's shattras, Awaken to Hrum-in-Thee and see the universe as it is, is the fourth.*

Even in Hrumma, most do not attain the first, and even in the monastery some do not attain the second. Of those who attain the second, only a few attain the third. Of those few however, most attain the fourth, and we say of them that they have Awakened, *and we dub them masters.*

After having Awakened, one grows simply by living, observing life with the viewpoint of the Awakened.

And as a master returns repeatedly to the inner Hrum, dwelling in trance on the other side, his perception sharpens on both sides. Little by little he is able to do knowingly what he could not knowingly do before. But regardless of how far one progresses in that manner, that is not the Ultimate.

The Ultimate is the condition you began at and never left.

—Panni Vempravvo to a crowd gathered at the Grandfather Tree at Harvest Festival in the Year of the Sullsi.

It was dusk when Eltrienn arrived at the hut above the firth and peered in through the open door. Only three men were there, fewer than before. Vessto was reading in front of the fireplace. Meditation hadn't gone well recently; trances eluded him.

"Brother," said Eltrienn quietly.

Vessto looked up, brightening. He went to the door, taking Eltrienn's arm, and led him around the outside of the hut to a bench at one end, with a view of the ridge across the firth. Eltrienn shook his head. "What I want to tell you is confidential; I can't have it overheard."

Vessto nodded, and they hiked up the narrow path to his outcrop, where they sat down together in the twilight.

"I'm leaving tomorrow," Eltrienn said, "on an extended assignment." He paused. "I'd like you to come with me; I need someone of your abilities. A holy man. A sage."

Vessto's face went somber. "Brother, I am no holy man, no sage. I see that now. Though perhaps I approached it. I am no more than an adept, favored with prescience." He examined Eltrienn's face and the surface of his mind, its tone, its color. All were neutral, telling him little. Eltrienn nodded acknowledgement.

"Such holiness as I may have had," Vessto went on, "I gave up to save Hrumma. One cannot take a banner, one cannot polarize as I have, and be close to Hrum."

The soldier face remained neutral, and almost the voice. "Then bring your banner and come with me. To the barbarian lands." He raised a hand to deter objection. "The nearer danger is not Almeon. It's Gorrbul."

He described then what had been learned about the emperor's plan, beyond what Vessto had read in Brokols' mind. "If Rantrelli succeeds in bringing down the amirr, it will damage what chance we have to save Hrumma and the worship of Hrum. If you leave with me, you can help, and Rantrelli's movement will wither and die."

Vessto sat silent a thoughtful moment. A realization had come to him: When he listened to the minds of men, too often he failed to hear Hrum. And from men's minds he garnered only knowledge; it was from Hrum that wisdom came. Well, now he would listen to Eltrienn; his access to Hrum seemed inoperative these days.

"What is your assignment?" he asked.

Eltrienn told him how the exchange of weapons for lumber and charcoal had halted. "I'm to see it renewed," he said. "And after that, I'm to stay with Killed Many, be of whatever help he's willing to have. Get him to move as soon as I can—surely before winter—and if possible before the Gorballis move against us."

Vessto looked long at him, feeling Eltrienn's sense of uncertainty, suspense, of no foreseeable result. "And what good will that do?" he asked.

Eltrienn shook his head. "I don't know. The amirr doesn't know. But if we sit here and wait, the Gorballis will attack, and may very well conquer, for Gamaliiu has a general of the Almites to advise him. Probably he will have thunder weapons. And while the Gorrbian army is here, the emperor's fleet will land at Haipoor l'Djezzer and seize the Gorrbian throne.

"Rantrelli would have us act like a yart surrounded by varks, that tears open its own belly with its claws. Suicide.

"We have no complete plan. But if we can upset and dislocate the emperor's, perhaps a road out will present itself. You said it: If we do all that we possibly can, as if there could be no help, perhaps Hrum will provide."

He stopped talking then, waiting for Vessto to respond. And Vessto realized that he'd ceased to believe his own prophecy. He'd really fallen from the grace of Hrum.

"What good can I be to you?" he asked.

"I'm to take an adept with me. I'd prefer it was you. The barbarians honor Hrum too, in their way. The clans have holy men, shamans, that they consult before battle. I don't know as much as I'd like to about them, but I believe they'd recognize you as a holy man."

Vessto sat gazing across the firth for perhaps half a minute. "I'll go," he said. His words had no energy, no confidence, no strength. "I'll go," he repeated.

Hearing the tone of Vessto's voice, it occurred to Eltrienn that he might have made a mistake, that perhaps Vessto wasn't the man to take. But instead of backing out, he asked, "Where shall I meet you? Can you be at the main gate of the Fortress when the morning sun reaches it?"

"Yes. But if I'm to go, there's something important I have

to do in town tonight. Wait for ten minutes and I'll ride in behind you on your kaabor."

He went into the hut then, and Eltrienn waited outside the door, heartened a bit because Vessto seemed to have gained energy from somewhere. Ten minutes later, his few needed belongings in a packsack of woven reeds, Vessto was ready to leave. Half of that ten minutes had been spent talking to the one disciple who was not in a trance. Then the brothers went to Eltrienn's kaabor. Eltrienn swung up into the saddle, reached down, hoisted Vessto up behind him, and they rode into Theedalit together.

It had been a busy two days for Brokols and Venreeno. The question of a sulfur supply had been solved the first morning; it had been no problem. At the same time he'd gotten to know, and Reeno had hired, an herbalist, Amaadio Akrosstos. Akrosstos had agreed to work with them on identifying and isolating saltpeter and producing gunpowder.

In Hrumma and the Djezes, herbalists were not only the pharmacists. They were alchemists, in the sense of doing empirical research with not only plant but animal and mineral materials, directed mostly at producing pharmaceuticals. In the process they'd accumulated a large body of general chemical information and technique, though without any comprehensive conceptual scheme to fit it into and theorize from.

Meanwhile Reeno had sent a man with a cart to the Tuuchei Gorge caves to get a load of nightbird dung.

Amaadio, with Reeno and Brokols, had developed a list of what he needed for the work, and Reeno had prepared a certificate of credit for him.

On the second morning, before sunup, Brokols, Amaadio, and Reeno had ridden out to visit an abandoned fishing hamlet, Hidden Haven, about three hours ride south of the city. It had seemed to Reeno to be a possible site for their explosives research, and after examining it they decided it would do. When they got back to Theedalit that afternoon, Reeno arranged for its temporary use and to get the road to it rebuilt.

As Brokols sat down at the telegraph key that evening, Venreeno sat beside him as if to monitor his message. Brokols couldn't see what good that could possibly do the man, who knew neither Almaeic nor telegraph code. *He needn't worry,*

Brokols told himself. He slid the circuit closer aside, and tapped the "in service and waiting" signal through 300 miles of atmosphere to clang Kryger's signal bell in Haipoor l'Djezzer.

They waited for two or three minutes before anything happened. Then Kryger's acknowledgement came, followed immediately by a minute-long rattling of the sounder while Brokols' pencil lettered the incoming message.

> THE DARD WILL ANCHOR AT THEEDALIT DAY AFTER TOMORROW STOP ARGANT WILL COME ASHORE AND CONSULT WITH YOU STOP MEET HIM AT THE DOCK STOP ACKNOWLEDGE STOP END

Day after tomorrow?! Hurriedly Brokols scribbled his reply, then put down his pencil and positioned his hand at the key; his sending finger began to tap, his lips moving as he sent.

"Message received. Stop. Strongly urge that ship anchor outside firth, repeat, outside firth. Stop. Sea serpents raising newborn in firth this season. Stop. Are considered sacred. Stop. They fled at entrance of *Dard* earlier, which upset the Hrummeans. Stop. It is now known here that the *Dard* killed two serpents. Stop. If ship enters and serpents abandon young to flee, severe local reaction probable. Stop. Brokols end."

Kryger's reply was virtually immediate, as if he'd composed it while sending.

> ACKD STOP BE AT DOCK TO MEET ARGANT STOP KRYGER END COMM

Kryger sat steaming, his jaw clenched, its muscles bulging like pahlnuts. Brokols had even managed to leak the killing of the two sea monsters! The man was a hopeless fool! He'd wireless Argant and Stedmer and tell them definitely to remove him. No option.

"*Meet Argant at dock.*" Brokols knew, as surely as if he'd been told, that Kryger was sending Argant to replace him. There wasn't the slightest doubt in his mind.

And he was just as sure that Kryger would not tell Stedmer to anchor outside the firth. For several minutes he brooded, then with abrupt decision jotted another message, dialed the ship's frequency, and sent the "in service and waiting signal." Three minutes passed before he was acknowledged.

His sending finger began to move, informing the ship of the situation with the serpents, instructing them to anchor outside the firth and send Argant in in the captain's pinnace.

All he got was an acknowledgement, with neither agreement nor rejection, or even any comment.

After Eltrienn had let him off at a sidestreet, Vessto strode down it, alone and purposeful, to a tall but otherwise ordinary apartment building, with shops on its ground floor silent and dark. He climbed the outside stairs to the roof. Dim smoky light shone from its small penthouse, where a holy man sat crosslegged outside the door. Vessto went across to it and stepped inside. Old Tassi Vermaatio sat there in beatific meditation on a prayer mat.

The Trumpet of Hrum put down his pack against the wall, walked over, and sat down in a full lotus to one side of the ancient sage, facing his profile.

This time he knew a trance would not elude him. He relaxed, breathed deliberately, slowly, as he'd been taught as a child. His eyes ceased to focus in the universe outside him. Briefly he observed vagrant thoughts float by, letting them pass until there were no more. His remaining tenseness had passed with them.

Shortly he perceived his principal aspects, his Kirsan and Nasrik, two softly glowing eyes already nearly touching one another. He bade them unite, and they became two in one. Then he perceived his life guides, his Zan and Naz, soft pyramidal luminescences; they too he bade unite, and they did. Kaz and Zak, they who provide, showed themselves as pale luminous cubes; and they became two in one. Then the Kozziu appeared, givers of energy, half a dozen vibrating triangles flickering with rainbow tints, seeming energetic beyond constraint; they merged by pairs and became three.

All of these aspects Vessto had seen before, though infrequently and not since he'd left the monastery. They had always appeared in pairs and sometimes had touched, but never had their pairs fully merged before. Now a single opalescent pearl displayed itself. It was new to Vessto, and he realized that he was outside the universe perceiving himself.

He'd long understood that his existence in the world of phenomena grew out of these luminescences, his shattras. Now he knew it beyond understanding.

Amusement swelled. All the luminescences moved to the

pearl, and they touched, pulsed, became one, to take the form of a single, twelve-faceted crystalloid pulsing softly with silver light. He contemplated it, and as he did, the he that watched seemed to expand, to absorb it, and felt a sense of one-ness, power, wisdom. And laughed, the laughter bubbling from some great depth.

Then Tassi was floating farther off as another crystalloid, and Panni as yet another, both laughing with him. A golden glow formed, seemed to envelope him, and he went beyond later remembrance.

When Vessto became aware again, his body still sat upright in the dim, silent room. Unfolding his legs, he arose, went to the door, picked up his pack, and stepped out onto the roof, chuckling softly. Eastward the silver light of dawn had begun to thin the stars. He chuckled all the way to the square, where he arrived while the last stars were fading.

Thirty-Four

There was a great deal to do, Brokols realized, but just now most of it wasn't ready to be done. So he and Reeno didn't feel particularly rushed. Their breakfast dishes had been cleared away—Arnello Bostelli had hired a houseman-cook for Brokols—and they were relaxing over satta in the long rays of a sun less than an hour above the hills. Birds twittered and sang among the plantings on their roof and other roofs nearby.

Neither man said much. Brokols was thinking about his dream, which hadn't evaporated at waking as so many did. Reeno was thinking his own thoughts, giving only peripheral attention to Brokols'. The houseman stepped out into the garden.

"Your Excellency," he said, "there's a soldier at the door with a message for you. Says he wants to give it to your hand."

"Huh!" Brokols got up, Reeno a moment behind, and went inside. It was a young senior private in clean kilt and tunic, capped instead of helmeted. He recognized the Almite and saluted, put the large envelope in Brokols' hand, saluted again and left. Brokols closed and bolted the door, then slit the envelope with his pocket knife while walking back down the hall toward the garden. Sitting down to his cup again, he drew out a sheaf of papers and began to read aloud.

> *Dear Elver,*
>
> *Earlier today you asked me to tell you about the sages of Hrum. It turns out that I have time to tell you, but as you are not here, I will write it down.*
>
> *At present, three men are widely considered sages:*

Tassi Vermaatio, Panni Vempravvo, and Vessto Cadriio. I'll start with Vessto. I know him best, and recently have gotten well reacquainted with him.

At age 27, Vessto Cadriio has come to be called, by some in Theedalit, "the Trumpet of Hrum." This appears to be from his foretelling some things regarding your ship, yourself, and the ambitions of your emperor—things in the nature of a warning—and also his preaching against Almeon.

Vessto is from a rather poor country province, Kammenak. He was trained in the monastery there but never experienced "the Awakening," and therefore was never dubbed "master." However, as a child he already showed certain Hrum-given talents that drew attention to him, and after four years in the monastery became a third-level adept—the highest is a fourth.

"Adept" refers to certain spiritual aptitudes conveyed by Hrum. Vessto occasionally produced what many came to call his "sayings from Hrum." Often, however, he did not show the neutral affinity that is normally a trait of sages and masters. He can be a dedicated partisan, as you well know, believing that Hrum intends him to do so.

Vessto will no longer be speaking against Almeon in the square, which will severely hamper Mellvis Rantrelli's efforts to depose the amirr. Instead, he has agreed to go with me on my new assignment, where he can be of real value to Hrumma.

Brokol's eyebrows raised at the last paragraph. Previously he'd been going to ask Reeno what Eltrienn had meant by the terms *Hrum-given aptitudes* and *neutral affinity;* neither had any meaning for him. The comments about "foretelling" had not impinged at all; he couldn't have told you they were there. The final paragraph took his attention off everything else however: Vessto was leaving with Eltrienn. He read on.

At age 58, Panni Vempravvo is known as "the Lamp of Hrum." Son of a fisherman, he was born in a village on a small inlet not far north of the firth. He spent longer as a novice than is normal in the monastery. Usually those who do not attain the Awakening within fifteen years are urged by the masters to leave. (Most leave sooner on their own or at a master's prompting.) But Panni Vempravvo was never urged to leave, and Awakened after twenty-two years in the monastery at Theedalit. Rather soon afterward, his observations on life and humankind began to bring him recognition as a sage.

Tassi Vermaatio was born in the hill village of Zarrnosi. He is said to be 94 years old. After meditating with him for an hour, one day a dozen years ago, Panni Vempravvo dubbed him "the Is-ness of Hrum," perceiving Tassi as having attained permanent one-ness with Hrum-In-Him and thus no longer having any other beingness.

Tassi went late to the monastery. As a boy and young man, he had labored in a quarry with sledge and chisel, cutting blocks of stone. He was renowned for his physical strength. At age 26, he went suddenly blind. This was not from some chip of stone in the eye; it simply happened. At the same time he received a call from Hrum, and entered the monastery near the marketing town of Kritallios. In less than two years he Awakened, at which point his eyes could see again.

For several years afterward he sat on the headland above the firth, in all weather and without a roof, draped with a woolen blanket, speaking occasionally to his devotees and allowing them occasionally to feed him, but mostly meditating. Once a day he got up, relieved himself, and walked about on the headland for a few minutes.

At age 50 he retired to a one-room penthouse in Theedalit, and within three years ceased entirely to speak, sitting in a state of permanent Enlightenment. He quite often laughs however. His breathing is usually imperceptible. He is said to take a small cup of satta once a day, and every week or so to eat a fruit or a meal cake of some sort. About as often, it is said, he voids his bowel and bladder into a bucket. Other than at those times, he rarely stands up anymore, and does not lay down at all. He is not known ever to be sick, and when he stands, he needs no help. It is said that to live with him is to slide gradually into a state of continuing bliss, but only two of his present followers have been with him for an extended period of years. Those two are dedicated to taking care of him. Others have emerged from their association with him to instruct in some monastery, or go back to the fishing boat, the farm field, or the herdsman's hut.

Panni is reported to have said that Tassi is above even the level of Play; he is simply at Perceive. Perhaps no one who has not had the Awakening—that is, no one but a master—has an inkling of what he perceives. Certainly I do not.

Eltrienn

Brokols had paused over the terms "level of Play" and "Perceive." Presumably Perceive was also a level of some kind. "Adept," "Hrum-given talents," and "Awakening" had little meaning for him. It was unlike Eltrienn to state things unclearly. But then, these were patently religious terms, not worth worrying about.

He and Reeno were about to leave when another messenger arrived, this one a page from the Palace. The wax-sealed envelope he brought was from Juliassa: Brokols was invited to attend a play with her that afternoon. If he accepted, a carriage would pick him up at noon, for lunch before the play. It said nothing about her father, but the messenger was to bring back his answer. Brokols invited the page inside and, sitting down in his study, wrote a brief reply: He'd be delighted, of course, but Reeno Venreeno would have to accompany him. By amirrial order, Reeno was to accompany him wherever he went.

THIRTY-FIVE

In Hrumma, "ladies" were not necessarily "lady-like." Its noblewomen felt no class compulsion to be driven in a carriage, and Juliassa Hanorissia was far more likely to do her traveling in the saddle or, for short distances, afoot. As was her aunt and newly-appointed chaperone, Torissia Korillias, who was only six years older than the namirrna, though somewhat more decorous.

But to take Brokols to the theater, even a bare half-mile from the palace, it seemed to Juliassa that a carriage was more appropriate.

"Do they have theaters in Almeon?" she asked as they drove down a stone-paved street.

He smiled. "Of course. We're not totally uncivilized."

"What are your plays about?"

He shrugged. "Historical events." What else would plays be about? "Kings and crises, mainly," he elaborated. One popped into his mind, but he was not about to mention it: The hunting and capture of the infamous "Contemptible Darmol," a Kelthian "holy man" who'd slunk from village to village on Kelthos, being hidden by the people and preaching religion. General Falthis had finally been forced to a distasteful but necessary extreme—he'd held a village hostage and prepared to kill its children one by one. Darmol had given himself up then and been beheaded in the square in the play's final scene, babbling idiocies until almost the last minute.

It hadn't been the final act in the historical reality, Brokols knew. The execution had triggered the last serious revolution in Almeon. The Kelthians had never recovered from their punishment: to this day they were sullen and worthless, and Brokols wondered if separating the man's head from his shoulders had been worth it. Certainly religion here didn't seem especially noxious, or noxious at all, though perhaps on Kelthos it had been.

"We have historical plays too," Juliassa was saying. "But the one today is a romantic comedy. To make people laugh."

"Hmh! That'll be quite a novelty for me, a play written to make people laugh."

The carriage stopped, and the footman climbed down to open the door for them and help them dismount. The theater was at one end of the park where he'd attended Festival. There was a shallow bowl-like depression, terraced with steps green with grass, a wide paved oval at one side as a stage. Silvery curtains, patterned with gold, hung behind it to conceal the waiting players. Facing it on the sloping sides, occupying the steps, were curved concrete benches in 120° arcs, spaced well apart on contours. They might have held a thousand, but just now they were little more than half full, and he wondered if many spectators would come late, as so many were inclined to do in Larvis Royal. It was a business day though; that may have been it.

The royal party started down one of the aisles carrying their own cushions, as was the custom, the namirrna and Brokols leading, Reeno and Torissia following. The crowd was chattering and laughing, a light and pleasant sound, Brokols thought. As he and Juliassa passed the first few arcs of benches though, the sound faded.

Then someone shouted, the words somehow failing to register on Brokols. A second, close at hand, reached him with a shock.

"Foreigner go home!" It was picked up quickly, growing, taking on a unity. Near the foot of the aisle, Juliassa stopped, at first not turning. It was a chant now: *"Foreigner go home! Foreigner go home! Foreigner go home!"* His hair crawled at the sound. She did turn then, face at first bewildered and shocked but stiffening quickly into anger. Sensing her reaction, their effect, the crowd shouted louder: *"Foreigner go home! Foreigner go home!"* Gripping Brokols' sleeve, she started back up the aisle, striding now, Reeno and Torissia separating to let them pass, then closing to follow.

"Foreigner go home! Foreigner go home! Foreigner go home!" The chants followed them out of the bowl and into

the carriage. Actually, the shouting didn't bother Brokols that much, after the original shock. He could understand it. But he almost cringed at what it had done to Juliassa. Tears of rage rolled down her cheeks. As they drove away, the chant began to break, to be replaced by a cheer, the last sound they heard from the theater.

Inside the carriage, the atmosphere was like a block of ice. No one spoke; one scarcely looked at another. The driver drove into the palace grounds and let them out at the main entrance. Brokols took Juliassa's hands and turned her to face him.

"Namirrna," he said, "it is best for you, and certainly for the amirr, if we do not see one another again. At least until this"—he gestured as if to indicate the theater crowd—"until this situation is over."

"No!" she cried, and stamped her foot. "I will not be dictated to by a crowd of ignorant fools!"

For a moment she glared at him, then abruptly her anger was gone. "I'm sorry, Elver," she said quietly, and putting her arms around the startled Brokols, kissed him on the mouth, ignoring her staring chaperone and the bemused Venreeno. Then she stepped back from him.

"You are wiser than I," she said, then added, "this time anyway." She grinned, taking him further by surprise. "And we will not attend another public function for now. In a little while this 'situation' *will* be over. Father told mother and me a little of what you're doing; it's why he agreed to let me see you today. And I can help you in your work! You'll see! I've often worked with Aunt Zeenia; it's been a condition of my staying with her. I've even helped pull a calf from a gleebor in difficult labor!"

He was overwhelmed by this girl, this not much more than child, it seemed to him. They talked for a minute or two more, then she had the carriage take him and Reeno home.

THIRTY-SIX

Brokols had warned the amirr of the *Dard*'s coming, and was spending the day in the Fortress, to be close to the wharf. He read a book on ceramics while he waited. Meanwhile, Hrummean defense forces were on alert. On the headland, the watchtower keepers kept a constant eye northward.

They ran up the signal flags just as the sun was crossing the meridian. A trumpet pealed from the Fortress's gate tower: the *Dard* had been spotted, presumably at the edge of visibility to the north. Which meant he had an hour or more. Yet Brokols found it difficult to turn back to his book. Most of an hour later, another flag was run up. The trumpet spoke again. Soft-booted feet, many of them, sounded on the stone stairs from the courtyard to the top of the wall. Brokols placed a bookmark, closed his book, and went onto the wall himself.

The mangonels were manned, blocks of stone piled ready beside them. Soldiers, and baskets of heavy, sharp iron bolts, were ready at the arbolests. Bowmen, longbows still unstrung but quivers full, stood about. A few men had gone to the parapet to look up the firth, until an officer ordered them back. They were not to show themselves. The Almites would, of course, have telescopes—the Hrummeans did—and it wouldn't do to show the ship their readiness.

Presumably—almost surely—there'd be no need to fight. But it seemed to Brokols that if it came to it, the Hrummeans might well surprise the Almites—his own people!—and cause them heavy initial casualties before Stedmer brought his cannon into action. Then, of course, it would be a different story.

The pintle guns wouldn't be the problem, or the *major*

problem. They were quick and could be aimed in any direction without turning the ship, but their rounds weighed a mere four pounds. More dangerous, if more ponderous, were the waist guns, four in each side, fired from gunports below deck. They'd be somewhat sheltered from the primitive machines on the Fortress wall, and immune to archery. Their explosive shells weighed more than thirty pounds. If it came to a fight, only the Hrummean marines, waiting at their oars now in nearby boathouses, seemed to have any prospect at all of silencing the cannon, and they'd have to storm the *Dard* in the face of rifle fire.

Brokols kept reminding himself how unlikely it was that it would come to that.

She rounded the headland beneath a smudge of smoke. Brokols stood watching at the parapet, dressed in his Almaeic finery. Apparently the serpents weren't fleeing this time; he was sure he saw one of them blow a spout of steamy breath, half a mile out from the Fortress, and another near the south shore. They could breathe with no more than their snouts breaking the surface.

In minutes the *Dard* was halfway up the firth. It was time to join the guard detail, he and Reeno, to go to the wharf and meet Argant. They started down. Presumably Argant would come ashore with no more than the master-at-arms and perhaps one other man. If an armed party landed, the guard detail was to meet them on the dock and insist that Argant come ashore alone. *I've changed from a peril to a resource here,* Brokols thought, and found the irony amusing. Slightly.

Allbarin's insistence that Reeno accompany him had seemed odd to Brokols. "He's the amirr's representative," the privy counselor had said. It hadn't seemed a very compelling reason to Brokols, but he saw no reason to object. And Reeno went nowhere without shortsword at his waist. Undoubtedly he could use it well. When questioned, he'd said his usual function was amirrial security, but Brokols wondered. In conversation once, he'd shown a surprising knowledge of the Gorrbian military, and it seemed likelier he had something to do with intelligence.

They left the Fortress through a pedestrian gate, followed by a decade of the guard, and walked down onto the wharf. This time there was no crowd; it was a business day, and only a couple of dozen bystanders stood by in little groups. The *Dard* was still some minutes short of anchoring.

Brokols' nervousness took the form of neither tremor nor knotted stomach. Instead, time and space seemed to alter. His attention focused totally on the approaching ship; he was spelled by it, emotionless, feeling as if everything was predetermined, with himself a spectator. She'd slowed, lost the foam on her bow wave. Soon after, she stopped, this time perhaps only three hundred yards offshore. He saw her bow anchor splash. The captain's gig was swung over the side on its davits, and suddenly Brokols' knees felt watery, as if they'd collapse to dump him on the wharf's timbered deck.

The gig began to pull toward shore, and from the height of the wharf at a little past ebb tide, there seemed to be four aboard her besides her oarsmen. Argant stood in the bow, looking shoreward, and Brokols was sure the man's eyes were fixed on him. A terrible thought occurred to him then: Reeno would turn him over to them, let them take him away! He didn't believe it, not even briefly, but the idea washed over him like a cold and numbing wave, leaving sweat behind.

Then an open-beaked head rose out of the water on a muscular, snake-like neck thicker than Brokols' thigh. It struck, and Brokols could hear the scream from where he stood, a very brief scream. For just an instant the beak held a man by the waist, arms and legs waving as he was lifted from the bow. Then serpent and man disappeared beneath the waves.

And it was Argant who was gone.

The gig began to veer. The oarsmen on the portside still rowed, but on the starboard side, the side toward the serpent, the forward oar flailed the air in seeming terror and the midship oar raised to stay out of its way, while the stern oarsman still stroked. Brokols heard the bosun bellow angrily, no doubt cursing them, then all the oars began to stroke again. The gig turned about, and with the oars once more in a semblance of order, started back to the *Dard*.

Brokols' fear was gone, replaced by fascination. When the gig reached the ship's side, most of her men climbed back aboard. The hooks on the davit blocks were set and she was hoisted from the water. And it seemed to Brokols that with Argant gone, there was nothing the ship could do except leave.

Midshipman Werlingus sat at the rattling wireless, pencil

moving rapidly on his tablet. Kryger stood behind his shoulder, watching the rows of letters form.

> SHIP AT ANCHOR OFF THEEDALIT WHARF STOP ARGANT SENT IN GIG WITH MAA AND TWO MARINES STOP LARGE SERPENT SNATCHED ARGANT FROM GIG WITH BEAK TOOK HIM UNDER STOP GIG RETURNED SHIP STOP REQUEST PERMISSION TO SHELL FORTRESS STOP END STEDMER

The midshipman reached to hand Kryger the tablet but Kryger waved it off, had already read it. He'd accepted the information without difficulty, despite how bizarre it was. What he could hardly believe was Stedmer's reaction. The man was insane!

"Send this," Kryger said. "Fire no rounds at fortress or anything else. Stop. Repeat. Fire no rounds at fortress or at anything else. Stop. Raise anchor and leave for Almeon. Stop. End communication. Mission Commander General Lord Vendel Kryger."

The midshipman's middle finger tapped the key, producing a rapid irregular pattern of clicks. When he was done, he looked back over his shoulder questioningly. "That's all," Kryger said. The young man had started to get up when once again the receiver began its tattoo. Werlingus paused, uncertain.

"Ignore it," Kryger said.

They left, the midshipman looking back worriedly over his shoulder.

Brokols watched the *Dard* leave, steam down the firth and out of sight, trailed by a streamer of black smoke which thinned in the breeze and gradually disappeared. The guards had returned into the Fortress when the ship was well underway, and only Reeno still stood with him.

"Well," Brokols said thoughtfully, then turned. Instead of going into the Fortress, he started up the street. "I want to message Kryger," he told Reeno. "Stedmer probably messaged him what happened. Perhaps I can add a little confusion to it."

Kryger had almost not answered the signal; he'd assumed it was Stedmer again. Now he sat looking at the message Werlingus had written down for him.

STEDMERS FOOLISHNESS IN ENTERING HARBOR HAS RESULTED IN ANTI ALMEON SLOGANS SHOUTED IN THE STREETS STOP HE HAS TAKEN HRUMMEAN HOSTILITY OFF GORRBUL AND PUT IT BACK ON ALMEON STOP RECOMMEND IMPERIAL REPRIMAND FOR STEDMER STOP END BROKOLS AMBASSADOR

Interesting, Kryger thought. He didn't trust Brokols though, and didn't take his advice. It wasn't wise to stir the water when things were proceeding so unpredictably. Besides, something was going on with the ambassador to Hrumma, and whatever it was, it didn't feel like patriotism. He wasn't sure what it felt like.

Thirty-Seven

One of the bystander clusters on the wharf had been Mellvis Rantrelli with several employees. Within minutes of the *Dard*'s departure, he'd put his people in rikkshas to visit certain places and people in the city, tell the story and call for a rally in the square immediately after business hours.

The turnout was far the best yet: There were at least three thousand there, he estimated. There was also more emotion than ever. A sea serpent, a Messenger from Hrum, had spoken through its action. There were random shouts for Brokols' deportation, his imprisonment. And scattered cheers.

Rantrelli waited till the inflow of people had nearly stopped, then climbed the platform and faced them, raising his arms. When the crowd had quieted, he spoke.

"People of Hrumma!" he shouted. "Hrum has spoken to us through his messenger, and we have heard him!"

There was loud cheering. He let it run its course, then raised his arms again. "And you are right! The foreign ambassador is an enemy, of Hrumma and of Hrum, and should be deported!" He waved his arms to forestall an incipient cheer. "But more serious—more serious—the amirr has endangered the country by not imprisoning him as soon as he was exposed for the enemy that he is!"

From the crowd a large voice bellowed, "Down with the amirr! A new amirr! Down with the amirr! A new amirr!" The second time through, it was joined by other voices, until most of the crowd was shouting. *"Down with the amirr! A new amirr! Down with the amirr! A new amirr!"*

Rantrelli watched with a feeling of satisfaction. The situation was ripening. Within a day the whole city would be in agreement, and every traveller would spread the story of it. Within a week he would send his people through all of Hrumma to call for moots. Within five weeks there'd be a new amirr, himself perhaps.

Wrapped in his thoughts, he didn't see someone mounting the platform to one side, didn't notice until the chant thinned and died. Then he became aware of the robed man standing with arms raised. The crowd was waiting, surly but listening.

"People of Hrumma!" Allbarin called. "I am glad to see and hear your concern for the safety of our country. It is well justified.

"For the Emperor of Almeon, its king over kings, desires to rule on this side of the ocean as well. And he has a plan of conquest! He intends that Djez Gorrbul attack us, send its army to invade. And while the Gorrbian army is engaged here, fighting its bloody way southward into Hrumma, an Almaeic fleet will land a powerful army at Haipoor l'Djezzer."

A murmur flowed through the crowd, and he stopped for a moment until it quieted, waiting.

"The amirr reluctantly sent an envoy to Haipoor, to warn Gamaliiu. The reply was as feared: Two days ago our ship arrived back with sacks containing the heads of the envoy and his party. After scanning the heads, I do not believe they were even received by Gamaliiu, or that he so much as witnessed their execution. And if they told anyone their message, it never reached Gamaliiu; otherwise he'd not have sent our people back as he did.

"So we can expect war, and with the large army that Gorrbul can field, it will be a fierce test of the people of Hrumma.

"The Trumpet of Hrum was right in his admonition: The battle is ours alone. We must fight to the limits of our strength and courage, expecting no help. If we do this—if Hrum is pleased enough with us—he will help us. But do not rely on intervention by Hrum. Rely only on ourselves. For only in that way can we earn his help.

"As for the Ambassador from Almeon . . ." Allbarin stopped then, drawing their attention from what he'd just said, back to himself. "As for the Ambassador from Almeon, he has seen our land and been touched by the sages. He has helped us with his knowledge. He continues to help, and has strengthened us."

Rantrelli listened, unsure of what to do. He'd lost the crowd, and groped now for ideas.

"Tomorrow we send couriers throughout the country," Allbarin was saying, "with instructions to the district defense commanders. We do not expect the invasion to come till late summer or early fall, but it is time to prepare our . . ."

Allbarin stopped. The crowd had been motionless; now there was movement in the back as people gave way to someone. It was Panni Vempravvo, and as they melted aside for him, a murmur spread through the crowd. "The Lamp of Hrum! The Lamp of Hrum!" The tall sage reached the platform and climbed its stone steps. Both Allbarin and Rantrelli stepped back, giving him the stage.

Panni smiled, a wide warm smile.

"Where is the Trumpet of Hrum?" he asked. He didn't shout, but everyone heard him. "What has become of the Trumpet of Hrum? Have any of you seen him lately?" He turned to Rantrelli. "Have you seen him, merchant?"

Rantrelli wagged his head, his jowls.

"I will tell you what has happened to him. He has Awakened! The other night he meditated till dawn with Tassi Vermaatio and saw Hrum. And Knew! Today he is far from Theedalit, on a mission for the amirr.

"Until now, Vessto Cadriio has had mainly knowledge, knowledge such as is given to those rare adepts who are also seers. His flashes of Wisdom were only flashes. Now he lives in Wisdom. It flows through him. No longer will Vessto Cadriio wear a long face unless he chooses to create it in Play.

"So rejoice that matters are beginning so well. And heed the words of the Trumpet of Hrum, and of Allbarin Venjianni. If you play fully the role of warriors or the role of workers, for Hrumma, Hrum may decide that the people of Hrumma are truly his foster children!"

He bowed deeply to them then, and the crowd began to cheer, less than wildly to be sure, but after a minute or so Rantrelli watched them melting away into the street, and the sound of their excited voices was like a flood through a rapids. He looked around. Allbarin had left the platform; he saw his white-robed back going toward a Fortress gate. Panni, however, still stood there, looking at him.

"Have you meditated lately?" the sage asked conversationally.

Rantrelli shook his head. "I was never any good at it. I gave it up years ago."

Panni nodded. "When one feels no true desire to meditate,

one can only pretend. When one desires to meditate, that is the time to meditate. If you ever desire to, you are welcome to do so with me. Whether you bring your body to my cave or we come together only in the spirit."

Rantrelli nodded, not heartened by the words or their friendly intent.

"Do you feel you've been defeated here this evening?"

Again Rantrelli nodded.

"It is all right to feel that way. But it is also all right to feel that you have had a victory here—that you created all this to bring you to some point, or to bring others to some point. It is all right to believe that you have followed beautifully and exactly an act which Hrum-In-Thee created in your script of life."

Rantrelli spoke then while avoiding the sage's eyes, his voice more plaintive than complaining. "It has never been real to me that we live a script. That our lives are pre-written for us and we simply go through the motions. If that is true, what purpose is there in life?"

"Ah! To speak of a script is simply a way of talking about it. Anything we say can only be a way of talking about it. But I will talk of it nonetheless. Before our body leaves the womb, before we have merged with it to enter the stage, we have ourselves prepared, or accepted, a script complete with furnishings. Everyone: villain and hero, vanquished and victor—everyone has their own script."

The sage chuckled, grinning at the merchant. "And there is no director, unless Hrum chooses to take a hand. Which is not often, not at all. And more: Each actor is born both knowing the script and not knowing the script, living it as best he can, revising, rewriting, creating the play, the action, moment by moment in the ever-changing circumstances of Hrum's stage." He looked almost archly at Rantrelli then. "It can even happen that one assumes a certain role in Act One simply to prepare a different role in Act Two."

Rantrelli peered cautiously at him. "And what use is meditation in all this?" he asked.

Again Panni laughed. "All or none whatever. Any player can benefit from Wisdom, Wisdom being simply the right action at the right time to attain the purpose of the role. And for some roles, meditation opens the channels to Wisdom. Wisdom is not Hrum whispering in your ear. It is not words. Any whispering is an addition by Hrum-In-Thee, which may make Wisdom easier to accept."

"And I may come to your cave and meditate with you?"

"If you wish. But you are used to comfort, and you may also meditate with me while kneeling alone in your garden, or even sitting in your admirable hot tub, while I sit on my mountain."

"And if I would meditate with you, what time would be best?"

"Follow your knowingness and your need. If you decide that a certain time is the time, it is. I am usually meditating from nightfall until midnight, and often well after."

Panni half-turned then, as if to join his two waiting disciples. "Go with Hrum," he said to Rantrelli, and walked down the steps.

Rantrelli watched them start across the square, then went down the steps to his own waiting people, and they walked to his carriage together. His employees said nothing, in keeping with Rantrelli's mood.

Leonessto Hanorissio had been told of the gathering crowd, and had gone to a window to watch. He hadn't been able to hear Rantrelli's talk, but the crowd's chant had reached him clearly, its volume stunning him. He'd seen Allbarin mount the platform, and if he couldn't hear his words, he'd seen their effect. Then Panni had arrived and spoken, and the cheers that followed were a different phenomenon from the earlier chanting.

After they'd dispersed, he'd returned to his office. Allbarin would tell him what had happened.

Which he did. "And do you believe it?" Leonessto asked. "That if we do all we can, Hrum will give us victory?"

"Milord, that is what the Trumpet said. But it isn't what Panni said. He said, in effect, that if we do all we can, not depending on help at all, Hrum *may* decide we are indeed his foster children. And it seems to me now that that is more the actuality of it."

The amirr looked at it thoughtfully. "Well, that's what we must do, in any case. Unless we'd give up."

And knowing his history, and what had been learned from Brokols' mind about emperors and a sad country called Kelthos, he had no intention of giving up.

THIRTY-EIGHT

Three years past, the steep-sided draw above Hidden Haven had held a decent wagon road. Then a mud and rock slide sloughed off the south wall, blocking road and creek, forming a pond behind the mass of dirt and rock until the water cut a new course around it, leaving a morass behind.

Now a unit of army engineers, tough brawny men with callused hands, had labored with crowbars, shovels and picks, kaabors and kaabor-drawn barrows. They'd dug and ditched and leveled until the draw was passable for a wagon again.

Amaadio knew it was passable because a wagonload of building supplies, two of lumber, another of baggage and food, and a ponderous wagonload of roofing tiles had all passed down ahead of him. To cross the mud, the engineers had rough-cobbled the new wagon road with native stones of whatever size. Amaadio Akrosstos winced and swore as the large army wagon lurched over rocks and down the draw, carrying his precious equipment. The glassware and light crockery was what he worried most about, that and the carboys of liquid reagents. He'd packed them himself in large baskets, not sparing the straw, that they'd take no harm. But he winced anyway.

He'd rather have stayed home and done the job there. But it was for Hrumma and for Hrum, secrecy was wanted, and there'd need to be explosions. Deliberate explosions! So they'd picked this Hrum-forsaken place. He'd shaken his head when they'd told him about the explosions; to a Hrummean herbalist, an explosion was an accident, something to be avoided. Dangerous, a significant source of injuries and death to venturesome herbalists, though fumes killed more of them or left them strange . . .

But the job would be interesting and different, and they were paying him well. Besides which, Trinnia had liked the idea of spending a week or two, even a working week or two, away from the city and close to a beach.

They left the slide behind, and now he could see past a shoulder of land to the inlet and the hamlet above it. They'd been abandoned since the slide had buried the road, but from a distance it looked as if people still lived there.

Reeno and Brokols had examined Hidden Haven before they'd chosen it, and when they'd decided, Reeno had made a hurried list of what needed to be done to make it useable. Juliassa had visited yesterday, with Torissia and three guards, on pretense of a day's outing.

It was small, even for a hamlet: six stone dwellings plus sheds and other outbuildings, built near the creek eighty yards above the beach. Below the slide, the creek was too muddy now for drinking or for Amaadio's professional needs, so the army had built a small weir upstream of the slide, with a pipe on trestles carrying water to the hamlet, where it filled a small cistern.

The hamlet had been there a long time. Its markets had been three inland villages. It had never been much more than a subsistence operation, in recent decades exporting its youth to Theedalit and the distant but increasingly prosperous east coast towns. So when the slide had blocked the road to their markets, the fisherfolk had left.

The inlet itself was deep and well-sheltered, some four hundred yards long and more than a hundred wide. Close beyond the narrow mouth, a rocky isle, like some great rude menhir, hid the opening, and in rough weather made entry a matter of skill and care.

Juliassa had found two weatherbeaten old skiffs upside down above the beach. Their gunnels had rotted enough that the tholepins had broken out, but there was a paddle beneath each of them, and she'd imagined paddling one of them out on the inlet or maybe beyond.

The inlet itself was occupied; some serpents used it as a nursery. That especially pleased Juliassa, and she wondered if a human could learn to speak with them. They were said to make sounds above water, but serpents were well known to be shy, or perhaps aloof. As far as that was concerned, she didn't even have permission to work there yet, but she had no doubt at all that she'd get it.

When the wagon train arrived, the only woman with it was Amaadio's wife; Trinnia Akrosstas had hired on as a cook. Besides Amaadio and Trinnia, Brokols and Reeno had brought a handyman, Carrnos Frimattos, and four builders who would reroof the buildings the project would use, and do minor repairs. They began with an all-hands project, all but Trinnia, tearing the thatch roof off the building most of them would live in. Dusk was settling, and they were dirty, sweaty, and tired, before they finished reroofing it.

Thirty-Nine

The next morning Brokols helped Amaadio build work tables and shelves. At noon Juliassa and Torissia arrived, followed by a hawk-eyed Jonkka with two pack kaabors in tow. The women wore rough clothes. Juliassa seemed quiet, for her, and businesslike, almost ignoring Brokols when she arrived. She gave Reeno a paper of some sort and he put her right to work. Climbing a ladder, she began to help the building crew tear old thatch from another building, a heavy, dirty, even somewhat hazardous job. Meanwhile Torissia led their kaabors back up the draw to the pasture the engineers had fenced, and left them to graze, then put baggage away in a separate hut that could be reroofed later. Jonkka had climbed another hut, where he squatted on the ridgepole, spying the country round.

During a rain break, a man arrived with a cartload of covered baskets—the guano. Reeno called Juliassa down from the roof, and Amaadio had her sweep the floor of a shed and empty the baskets so he could see if the guano was dry. That done, Reeno gave her a pitchfork and a great, deep-bellied wheelbarrow, to haul away old roof thatch and burn it.

Brokols wondered what was going on; why they were giving a namirrna orders like that, and why she was obeying them.

They worked till the sun was low, then bathed briefly in the inlet before supper. When they'd eaten, Juliassa slipped away from Torissia in the dusk, to the beach again. Jonkka saw her leave, and followed. She walked along it to the skiffs and dragged them into the water, filling them and weighing them down with rocks so the seams would swell shut.

When she'd finished, she sensed a movement in the dusk, or perhaps a sound, and looked up. Thirty yards offshore, a very large old sea serpent watched her, its head half a dozen feet above the water. On an impulse she called to it in sullsi.

"Hello! I am called Juliassa. What are you called?"

The answer came in sullsit as atrocious as her own—differently atrocious, full of hisses and sonorities—sullsit spoken slowly, accommodated to different vocal equipment. "Hello, Suliassa. I am called K'sthuump. You must be the human told about, friend of the sellsu Sleekit."

"I am! I am! Do you know Sleekit?"

"I know of Sleekit, and of you. Sullsi love to tell stories. His, of you, are new and widely told now. Excites to think of talking with land people! How wonderful that I meet you! People say Sleekit ssould have gotten more stories from you. Land people must have stransse and marvelous things to tell."

"I'm afraid he spent most of our time teaching me to speak. It wasn't easy. I had to spend so much of my time with him, to master it, that I did hardly any duties."

A resonant grunting issued from reptilian lungs, and she realized K'sthuump was laughing. "You do well. K'sthuump loves you. And it would not be easy to tell sullsi of land things, things they have never seen or dreamed of. They would have no picsures for them. It is easier for me than for Sleekit to receive your stories. I will see your mind picsures beneath them. I would love to spend time talking with you."

"And I with you!" Juliassa said. "But I have many duties here, my pack and I. My tribe prepares for great death fight with another. I must help it prepare. I can talk with you mainly at night."

"Ah!" The exclamation was a sort of laryngeal grunt. "At night is my main time of duty. I am the old mother, old beyond breeding. At night I patrol outside, listen for sarrkas. Very soon I must go. When light leaves the sky."

"Can we talk other times when the light is dimming?" Juliassa asked.

"I will be here every time. If you are here also, we will talk. I wiss to know more of this great death fight."

"A question," Juliassa said. "Have you heard that the big-ship people killed two of the Vrronnkiess?"

"All of the Vrronnkiess know it."

"The big-ship people are one tribe which my tribe will

fight. We do not know how we can beat them, but we will try, and maybe Hrum, the Great Sea Lord, will help us."

A sound resonated from the serpentine throat, like the *Hrum* uttered by monks at meditation. Juliassa wasn't sure what to make of it. "One of the Vrronnkiess killed a big-ship person yesterday," she went on. "Did that clear half the blood debt?"

"Vrronnkiess are different from sullsi. Recognise no blood debts. It was that . . . to kill the big-ssip person seemed the correct act."

"You know about it then. Did you see it?"

"Not as you mean. I was not there. It is known."

"How is it known?" the girl persisted.

"Humans are like the sullsi; one human does not know what other humans know. Every Vrronnkiess knows what every other knows."

The voice stopped, as if K'sthuump was contemplating Juliassa. Or her pictures. Then the serpent spoke again. "If one of us learns something, we all know it. If it is important to all Vrronnkiess, then we are *aware* that we know it. And the coming of big-ssip people is very important." The old serpent floated quiet for a moment, then went on. "Stransser things will happen than human and sullsi talking, serpent and human talking. A time of testing is coming, has come, to the world."

Neither said anything more for a minute. "I must go to duty now," the serpent said finally. "K'sthuump loves Suliassa." She began to swim away, holding her head high above the water.

"Juliassa loves K'sthuump!" the girl called after her.

There was no answer. The serpent receded into the thickening darkness, till at a hundred yards she could scarcely be seen. Then she dove, disappeared, Juliassa staring after her, feeling loss at the departure. *I'll learn to be an adept*, she told herself. *I'll get Panni Vempravvo to teach me, so I can see K'sthuump's pictures, and I can learn the stories the serpents tell. Right after I marry Elver*. But she felt no confidence. Not even all the masters had adept powers, and she'd never shown the slightest talent for them.

Thoughtfully, unsmiling, she turned to walk back to the hamlet. She didn't remember Jonkka until she almost ran into him where he squatted in the dark.

"I saw the serpent," he said. "It sounded like you were talking with him."

"With her," Juliassa corrected. "She speaks sullsit. K'sthuump is an old mother of her pod. Like a grandmother, I guess. She has to stand sentry duty now, outside the inlet. To listen for sarrkas."

"Hmm. Juliassa Hanorissia, you are an unusual person." Jonkka got up and they started for the hamlet. Before they got there, they met several of the others going to the shore: Brokols, Reeno, and Torissia. Juliassa and Jonkka turned back and went with them. The men gathered dead branches from shrubs at the foot of the cliff, and with a match, Reeno lit a small fire on the beach.

They sat around it talking, and Juliassa began to tell about K'sthuump.

"Really?" Brokols was impressed, not skeptical. "You talked with a serpent? What did he say?"

"She. K'sthuump is a she." Juliassa described the conversation.

Knowing at a distance, from one mind to another. It bothered Brokols to hear her accept such superstition so uncritically. "I find that hard to believe," he said cautiously. "That the serpents can know what each other knows—without talking about it, that is. There's no medium for direct thought transfer." He paused thoughtfully. "Unless it's done through water somehow."

She stared at his face, lit by flickering firelight. "Do you mean," she said, "that you've spent all these days with Reeno Venreeno and don't believe that one person can read another's thoughts and see their pictures?"

Brokols peered at her. "Are you telling me," he said slowly, "that such powers exist? And that Reeno . . ."

"Of course," she said. "And Allbarin and . . ." She stopped, suddenly chagrined, realizing she shouldn't have told him, that undoubtedly he wasn't to know, and turned to Reeno.

Chills washed over Brokols in long waves almost painfully intense, as ambiguities, mysteries, scores of unfitted data began falling into place. Everyone felt it a little. Reeno watched intently, and when Brokols had settled out somewhat, spoke to him.

"That's right, Elver. You needn't wonder any longer."

There was another silence before Brokols said anything. "And Eltrienn?"

"No, not Eltrienn. And not Juliassa or the amirr. Fewer

than one of us in a thousand. The sages, most masters, all adepts. And almost no others."

Brokols sat a moment longer, seemingly lost in thought, then stood up and looked around. "Excuse me," he said, "I have to go away. To be alone." He started off, began to jog.

"Elver?" Juliassa called tentatively. Reeno stilled her with a gesture.

Brokols stopped, looked back. "From how far away can you—look into someone else's mind?" he asked.

"If I can see you, and if there aren't many other people around, perhaps a hundred feet. In a crowd not more than—twenty perhaps. In an excited crowd I might have to touch you." He shrugged. "Apparently serpents are much more able than human adepts. But then, they're the Messengers of Hrum.

"And if it's any help to you, I can't read you freely now, because you know about us, about adepts. When a person knows he can be read, or suspects it, his mind curtains itself automatically. To read you at all now, I'd have to question you. Questions can bring things to the surface of the mind, or near it—not necessarily the things we're interested in—and lets them be seen.

"The exception is emotions. Those we can always get."

"Thank you," Brokols said quietly, then walked away and disappeared.

Reaching the plateau top, Brokols stopped. The sky seemed infinitely deep, its stars myriad and sharp, but though he was aware of them, he found neither awe at the sight nor joy in its beauty. Facing north toward Theedalit, he spoke aloud. "I trusted you people. I trusted you and came to—to love you. I'd never loved my own people, never knew it was possible, and I came to love you. And you fooled me, and used me, maybe laughed at me."

He began to run, ran hard, stumbling occasionally on stones and clumps of grass. He slipped in gleebor shit and fell heavily, jarring himself, got up limping and ran again, though only trotting now, until after a few minutes he flopped down exhausted and rolled over on his back, breathing hard.

So what now, Elver Brokols? he thought wryly. *Do you go away somewhere? Find your way north to Djez Gorrbul to throw yourself on the mercy of General Vendel Kryger? Steal a rowboat and cross the ocean to Almeon?*

Less than one in a thousand. And the rest were exposed to the few. No, not so, not broadly. Mainly their emotions. He grimaced. He wasn't proud of all his emotions.

What would it be like to have such an ability? To be exposed to everyone's emotions. Undoubtedly it was a matter of getting used to it. And the others were used to them.

And I prefer these people to my own. Even now. The realization didn't surprise him at all. *I never did fit in well at home. Kryger knew that. He knew I wasn't a proper Almite. He knew me better than I knew myself.*

And Reeno knew him better yet! Much better. Reeno had browsed his thoughts, breathed in his feelings—and had never visibly shown distaste or amusement at them. And Allbarin. Allbarin had manipulated him with questions, picked his brain, harvested his memories, but always with courtesy, somehow with seeming respect.

And Vessto, and Panni. And Panni! Brokols stood up. "Panni!" he called aloud, though not loudly. Somewhere in the darkness a gleebor snorted, startled at his voice. "Panniii!"

Chills flowed over Brokols again, wave after wave, the short hairs on his neck bristling, and he felt his face grinning. *"Panni!"* He barely breathed it that time.

He stood there until the chills stopped. It seemed to him he could almost see the sage sitting straight-backed in the grass on his hill, his mountain, skinny legs folded under him.

After a few minutes, Elver Brokols started trotting again. Great Liilia had just risen, swollen, lopsided, lighting the plateau. *Liilia!* Brokols chuckled wryly in his mind. *Almost the same name as Lerrlia!* He threw the moon a salute as he jogged.

He returned to the hamlet, rolled out his pallet and lay down. It took him very little time to go to sleep.

FORTY

Brokols dreamed richly that night, and awoke to grayness. He went to the window, clutching his blanket around himself not from modesty but chill; he'd lost much of his squeamishness over skin. The fog made it impossible to tell whether it had just gotten daylight or been light for some time, but he assumed the former because no one else seemed to be up.

Wrapped in his blanket, he limped quietly to the door and looked out, his attention still caught by his dreams. It seemed he'd been swimming in the night with Sleekit and a number of other sullsi. A serpent had come and told them mentally that the fleet was about to arrive. Brokols had felt a surge of exultation, not because the invasion was about to happen, but because of something he'd been going to do, he and the sullsi.

Sometime before that he'd dreamed of being with Panni. Panni was going to teach him to be an adept, but said he'd never be able to read minds—that people from Almeon couldn't be taught. He'd teach him to do other things. And somehow Brokols had been down at the shore, trying to catch fish, but he kept getting the line caught on an old sunken log, which turned out to be Sleekit, dead.

He'd awakened at that and gone to the men's privy to relieve himself, then went back to his pallet and dreamed about Sleekit alive. It seemed to him that Sleekit dead and Sleekit live were simply different chapters in the same dream, with Sleekit live the later.

Now, staring out into the fog, Brokols' attention was stuck

on what the dream might mean, which was ridiculous because the content of dreams meant nothing. That was well known. It might have grown out of the soreness of his thighs from last night's run, or of sleeping in a strange place.

Reeno got up then, and together they walked to the cistern and washed their faces in the cool water of the overflow pipe. Neither mentioned the evening before. Both made a point of being courteous, and Brokols of being friendly, since he'd been the one who'd walked out on the others. They could hear Trinnia in the kitchen, dumping the stove grates.

Their workday started early and lasted long. By morning's end they'd finished building shelves, workbenches and tables in the work-building. Juliassa had been carrying tiles up a ladder for the roofing crew, which through the afternoon had included Reeno, Brokols, and Frimattos the handyman. (Torissia had helped Trinnia in the kitchen.) By supper, the retiling of roofs was largely finished.

They'd bathed in the inlet again, all of them naked, even Brokols. Everyone except Jonkka, who stood nearby on guard. All of them took the nudity so casually that the Almite found it not really embarrassing after the first minute or so. Although his chest hair drew the attention of the Hrummeans, who had none. He made a point though of not letting his eyes stop on Juliassa except a couple of times when she was in the water almost to her shoulders.

Supper was excellent, with baked fish; *perrni*, a starchy, somewhat sweet tuber that cooked out pink-colored and mealy-textured; bread; stewed pinkfruit made a bit tart with sourdrupes; and the invariable satta.

Tomorrow morning they'd begin working on the guano, to see if they could extract a substance which, mixed with sulfur and powdered charcoal, would flash when ignited in air. Brokols had little idea of how to go about it, but presumably Amaadio did.

Brokols went to bed early, thoroughly tired.

He sat up abruptly, sure that something outside had wakened him. Though foggy again, this time it was definitely early, more nearly night than day. He pulled on clothes, including a sweater, and on an impulse buckled on the belt that held the shortsword Reeno had urged on him. Then he went out, looking about and listening. He saw or heard nothing out of the ordinary, and again on impulse walked quietly toward the beach. The fog grew thicker as he neared the water.

Near the bottom of the descending path, he heard something and recognized it immediately: two voices speaking sullsit—Juliassa and a sellsu. At eighty feet he saw them vaguely through the fog, on the beach. She'd dressed against the chill. He stopped, in order not to interrupt, but as the sellsu spoke, Juliassa looked up the path toward Brokols and waved. He started down to them, and a moment later could see a large serpent, presumably K'sthuump, lying barely awash off the beach, with her head up, listening.

By the time he got there, Juliassa and the sellsu were fully caught up in their conversation again. Brokols sat down on a rock to listen and watch, intrigued without understanding a word, simply by the sound. The light grew a little stronger. Finally the sellsu humped his way into the water and disappeared.

K'sthuump spoke. She and Juliassa had half a dozen exchanges; then K'sthuump too disappeared, and Juliassa turned to Brokols. "Good morning," she said.

"Good morning."

Juliassa grinned. "Torissia isn't going to like our being alone together."

"Why? I'd thought that Hrummeans . . . I mean my impression's been that Hrummeans—don't see anything wrong with a couple being alone. Even if they . . ." He stopped. He'd been getting into something he wasn't ready to finish.

She peered at him quizzically. "Even if they what?"

"Even if they—couple." As when he'd talked with Eltrienn, he'd used an Almaeic word which was more clinical than lascivious.

"You mean fuck?"

He felt the blush, back to his ears, and nodded.

"It's considered poor behavior for girls from noble families, though sometimes they do it. I wouldn't hesitate with you, if my father weren't the amirr. For an amirr's daughter, it would be entirely unacceptable."

"Then you haven't. . . ?"

Her smile made his loins stir, and he was glad Reeno wasn't there to read his emotions. Then she sobered. "No. Tirros has been trial enough for my parents."

Having said it, Juliassa seemed less there, her attention

elsewhere, and Brokols waited. When she stood up, he saw a shortsword at her side, too.

"We're not too many miles from Sea Cliff here," she said. "Fifteen maybe. And no one knows where Tirros went from there." She patted the sword. "I'm not supposed to slip away from Jonkka like this. He's not going to like it."

Brokols looked questioningly at her. "Surely Tirros wouldn't harm his sister?"

Her laugh was unpleasant. "You don't know what he did, do you?"

"He killed Stilfos."

"More than that. Afterward he came to Sea Cliff by night and robbed my aunt. He knew where she kept her money. Then he tried to rape me, but I jabbed my fingers in his eye and ran away screaming. That brought everyone out, but he got away in the dark. He left his horse, his boots, his belt with sword and purse—everything. Except he did take his pants with him."

Brokols stared, mouth open.

"He'd have killed me, you know. Sometimes I still dream about it, feel myself being smothered by the pillow, and I wake up gasping and sweating. I suppose I will until he's caught and executed."

Her expression was suddenly grim. "Can you use that sword?" she asked.

"Why, yes. Rather well."

"Let's see your drill."

A bit uncomfortable at her new mood, he drew his sword, took a guard position, and went through a rather lengthy practice evolution. His movements were a bit imprecise, from more than a year without practice, but all in all it went rather smoothly. Done, he watched for some sign of approval.

After a moment of consideration, she spoke again. "That wasn't bad. Tirros is no better; probably not as good. And he's a coward; he's unlikely to test you. He wouldn't come within sight of Jonkka; Jonkka would cut him into mincemeat, and he knows it."

Brokols felt aggrieved and a bit jealous at the implied comparison with the guard. "Is Jonkka always with you?" he asked. "Except when you slip away as you did this morning?"

"Not at the palace or at Zeenia's," she answered, "but away like this, yes. And at Zeenia's now, if we were there. I should go back before he wakes up. He'd scold me." Smiling she added, "With him around, Torissia really isn't necessary." She paused. "But first help me take the skiffs out of the water."

They walked over and took the stones out of them, then dragged them up the beach and turned them over. Afterward they started up the path side by side, and her hand found his, holding it. She was longlegged for her height, and not too short to match steps with at a stroll.

"Where does Jonkka sleep?" Brokols asked.

"You know the wagon parked outside our building? The shed Torissia and I sleep in? He sleeps under it! The wagon, I mean. He has some stout threads strung outside our window at night, fastened to a bell beneath the eaves. He doesn't worry about the door because we bolt it from inside. But of course, that doesn't keep me in.

"He brought a little soldier's tent, but he says he won't use it now. He says it invites an attack."

They ran into Jonkka on the path, looking for Juliassa. The guard glowered, more at Juliassa than at Brokols, but all he said was, "Namirrna, I cannot protect you if I don't know where you are."

She nodded. "I know. But Sleekit came in the night. Flopped his way all the way up from the water and called to me. I'm not surprised he didn't waken you," she added archly. "You were sleeping like a rock when I came out."

Jonkka failed to wince.

"He'd been at Sea Cliff looking for me; he'd come all the way down from the Gulf of Storms. Then yesterday a serpent recognized him and told him where I was.

"And if Tirros came after me on the beach, all I'd have to do is run into the inlet. I told Sleekit and K'sthuump about him—Sleekit hated him already—and they'd take care of him. Sleekit definitely would."

As they'd talked, they'd reached the buildings. Now they sat down together on one of the benches left by the previous inhabitants.

"Why was Sleekit looking for you?" Brokols asked.

She shrugged. "I asked him the same question. All he could say was that Hrum—'the Lord of the Sea' they call him—told him to. He says he'll stay around the inlet here until Hrum tells him what to do next."

Hrum! It seemed to Brokols a dodging of responsibility for one's own impulses and fancies, to say they came from some supernatural force or being. Perhaps the water people weren't as intelligent as they were credited with being. But then, the Hrummeans believed in him too; certainly Panni did and presumably Allbarin and Reeno, and Eltrienn.

From the kitchen came the sound of stove grates again; it took his attention off the sellsu. A new day was at hand, and there seemed little doubt that within a few more they'd have their first successful batch of gunpowder.

Forty-One

Amaadio was more than an ordinary herbalist. He was a supplier: He produced pharmaceuticals for sale to other herbalists. At Hidden Haven he did his work in a communal summer kitchen with the ends open, large windows in the two walls, a large brick stove and tiered oven. For six days, with their help, he separated guano into its constituents and tested them. Reeno gave Juliassa what Brokols thought of as the worst job. She worked in a shed, breaking up guano, putting it into a leather sack a quart at a time and beating it with a bat, then pulverizing it in a pestle to the consistency of flour.

Amaadio stirred or shook weighed portions of it into water or some other solvent, in a flask or retort or beaker, with or without some further reagent. Some of the solutions and suspensions he boiled. Some he boiled dry. From some, he decanted off the fluid and spread the wet residue to dry. From others he skimmed off a precipitate. And from the solids he obtained, he took portions and dissolved them in presumably some other solvent.

From some of the stinks, Brokols was glad the building was so well ventilated.

Brokols' main job was to pulverize sulfur; crush, grind, and pulverize charcoal; and mix small, carefully weighed amounts of them thoroughly with various powders that Amaadio gave him, then put the mixture in small bowls. Before he mixed anything though, Amaadio examined the constituents, settling for nothing but the finest flour-like texture, and mixing had to be thorough beyond what Brokols considered all reason.

Reeno's job was to weigh guano samples, solvents, and reagents, and keep records of everything. No solid from any of Amaadio's brews escaped labeling and recording. And as Amaadio separated one derivative and subderivative after another, Reeno's lists grew long. Brokols came to realize why the herbalist had brought so many bowls and built so many shelves.

The work was neither hard nor intense, simply unrelenting. Both Brokols and Juliassa prepared the raw materials in quantities well in advance of Amaadio's needs, on the assumption that they'd need more when his tests were done. The first day found one ingredient of guano that flashed nicely when, mixed with sulfur and pulverized charcoal, it was ignited in air. The second day produced another, plus a third derived from the first. The next morning produced a fourth that flashed, derived from the third. By that day's end, Amaadio said he'd gotten all there were to get, but threw none of them away yet.

Brokols had no idea whether any of the derivatives was saltpeter or not, nor of course did Amaadio. If none of them were, hopefully one of them would do as a substitute.

Each evening Juliassa went to the beach and talked with Sleekit and K'sthuump, soon after sunset.

The fourth day they tested each of the candidate ingredients in various proportions with sulfur and charcoal for maximum vehemence of flash, on the assumption that this equated with explosive power. And again threw nothing away. Brokols, remembering his courses in Almaeic history, tried burning them damp; one flashed, the others didn't. From that point they gave their attention to the one that flashed damp, and rightly or wrongly, Brokols named it saltpeter. The fifth day was given to making a quantity of it.

On the sixth afternoon they settled tentatively on a mixture of twelve parts "saltpeter," three parts charcoal, and two of sulfur. The recipe was a grave disappointment to Brokols; he'd hoped that saltpeter would prove to be necessary in only small quantities. This one required that they process guano in quantity, a nuisance. As far as that was concerned, he didn't even know whether large quantities were available.

Among Amaadio's goods was a basket of small ceramic pots with narrow mouths. After supper, while Juliassa went to let the serpents know that the noise was no threat to them, Amaadio filled three of them with powders: one with the mixture that had flashed best, one that contained only two parts saltpeter (a wild hope), and one that contained seven. After sealing them with a fiber wick moistened with lamp oil, they lit them one at a time behind a large rock. The grenade with the low saltpeter mixture didn't even blow the wadding out. The one with the 12:3:2 mixture exploded most violently.

That night Brokols lay on his pallet staring through the darkness at the crossbeams. They'd occupied their minds for more than a week with the production of gunpowder. Now they'd made it, and presumably the manufacture of grenades would be no problem. Amaadio was familiar with what presumably were fulminates, and had three of them in mind to test for fuse caps. Time fuses seemed unfeasible; they had to get into production too soon. They'd have to settle for impact grenades, and hope that they came up with a fuse which wasn't too touchy. Amaadio felt that the putative silver fulminate—silver something anyway—would serve.

But of what avail were grenades to them, really? They could kill and demoralize Gorballis with them. It was even conceivable that with them they could save Hrumma from Gorrbian conquest. But the real threat wasn't Gorrbian. When the imperial army controlled Djez Gorrbul, grenades wouldn't help, and the belief that some god would intervene was wishful thinking of the worst sort.

He turned onto his side, jaw clamped. The Hrummeans were right about one thing though. It was better to tough it out and fight with what you had, than to lie down and wait.

Forty-Two

After breakfast the next morning, Reeno sent Juliassa riding off to Theedalit, with Torissia and Jonkka of course, carrying a request for a squad of soldiers to come to Hidden Haven the next day. Then Reeno, Amaadio, and Brokols sat down together, reviewing and redrawing their flowcharts and lists for producing grenades in quantity, including tests of impact fuses and of ceramics and fragmentation designs.

Finally they apportioned the list of tasks among themselves.

The morning was gone before they knew it, and Juliassa was back by midafternoon. The soldiers would leave Theedalit next morning, to arrive by midday.

The afternoon was spent preparing to leave, repacking Amaadio's laboratory gear and most of their personal effects. In the time that remained, they went over the flowcharts and lists again, searching for oversights or anything that might need changing. Then they all went swimming before supper.

After supper, Brokols and Juliassa walked back to the beach with Jonkka and Torissia. Sleekit was there, and K'sthuump, and Juliassa talked with them again, but only briefly. Brokols wondered what she'd told them that sent them off early, but he didn't ask. He had other things on his mind.

Juliassa turned to her bodyguard. "Jonkka," she said, "Elver and I are going up the beach a little way, to talk privately. You can watch us from here."

Jonkka nodded. "Yes, namirrna, as long as it's light enough that I can see you."

She turned and fixed her aunt with her eyes. "Torissia, you stay here too."

"But Juliassa . . ."

"You can watch us from here. What harm do you think it can do to talk?"

She didn't wait for a reply, but took Brokols' arm and led him up the beach about two hundred feet. There they sat down on one of the overturned skiffs, facing west and a sunset banded rose, dusty gold, and deep purple. "Something's troubling you," she said. Her voice had lost the peremptory tone she'd used on Torissia, had become concerned. "I hope you'll tell me what it is."

"Namirrna, I'd rather not. It—you might find it discouraging. And I'd rather not depress you."

Taking his left hand between hers, she looked at him. "Maybe I can help," she said, and smiled. "Especially if you call me Juliassa instead of namirrna."

He returned her gaze for a moment, then shrugged. "We can make grenades now," he said, "but I don't see how they can save Hrumma. I don't see how anything can." He stopped, to see what effect his words had had on her. Her expression was sober but not disquieted, so he went on, telling her of his thoughts the night before.

"It's more than that though," he added. "I have no country. In Almeon they'd think of me as a traitor, and they'd be right. I'm not sure just how it came about, but that's what I've become. I suppose because, from here, I could see more clearly how my people live. The government and—and the beliefs and oppressions . . . in my heart I'm no longer an Almite, and better to be a traitor to my country than to myself. Perhaps I never truly was an Almite.

"I'm not a Hrummean either, of course, but I think I could come to be one. I really do."

Once more he paused. "And when the emperor takes over Hrumma," he said slowly, "my life won't be worth a copper."

She still held his hand; now she squeezed it. "I can help," she said, then got up. "But first, help me with the boat."

"The boat?"

"Pull it into the water. I'll bring both paddles. We can go to another beach. Jonkka's getting ready to call us in or come to us, and we still have a lot to talk about."

He stared at her, his stomach knotted now. Her gaze was steady. "Please," she said. "And when you move, you must be fast."

Bending, he turned the boat over, then grabbed its bow

and pulled it quickly, strongly into knee-deep water, feeling it float, handling it past him. She was there with the paddles and clambered in, to move crouching to the bow as he scrambled over the stern. Jonkka would be running up the beach now, Brokols thought, must be almost there, ready to plunge in after them. He didn't take time to look. Juliassa was already digging with her paddle as he snatched the other from the bottom. The water shoaled off sharply, and they moved quickly out of reach.

A hundred feet out, Brokols, panting, turned and looked back, feeling unpleasantly like an adolescent prankster. Jonkka and Torissia had run to the other boat and found no paddle; they were standing there watching the fugitives.

"Jonkka," Juliassa called softly, "we'll be all right. Sleekit and K'sthuump will protect us if there's any need. And Elver has his shortsword."

Jonkka didn't call anything back, nor did Torissia. Juliassa began to paddle again, slowly, and Brokols followed, feeling guilty, as if they'd committed a betrayal on her bodyguard if not her chaperone. He also felt water on his knees; its seams may have swelled more or less shut, but the skiff was hardly watertight.

"Do you feel bad about running away from them?" Juliassa asked.

"It seems—treacherous. For me."

"I understand. But to me— A namirrna has more restrictions on her than almost anyone. I learned a long time ago to take things in my own hands." They continued to paddle slowly toward the opening to the sea. "That's how I got to come and help you make gunpowder." She used the Almaeic word for gunpowder, the only one available.

"What do you mean, that's how you got to help?"

She continued paddling, talking without looking back. "In Hrumma, there are arbiters for family disputes. It's somewhat embarrassing for a family to turn to one; they're a last resort. When I told my father I wanted to come out here to work for Reeno and you, he said no. Then I made promises of how hard I'd work, and what I'd do when I got home in return for permission, and he still said no. So—I took him to an arbiter."

Brokols stared at her back, amazed at her tenacity of purpose and almost aghast at her audacity.

"If the arbiter found against me," she went on, "I'd have

been in real trouble. He'd have assigned me heavy amends; I'd probably have spent the rest of the summer on my knees, scrubbing floors at the Fortress.

"But he didn't. He questioned us, and finally ruled that I could, that father's denial had been arbitrary and without a reasonable basis. I have both a chaperone and a bodyguard. You and Reeno are both nobles, and Reeno has an outstanding record in government service. And your decency is better known than almost anyone's in Hrumma, if you're as open to adepts as father admitted."

Her rundown didn't make Brokols feel much better. He wondered what kind of decency report he'd get after this.

"The conditions were that I'd have to get a good work report from Reeno," she continued. "And that if I didn't, I'd have to work double shifts in the palace kitchen every day for ten weeks, and lose all rights to arbitration until my majority."

She smiled back over her shoulder. "They don't want people turning to an arbiter for everything that comes up. They make it risky."

Brokols was impressed. "And how long is it till your majority?"

"Until I'm eighteen or married, whichever comes first. But I knew I'd get a good work report."

He said nothing more then, and she didn't either. They were passing through the opening into the sea. The great jutting rock outside it protected them from the seas even here, but he could hear the surf both to left and right, and wondered where this wild namirrna had it in mind to go. The water in the skiff wasn't more than an inch or so deep, but the craft didn't seem fit for rough treatment.

"Steer left," she said, "and we'll beach it."

He did, and they pulled it farther up from the water than seemed necessary to him, then turned it over between two big rocks. Turning, he looked at the sky. All but the last faint wash of twilight had left the western horizon. Overhead, stars shone sharp and distant against deep black, the brightest of them by far no star at all, but Little Firtollio, the lesser moon, a tiny demidisk of silver-white.

Somewhere out there his ancestors had been born. And hers, in a manner of speaking. It made no difference though. This was the world they'd been born on, grown up on.

She took his hand again and they sat down crosslegged on the sand. "You talked about when the emperor conquers

Hrumma. Suppose he does. What could you do? Is there any place you could go then?"

He hadn't thought of that. "Well . . . I couldn't pretend to be Hrummean. I don't sound Hrummean, and except for my size I don't look Hrummean."

"So what else could you do?"

"I—could die fighting. That will probably happen before the war is over."

"All right. What else could you do?"

"Huh! Well, I suppose I could go to the east coast and try taking a small boat to the barbarian lands. And see if I could learn to be a barbarian."

"And take me with you," she said. "What else could you do?"

"That's about all I can think of."

They sat without saying anything more for half a minute. Then Juliassa got up, still holding his hand so that he got up too. "I want to show you something," she said. "It's just over here a little way."

They walked south on the beach some fifty yards, then she led him back through an old rockfall. And there, opening toward the ocean, was a wide cave mouth. Its front had been partly walled with loose stones, leaving a wide door, and they went to it. Looking in, he could see little except that it wasn't very deep.

"I came out in a skiff by myself, yesterday morning," Juliassa said, "and found it. It looks like a place lovers might have built. And I came again last night after everyone had gone to bed. I needed to be alone."

No wonder, he thought, *that Jonkka could look so exasperated sometimes. Especially with Tirros running loose.*

She took both of Brokols' arms with her hands and stood close in front of him. "I'm going to marry you, you know," she said, then leaned against him and kissed him on the mouth. He felt her firm breasts pressing his chest, and suddenly it was difficult to breathe. She pulled his arms around her waist, looked into his eyes and kissed him again.

Then she was unbuckling his sword belt, unbuttoning his shirt, and he found his own treacherous hands beginning to undress her. When they were naked, she stepped back and they looked at each other in the starlight.

"I love you, Elver," she said simply, and he wondered if it was true or if she only thought it was.

She led him into the cave, to a pile of beach grass there, with a robe thrown over it. The grass was fresh; it smelled like new hay, not at all like some that had lain there for three years. And the robe, he was sure, was hers. She'd set it all up, set *him* up, he realized. She was sixteen, and she'd set him up.

Her hands began to caress him, and his own followed her lead. He was glad to have been set up. Honestly earnestly glad.

He wasn't too engrossed to feel a moment's gratitude to Lerrlia, either. And to Tirros! Except for them, and the brief intensive training they'd provided, he'd give Juliassa little pleasure for her efforts, little return on her love this night, if love it truly was.

Forty-Three

Great Liilia was nearly full, and about midnight shone into the cave, wakening them. Considerably later they got back to the inlet's beach where the other skiff lay. The moonlight showed Jonkka asleep there, a brawny forearm shielding his eyes from the moon. Their skiff scraped the sand and Jonkka rolled instantly and silently to his feet, his sword somehow in his hand. It startled Brokols without frightening him, and he made a mental note to be careful if he ever had to waken the man.

They said nothing to Jonkka nor he to them. The man waited stolidly while they drew the skiff up beside the other, and Brokols' covert glance showed no sign of anger or even sullenness on the bodyguard's face. They walked back to the hamlet together without a word and went separately to bed. Their work here was done. They could sleep late if they wanted to.

Late that morning a squad of mounted infantry arrived to watch the hamlet for them while they were gone. Nothing was to be disturbed and the soldiers were to stay out of the workshop.

Frimattos and Torissia had already led the kaabors down from pasture and they'd been variously saddled or harnessed. Now they hitched the teams to the wagons they were taking back with them, and on spring seats or in the saddle, rode up the draw to the road at the top.

The day's shower had come early, sparing them and wetting the soldiers instead. The weather was typically humid but less hot than some, and a breeze kept it pleasant. Brokols and Juliassa rode a bit ahead of the others, Brokols remembering the night and wondering what Juliassa was thinking about. He'd worried, as they'd paddled back, that there might be an irreparable breach between Juliassa on the one hand and Jonkka and Torissia on the other. But as far as he could see this morning, the only effect was that Torissia avoided her niece's eyes.

"I'm relieved," he murmured to Juliassa, "that Jonkka isn't mad at you. Or Torissia either."

Juliassa giggled. "She can't be. She woke up when I came in last night and asked if it was me. I told her yes, and she said 'oh,' as if she was disappointed.

"So I put one and one together, her disappointment and the fact that Jonkka wasn't angry at us, and questioned her. Finally she confessed. After we got away, they'd stood on the beach side by side, watching us paddle down the inlet, and she was thinking about what we were probably going to do. Then she realized they were holding hands. Next, Jonkka's arm was around her shoulders and her arm was around his waist. Before long they were undressed." Juliassa giggled. "And after that. . . . She says she's in love with him.

"Actually I'm surprised. Mama's family—Torissia's—are nobles, and have been for a long time, even though they're a minor family. And Jonkka never seemed the type to seduce a noblewoman." Juliassa dimpled. "Especially on duty!"

"Maybe he *was* doing his duty," Brokols said. "Although enjoying it, I'm sure."

She looked questioningly at him.

"Maybe he was still protecting you." He chuckled. "I don't suppose Torissia will tell on us now, will she?"

Juliassa's eyes widened, then she laughed. "Never. Nor I on her."

Brokols rode along thoughtfully. "Will she feel bad that they can't marry?"

She looked surprised. "Oh, they can marry."

"They can? But—but wouldn't she lose her nobility then? Be outcast from her family?"

"Oh no. She'd lose her inheritance, and their children would be commoners. What would probably happen though is that her family, after they'd looked into his record and gotten to know him,. would adopt Jonkka as an honor-nephew. With what's called untenured adoption; they could reject him later for cause. If he abused her, for example. That way any children they had would be noble and she'd still have her inheritance.

"And quite probably they'd appoint him in some supervisory capacity on their estate or in their stone quarry."

Brokols nudged his kaabor closer to hers, reached and took her hand.

"How do I go about marrying you?" he asked.

She smiled and once more his heart melted. "First you ask me. Then, together, we ask my father. After that . . ." Her face turned from sweetly girlish to determined. "After that—we'll see whether any more will be necessary.

"This evening you'll have supper with us; I'll arrange it with my mother. We can ask them then."

Brokols wasn't as nervous at the prospect as he might have expected. Not after last night. He'd fight the amirr for her if he had to. Although clearly, Juliassa was the fighter.

Forty-Four

The two of them, Brokols and Reeno, walked through the Fortress's north gate into the broad, tree-ringed, flagstoned courtyard, scattering a flock of busy varrpio feeding on seedbursts from the linntis trees. There seemed to be more activity in the Fortress than when they'd seen it last. Uniformed men walked swiftly or trotted, as if carrying messages. Together they went up outside stairs and down a corridor to the amirrial waiting room, where they sat for a time until the amirr could see them.

Allbarin was with him.

"We have made grenades, Your Eminence," Brokols said, "and we're preparing to produce them in large quantities."

"Good. Good." The amirr's voice showed no enthusiasm. It was simply matter-of-fact. "I expected you would. You've done well."

"The herbalist, Amaadio Akrosstos, was instrumental, sir. Without his professional skills, or those of someone comparable, it's doubtful we'd have succeeded."

"Without your knowledge of the possibilities," the amirr countered, "it's certain we wouldn't have."

"Yes, sir." Brokols stood without saying anything for a moment. The amirr waited. "Sir, I need to point out that while grenades may have an important influence in Hrummean successes against Djez Gorrbul, there'll remain the Almaeic army and fleet. And grenades are not likely to make much difference against them."

The amirr nodded. "I understand. We will do what we can. All we can. Grenades will help." The hazel eyes examined

Brokols. "I'd think you'd find satisfaction in our predicament. You are Almaeic, after all."

Brokols' mouth twisted, his lips tight. "Satisfaction? Almeon is not a happy nation, Your Eminence. I wonder if it ever has been. The more I see of Hrumma, the less happy I am at the prospect of its being ruled by the emperor. Or of my return to Almeon. As far as that's concerned, considering the opinion Lord Kryger seems to have of me, I could very well end up executed as a traitor."

He paused. "If I have been of service, as you say, I'd like to ask a favor of Your Eminence. I'd like to become a citizen of Hrumma."

The amirr's brows arched. "A citizen of Hrumma? We have a precedent and procedure for that. An occasional Djezian refugee requests citizenship. You need to present a written petition, with four sponsors, to a magistrate. Who'll question you, and probably one or more of your sponsors. Then he'll decide yes or no, or possibly question others."

The amirr looked curiously at Brokols. "Who might you ask to sponsor you?"

"I'll ask Reeno—and Panni Vempravvo. And your daughter. I'd ask Eltrienn Cadriio, but he's gone; perhaps Arnello Bostelli would agree to be the fourth."

"You know Panni?"

"Not as well as he knows me. He . . ." It occurred to Brokols how remarkable, how seemingly inexplicable it was that Panni had come to him. "He took an interest in me, and we talked at some length."

Allbarin broke in then. "You need not ask Bostelli. I will sponsor you. I can help you write the petition in my office when we've finished here. This is His Eminence's last audience for today, unless something or someone else unforeseen has come up."

Brokols looked surprised, but not as surprised as the amirr. "Thank you, Allbarin," he said. "If I have two adepts, a sage, and the namirrna as sponsors, I'd rather expect a favorable decision." He looked at Venreeno. "Reeno, will you agree to sponsor me?"

Venreeno nodded. "Without hesitation, Elver."

Brokols turned back to the amirr. "Then with your leave, Your Eminence, I'll write my petition and go to find Panni. Your daughter plans to have me invited to supper at the palace. I'll ask her then."

He left the room with Allbarin, leaving Venreeno with the amirr. "Reeno," Leonessto said, "he said two adepts and a sage. Does he. . . ?"

"Yes, sir. The subject came up in a group conversation around a fire on the beach, and he suddenly realized what had been happening."

"Umm. How did he respond? Well enough, I take it."

"Quite well. It shook him, as you'd expect, but he adjusted without real difficulty. He is, Your Eminence, as good a man, a person, as Cadriio said, and more than that, he is stronger and more capable than he imagines."

"Well good! And was Juliassa as useful as she should have been?"

"Yes, sir. I gave her some of the dirtiest, hardest, most unpleasant tasks. She did them conscientiously, rapidly and well, with minimal supervision. It's my impression, Your Eminence, that your daughter is very capable and does what she says she'll do."

Leonessto Hanorissio grunted. "Indeed. Whether it meets with my approval or not."

There were six of them at supper: the amirr and naamir, Juliassa and Torissia, Brokols and Reeno. It had been a miniature feast, and Brokols, by nature a moderate eater, felt a bit stuffed. The table had been set on a veranda, where they could watch the sunset afterward, and he leaned back in his chair, listening to two flute-birds in a sing-off from opposite ends of the garden.

For a fee, that afternoon, a youth had led him to Panni's cave on saddle kaabors that Brokols had hired. The sage had signed his petition, and he'd gotten Juliassa's signature before supper. He'd told the amirr of it while they ate; the amirr had seemed pleased.

Now, Brokols decided, it was time to bring up his and Juliassa's wish to marry. She'd intended to do the asking, but Brokols had said it was his place to, and she'd assented.

"Your Eminence?" There was significance in the way Brokols said it, and the amirr put down his wine glass.

"Yes?"

"Your Eminence, your daughter and I would like to marry."

The naamir looked worried at this, her eyes moving quickly to her husband, then to her daughter. Leonessto Hanorissio frowned only slightly, pursing his wide strong mouth. "Do you feel you know one another well enough?" he asked.

"We've talked at length," Juliassa broke in. "Beginning as early as when we met at Sea Cliff. And we've worked together."

The amirr didn't look at her, keeping his eyes on Brokols.

"I'm satisfied that we do, Your Eminence," Brokols answered. "I'm also quite satisfied that I love her, and that she loves me."

"She is a noblewoman. Can you protect her?"

Brokols was taken aback at the question. It hadn't occurred to him that that would be a criterion. Perhaps it was a matter more of tradition than need. "Yes, sir," he said. "I can."

"I've had him demonstrate his sword drill for me, father. He was quite skilled."

The amirr looked at her, nodded acknowledgement, then turned his chair to face an area of open grass and gestured at it. "Show me," he said.

Brokols got up from the table and put his hand on the hilt of his shortsword. "Would Your Eminence prefer that I use a saber? It's the weapon with which I am most familiar."

"The shortsword," Leonessto answered. "It's what a man is most likely to be carrying, except in war."

Brokols nodded and stepped out onto the grass, where he drew his blade and took the guard position. Then he began his drill, thrusting, parrying, riposting, feet nimble, body dodging imaginary stabs and strokes but always balanced. And it seemed to Brokols that he'd never done it as well before. When he'd finished, he turned and bowed to his audience, forehead moist, trying not to pant visibly.

"Not bad," said the amirr. "Quite good in fact. Particularly for someone who's just eaten a large meal." He waved Brokols back to his chair, and when the Almite was seated asked his next question. "How do you intend to support her? We accept your nobility, but you have no property, and so far as I know, no profession beyond ambassador."

The question took Brokols unprepared; he'd given it no thought. In Almeon he'd been a bureaucrat, and the son of a very wealthy family. "Currently I'm employed by yourself in the development and manufacture of weapons," he answered slowly, "and Hrumma faces serious and certain war. Also, I've served in the emperor's cavalry as an officer. So I suppose the army is the most appropriate place for me."

The amirr had withdrawn his gaze. The others sat waiting.

At last he looked across at his daughter. "I suppose you're quite set on this," he said.

Brokols had never seen her avert her eyes before. Now she looked down at the table cloth in front of her, no doubt the way a noble maiden of Almeon was supposed to under the circumstances. "Yes, father, I am. *Quite* set on it."

"Umm. I suppose . . . I'm quite unprepared for this, you know. You're barely old enough."

Her eyes remained downcast. "I'm nearing seventeen, father." She glanced up then, smiling. "I know you think of me as your little girl, but I've been marriageable for more than half a year."

"True. But usually these things follow a longer acquaintance than yours. It allows a father time to get used to the idea." He paused. "Well," he said, then turned to his wife questioningly. Her nod was barely perceptible, and he turned to Brokols again. "When your petition for citizenship has been approved, I'll write my approval of the marriage. You then take it to a magistrate, who'll question you both. Unless he finds something clearly objectionable, he'll approve it. The procedure is not intended to discourage or hinder marriages, but simply to avoid the more obvious mistakes.

"Then—hmm. You're not familiar with procedures here. You can be wed in four weeks from that time, assuming of course that the magistrate doesn't veto the request. As the groom, you won't have nearly the pre-marital preparations that . . ." He paused, frowning. "I suppose your lore of being a husband in Almeon differs from ours in some respects. If you're to be my daughter's husband . . ." He turned to Venreeno, who'd said little all evening. "Be his tutor please, Reeno. Lord Brokols has no uncle here."

"Of course, Your Eminence."

The amirr returned his attention to Brokols. "Because she's a maiden, you'll be able to see Juliassa only once a week, at supper here, except for a few formal requirements having to do with your engagement." He looked at Juliassa. "And you'll have to forego assisting them in their work, unless there's something you can do that requires no contact with Elver and can be fitted around the social requirements of a bride-to-be."

"Father—"

He stopped. "Yes?"

"Those are not law. They're tradition. And we're . . ."

He interrupted. "Young lady, tradition gives us values, teaches us discipline. It's as important as law."

She met his eyes, carefully avoiding defiance. "I've read my history, father," she said quietly. "In some wars, at least in the last war, in '23, noblewomen did work they'd never done before except perhaps in other wars. And haven't done since. The namirrna, Delorra Sabontinna, drove supply wagons to Kammenak, like a man. Where her fiance was fighting. And when he was wounded . . ."

"Leonessto." It was the naamir who spoke. "Perhaps she could help them and then come home at night, or some other arrangement could be made. It would serve as an example to the country."

He'd stared in some surprise at his wife's interruption; now he frowned thoughtfully. "Yes. Well. Perhaps." His gaze moved back to Juliassa. "Your mother and I will give it some thought, see what we come up with."

She averted her eyes again. "Thank you father."

"Elver," he said, "Reeno will take you to the magistrate in the morning, to see about your citizenship. Then we'll see about a formal betrothal, and Reeno can talk to you about being a Hrummean husband, though it may be that you learn much the same lore in Almeon."

He got up. "Now if you two young lovers will say good night to each other, I'll have a carriage take Elver and Reeno home."

Juliassa went to her father and kissed his cheek, saying nothing. She was doing an excellent job of being the well-bred namirrna this evening.

When Elver kissed Juliassa goodnight in the garden, Torissia looked the other way.

The amirr and naamir retired to their private sitting room, where wide doors stood open onto their balcony. He'd called for brandy, and when it arrived, he sent the servant away.

"I was surprised," he told his wife, "that you took Juliassa's part in our discussion."

She smiled quietly and looked him in the eye. "I believe her point was valid. And I remembered how we tricked my parents and met privately in the vacant herdgirls' hut during our engagement. More than once."

He grinned ruefully. "But we'd already made love. To be apart for four weeks after that seemed intolerable."

"Perhaps they've made love."

He grunted. "Not likely. They'd have had to escape more than Torissia. Jonkka was guarding her, and he takes his duties seriously."

"Love finds a way. Ours did."

He smiled fondly. "So it did. Hmm. We *were* young once. I'd forgotten." He got up and reached for her hand. "It's getting dark. Why don't we sit on the balcony awhile and watch the last of the sunset."

"So," Brokols said, "what is this education for Hrummean husbands-to-be?"

"It varies with the experience of the youth. Or man." Venreeno sipped his watered wine, then looked at the Almite. "If you'll excuse me for mentioning it—it's very relevant here—I believe you were drugged by the mirj and spent a night in sexual relations with an apparently very experienced young woman named Lerrlia. That takes care of part of it."

Brokols looked hard at him. "You're not telling me you put a young man with an experienced woman to. . . ?"

Venreeno laughed aloud. "No no! Oh, some uncles do, I know. If the young man is seriously bashful, or unnaturally introverted or selfish. But most aren't, and chances are they've already had some experience without any uncle. Perhaps at Festival. And perhaps with their fiancee, as I suspect you did one night on the beach." Venreeno's calm gaze was focused on Brokols, who reddened.

"Just a moment," Brokols said. "What are your qualifications? You're not married. Are you?"

Venreeno shook his head. "Not at present. I have been, but my wife died as yours did, in childbirth. Or soon after, actually. And I hope to be married again: I've talked of it with a certain lady with whom I share mutual respect and admiration.

"And no," he went on, "uncles who take a bashful youth to an experienced woman don't do it to give the lad pleasure. The woman, often the widow of a happy marriage, will teach him the things that pleasure her, and discuss with him how such things are for her and for other women.

"Of course, I don't have to point out to you that sex, important as it is, is only one aspect of marriage. Or that for a good marriage, in bed, the kitchen, the field—in all things—more than enthusiasm is needed, although that can help. And certainly there's far more than simply the pleasure of the groom to be considered. There are two sides to pleasure—to all of marriage—with wisdoms and techniques for both sides."

"And Juliassa . . ." Brokols said a little worriedly. "Is someone. . . ?"

Venreeno smiled. "Someone. I got the mental impression that it would be her Aunt Zeenia. I believe you know her.

"A good uncle, or a good aunt, will try to see that the soon-to-be-wed knows these things. The principles of being a good, thoughtful, and pleasurable spouse. And that the spouse-to-be feels reasonably confident about his or her ability.

"Of course, a lot that you need to know is personal—things you learn from each other after you're married. People differ one from another. But with your permission, I'll tell you the basics somewhat as they were told to me, colored of course by my own experience and observations. . . ."

Venreeno talked and questioned and listened through most of the evening. When finally Elver Brokols got to bed, his head was buzzing.

FORTY-FIVE

Almost everyone who saw his gaunt, robed figure knew who he was. And did a doubletake. One just did not see an elder sage walking alone in the city; invariably some of their disciples were with them, certainly when there was something to be carried. But Panni Vempravvo had told his people he must go alone this time, and that he might be back before winter.

Though somewhat bulky, the parcel Panni carried wasn't heavy. It consisted of a spare robe wrapped around a few belongings—eating bowl, toothbrush, prayer mat, and three or four rags for whatever uses. He carried it over his shoulder, tied to the end of a three-foot-long stick.

No one offered to carry it for him, or rather, no adult did, though several felt an urge to and somehow held back. Only a boy about eleven actually offered, an offer that was accepted. Accompanied by half a dozen playmates, he carried it until Panni stopped, straight-faced but twinkly-eyed, put out a hand and received the bundle back. Then the sage bowed deeply to the boy and turned up a narrow, climbing sidestreet. The children turned back toward the small square where they'd been playing.

Only a block farther, Panni came to the building whose penthouse was occupied by Tassi Vermaatio. His skinny legs climbed the many steps slowly but without pause, and he reached the top with no sign of labor, not even sweat. Crossing the roof to the penthouse, he entered and stopped. There were eight men there besides Tassi. Three still sat on a bench, eating supper; another was washing his bowl. Panni's eyes went to Master Dazzlik, the head of Tassi's household, who got up from his prayer mat and bowed. Panni bowed back, put down his bundle, and spoke courteously.

"I would like to stay here, on the roof of your penthouse, and meditate." There was more, unspoken, not even articulated mentally.

Dazzlik's answer was partly voiced, partly silent. (Sense of: We have been waiting for you.) "We are happy that you have come." (Sense of: Your needs will be seen to.) He turned to a youthful disciple and spoke mildly. "Felsettos, bring supper to the Lamp of Hrum. Then obtain a ladder by which he can mount to the roof."

That said, the master bowed again and lowered himself to his prayer mat, paying no more attention to the visiting sage. Folding his long, skinny legs, Panni too sat down, opened his bundle and took forth his bowl. The young disciple went to a sack hanging on the wall and took out a leafy green head of sallto as large as his two fists. He presented it to Panni with a bow, took the sage's bowl and brought it back full of a vegetable stew with bits of meat. Then he hurried from the room. Panni began with the sallto, eating slowly so that it lasted till Felsettos returned, sweaty and breathing hard, to bow again.

"The ladder is outside the door," he said. "Orros Vencarmos, who has the honor of owning this building, says the ladder is yours as long as you wish to keep it."

The sage's eyes met Felsettos', and without speaking he grinned. Picking the morsels from the stew one by one, he ate them slowly, drank the broth, licked his fingers and wiped them on a rag, unfolded his legs, got easily up, and washed his bowl in the pan provided. Then he gathered his bundle loosely in one hand, went outside and climbed the ladder to the roof of the penthouse. Laying out his prayer mat, he sat down on it, facing south across the city, the lowering sun brightening his right profile, and almost at once entered a trance.

Elver Brokols no longer fooled himself that he would, or could, play both sides of the game. So it felt peculiar to him to sit again at his wireless; peculiar and somehow dangerous. But it also seemed necessary to continue the pretense with Kryger. And to otherwise mislead, perhaps confuse, and just possibly learn something.

Almost he wished Kryger's sounder would remain silent, but after a moment his signal was acknowledged. Looking at the message he'd drafted, Brokols began to send:

"Have returned to Theedalit from week with army unit. Stop. Hrummean discipline and morale excellent. Stop. Have had crossbow constructed and interested army in it. Stop."

The two statements out of three were deliberate lies. He had, of course, not been with the army. Also the expert Hrummean longbowmen had greater range and much faster rate of fire than crossbows could provide, and their accuracy was excellent. But he was willing to bet that discipline and morale were strong indeed.

"Government has accepted that Djez Gorrbul is the threat. Stop. Almeon too far away. Stop. Public belief increasingly follows government position. Stop. Brokols end."

After a few seconds the sounder began to rattle.

MESSAGE RECEIVED STOP CONTINUE EFFORTS STOP
KRYGER END COMPLETED

The sounder stilled, and Brokols frowned at Kryger's reply. It told him nothing new, nothing of value. "Kryger end. Completed." No questions, no probing—the apparency of disinterest. Perhaps Kryger had written him off as too uncertain a quantity to waste attention on.

I'll keep checking in from time to time though, Brokols told himself. It was desirable that Kryger not speculate too much on what he might be doing here in Hrumma, and it seemed to Brokols that such speculation was more likely if he stopped reporting entirely.

It was not long after daylight, and his disciples were eating their morning porridge—when Tassi Vermaatio got up! It took all of them by surprise except the two masters. When he stood, the ancient skinny calves, the scrawny arms, looked somehow even more fragile than usual.

It was not the customary time of the week for him to stand up. Just two days earlier he'd relieved himself, sipped satta and eaten a crust.

He looked around interestedly, his gaze absorbing who was there, and he bobbed his head, acknowledging their presence. Then he went to the door and outside. Two of the younger disciples hurried after him without orders from the masters, who continued eating unconcernedly. To their astonishment and concern, the old man stepped to the ladder and climbed slowly to the flat roof.

Panni's head turned toward him, eyes focusing, and he grinned. Tassi grinned toothlessly back, and without a mat, sat down a few feet away, legs folded, back straight. Both sages' eyes slipped out of focus then, and they returned to their trances.

FORTY-SIX

For a very long time, ships in the waters around Hrumma and the Djezes had been single-masted square-sail craft, undecked, that used oars when the winds were contrary. Shipping had always been much more important to the Hrummeans than to the Djezians, and eventually, several millenia before the first Almaeic expedition, a Hrummean invented the keel, making taller masts practical. Not long after that, someone else had reinvented the fore-and-aft rig and built the first sloop on the continent. Its greater agility in coast-wise shipping had rather quickly made it the standard, and oars soon disappeared from merchantmen. Over the last millenium and a half, the Hrummeans had built a few larger ships for the long runs of the Djezian trade, requiring a second mast, thus reinventing the schooner. But their domestic shipping almost never called for so large a ship. Even for trade with the Djezes, sloops were usually adequate, as well as cheaper to build and operate.

That of course was on the west coast. The Djezes didn't have an east coast.

When the treaty with the Kinnli Innjakot established a regular Hrummean lumber and charcoal trade from Agate Bay (and later iron trade from Iron Island), schooners became important out of Hrummean ports on the east coast. And the two largest vessels out of Gardozzi Bay were built as topsail schooners, increasing both size and speed.

The boat that Eltrienn and Vessto rode was a schooner, carrying considerably more passengers than crew aboard.

Eltrienn and Vessto had left Theedalit on kaaborback with

a second centurion, Danntis Deltibbio, and as they rode, Eltriенn had drilled the other two on the basics of the barbarian language. When they left Gardozzi Bay, the once deputy-factor, Ressteto Istroovio, had added his greater fluency to the language lessons. Both Eltrienn and Ressteto were surprised at how rapidly Vessto learned; an adept gets the images and concepts along with the words.

And Eltrienn especially was surprised at other things about Vessto. He'd changed dramatically overnight, that last night at Theedalit.

The schooner arrived in Agate Bay at night, just ahead of a following squall, and rode the hook in the lee of the raw stone ridge that was the south point. Dawn broke to skies freshly clear except for scattered tatters of cloud, a few first and second-magnitude stars, a light cool offshore breeze, and a long swell that rolled the schooner slowly, her mast a silent metronome sweeping a considerable arc. Some of her passengers manned the capstan, raising the anchor, and she tacked her slow way up the bay, sunrise catching her within sight of the Agate River.

The wharf was still there, a half-mile upstream, and the sawmill with its undershot waterwheel, the kilns for brick and tile, the broader kilns for charcoal. They could see them as they approached the river. But the captain anchored outside its mouth, and the Cadriio brothers, with Ressteto Istroovio, rowed themselves to shore in a small boat.

No one was there. Lumber still lay piled on the wharf, seasoning beyond dryness in the sun. A quick inspection showed that the cabins hadn't been occupied or despoiled—a hopeful sign—but the broad blood stain in the old factor's office clouded the morning for Eltrienn, and left a tight-lipped cast on Ressteto's face. Vessto was not affected emotionally, but he could feel Ressteto's emotion, and kept his face somber in respect for the others.

They started on foot up the river, the four of them, past decks of logs still piled on skids, wood borers chewing audibly inside them, a slight dry, grinding sound. Beyond the millsite, the wagon road became a broad footpath, with here and there the marks of split hooves in the dirt. A heavy-haunched kaabor, a draft animal, ventured down to drink, saw the Hrummeans coming, and wheeling, loped noisily into the thicket of a second-growth forest. *Encouraging,* Ressteto thought. *The Innjakot haven't butchered them. If things work out, we can bait them up with grain and catch them—use them for logging again.*

The next life they saw, aside from flitting birds, was a party of warriors coming toward them.

"Ressteto!" one of them called as they approached. "We did not know if you would come back or not."

They met, shook hands. "'I had thought not to," Ressteto said. "Since my cousin was killed. The chief who is my uncle was not in favor of it, for he loved his son, and it turned him against your people. But the great chief of my people sent this man, Eltrienn, to talk with Killed Many. I think you know Eltrienn. This is his friend, Danntis. And this is Vessto, Eltrienn's brother, a great shaman from my country. He is with us to make sure we do not offend Hrum."

"Hello, Strong Grip," Eltrienn said. "I have not seen you for several winters."

"I remember," Strong Grip replied. "You lived in our village and learned to hunt." He turned to Ressteto. "A boy saw your big canoe coming. He ran and told Killed Many, who sent us to meet you. If he'd known it held such important chiefs, he would have come himself."

Strong Grip took them a long mile farther upstream to the Great Village of the Kinnli Innjakot, and to Killed Many. The Great Chief met them with several of his principal warriors, including his younger brother Bloody Sword, and greeted the Hrummeans courteously and solemnly.

Clearly, Killed Many too wanted the sword trade continued. Bloody Sword said nothing, didn't even scowl, but his sullen face expressed what his mouth didn't. For whatever reason, he hated the outlanders, and was here peacefully only under duress.

"Come in the warrior's lodge," Killed Many said. "We will drink howwas and talk about our children." He called to a woman who stood nearby, ordering that howwas be heated and brought in to them, then led them into the lodge, turning to Eltrienn as they entered. "You saw that no one has disturbed the places of the sword chief Torillo," he added pleasantly. "I have not allowed anyone to live in them or use them for anything."

"Yes, we saw that," Eltrienn said.

The Great Chief sat down on the ground, and the others followed his lead.

"There is blood in one of them," Eltrienn went on, "but we

have come in friendship. There'll be time enough to talk of blood debts after the Djez is defeated."

The Great Chief nodded. "Always blood is spilled. Some gives rise to pleasure, some to grief. You remember Yellow Hair, my oldest. He was killed this summer in his first blood battle, with renegades of the Aazhmili. All of the renegades were killed; Yellow Hair killed two of them. I was very proud. Also I wept."

Eltrienn nodded. "I heard that you beat the Aazhmili, who are great fighters, and that they have joined your people. And that a tribe farther north has also acknowledged you chief."

"*Two* tribes farther north," said Killed Many calmly. "The Icy River People and the people of the Great Fen River."

"Do you hope to obtain swords for them all? To help conquer the Djez?"

More than Vessto felt the flash of rage from Bloody Sword then, and he seemed about to speak, but the Great Chief spoke instead.

"Yes. We would like to obtain many more swords as soon as possible. We do not *need* those swords; our warriors can defeat the Djez with spears and bows and war axes. Still, it would be good to have more swords, one for each warrior. And that is very many swords now, for we have very many warriors." He paused. "You cannot make swords fast enough for us. I wish to take my warriors into the land of the Djez soon—by the time the leaves turn color. It would be best if, besides selling us all the swords you can, you taught us to make swords for ourselves."

Eltrienn met the chief's eyes calmly. "We can bring swords more rapidly than you think. As for making swords, there is much to learn and also much to do. You must find the right kind of rocks underneath the earth, and they are present only in a few places. Then you must dig deep pits to get them, and learn to make them into steel. But before you can make steel, you must make the right kind of furnaces, things of very great heat, and know certain kinds of earth to cook in them, and just how, and how to work the melted rock when you have done all those other things. And then, of course, how to make the swords from it so they will be strong without weighing too much. These things take time to learn and do."

He paused, looking thoughtfully at the ground, then back up at the Great Chief. "I would like to make a proposal. If indeed your warriors go to fight the Djez before the leaves turn, I will see that skilled men come a year from now and teach you to make steel yourself. And this summer I will have as many steel swords as possible sent to you. Many hundred of them."

One of the other warriors spoke then, a chieftain of one of the Innjoka clans. "There are those among us who do not trust you to keep your word," he said. "Your people are not honorable. And there are those who say it is better to wait, to find out ourselves how to make steel. Your people found out how to do it; so can ours."

Eltrienn settled his gaze on the man. "Excuse me for not knowing in all cases the thinking and understanding of your people. In what way have you found us lacking in honor?"

"Your people left our land without taking blood for the death of their factor."

Eltrienn shrugged. "A blood feud would only widen the breach between your people and mine. My people have enemies enough in Djez Gorrbul; they don't need more.

"As for finding out yourself how to make steel, it is true, you could. In time. Meanwhile you would grow old and feeble, too old to make war on Djez Gorrbul. You might easily die of old age before then."

None of the barbarians answered that.

"Your Great Chief does not wish to grow old and feeble waiting. Nor does he wish the different tribes to become restless, perhaps to grow apart again and waste their strength fighting each other. He wishes to depart with his warriors to the Djez before the leaves turn. And I can bring thousands of new swords to Agate Bay by leaf turn.

"Meanwhile, your warriors without swords can drill with practice swords of stout wood, clubs with a thin handle like a sword's, cut to weigh the same as a sword weighs. So that when they hold a sword of steel, they will be ready to fight with it."

Bloody Sword spoke then, scornfully. "Real warriors do not play with wooden swords."

Eltrienn seemed to ignore the man, keeping his gaze on the Great Chief. "And as for the murder of the factor, that was not an act of the Agate River People. It was the impetuous Bloody Sword, long known as 'Always Fighting,' who thrust his blade through the throat of a man sitting down with no weapon in his hand.

"But I realize that the murderer is the Great Chief's brother and has his protection. And we are more interested in seeing Djez Gorrbul beaten than in vengeance on the brother of a friend."

Bloody Sword got abruptly to his feet, his face seeming to swell. "You outlanders are cowards! You are women! You are too cowardly to take vengeance and too womanly to fight! You want the tribes to beat the Djez for you because you cannot beat them yourselves!"

It was Ressteto who answered. "The murdered factor was my uncle, and one of our people saw him killed. He had no sword, only a knife on his belt. That was not fighting, that was murder, and shameful. And we were few, with few of us armed. We wondered what had happened to the honorable Innjoka. Had they taken to killing the unarmed? It was more important for me to take the story back to Hrumma than to be murdered myself at Agate Bay."

He stopped then, staring up hard-eyed at Bloody Sword, the only man there on his feet. Bloody Sword had stiffened at the word "shameful," and when he answered, his voice was hoarse with emotion.

"I will give you a sword and you may strike the first blow. Then I will kill you."

Ressteto shook his head. "My high chief, the amirr, has forbidden my family vengeance in this. But to show that Hrummeans are strong fighters, I challenge Bloody Sword to wrestle."

Bloody Sword barked scornfully. "Wrestling! A sport for boys, not warriors! But yes, I will wrestle you. And break your neck."

Killed Many didn't even get up, simply bellowed sharply. "Sit down! Until I give you leave to stand!" His glare stilled the truculent Bloody Sword, who reluctantly sat, still looking scornfully at the Hrummean. Now Killed Many turned a mild gaze to Ressteto.

"Would you be willing to wrestle one of the best wrestlers among the Kinnli Innjakot? He is just now on guard outside the council lodge. This would not be a match between enemies, but between two men who enjoy contesting. And I would be interested in seeing how well you do."

Ressteto nodded and got to his feet. "It would indeed be an interesting contest," he said. Eltrienn looked at him, unsure about this, although Ressteto seemed confident enough.

The man had conspicuously thick strong hands and wrists; probably he'd been taught smithing while still a growing boy. But he'd need more than strength.

The chief got up then, and the others, and they went outside. "Saarho!" he called, and one of the warriors on guard there turned to him. "One of the outlanders wishes to wrestle. Will you oblige him?"

The barbarian grinned and nodded. He wasn't built like a saarho. He wasn't especially large and was more slender than Ressteto, but sinewy, looking as if he'd be very quick and agile.

Killed Many turned to the deputy factor. "And you still wish it?"

Ressteto's smile was no grin, but it showed his satisfaction. "I wish it."

"Then prepare yourselves."

As Ressteto pulled off trousers and shirt, the barbarian removed his sword belt and leggings. When they were ready, Saarho wore only his loin cloth, Ressteto his codstrap. They faced each other a dozen feet apart, ready, examining each other. And with Ressteto stripped, it was clear that he had more than powerful hands and wrists. From the look of his muscular legs, buttocks, torso, he was a Dancer before Hrum, a gymnastic dancer. It wouldn't have surprised Eltrienn to learn he was one of the best wrestlers at Gardozzi Bay.

Killed Many eyed the Hrummean appreciatively. "Ready—Begin!" he barked.

The two men sidled toward each other, hands raised to grapple. Then they closed, feinting, gripping, heels moving to trip, tugging, pushing. Suddenly Ressteto seemed to fall toward Saarho, twisted, bent, and the barbarian was off the ground, feet arcing high as Ressteto pivoted him over his hip, holding wrist and upper arm, and cast him to the ground, keeping his grip on the wrist. They heard bone snap, and a suppressed cry of pain, little more than a grunt. Ressteto let go the arm, and the man rolled onto his side in agony.

Killed Many pursed his lips, impressed, saying nothing for the moment. It was Bloody Sword who spoke, his throat tight with anger.

"A warrior does not wrestle his enemy. He fights him with the blade. I challenge any of the cowardly outlanders to fight me with the sword, to the death."

It was what Eltrienn had been waiting for.

"Great Chief," said the centurion, "I prefer not to kill a warrior who has proven so valuable to you by his valor in war. But I am a warrior by choice and training, and if you say it is all right, I will accept the challenge of Bloody Sword."

Killed Many didn't answer for a few beats, then nodded. "It is your right. The sword you wear is not as big as that my brother carries. Would you prefer to use another?"

"This sword is like part of my body. My deadliest part. And when we are done, I will offer the chief my regret at having killed his brother who had fought so well for him in his conquests."

For just a moment Bloody Sword's eyes lost their arrogant assurance, replaced, after a moment of uncertainty, with blood rage. Killed Many's face had gone grim. He looked the two over. The men were similar in height; Bloody Sword, broad and deep-chested, weighed the most.

"Draw your weapons!" the Great Chief ordered. They did. "Ready— Begin!"

Bloody Sword strode forward, arm partly extended, sword crossways. Eltrienn, instead of meeting him, circled to his own right, away from the barbarian's sword arm. He'd never seen a barbarian fight with the sword, and intended to feel the man out.

Bloody Sword was having none of it. He pounced, slashing at the Hrummean, who jumped back, then darted forward, bent arm straightening, thrusting, blade tip slicing a pectoral muscle, glancing off the breastbone. The barbarian bellowed, swung backhanded, the move quicker than anticipated. Eltrienn leaned away, nearly hit, Bloody Sword's blade striking his own, but Eltrienn simply rotated his wrist and leaned forward again in a short thrust, then jumped back. And now blood flowed from the barbarian's left jaw and ear as he brought his sword back to guard; three inches lower and his throat would have been cut.

Eltrienn's blade tip moved again in small circles, like the head of some poisonous snake preparing to strike, and Bloody Sword's reaction was exactly what he'd expected. The barbarian rushed at him, blade chopping, and Eltrienn jumped back, circling right again, sword slashing back-handed, striking the heavy left deltoid and finding bone. Bloody Sword recovered balance and guard position, bleeding freely but not stumbling as Eltrienn had hoped.

The warrior paused then, brows knotted as if he analyzed

his opponent. Eltrienn showed only his side, his blade tip circling again before the bleeding face.

The barbarian moved suddenly, thrusting this time. It was an error. He could not hope to fight the Hrummean's style unpracticed; his best chance lay in his usual approach—violent strength. Eltrienn parried the heavy blade to his right, then his own long thrust penetrated below the short ribs, through abdominal wall, intestines, abdominal aorta, and he was away again, circling right.

Bloody Sword's reaction was instinctive: *Chop! Slash!* At an opponent who wasn't there. He staggered, rapidly bleeding to death internally. Then the quick saber took him in the throat and he fell, dead as he hit the ground.

The centurion did not exult. Turning to Killed Many, he lowered his sword tip to the ground. "My regrets, Great Chief. You have lost a brave and strong warrior."

Killed Many gazed steadily at him for a long ten seconds, then down at his brother. Tears welled but did not overflow, and his voice confessed no grief. "It was as he wished, to die fighting," he said drily. "Sooner than he wished, no doubt, but by his own insistence. Now we must bury the warrior as befits one who fought so well against our brothers the Tchook and Aazhmili." He turned to the guards standing near. "Take him. Clean him. Dress him in his ceremonial robe. Put his headdress on his head."

He looked back at the Hrummeans, their faces blurred through his tears. "You are invited to his funeral. It will be this evening. You owe no blood debt to me or to his wife and daughter, who will live in my lodge, and he has paid his."

That evening the body of Bloody Sword was laid on its funeral pyre, and the fire was kept burning far into the night. Beer was drunk, the weak sour beer that was a principal product of the grain field grown at every barbarian village.

The next morning a warrior ceremony was held in the clearing in front of the warriors' lodge, and Eltrienn Cadriio was made "brother to the Kinnli Innjakot" for his warrior skill and his honorable deportment.

When it was over and more sour beer drunk, Eltrienn asked Killed Many why he'd denied Bloody Sword permission to wrestle but had allowed him to fight with the sword.

The Great Chief eyed him thoughtfully. "To refuse him permission to accept a challenge was a rebuke, which he had more than earned for repeatedly making problems. The greatest of which was ending the sword trade. But to make him retract his own challenge would be a major insult not lightly given.

"Beyond that, if he'd wrestled the deputy factor and lost, he'd have hated your people beyond all sanity, and probably made further serious trouble. While if he'd won, you'd have lost very much face. It had been your man's challenge, and the worthiness of your people was already in question. It would then have been difficult for me to negotiate with you. I would have had to offer terms so poor that you would surely have refused them.

"And yet I want more swords.

"But if he beat you with the *sword*, I could have burned your body with high honors and negotiated with the others of your people, because you would have shown yourself no coward and restored your people's honor. While if you beat him . . . well, that is what happened."

He shrugged. "Let us talk terms."

They agreed quickly. The Innjoka tribe would trade a perpetual wood supply in return for 3,000 steel swords by the equinox, half of them by the second full face of Great Liilia, which was about six weeks away.

Ressteto's brows rose at that for just a moment, but Killed Many wasn't looking at him. The attention of the barbarian was on the centurion.

When the negotiations were over, Eltrienn introduced Vessto to the Great Chief, calling his brother "a listener to Hrum." Then the Hrummeans accompanied the chief to watch his principal officers training a cadre in his new tactics, men who would return to their clans and train the warriors there.

Later, sitting in the factor's office at Agate Bay, Ressteto asked Eltrienn how he planned to deliver so many swords so soon.

"Partly by not relying entirely on your uncle to make them. Before I left Theedalit, the amirr ordered that every smith in Hrumma who's a competent armorer was to start making swords. I'd worked with the royal armorer to provide a system, a sequence of actions, that would allow a smith to make swords faster than before." He shrugged. "Ettsio forfeited his monopoly when he abandoned it, and at any rate, it's important that the barbarians move before autumn, with as much strength as possible.

"And if necessary, which it probably will be, the government will make up any deficit for the first 1,500 from government armories, replacing them out of new production. Leonessto authorized it."

Ressteto nodded. With wealth, his uncle had grown arrogant and hard to get along with. His sons and nephews still were loyal, but they'd feel no indignation for him. And what could Ettsio say against Eltrienn, who'd avenged his murdered son?

Although . . . "By what authority," he asked slowly, "did you promise the barbarians that they'd be taught to make steel?"

"They'd soon learn anyway."

Ressteto's eyebrows raised. "How?"

"The least we can expect the barbarians to do is conquer the border duchies. If they get no farther than that, they'll get that far. And when they capture some Djezian smithies, they'll almost certainly think to take some smiths captive.

"Besides," he added, grimly now, "we face a dangerous war—more dangerous than any since we last threw out the Gorrbian overlords. If we take no chances, our prospects of winning are poor."

On the assumption that Eltrienn could get an agreement, the schooner had brought men to start work in the woods and the sawmill, and at the charcoal kilns. These men now came ashore to work under Ressteto, the new factor. Their families, and more crews, would come later. With the new urgency for steel and swords, the need for charcoal had also become urgent. It would have priority.

Then Eltrienn wrote a report and gave it to Danntis Deltibbio to take back to Hrumma. Eltrienn and Vessto would stay with the Great Chief as advisors in his preparations.

FORTY-SEVEN

Having nothing to protect him from the nighttime chill, Tirros Hanorissio slept by day in the shade of cliff or rock, and hiked, often staggered, the beach at night. He ate dead fish he found, and several times over the days and nights lay ill from it for hours, waiting fruitlessly to die. His senses were dulled by hunger and hopelessness, and by the defeat of whatever psychotic compulsions drove him.

At no time did he cease feeling sorry for himself, somehow wronged by others. But the emotion had no force, and he felt too defeated to plan revenge or even dream of it. He was incapable of planning anything, or of looking ahead at all except for the vague unexamined impulse to get out of Hrumma north to Djez Gorrbul. His progress was slow, partly from hunger and partly from self-pity, resting by day and traveling almost solely by night. He also rested much at night, sleeping readily if restlessly, to wake shaking with cold. He swam inlets and even the Firth of Theed, to avoid towns and fishing hamlets.

An uncounted number of nights later he reached the Great North Firth, fifty miles long, and far too wide to swim across. Yet hiking round it seemed dangerous too. There was a sizeable town at its head, he knew, and fishing hamlets on its flanks, and in his mind, every man was watching for him.

He slumped down on the beach and peered across the firth, the opposite headland beyond sight in the dawn. North from it, he'd heard, the shore in places rose sheer from the ocean, even at low tide, waves booming on spalled cliffs, slashing and foaming among basaltic fangs. It occurred to him to leave the shore and travel overland, but that seemed more dangerous than the sea. It even occurred to him to try swimming across the firth; drowning would be better than starvation or capture.

Instead though, and by daylight now, he began to follow the shore along the firth, till on a tiny side inlet he came to a hut. In front of it, an old man sat mending a fishtrap. There was also a kienna, gray-muzzled and fat, but she merely raised her head and hissed, ceasing even that when the old man spoke sharply to her.

The old fisherman assumed that Tirros was some mariner lost, and meanwhile Tirros's wits began to function. He'd fallen overboard from a coasting sloop, he said, several nights back. The old man fed him, lightly enough that he didn't get sick, then loaned him soap and razor and a small mirror, and left to tend his fishtraps, saying he'd be back in a couple of hours and row him up the firth to a village.

When the old man returned, the "castaway sailor" met him at the door with a cutlass that had been hanging on a wall, and cut him down. The kienna was already murdered. Then Tirros left, wearing clean tunic and trousers—the shoes were too tight—with the old man's small cache of coins, the loaf and a half of bread he'd found, a head of cheese, and a large sausage too strongly spiced to spoil quickly, all stuffed into a sack. And a blanket in an oilskin bag. The cutlass rode on one hip and a fishknife on the other.

By now Tirros was functioning well enough that he'd also thought to fill the old man's waterskin and take a half-full wine crock. Then he untied the rowboat and started rowing across the firth. Away from the firth's south wall was a southerly breeze brisk enough that Tirros stepped the little mast, no more than eight feet tall, and spread the small sail.

He continued to travel mainly by night, occasionally visiting the mouth of some stream to refill his waterbag, hiding out on some small island or isolated beach through the day. If the wind was adverse—rarely was it lacking—he holed up till it blew right again, for he did not care to row.

Little by little he moved northward toward the Gulf of Storms, across which lay Djez Gorrbul. He'd have to coast his long slow way around the gulf, of course, but he could do that.

Forty-Eight

The rikksha stopped at the main gate to the palace grounds. Brokols got out and paid the runner. Reeno was no longer with him. Someone, probably Allbarin he thought, had decided they needn't monitor him any longer, and the way things stood now he no longer needed a bodyguard, although his home was still guarded.

The gate guard saluted him casually through, and he walked up the paved drive to the palace. A houseman had been waiting for him at the door, and led him through the building to a sitting room where he was met by the amirr, his wife and daughter. The namirrna hadn't been continued on the grenades project after all, but been given a different job. She rode east out of Theedalit each morning and worked cultivating plots of medicinal herb that would be processed and shipped to Kammenak for poultices, to be used on wounds when the war started. To Brokols she looked—not tired, really, but less lively than usual.

Smiling, the amirr stood at once, stepped forward and shook Brokols' hand. "It won't be long," he said, "before we can dispense with having you met at the door and conducted to us. But as the namirrna's fiance, you understand . . ." He gestured. "Sit! Sit down! What news do you have of your project?"

"All good," he said, then addressed himself more to Juliassa than her parents. "Yesterday we tested cast iron grenade casings from the Theed Valley Ironworks. Two, actually: one for throwing by hand and a larger one for ballistas. They're serrated, and blow apart into ugly fragments with quite adequate penetration. And this morning we finished the tests of Amaadio's fuse designs. The fuses were the most worrisome aspect of the whole project."

"How so?" It was the amirr that asked.

"The imperial army uses a fuse that explodes the grenade five seconds after the head is turned a quarter turn. But it would take us too long to develop and manufacture them here, so we've settled for impact fuses; the grenade explodes when it strikes. Which could make them dangerous to transport over rough mountain roads. We've settled for a design in which the fuse is not fully armed until the grenade is ready to be used. It's not entirely safe—the fuses won't be installed at all until they get to Kammnalit—but I'm not afraid to handle them myself."

The amirr looked unhappy. "Cast iron cases? I thought you'd meant to use ceramics. We're making a lot of demands on our ironworks these days."

Brokols nodded. "I understand. Reeno's been quite reluctant to go with iron, but with the ceramic casings, the fragments didn't penetrate enough."

A houseman had come in while Brokols was finishing. "I believe supper is ready," the amirr said, and got up to lead them into the summer dining room. "If iron it must be," he went on, "then iron it must be. The price of iron is getting much too high, and the prices of things made of it, but it seems we have little choice."

Brokols thought the amirr's concern was overblown. This society used enough iron that obviously it had a significant capacity to make it. And he didn't know about the arming of the barbarians. It wasn't public knowledge, and there hadn't been any particular reason to tell him.

At supper they talked about other things—about agriculture in Almeon and how things were done there. The talk introverted Brokols a bit, making him compare life there with life in Hrumma. It would be difficult to live in Almeon again, even if he'd be welcome there. Almeon was beautiful—greener than Hrumma, more fertile—but the way people lived, the oppressions there, would be hard for him to take now.

They'd made a mistake sending him to Hrumma, he realized. He'd been a misfit at home, but had learned early to conceal, to conform, to fool even himself; there'd be a lot like him there. And he'd never realized it until he'd come to know Hrumma. Nor had Almeon built cultural defenses in him—a set of "we're the best because. . . ." They hadn't needed to, when he'd known so little of any alternative until he was grown.

He wondered if the Djezian culture had impacted Glembro Dixen at all like the Hrummean had impacted himself. Kryger, he assumed, was beyond being appreciably touched; Kryger *was* Almeon.

Almeon was much more advanced technologically, of course. The fruit custard he was eating was delicious, but he couldn't help thinking that it would have been nicer chilled.

Hrumma had excellent artisans though, and he wondered if he knew enough about electricity, and about physics and chemistry in general, to get them started on a refrigeration plant after the war.

Hrumma after the war? A free Hrumma? He'd forgotten about that problem, and remembering it, his spirits slumped.

After supper he sat in the garden with Juliassa, on facing chairs under Torissia's chaperonage. The youthful aunt sat far enough away to give them privacy of conversation if they spoke quietly. From a hedge, a flute bird warbled a liquid cascade of notes.

"I dreamed of you again last night," she said smiling. "It was—most pleasant."

Brokols nodded. "And I dreamed of you. That was my first dream. Then, when I'd gone back to sleep, I dreamed another dream less pleasant."

Her gaze was direct. "Tell me about it. About the later dream that was less pleasant."

He didn't start at once. It had been realistic, as dreams go, like the dream in which the Almaeic army had been embarking in the time of lenn harvest.

"I dreamed," he said, "that the army had left Almeon. But the training camps were full of men, a second army. I watched them train. They were new, green. Their cadre was cursing them, working them hard."

He looked bleakly at Juliassa. "It seemed that the fleet planned to return to Alemon when they'd unloaded the first army, to get the second and bring them over." His lips were thin, straight. "And with two such armies, it seems to me there can be no possible victory over the empire."

Juliassa didn't answer for a moment, but neither did she look frightened or dismayed. "We'll just have to follow the advice of Vessto Cadriio then," she said. "And Allbarin and

Panni. We'll have to do all we can, and hope that our efforts will bring Hrum's intervention."

"What further can *I* do?" Brokols asked. "Besides die in battle eventually."

"You might take your dream to Panni," she said.

The suggestion took Brokols by surprise, and he decided that he would, the next day.

He saw Panni sooner than that, that night in another dream. Panni wasn't in a cave or on a hilltop. He was sitting on a roof somewhere, with an exceedingly old, spidery-looking man that Brokols somehow knew was Tassi Vermaatio, the Is-ness of Hrum. They went somewhere together, the three of them, and did something that Brokols couldn't afterward remember. But when he woke to gray dawn and morning birdsong, a thought stuck in the front of Brokols' mind: Go talk with K'sthuump.

Forty-Nine

The next morning Brokols talked with Allbarin and got ready agreement. Nor did Allbarin have any difficulty with the amirr. Yes, Juliassa could ride with Brokols to Hidden Haven, properly accompanied. So a mounted courier was sent to the herb farm where she worked, to send her home, while Brokols went home and packed his own gear.

It was noon before they left Theedalit—Brokols, Juliassa, and Torissia, with Jonkka and two other guards—riding kaabors. Two pack animals followed, with sleeping and cooking gear and food. Brokols couldn't help thinking of the train of gear and retainers that would accompany a princess of the imperial house, were she to set out on an overnight outing in the country.

The daily thundershower obligingly let them get out of town, then in booming tones announced itself as storm instead of shower. Violently it slashed and beat on hooded oilskin ponchos for more than half an hour, while it marched across the plateau on electric legs, inspiring thoughts of charcoaled death. In the minds of the Hrummeans it resurrected the storm god, Borrsio, from his relegation to superstition, reestablishing him as a genuine aspect of Hrum, at least for a little while.

It ended abruptly, and the sun emerged to laugh at them. Humans and kaabors steamed, and the ponchos came off. All that was left of the storm was its tracks—puddles on the hoof-beaten road.

They reached Hidden Haven in midafternoon. The soldiers were gone, had left after the project had decided they didn't need the place anymore. Juliassa led at once to the inlet. There'd been concern that they'd miss K'sthuump, for it was the time of summer when the serpents departed the firths and inlets to travel north. They still could be seen in the Firth of Theed, but the departures generally began in the south and worked northward.

But at Hidden Haven too the serpents hadn't left yet. A juvenile, less shy than before, raised its head to breathe, its pink, still scaleless neck no larger than Juliassa's arm. Juliassa called to it; it whistled shrilly in acknowledgement and disappeared. Brief moments later, K'sthuump showed herself, swimming toward the beach, talking as she came.

"Suliassa! I had not thought to see you again! It is good! It is good! How go the preparassions of your tribe for the great death fight?" She asked the question cheerfully, as if the matter wasn't deadly serious, then grounded herself on the shoaling beach, barely awash, her head raised on arched blue neck.

"I'm glad I found you here," Juliassa said. "I was afraid you'd be gone already."

"Ah! I will not go. I will stay here. I am too old to go again with the people to the northern waters. Too slow to keep up. I will wait here for them to come back."

Juliassa didn't say anything for a long moment. It seemed to her that K'sthuump might easily die if she stayed here alone all that time—most of a year. The serpent read her emotion and what lay beneath it.

"Or maybe die, come back as young. I can't use this old body forever; it wears out." A series of grunts/laughs came from the long throat.

"But I won't know you in a different body," Juliassa protested. "And you won't remember me."

"Perhaps. But if we wiss it to happen, we will meet again. As perhaps we have in some life before." K'sthuump looked at Brokols, who'd understood none of the sullsit they'd spoken, then said to Juliassa: "Your mate has something to tell me. Perhaps this is good time to say what it is."

Juliassa glanced at Brokols and nodded. "Elver," she said, "say what you want to tell K'sthuump."

He told the old serpent his dream of the training camp,

and that it seemed to him the fleet would go back for a second army; maybe even a third, if the emperor deemed it necessary for complete conquest. He spoke in brief sentences, letting Juliassa interpret each in turn, suspecting all the time that the serpent didn't need the interpretation. "I told the dream to a wise man called the Lamp of Hrum," he finished, "and he told me to talk with you about it."

"Ah!" The serpent made a long cooing sound, remarkable from her scaly neck. "Of course!"

The slit pupils fastened on Brokols, the being looking out through them at the Almite, the big-ship person become Hrummean. "You have made grenades to war with, have you not? The stones that go boom?"

He nodded. "That's right."

"Can you not make very big grenades and destroy the many ships with them when they come to the Dssezes? Then they cannot go back and bring more enemies."

He stared. It would take some doing, but it definitely seemed possible. And a sea serpent had suggested it, a creature to whom empire, explosives, perhaps even conquest were foreign concepts.

"Thank you, K'sthuump," he said. "I believe we can. Your suggestion is all that I need to begin."

Then, while Juliassa and K'sthuump carried on a private conversation, Brokols walked back up the path to the hamlet to examine the buildings there. They were the way the grenade project had left them.

Now they might need Hidden Haven again for a new project; his mind was playing with the problems. Attach an explosive charge to the hull under water, then explode it so the ship would fill and sink. It would take a huge amount of powder of course, for 200 ships. And how could they attach explosives to them? The sullsi, of course! They could swim considerable distances underwater and had arms and hands. It would take a lot of them though, and he'd need to find a way to explode the charges.

He took an armload of firewood back to the beach, arriving to see three sullsi swimming up the inlet in a playful synchronized formation, all clearing the water at once in a vee of three. They too beached themselves, in their case out of the water. For a moment Juliassa didn't recognize Sleekit; his nose was swollen and his voice different.

"Juliassa!" Sleekit said. "You may have saved me a difficult decision."

"How so?"

"It seemed to me I shouldn't leave. Hrum had called to me to return south, and the reason had to do with you. Yet as far as I could see, I had accomplished nothing by coming back.

"But you were gone, and this is not a good place for sullsi in the season of cold water; food will be scarce for us, is already so. Could it be that I was mistaken? That I had heard falsely? What was I to do?"

"I'm very glad you came," Juliassa said. "Although I too don't know why you were called."

She turned to the other humans then and translated briefly for them.

"I don't know why they were called, either," Brokols said. "But we do need them. We need someone to attach ship-killing devices to the Almaeic fleet. The job requires hands and arms, and the ability to stay under water for a longish time.

"But Sleekit and his two friends won't be enough. There's to be 200 ships, each requiring its own ship-killing device. And each device will probably require two sullsi to attach it. If a pair of sullsi can attach devices on two different ships, it'll require 200 sullsi. If they can attach them to four, it'll take 100. Ask him if he can get us 200 sullsi."

Juliassa and Sleekit talked at some length. No doubt it had taken some explanations to make the matter clear.

"When?" Sleekit wanted to know.

"Soon. We might need them in as soon as fifty days," Brokols said. "It depends on when the fleet arrives."

She passed it on to Sleekit in her slow-paced sullsit. When she'd finished, the big sellsu lay there for a bit without speaking. When he did speak, it was a brief exchange in rapid sullsit to his packmates. Then he turned to Juliassa and talked to her at the slower pace she was used to and could understand.

She looked at Brokols. "Sleekit says he'd be glad to help, and he supposes he could interest some adventurous sullsi—perhaps 10 or 20, perhaps a few more—but not 200."

When she'd finished, Sleekit spoke again. "The sullsi feel no attachment to the Hrummeans, nor worse than distaste for the big-ship people. And to help would be a hardship; the sullsi follow the movements of the yerrcha, in order to keep themselves fed in their numbers. When one is away from the yerrcha, one must travel slowly in order to fish a lot."

Fifteen or twenty, perhaps a few more. Brokols pursed his lips, then spoke. "Tell him the big-ship people are dangerous to the sullsi. Long ago, many sullsi raised their young on the beaches of Almeon, the land of the big-ship people. Then the big-ship people began killing the sullsi for their flesh, their fur, and oil, until the sullsi stopped going to those islands. Now they are said to raise their pups on cliffy beaches of a great wild continent where they must worry about a very dangerous land people, very savage, called sauroids in our language.

"If the big-ship people conquer Hrumma and the lands to the north, as they intend to, they will probably hunt you here, too, till all of you are either dead or have found a new and distant place.

"What I want to do is destroy the fleet of big ships. Then perhaps they will not conquer us here, and the sullsi will be safe. But I'll need the help of many sullsi. At least 100."

Sleekit gazed long at Brokols. Then K'sthuump spoke to the sellsu. "Suliassa's mate tells the truth," K'sthuump said, "at least the truth as he knows it. It seems that the big-ssip people actually did those things, and might well do them here if they win in the great killing fight."

The sellsu's eyes hardened. "This gives the situation a different look. Knowing this, my people would want to help you. But in fifty days? Or sixty? If I were to leave at once, that would not be nearly enough time. They would be far away by the time I could catch and tell them." He turned to K'sthuump again. "Unless the long necks help."

K'sthuump nodded her head and sinuous neck in an apparent affirmative. "I will give this matter the taste of urgent, that my people will not only have the knowledz in their memory, but will be aware of it at once and tell any sullsi that they see. Young Vrronnkiess males, unmated, do not come south with the families. There will be some where the sullsi are now. And the sullsi are almost always willing to stop and listen to my people.

"Meanwhile, my people must also consider what may happen to our nursery sites if the big-ssip people prevail." She paused to concentrate for just a moment. "Now," she said, "every one of my people knows, and knows that they know."

"Then the three of us will wait here until we know what part we have in this," Sleekit said.

When Juliassa had resumed the conversation for him, Brokols spoke. "I believe I have a special role for you three right here," he said. "We humans must first make such ship-killers, and they are something that has never been made before. We will have to try this and try that until we have made one that does what it's supposed to. You can help us test them."

When Juliassa had finished translating that, she paused, then continued on her own. "And I can have the flesh of land animals sent for you three to eat while you're here. You too, K'sthuump. So you don't have to work long hours fishing. I'll send off for it tomorrow."

She paused, her attention on Sleekit's swollen, somewhat distorted face. "What happened to your nose, Sleekit?"

He snorted ruefully. "I am no longer young. I begin the change of life."

"Change of life?"

"Male sullsi change when they get old, ready to stop breeding." Sleekit held out a hand, and Juliassa became aware that it was changing too. Hand and arm both had thickened, and the hand itself had grown larger. "Before long I will have a sword on my face. My hands and arms will be thick and strong. I will bc a protector, able to speak only with difficulty. And the sarrkas will fear me."

He grunted the string of clicks/coughs that passed for chuckling among the sullsi. "I will no longer float on my back with the pack around me and tell stories." He gestured at the other two sullsi. "Triivarum and young Krootar here will be the ones to tell this story. My place will be to listen for sarrkas, and to drive off or kill any that come around. Great sagas are told about certain protectors; perhaps I will be the subject of a saga instead of the teller."

All three sullsi laughed then, but Juliassa looked sober. It seemed to her she'd be losing a good friend, though she didn't say so. Sleekit seemed content or even happy at the prospect of being a protector; she wouldn't deliberately impose her unhappiness on him.

Then his gaze caught hers. "I will miss talking to Juliassa, when the change is complete," he said. "But I will enjoy hearing her talk to me."

No one had anything much to say after that. Jonkka laid a fire with dead twigs from a bush and some of the wood Brokols had brought down, then lit them with a large waxed match from a pouch he carried. The humans cooked and ate their supper around the small fire. When she'd finished eating, Juliassa asked Sleekit and K'sthuump questions about their people, and after a little, K'sthuump and the sullsi swam away.

FIFTY

Accompanied by her chaperone and guards, Juliassa spent the evening on the beach, talking with Sleekit and K'sthuump. In the hamlet, Brokols and Reeno sat down together at a table to sort out design problems and rough parameters. Reeno jotted notes as they talked, ending up with a list.

1. *The mine must be waterproof.*
2. *It must be easily attachable to ships.*
3. *It must explode under water.*
4. *It must be big enough to sink a ship, but small enough that a single sellsu can handle and control it while a second sellsu attaches it to a ship's bottom.*
5. *It is important that all the mines explode within a few minutes of each other, so that when some explode, divers will not have time to find and remove others from the remaining ships.*
6. *Also, a lot more gunpowder will be needed, and other sources of saltpeter may need to be found.*

Reeno gave his notes to Brokols, who read them back aloud. "What did we overlook?" Reeno asked.

"Probably something," Brokols said. "But let's start with this. What will we use for the casing? Kegs? (He used the Djezian word, with a description, having never heard the Hrummean.) I don't believe I've seen a keg or a barrel in Hrumma."

They talked for more than another half hour, again with Reeno taking notes. They ended up with another list.

1. *Ceramic containers will be used for the mines. The mines must be buoyant enough that a sellsu can swim with one. A light, strong ceramic crock must be developed with a flotation chamber.**
2. *Consider two sullsi working together. They transport the mine underwater. It has two large ear-like brackets at the explosive end. The brackets are attached to the ship with lagscrews. One of the sullsu can carry the lagscrews and wrench in a pouch strapped to one arm. We need to decide quickly on lagscrew specifications so the wrenches can be made.*
3. *The fuse must be contained inside the mine. It must provide sufficient delay for the sullsi to get away from the blast zone.*** A clockwork within the flotation chamber would seem to be the solution. The clock would activate a spring-driven striker which would fire the charge.*
   All the fuses could be set to go off at a given hour. That should give a single team of sullsi plenty of time to emplace at least two mines. Thus 100 sullsi teams—200 sullsi—could mine the whole 200 ships within a few hours in one night, if they don't have an unreasonable distance to swim.
4. *A charge of thirty pounds of gunpowder blowing up against the hull under water, should make a big enough hole, but this needs to be tested. Such a mine, with flotation chamber, need be no larger than, say, a ten-gallon crock.*
5. *The clock could be set and started, then installed in the flotation chamber. When the clock is installed, the end of the chamber would then be installed and snugged against a leather gasket by tapping in small dry wooden shims that would swell in the water. The clocks will need to be tested in advance for reasonable accuracy.*
   *The clocks and the spring-driven strikers are crucial parts of the project.**** There are only two shops in Hrumma*

**Wood suitable for watertight kegs is practically nonexistent in Hrumma, and Hrumma had no shops with equipment and trained labor to make kegs.*

***Brokols had seen explosives used underwater to blast holes in rock for bridge footings in Almeon. The blasts had killed large numbers of fish and would no doubt be dangerous to sullsi.*

****In Hrumma, most mechanical clocks are driven by suspended weights. Reliable spring-driven clocks are expensive.*

that make clock springs. Need to get started at once on obtaining clocks and springs.

6. *Have Amaadio look into another source of saltpeter, as this will take a large amount. Maybe saltpeter can be made with manure from farms, nightsoil wagons, or pit toilets.*

"Is that it?" Reeno asked after reading the list aloud.

Brokols sighed. "I hope so. It's a start at any rate." He leaned back in his chair, looking depressed, disheartened. *So much to do in so little time! So many things that could go wrong! So little time for testing, so many assumptions. So much opportunity for failure!* He wondered if it was worth starting.

Reeno read Brokols' emotions and the sense of what lay beneath them. "Let's go for a hike," he said. "Up on the plateau. Run a bit, walk a bit. I've got a bottle of brandy in my bedroll, for when we get back."

Brokols smiled wryly at him. "The gentleman shows foresight and understanding," he said, and got up. "Let's go."

They ran a good bit and walked more, stopping now and then to admire a marvelous night sky. When they got back, Brokols had destimulated, and after a short drink of brandy went readily to sleep. That night he dreamt unusually coherent dreams, of both success and failure, each with a somehow satisfactory conclusion. He remembered little of them in the morning, except that Panni had been part of them, and Tassi Vermaatio. He felt a lot better.

Fifty-One

The water in the Gulf of Seechul was remarkably calm, with only a slight ground swell. Stars strewed the sky and reflected on the oil-smooth water below. Two related packs of sullsi lay floating semi-vertically in one group, digesting, facing a young sellsu who recited the Tale of Zeltis Long Nose, a romance, a favorite, very old. None of the others made a sound. They'd wait till the youthful reciter was done, then discuss his style and delivery. He was free to tell the story any way he pleased, so long as he did not change what happened—the givens, the "facts" of the story. That, and that only, would bring interruption.

The presentation was interesting, with assonances in most lines, a rather daring effort for a sellsu. Mostly they left such technique to the Vrronnkiess.

Three protector sullsi, singlemindedly alert, had posted themselves on the packs' perimeter to listen for sarrkas and the rare but frightening rokkas. Rising and falling slowly on the ground swell, the rest were absorbed in the tale, waiting for the part in which Zeltis confronts the great sarrka chief. For the young of the year, it was their first hearing of this, one of many sagas.

It was no predator or protector that interrupted the saga's spell, but a young serpent swimming up to them on the surface. The mood broken, the teller fell silent, and his audience assumed the ready attitude. The senior pack leader confronted the serpent.

"Did you not hear the saga teller?" the leader asked severely. The serpents had their own sagas, sung instead of told. It was unheard of for either species to interrupt a telling by the other.

"Yes. It sounded like a very fine telling; my deepest regrets for interrupting. But I have an urdsent messits for the sullsi. Other packs will be hearing it also. It comes from Sleekit, the sellsu who taught the human, Suliassa, to speak your tongue. You have heard of Sleekit? It was passed on to me, and to all Vrronnkiess, by an old mother named K'sthuump."

"We have heard of Sleekit. What about him?"

"Then you've heard of the great death fight whitss the humans of the south expect to have with the big-ssip people. Sleekit returned to the nursery beatses, believing to be called there by the Lord of the Sea."

"Yes yes." The pack leader was impatient to hear the message, but it would be both futile and discourteous to hurry the serpent.

The serpent told them what Sleekit and K'sthuump had learned about the big-ship people: That they had butchered the sullsi across the ocean till the survivors had fled, and that they would no doubt do the same here if they won the great killing fight. Then he told them what the humans of the south wanted the sullsi to do. The serpent was young, not yet of breeding age, but had the talent of a saga master, and knew everything about the matter that K'sthuump did. When he was done, he floated quietly.

The sullsi also floated quietly for a long minute, starlight glinting on sleek wet heads. It seemed to them that they faced the near destruction of their kind unless the big-ship people were defeated.

They conferred. When they were done, the two packs had given the Almites a new name—the sarrkas people—and ten of their twenty breeding males would turn back to help the humans of the south. The protector sullsi would stay with the pack and its juveniles.

It seemed to the sullsi that those who went back would soon be living the greatest saga ever, and two of them were saga masters.

The young serpent, Tssissfu, would travel with them. Tssissfu would stay in touch with K'sthuump, and through K'sthuump with the humans, so the sullsi could be informed as plans developed. Meanwhile they'd head for the islands that formed an inner channel off the coast of Djez Gorrbul.

Fifty-Two

The old man wore a robe of stealth-hawk skins, and a wooden mask carved in the likeness of a stealth hawk's fierce visage. He was the chief shaman of the Innjoka tribe, and recognized as more powerful than any other shaman among its clans. Drums beat a steady resonant meter, but he did not dance, simply sang a song to Hrum in a voice that alternately keened ashrill and droned in the deepest bass.

Several other Innjoka shamans, including shamans of clans besides the Kinnli Innjakot, stood arrayed behind him to both sides. Vessto Cadriio stood in the place of honor, almost at his right hand, only half a step back. In front of the old man, facing him, was a large crowd of warriors, mostly Kinnli Innjakot but with fighting men of every Innjoka clan and the hostages and cadre of every other tribe.

When the old man was done singing, the drums stopped too. He looked the crowd over, then despite his age, spoke in a voice that all could hear.

"Warriors of the Innjoka and the united tribes. Hrum has sent the southerners to you to show you the way Hrum wishes you to fight when you make war on the Djez." He paused for effect. "But you have been obstinate! You have not been willing to change! You are more willing to be killed by the Djez than to learn new ways that would make you greater warriors!"

His piercing eyes scanned the sullen faces before him.

"When told to drill with the long spears, to stand against soldiers riding kaabors, many of you refuse, asking, 'What manner of fighting is this? Warriors do not stand still and let 'others rush at them,' you say. 'Warriors attack!' But the Djez who charge on the backs of kaabors do not care what you prefer! They will be happy to ride their kaabors trampling over you. And they will, unless they are met by rows of men standing firm behind their long spears.

"And when you are given a shield to use in sword drills, you refuse to use it. You say a warrior doesn't need something to hide behind. That is all right if you would rather die than kill. Otherwise it is the quibbling of a sulky child. You fail to differentiate between a duel and a battle between numbers of men."

The old shaman stared at the warriors with asperity. "Now Hrum is giving you one more chance. Two great swordsmen will fight before you, one in the old way, one in the new. If you learn nothing from this, Hrum will abandon you as foolish children. He will not travel with you when you go to fight the Djez. If you refuse to accept his gifts to you, of better ways to fight the Djez, there will be no more gifts, and Hrum will turn his back on you."

Their faces still were surly, but they stood attentive and quiet nonetheless.

Two men came out of the warriors' lodge then: Eltrienn Cadriio and a warrior named Quick, who was famous among the Innjoka clans for his skill with the sword.

Before the crowd, the two faced off. On his left arm, Eltrienn carried a stout wooden buckler, two feet in diameter and covered with tight-stretched bullhide. His right hand held a wooden sword. Quick carried a wooden sword in his right hand and a wooden knife in his left.

They fought for two long minutes, and Quick was quick indeed. Twice Eltrienn was nearly touched by the knife. But the sword strokes he countered nicely with his own sword and shield, and when it was over, he had touched Quick four times, the last one on the ribs. The old shaman called the exhibition finished. The contest had given the warriors something to think about.

As the two contestants turned to enter the warriors' lodge, a newly arrived decade of Hrummean cavalry galloped into the village. Steel swords raised, they charged the mass of warriors, sheering off at the last moment. Then they stopped their mounts at the edge of the mustering ground and dismounted, having sheathed their swords.

It was Killed Many who stepped before his warriors this

time. "Now," he said, "maybe you can see why we need the long spears, and men who will stand firm with them in lines. If the foreign kaaborwarriors had wanted to, they could have ridden over you, and many of you would have died. But if you'd stood firm behind long spears, the kaaborwarriors would have died instead, or turned away."

He stopped then, and waited a silent minute before saying any more. "When the first leaves turn, I will lead the united tribes to fight the Djez. Every man who goes with me will have drilled satisfactorily with his weapons. The older men will carry the long spears, to hold off or kill the charging kaabors, for the older warriors are strong and steady but no longer so quick. Many others will carry a sword. And shield! No shield, no sword! Those who will not learn to fight in the new ways, will be left behind."

He glared around him at the tribesmen, and when he spoke again, it was an angry shout. "Those who will not learn would be liabilities in battle against the Djez! They can stay home and help the women cut firewood while the men go off to fight. Now—" He looked back at the warriors' lodge, and called a name. His two household squads came out—ten men; barbarian squads had five warriors each. "These warriors have drilled with sword and shield until they have mastered them. I invite any other squads to fight them, right now. See how well you do against them without shields."

Two squads volunteered. The fight lasted brief minutes, refereed by the shamans, and when it was over, more than the shamans could see that the warriors with shields had gotten much the best of it.

"Now," said Killed Many, and his voice was a growl, "who will go with me to make war on the Djezes?"

The response started slowly, with scattered men pushing through the others and shouting the name of Killed Many. But it grew quickly to a clamoring mass of fighting men crowding around the Great Chief.

In midafternoon a schooner landed at Agate Bay. Her timing was fortuitous. She unloaded 500 new steel swords. She also unloaded three more logging crews complete with kaabors for skidding logs. Large piles of charcoal were waiting on the wharf, and when the swords had been unloaded, men with wheelbarrows began loading the charcoal into the holds.

* * *

The next morning the Cadriio brothers, with Killed Many's principal subchief, rode north on the trail to the Aazhmili lands. Behind them came other prominent Innjoka warriors, the principal shaman, two squads of Killed Many's household warriors, and the decade of Hrummean cavalry. And the cadres from the north who'd been trained in the new ways and would teach them to their people.

They'd force a march to the Icy River, where the warriors of the northern tribes were gathering, and cajole and coerce until they too accepted the new ways.

So much to do, Eltrienn thought, *and so little time*. But so far, he reminded himself, things had gone surprisingly well.

Fifty-Three

The schooner *Karassia* had been one of the largest vessels in the Djezian trade, larger, really, than was often called for. Now King Gamaliiu had closed the port of Haipoor l'Djezzer to Hrummean shipping, and though minor ports in Djez Gorrbul still were open, along with the ports of Djez Seechul of course, trade was down seriously.

Then, two weeks ago, the *Karassia* had been caught in a white squall while approaching the firth, driven aground, and the wind had stripped her of canvas and masts, though dropping soon enough that she hadn't broken up. Her owner had had her cargo lightered into harbor, leaving the wreck where she lay for the time.

With trade what it was, the government had been able to buy her cheaply. Shipwrights had patched her hull, then a salvage barge had dropped anchor hooks on the shelf a hundred yards offshore, and at floodtide, oarsmen rowed the barge to within fifty feet of the derelict's sternpost. A workboat took a line to her, and with it a cable was pulled across. Then eight burly oarsmen at the capstans had winched the barge seaward by the anchor chains, pulling the *Karassia* off the shoal.

They tugged her into harbor, where the navy jury-rigged two short spars on her. They'd bear enough canvas to take her down the coast not many miles. Thus rigged, and rocks loaded for ballast, a naval crew had sailed her back out of the firth by the first light of dawn, an hour when few or none would notice and talk. A light sloop trailed her to bring her crew back.

* * *

Elver Brokols and Reeno Venreeno had been intensely busy on the submarine mine project the past three weeks. Their days had been long, their nights short. Part of the time they'd been in the capital and part at Hidden Haven. Juliassa had worked with them, just as long and hard as they, and had ridden most of the courier trips.

To get manufacturing started, they'd had to finalize certain design features before they felt ready. The cylindrical casings were no thicker than thought necessary for sufficient strength. As designed, they'd hold forty pounds of gunpowder in the charge end if need be, but no more than that. With thirty pounds plus a weight added to approximate the fuse mechanism, the flotation chamber tended to float the mine to the surface, though two sullsi, or one for that matter, could easily hold it down while swimming underwater. Adding a couple of pounds gave neutral flotation. With forty pounds, two sullsi still could manage it easily.

With this established, several ceramicists began to make casings.

Meanwhile a clockmaker's shop had undertaken to produce reliable spring-driven clocks and firing mechanisms, and Reeno had assigned a man to test them in every position—rightside up, upside down, and sideways. The designs were successful. Test clocks proved accurate to within five minutes over a ten-hour period—quite good considering they were spring driven. Production was begun, with each day's production tested overnight.

The clockmaker and his workers had no notion of what the clocks were for. All they knew was that they'd been sworn not to tell that they were making clocks for the government.

Meanwhile Amaadio had found that gleebor excrement was another source of "saltpeter." They'd use nightbird dung as long as it lasted—it was more concentrated—but if the supply ran out, they now had a backup source, pre-dried for easy processing.

Followed by the sloop, the sturdy *Karassia* entered Hidden Haven and dropped the hook in the middle of the inlet. After unseating her spars and wiring them to cleats, the *Karassia*'s crew was taken to the sloop, and they left the inlet.

Brokols and Reeno had decided the test should be at

night—that's when the actual mining was planned for—so with Juliassa, Torissia, and Jonkka they mounted their kaabors and went riding on the plateau to relax. The military guard detail remained at the hamlet.

A breeze, cool and dry for the season, ruffled hair and brightened spirits as they rode; meadow flowers bobbed and danced in it. Birds called, swooped, darted at insects. Harriers sailed swift and low, stooped at rodents and rose again.

They were back in time for supper, then walked down to the beach. The three sullsi had arrived, and K'sthuump, and they waited together till dark, Juliassa asking questions and answering theirs. She was getting to know a lot about the sea people. Finally it was dark. Two of the sullsi (not including Sleekit, whose metamorphosis made his hands less dexterous and his strength greater than representative) swam out with a mine charged with thirty-two pounds of gunpowder.

They kept well below the surface, and rose beneath the hull. Even their excellent night vision was inadequate, so that they worked by feel and by their inborn sonar. Their short auger started the screw holes without difficulty, and they had no trouble attaching what they hoped was a ship-slayer.

Then they swam back to shore and, with the humans, lay around for a while; the timer in the mine had been set to allow for difficulties.

A muffled boom ended their wait. The sullsi hurried out to the *Karassia*, Brokols and Reeno following in a rowboat with Juliassa. The sullsi dove to examine the hole, and although the ship was settling notably before the humans got there, they boarded her and went below with a lantern to see how flooding was progressing. The hole was five feet wide; water was rising rapidly in the hold. Pumping would have been futile without quick and effective patching, and the ships of the fleet would hardly have patches prepared. Why should they?

The old schooner was doomed. The humans got hurriedly back into the rowboat and pulled away, then sat and watched the *Karassia* sink in fifty feet of water. When she disappeared, they exchanged quiet congratulations and hugs, more in relief than exhilaration.

"Well," said Venreeno, "we've got our ship-slayer."

"Yes, we do," Brokols answered. It occurred to him that the mines might slay more than ships. Some of the crew members might be below, close to an exploding mine, might be killed, or made unconscious so they'd drown. He felt no dismay at the thought—they weren't his countrymen anymore—and wondered at his lack of feeling.

Reeno looked at K'sthuump and the sullsi. "Juliassa," he said, "interpret for me. Are any of you familiar with the islands along the Djezian coast, and the first great harbor behind them? We call it Haipoor l'Djezzer, and it's where we expect the fleet to anchor to land the troops."

All three sullsi, and K'sthuump too, knew the harbor, knew the entire Inside Passage between the islands and the low mainland shore. Both species had well-developed curiosity, and few accessible places were unknown to them. K'sthuump, whose long neck provided an elevated viewpoint, had the best mental images of the place. With their help, Reeno and Brokols began to work out the details of just how the mission would be carried out.

FIFTY-FOUR

The distance from Theedalit to the defensive positions at the north end of the Isthmus of Kammenak was some three hundred winding miles. Brokols rode for seven days to get there, and it showered on all but one of them. He'd left Reeno behind to look after the production of mines and grenades, and a youthful lieutenant, Gorrvis Vendorrci, had been assigned as Brokols' aide for the trip. Like Eltrienn, Gorrvis was a native of Kammenak.

Much of the distance was over rolling plateaus cut deeply here and there by valleys, mostly narrow. The streams were high in that season, and some of the fords worrisome. The isthmus itself was rugged hills—steep longitudinal ridges separated by canyons—and its streams were creeks that in the dry season, Brokols suspected, would become mere trickles or dry up.

He saw almost no settlement on the isthmus; all the traffic on the rough and rocky roads was wagons with military supplies. The dwellings were mostly huts, according to Gorrvis for herdsmen and the rangy, nipping kiennos that helped move the herds from place to place. Almost all the herds were vehatto; you could hear their plaintive high-pitched cries a mile or more. The land was too steep for decent gleebor pasturage.

The two men were hungry, saddle-weary, and pungent with sweat when they arrived at regional defense headquarters five miles from the Gorrbian border. A sergeant ushered them into the sprawling command tent and presented them to general Doziellos. The general stood up to greet them and shake Brokols' hand, looking him over with interest. "So you're the one responsible for grenades."

"Basically. I was familiar with them—we have them in Almeon—and in a general way I knew their construction. An herbalist solved the key problems."

The general nodded. Brokols wondered what that meant, if anything.

"The report I was given," said the general, "says you've been an army officer in your own country; that you're to look us over and suggest possible changes we might make."

"That's right, General. But don't expect too much. I am not a tactical genius. In fact, I was a rather low-ranking officer of cavalry—a senior lieutenant, the executive officer of a squadron."

Again Doziellos nodded, this time a sharp little nod. "Well," he said, "let's go see how we look to you."

First they visited an advance ridgetop fort. It was a simple strongpoint, its thick walls of dry-laid rock about fifteen feet tall. In front of it the ridge ended, sloping down to an undulating plain and Djez Gorrbul.

Doziellos and Brokols stood atop a wall, Doziellos pointing. All along the border there were three forts on every ridge top and six in each intervening canyon. Those on the crests were walled on four sides, while those in the canyon bottoms were a single wall across the canyon, with another back about two hundred yards and several more behind that at varying intervals. The canyons were the natural routes up the isthmus. Any attack on the canyon strongpoints would come under fire from one or more of the ridge-top forts. The idea was to deny an invader access up the canyons.

"Why not bigger walls?" Brokols asked.

"It's partly a lack of decent building stone," Doziellos explained, "and the difficulty in storming them as they are. The rock around here is pretty rotten. But mostly it's a matter of policy. The intention is less to stop the enemy here than to cost him dearly."

"How wide is the isthmus?" Brokols asked.

"For most of its length, from five to six miles."

"Even with the long haul for building stone," Brokols said, "I'm surprised you haven't built a wall all the way across down there." Brokols pointed to the plain at the toes of the ridges. "Considering how long you've had troubles with the Gorrbians. You could have done it bit by bit, taken a century if you wanted."

Doziellos grunted. "A thousand years ago we started to. Darrto Pileggri, the principal sage then, warned against it, but he had no military background, and he was ignored. But the Gorrbians didn't like us building it, so before we'd gotten well started, they brought an army and overran it, then drove on up the isthmus. Fifteen weeks later they took Serrnamo, our capital then, and we lived with their heel on our neck for fifty-six years.

"After our war of independence, we developed the system we have now. The ridgetop forts are costly to attack; the Gorrbians learned that the hard way, more than once. And they're hard to bypass, because of the canyon strongpoints, while as you can see, the ridge sides are too steep for kaabors; it's hard enough for a man to walk along them. Our archers and arbalesters can shoot anyone that tries.

"And we have sentries out at night, with kiennos, watching for infiltrators."

Brokols nodded thoughtfully. Archers like those he'd watched could exact a heavy price. He'd seen men shoot five arrows in ten seconds and put all of them in a straw dummy at sixty yards. He'd seen the same thing tried at 150 yards with two hitting the dummy! "But if the Gorrbians do take one of the ridgecrest forts," Brokols said, "they can direct their own archery at your canyon bottom positions from above."

"True. If they capture a ridgecrest position, we'd likely pull out of any bottom strongpoints they could fire on. Back from the forts, we'll use ambush, cavalry strikes—whatever's appropriate to the position and strength of the enemy. We've studied and mapped the entire isthmus from this point of view. The function of the strongpoints is to blunt and slow enemy attacks and make them pay heavily. Your grenades will contribute to that. And the dam you saw below the headquarters? We can open it. There's one in each canyon.

"Yes, we quite expect them to overrun the strongpoints if they have the will."

Brokols nodded slowly. "I presume you've been told that the Gorrbians will probably have cannon, and what those are like."

Doziellos nodded. "Yes, and that if they do use such monstrous things, they can hammer our strongpoints to rubble.

We'll have to adjust to that if it happens. It may be necessary to abandon our strongpoints early, and fight on the move, though I hope not."

"Perhaps there's a way to avoid that," Brokols suggested.

"If there is, I want to know about it."

"Well then," Brokols said, "here is what you watch for. . . ."

Fifty-Five

The harvest crew didn't actually stop work to watch. But they paused from time to time, just for a moment, not long enough to anger the field boss, who himself was watching the long train of tawny dust that rose to the north up the road. The scythes missed only a sweep or two at a time, the long-tined wooden rakes no more than a couple of strokes. The women who piled the lenn vines on the many-branched drying poles looked northward for just a breath or two, wiping away sweat with a long sleeve before raising another load on their pitchforks.

The dust was raised by booted feet, by hundreds of soldiers in a column of twos, carrying light packs. The route was long, and their duffel bags were being hauled on wagons. For Almeon the day was hot and humid, and their officers set a hard pace of four miles an hour. So they sweated, and the dust that rose from their boots formed mud on their faces. Sergeants ranged alongside snapping, shouting to close it up, whacking occasional laggards with their batons.

They didn't know, most of them, how much farther it was to Larvis Harbor, they only knew they'd be glad to get there. Even though it meant going to war. Because the rumor was, they'd be on ships for sixty days, and there'd be no way to drill them aboard ship.

While at the other end of the voyage—Victory! Victory over the droids, that looked like people but weren't.

Then, far ahead, an officer bellowed for double-time, and the command was passed along the column. Muttering curses, the troops broke into a trot. Ahead, their road joined another in an inverted "Y," and on the other branch of the "Y," some distance farther back, a column of cavalry had been spotted. The major wanted to reach the "Y" first; that would block the road, and the Dard-cursed riders would have to eat their dust instead of vice versa.

As the lead company passed the harvest crew, the laborers did stop briefly to watch. So many soldiers! Their field boss shouted then: "Get to work, Dard blast ye! Or I'll uncoil me lash!" They bent again to their labor, a few of the youngest wishing they were off to the droid land as a soldier.

The cavalry commander saw what was happening, and ordered his troopers to a trot, then a canter, and at the last a gallop. They thundered into the junction not more than three dozen yards ahead of the foot troops, then slowed, while the infantry battalion jammed to a stop. The infantry commander stood glowering at the mounted troops, smelling their sweaty, farting animals and grinding their dust between his teeth.

FIFTY-SIX

The return trip to Theedalit took Brokols and Vendorrci twelve days, five days longer than the trip out. Brokols had taken sick early on the second day out of Kammnalit, puking and shitting, sweating and shaking, and occasionally babbling out of his mind. During his semi-alert periods, the first two days, he wondered if he was going to die. It was over with, though, on the morning of the third. He'd rested on the third and fourth, and would have rested longer, but he had a wedding to go to in Theedalit—his own. Instead, for the first two days back on the road, they'd taken it easy, resting often in the shade, snacking.

When he'd just begun coming down with it, they'd stopped at a hamlet, where Vendorrci had rented an unused hut and helped the trembling Brokols to bed. Meanwhile a youth had ridden to a village some miles away to bring a master who lived there. Brokols couldn't remember what the master had done, but he had the distinct if subjective impression that the man had saved his life. The people there said that child fever was going around; apparently he'd been infected, and it had hit him far more severely than it did Hrummean children.

When they got back to Theedalit, he looked and felt pretty much normal, perhaps a little weak. He luxuriated in the hot tub while his houseman took his Hrummean road clothes to a washerwoman. (Brokols never wore Almaeic clothes anymore.) A long night's sleep in his own bed completed his recovery.

He was not allowed to see Juliassa, or allowed in her home while she was there, as was the custom during the week before the wedding. Instead, on the second morning he was taken to a wedding grove to practice the ceremony. In Theedalit there were one or more wedding groves in every park, large or small, and one in the garden of the amirrial palace. The groves were sacred to Hrum, and they were where weddings were held. In each there was a round gazebo about twenty feet in diameter, where the actual ceremony was performed. The gazebos were pillared and without walls, but trellised and vine-grown behind the alter, which was on the west side.

In an earlier stage of Hrummlis, night had been regarded as the time belonging to Makklith, the female aspect of Hrum in charge of sex and birth. Thus tradition had weddings taking place at dusk, to represent the change from singleness to marriage. The wedding would be presided over by a master, but for Brokols' practice, Reeno Venreeno presided, and Gorrvis Vendorrci stood in for the bride. Beside the alter were two open bronze lamps on tall stands, and a fire was lit in each of them, as during the actual ceremony.

Venreeno himself had been remarried while Brokols was off in Kammenak.

There was no set wording for the service. The master would speak as Hrum-In-Him prompted, although the thoughts expressed were custom, and did not vary, however phrased. Reeno said those same things during the rehearsal—reflecting ideas they'd discussed earlier in their talk on being a husband. They practiced the ceremony twice, then Reeno declared it enough.

After that, Brokols went to his apartment, and with his houseman packed his things. He didn't have a lot; he'd rented the place furnished. Then he had his chests and boxes loaded on a wagon and hauled to a small house near the palace, bought and furnished for the couple by Leonessto. Juliassa's things had already been moved in and arranged as she wanted them. Brokols was leery about moving or even touching any of it, so he had most of his piled temporarily in a storeroom.

An exception was the wireless; a room had been set aside for it.

The next morning he went to Reeno's office and got updated on both the grenade and mine projects. Gleebor manure was being used to make saltpeter in quantity now. A large quantity of grenades had already been shipped to Kammenak by boat. Also, a dozen or more mine casings were being built each day, though only a few had yet been loaded with gunpowder. Production of clocks and trigger mechanisms had been slower, but even so, the current rate of production was predicted to fill their needs, and production was increasing with the experience of the artisans. Three east-coast schooners had been chartered and brought around to transport the mines and personnel, and K'sthuump had assured Juliassa that week that more sullsi were enroute to the islands off Haipoor l'Djezzer than were actually needed.

Brokols was a bit uncomfortable about the time prediction. After all, it was based on a dream!—the dream he'd had of the fleet leaving Almeon during lenn harvest. It had seemed so real and compelling when he'd dreamed it, but now, in the cold light of logic . . . every time he thought about it, he had a pang of anxiety.

But the dreamed departure time was much earlier than originally expected, so it didn't really prey on his mind. Much better to err in that direction than in the other, although it would be a terrific nuisance to be more than a couple of weeks early.

FIFTY-SEVEN

Brokols had been freshly barbered and manicured. And he'd bathed thoroughly, of course. Wearing a simple unadorned robe of perfect whiteness, he stood at one side of the gazebo, wrapped in a sense of unreality, as if in a dream.

On the opposite side stood Juliassa, similarly robed but with a loose, plaited belt of gold cord round her waist. To Brokols she looked incredibly beautiful. Her hair, more copper than blond and grown now to shoulder length, had been brushed straight, and it sheened in the lamplight. Her eyes were downcast, her smile demure, but he had no doubt that would change when the ceremony was over.

Master Jerrsio presided at the alter. Nearly half the gazebo was reserved for the master and the two celebrants. The amirr and naamir stood together in the center, and behind them, standing guests filled the rest of the gazebo, to spill broadly out across a lawn roofed and made sparse by huge spreading trees. Lamplight and shadow fluttered on intent faces. To Elver Brokols it had the feel of another world, another time.

Near Juliassa, at the edge of the gazebo, a seated musician had been playing dreamily, unobtrusively, on a lap harp. Now she began to stroke the strings more strongly, and a flutist behind her began to play, generating music unlike any that Brokols had heard either here or in Almeon. It made gooseflesh flow from his scalp to his legs, and he felt as if he enclosed his body instead of being enclosed by it.

Master Jerrsio looked at Juliassa, then at Brokols, and gestured them to him. They walked toward each other, eyes meeting, and again Brokols' scalp prickled, then they turned and faced the master.

"Good evening," Jerrsio said. "It is the time. Are both of you here because you wish to be here?"

"I am." They said it in virtual unison.

"Excellent. Now I will speak to you of certain things that are a part of marriage."

His eyes were level, calm, direct. Safe. "Love one another," he said, "but do not bind one another with your love. For you are separate beings, and it is better that there be space between you, for freedom of life and movement. Fill each other's cup, but drink each from your own. Sing and dance together to life's music, but let each of you be separate, as the strings of Yelldas' harp are separate, though they vibrate together and contribute to the same music.

"Love can be joyful, and it need not be painful. Let your love be neutral, not clutching, not demanding. Let it be free of 'must' and 'must not.' Do not command where to go and how to be, but find pleasure in letting the other live. Mention, do not demand; suggest, do not insist. And let the mentioning be light as air, the suggestion without force.

"Admire one another but do not adore one another, for adoration is rope that restricts and glue that immobilizes. Enjoy each other. Give freely to one another and accept from each other, but do not force what you would give, and do not demand what you would accept."

Jerrsio paused, still looking mildly at the couple in front of him. Brokols stood bemused by his words, aware of little else. Reeno had said somewhat the same things to him, both in his lesson on being a husband and in the wedding rehearsal. But from Jerrsio the words struck deeper.

"Have you understood what I have said?" Jerrsio asked.

The replies came in unison again: "I have."

"Good. Does either of you feel any reservation about what I have said?"

"No."

"None."

"Good. Then in the name of Hrum, I bless the marriage which Hrum-In-Thee has created. Go and share your love each with the other."

The master grinned then and gestured them together. The couple embraced and kissed slowly, tenderly, while the crowd applauded, then they all flowed into the palace.

Food and drink had been set out in the party hall, but that was for the guests. Leonessto and Morrvia steered the couple into a small room and toasted the marriage, then sat down with them for a light and private meal. When they'd eaten, the amirr rang a hand bell. A servant came in, and Torissia, and while the servant cleared away the food and dishes, Torissia led the couple to the small, third-floor bridal suite, leaving them alone there. Her trial as chaperone was over.

FIFTY-EIGHT

The newlyweds had planned to go to Sea Cliff the next day. Not for a vacation; they both had far too much to do. But Sea Cliff was a better place to do what they intended. Sleekit and K'sthuump, and Sleekit's two packmates, had come to the firth, so that Juliassa could keep track of the sullsi volunteers through the Vrronnkiess telepathic network. That morning they'd started off swimming south to Sea Cliff.

The intention was for Brokols to get a good working knowledge of sullsit, so he could help oversee the sullsi in mining the Almaeic fleet.

They delayed leaving for three days though, because when Brokols approached to mount his kaabor, it kicked him in the leg and broke his shinbone. A clean break, fortunately. Casts hadn't been invented yet in Hrumma, and the technology for pinning broken bones was well beyond them. Such a break required leaving splints on for a dozen weeks or more, while crutches were used.

This meant a change in operating plans, of course. Now Brokols would stay behind when the schooners left. Jonkka would learn sullsit with him (a project that had the big guard worried), and he'd go with the minesetting flotilla in Brokols' place, to help Juliassa oversee the mining.

The three extra days in Theedalit were not wasted. An omission had occurred to Brokols, an overlooked opportunity. If the emperor's fleet had sailed, there should be at least occasional wireless traffic between its flagship and the rest.

And if they'd left when he thought, they'd probably be near enough now for him to pick up their calls.

So he had his chair wheeled into the wireless room, prepared to spend as much time as it took, tuning up and down the shortwave band looking for wireless traffic. The first evening he'd gotten a surprise. He found traffic that proved to be between Kryger and the Gorrbian invasion base at the northern end of the isthmus. Either Kryger had given up his backup set, or he'd had a spare. Their language was Djezian, of course, and its alphabet was different from Almeon's. But the sounds were mostly similar, and Kryger had chosen to wireless Djezian messages with the Almaeic alphabet rather than develop and learn a wireless code for the Djezian.

It was a valuable frequency to know, and it made Brokols more willing to stay behind when the flotilla left. He could monitor the invasion headquarters' reports to Haipoor.

The next day he ran into wireless traffic near the edge of his instrument's ability to receive. (His was considerably less sensitive than Kryger's larger set.) But he got enough signal to know it was the fleet. His plans were *not* too advanced. Hopefully they were advanced enough; somehow he felt they were.

Fifty-Nine

The fishing boat *Merrias Lar* wallowed and staggered as the two men at her steering oar held her at an angle across the waves. She wore no canvas that night, not even her jib, getting her steerage from the brawny backs of eight men at the oars. The wind was a hoarse bass, the foaming surf a distant growl, but through the darkness, the skipper had seen a gap in the breakers, the sort of gap that should mean a stream mouth, and they angled toward it, hoping to reach its channel before the surf grabbed them.

They rode a wave in diagonally, the steersman fighting the oar, and shallow though they drafted, both skipper and steersman tensed, half expecting to run aground. Then they were through, into a river channel some sixty or seventy feet wide, flanked with rushes eight feet tall or more.

The skipper knew what it was, or thought he did. On the Gulf of Storms, much of the Djezian shore was marshland. Several rivers came down from the north, each forming a delta at its mouth, emptying into the gulf through multiple channels. This would be a lesser channel of the River Bron, the skipper told himself, unless they'd been driven farther west than he thought.

He walked between his oarsmen, slopping ankle deep in water they'd shipped, to the bow where he took up the sounding pole. This lower reach of the channel was deep; he couldn't find the bottom with it. Some two hundred yards upstream, they came to a rough wharf, shored with logs laid end to end behind stout pilings, and semi-decked with ill-sorted poles. On it a row of boats lay upside down.

He waved a thick arm, then gestured. "We'll land here," he said quietly, and the steersman angled them toward it. Two of the seamen crouched, and as the *Lar* drew close alongside, they jumped, lines in their fists, and made fast to pilings.

"Take up the decking and bail her out," the skipper ordered. "We'll wait here till the storm eases." Then he and his steersman got out and examined the boats on the wharf. There were ten of them, a somewhat varied lot, of a size for fishing. But why here? There was no hamlet in sight, no habitation at all, no racks or reels for drying nets and lines.

The rain, which had become intermittent, had turned off now, at least for the moment, and stars shown through breaks in the clouds. Great Liilia peered at them through scud, lighting the scene.

He went to an end boat and called to his men. "Help me turn her over," he ordered. They did. It was a fishing boat, fairly representative of the others there, a bit over twenty feet long—maybe twenty-two or three, with an eight-foot beam, and a sixteen-inch keel that ran most of her length. Stowed beneath her were ten oars plus a steering oar. And a stubby mast with folded canvas, the sort of thing you might give a landlubber to sail.

"Look at all the benches in her!" the steersman said. "I've never seen the like!"

The captain's eyes took it all in. These were no seats for a single oarsman, but ran across from flank to flank. "Aye," he said. "And the size of her water cask." He stepped quickly to the next boat in line, and they tipped it enough that he could see her equipage. "The same, or close enough," he muttered. "They'll seat thirty men, about."

"What in Hrum's name are they for?" one of the men asked.

They looked at one another. Several had the same thought. They tipped up two more; each had benches like the first two. "One'll get you three," the steersman said, "that there's boats like these in every channel around here. And these ten alone would carry three hundred men."

"Aye," said a sailor. "Meanwhile I'll bet there's damned little fishin' gettin' done. Old Gamaliiu probably commandeered every boat on the south Djezian shore."

The skipper's eyes were hard. "Let's turn this one back over," he said. "Then bail the *Lar* and stretch the awnings.

We'll catch some sleep and leave as soon as the wind allows. Usippi, the first watch's yours."

"And take the hatchets to these?" one of the men asked, gesturing at the Gorrbian boats.

The skipper scowled; the thought of holing a boat made a bilious taste in his mouth. "No," he said. "We'll leave 'em as is. They're just ten out of however many; and if they know we've found 'em, they'll be warned and set guards.

"Leave no sign we've been here. We'll take the word home and let Leonessto and his folks decide what to do about 'em."

SIXTY

. . . and their powder charges were uniform. Because instead of teaching the Gorballis to make gunpowder, which would not have been suitably uniform and would thus have resulted in inaccurate fire, Lord Kryger appropriated much of the standardly manufactured powder in carefully weighed powder bags in the magazines of the Emperor Dard. *This permitted excellent accuracy. He also gave the Gorballis most of the* Dard's *explosive shells, and had the cannon barrels cast and rifled to accommodate them.*

Captain Stedmer at first refused to surrender either powder or shells. By wireless, Lord Kryger then took the matter to the prime minister, who authorized him to confiscate them if necessary. At that, of course, Captain Stedmer gave in.

From: Memoirs of Midshipman Erlin Werlingus

General Doziellos stood on the wall, peering through his telescope. Two days after Brokols had left Kammenak, lookouts at the advance forts had reported Gorrbian army engineers setting up a vast camp on the plain across the border. Now, this morning, they'd reported the appearance of numerous small haystacks associated with paddocks for the Gorrbian kaabors. Hay would be brought in, of course. But a dozen of the stacks had each a wagon and cart parked near it, with tarpaulins tied over them. Much as the foreigner, Brokols, had said might happen.

Lowering the telescope, Doziellos turned to his intelligence aide. "Major, d'you see those haystacks? With the covered carts by them? I want you to carry out Cannon Plan Two tonight. Find out if there's anything besides hay in them."

The man lowered his own glass. "Cannon Plan Two. Yessir. And for what it's worth, sir, my guts tell me we'll find what the foreigner said we would." He'd wrapped his tongue cautiously around the foreign word, *cannon*. It'd be interesting to see one, especially in action, but not pointed in his direction.

Their uniforms were dyed black and their faces smeared with charcoal. They moved through the starlit night almost as quietly as a barbarian hunter.

Lieutenant Vendunno could see the haystack now, and more dimly the wagon. He stopped creeping, the two men with him following suit. After examining what he could see and hear of their immediate surroundings, he signalled—made three low sharp hisses—and continued toward the haystack. His two men should be creeping to examine the cart and wagon.

There seemed to be no sentries around. Probably the Gorballis saw no need of any and preferred not to draw attention to the haystacks. Or maybe they were just hay. Nonetheless he slowed as he neared the stack, and lowered himself to his belly, crawling.

The hay smelled fresh-cured. When he reached it, he burrowed in, forcing his way, eyes closed to protect them, feeling ahead of him as he crawled, breathing dust, and quickly touched something hard that felt like stout timber. He stopped, felt around, discovered a rather small thick wheel. Pushing against the weight of hay, he got to his knees, hands probing higher now. Leaves and chaff itched inside his uniform. He felt hard cylindrical metal with the texture of unpolished iron.

On hands and knees once more, he backed away carefully, trying to disturb the hay as little as possible, then stopped and rose to his knees again, feeling above him. The iron was still there. His hands crawled, found an end of it. With a hole! A hole that his hand said was about the width of his palm.

Lowering himself again, he crawled backward out of the stack and looked around. He wished he could take off his uniform and shake the chaff out. Both his men were ready and waiting for him. Without a whispered word they crawled toward their own lines. When they were well away, they heard trotting hooves, and flattened till the Gorrbian security patrol was well past. After that they rose to a crouch and hurried, but not carelessly, until the ends of two ridges rose on each side. Inky shadows filled the canyon bottom, and a low voice challenged: "Who's there?"

"Borrsio's grandsons," Vendunno answered quietly.

"Advance and be recognized."

They did, one of the sentries stepping out to peer closely at them, while others unseen surely stood by with bent bows, naked swords, and one with trumpet ready to blare.

"They're all right," said the first, and the reconn patrol walked through, still quietly.

"Maatio, what did you find?" Vendunno asked at last.

"The cart was full of cylinders, sir, tapering at one end to a sort of blunt point. About this big around." He indicated a diameter of roughly four inches.

"Not iron balls then?"

"No, sir."

Vendunno looked at the other man. "And you?"

"The wagon had sacks in it. Felt as if they were full of sand."

Unconsciously the lieutenant began to walk faster, eager to report. It was pretty much as Doziellos suspected. The only difference was that the carts held cylinders instead of iron balls. Verdunno wondered if he'd be going out there again tomorrow night.

Doziellos had sent patrols to check out two haystacks that had carts and wagons by them, and two that did not. They'd checked out as he'd expected: The stacks with carts and wagons concealed what could only be the "cannons" the foreigner had warned about. Those without wagons and carts seemed to be simply hay.

So, he thought, *twelve cannons then*. The only false note was that the carts held cylinders four or five inches across instead of iron balls. He didn't know what that might mean, but cannon they surely seemed to be, which meant carrying out Plan Three tomorrow night.

Great Lillia's crescent was setting later and thicker each night, casting more light. And they didn't want to be spotted by Gorrbian sentries or security patrols, so they hadn't started till well on toward midnight. Vendunno wasn't as relaxed about this one. Last night only three patrols besides his own had gone out. Tonight there were twelve, all told, which tripled the odds of someone being spotted and alarming the whole damned Gorrbian army. And last night they'd chosen haystacks with no squad tents close at hand. Tonight they couldn't do that.

He was glad he'd been given the same stack as before. The nearest tents to it were a couple hundred feet away. It didn't help stealth any, though, that Maatio was carrying two tied leather sacks of cement mud slung over his shoulders. They made it harder to sneak. And they couldn't hide for long to avoid security patrols because the damn cement would start setting up, and they needed it liquid enough to pour.

About halfway there they heard hooves again, and lay flat in a slight depression where the grass was longer. *Be a hell of a thing if they rode right into us,* Vendunno thought, but they passed a hundred feet away, and he relaxed. Nothing more happened all the way to the haystack.

Vendunno found the cannon muzzle again without burrowing in, just stood outside and groped, then removed an armful of hay and took one of the bags from Maatio. Its lashing had been untied. He poured the mud into the bore, then poked his hand in, pushed the mud deeper, and repeated with the other sack. They'd brought two in case something happened and they lost one of them, but it seemed to him he might as well use them both. When he was done, he stuffed both bags in his waistband, and they tidied up the haystack as best they could.

They'd crawled back maybe a hundred yards when they heard shouts from east aways, then more shouts. Hooves drummed in that direction. "Let's move it!" Vendunno husked, and crouched, they started running through the darkness, back toward the canyon.

General Doziellos needed to know what the results had been. Thus he waited in the dark, in the mouth of Canyon Three—what the troops had nicknamed Headquarters Canyon. Each returned spiking team had been put on kaabors and brought to him when they checked in at a sentry point. At least six cannons had been spiked with concrete. Maybe more, depending on whether the two teams who hadn't gotten back had spiked theirs before they were discovered. Four other teams had sneaked back without reaching their targets; theirs had been close to Gorrbian tents, and with the uproar, it had seemed both futile and suicidal to go on with it.

So there were between four and six cannons not spiked.

He'd hoped they wouldn't have to use Plan Four, but he'd prepared for it; it meant more casualties than he liked to take. His lips thinned. Before this year was over, he told himself, he'd be calloused to casualties.

So. Plan Four, and carry it out tonight. Odds were that the Gorballis didn't realize what the prowlers had been doing. But by daylight they'd almost surely notice that some of the haystacks had been disturbed—the stacks concealing the cannons. They'd discover what had happened, and set strong guards on the cannons that remained.

And it was important to nullify all of them.

He gave the order. Messengers climbed into their saddles and rode out of the canyon, trotting their kaabors to the cavalry troops waiting for this contingency. With as much neutrality as he could muster, he dropped a hint to Hrum that he'd like this to work. And that he'd prefer to have as many of his men as possible get back safely.

Then, grim-faced, he rode up the canyon some three-quarters of a mile and took the trail that slanted up Ridge Four, the highest, the backbone of the isthmus, toward its first-line fort. He'd be able to see at least something from up there, although dark as it was, he might not know what he was seeing.

Doziellos stared into blackness. Surely, he thought, they should have struck by now. But he hadn't seen or heard a thing, except for night fires, tiny in the distance, a sign that the Gorballis had become more watchful. Stealth wouldn't buy much now; they'd been alarmed. The best he could hope for was to confuse them. Ride in, quietly until you'd been discovered, then charge hard, carry out your missions, and flee.

He was too far away to hear the shouts or even see the fire arrows as they arced toward some of the haystacks. He hoped they hadn't fired stacks that hid cannons. The idea was to fire stacks that concealed nothing—draw attention to them and the men who'd fired them—while other kaabormen spiked the remaining unspiked cannons. But it was awfully damned dark out there; it would be easy to make mistakes.

And now he could hear trumpets, distant and faint, and Gorrbian because he'd sent no trumpets out. A few minutes later there was a tremendous roar, a great flash of flame, and what seemed to be burning hay blew billowing. A minute or so later there was another explosion, and quickly a third. He clenched his jaw in chagrin; it seemed to him they'd lit some wrong haystacks. A fourth followed several minutes later.

Things quieted then, and after several more minutes of futile staring he rode grim-faced out of the fort and south along the ridge.

His forward headquarters were south along the crest at the third fort. From there his signalman could see all the forts on all the ridges, and read their semaphores and signal torches. The isthmus was a lousy place to invade, but it was even worse to courier messages. Luckily it wasn't the season for fogs this far north.

Arriving, he got off his kaabor. An orderly took the reins and led it to the stable to be rubbed down and fed. Doziellos found himself wondering again how many cannons they'd missed. Maybe the gunpowder that blew up was at cannons spiked earlier; maybe they *had* gotten them all.

Go to bed, he told himself. *Get some sleep. You've done what you could. They'll tell you what happened in the morning.*

Sixty-One

Marshal Grimmuh Formaalu grimaced at the cannon. Its bore was clear, but its carriage charred and overturned, a wheel broken, by the explosion of a powder wagon. "So only two are usable! Shit!" Turning in his saddle, he scanned briefly the rugged ridges across the border, their forts reddened by the rising sun, and the narrow canyons which were also fortified. His thick right arm made a backhand slash of rejection. "It makes no difference," he said to no one in particular. "We'd take them if we had no cannon at all."

He turned his scowl on a junior aide. "Have our best gunners assigned to the cannons that aren't ruined. And get this one onto a new carriage; it might as well be ruined too, the way it is now. Take one from a ruined cannon. Have a platoon of foot assigned to each of the two as protection, and see that the remaining powder and shells are protected too. Right away!"

The aide's hand snapped a salute, fist to breast. "Yessir!"

Then Formaalu touched spur to a flank of his ungelded white kaabor. Wheeling, it broke into a powerful canter in the direction of field headquarters.

His executive officer, Colonel Arruh Mustorru, spurred to keep up, thinking that the old man rode the same way he did most other things: abruptly, plunging, with little finesse and lots of energy. Better to be his EO or his aide than his kaabor. Or one of his harem. Or his enemy.

Doziellos, after a few hours' sleep, was briefed on the morning's observations. Apparently the Gorballis had two functional cannons, not as bad as twelve, but bad enough. They were peculiar looking things: a massive iron tube on a heavy wooden carriage with wide solid wooden wheels. They'd be damned tough to drag through the hills.

He had no doubt the Gorballis would attack soon; you didn't ordinarily bivouac an invasion army on a border and then wait around for very long. He'd see soon enough whether the foreigner's description of what cannons could do was an exaggeration or not.

Meanwhile there wasn't much he could do at headquarters, so he ordered his kaabor brought and started riding along the ridge to the forward fort, his immediate staff following. They'd passed the second fort when he heard a distant boom. *That must be a cannon shooting,* he thought. Then, much nearer, seemingly from the forward fort, another boom! Puzzled, alarmed by the nearer explosion, he spurred his mount to a trot. A minute later another distant boom, and another from near the fort failed to clarify anything for him.

He was less than a quarter mile from the fort when a third and fourth distant booms were followed by a loud one that sent rocks and shards erupting skyward from the fort's rear wall and one more distant from the next ridge west. Shocked, chagrined, he drew up and stared. The foreigner's description hadn't prepared him for this; what kind of iron balls would send rocks high into the air?

As another distant boom sounded, he touched spur to flank again, sending his kaabor forward at a trot. Seconds later there was a roar from within the fort, and screams, and he spurred to a canter. Short of the fort, he reined his kaabor back and dismounted.

"Abrullo!" he shouted. "Vembroosi! Come with me. The rest stay here." Then he darted for the rear gate, others dismounting to hold the vacated kaabors. His orderly also stayed with the general, without being ordered to. It was standard that he do so.

A fifth shell roared against the front of the fort as Doziellos and the others ran in through the rear gate, the only gate. The explosion drove blocks of dry-laid stone from the wall, and others above them fell. These things Doziellos heard and saw in an instant, and they jarred his overloaded senses so that for a moment he wasn't aware of the screaming. Then he heard, cursed, and bellowing orders to the garrison, trotted out the gate, leaving them to remove their wounded. Outside he shouted orders to his signalman, who also dismounted. The signalman unfolded and braced the staff of his signal flag, and began to signal the next fort for stretcher men, and to let them know what the situation was.

Meanwhile his orderly and the two aides followed Doziellos, skidding down the steep side slope a little way, then scrambled along it past the fort. It stood on a prominence just where the ridge began falling away toward the Gorrbian plain. Doziellos stopped a hundred and fifty feet past the fort. He had a clear broad view of the Gorrbian positions. For a moment he simply looked, scanning. Behind him, more shells struck the fort. He saw a puff of smoke, and with his telescope looked at it. The Gorballis had pulled their two usable cannons to about eight hundred yards from the fort behind him, and the fort on the next ridge west. They were bombarding both of them.

And forming up in five broad columns of twelve was an infantry division, its front ranks about four hundred yards from the mouth of the canyon.

The shelling continued. A round fell short of the fort, its explosion stunning Doziellos, showering him with dirt and fragments of rock. Then he heard trumpets and saw the five columns start forward. The flanking columns, he realized, were to take the ridgetop forts while the cannons held the garrisons down. The central three columns would attack up the canyon while the ridgetop bowmen were prevented from shooting down at them effectively.

Doziellos got up and dashed for the rear of the fort again, to his signalman, gasping for breath from the uphill run. He pointed to the lead fort on the next ridge and the second fort on their own. "Signal them that an attack is beginning up Canyon Three and Ridges Three and Four." He turned to an aide. "Ride down the ridge into Canyon Three. Have them hold their positions as long as they possibly can, then fall back to the next. Got that?"

The aide nodded and repeated. He hadn't dismounted; now he simply turned his kaabor and started slanting precariously down the ridgeside.

Doziellos turned to the fort then. Its surviving garrison had gotten out and were crouching behind the rear wall. "Centurion!" he called.

The commander trotted over, looking unsure, concerned. "Centurion, Gorrbian infantry are starting to attack up the ridge. Their cannons will have to stop when their infantry get near the top, and their men will be winded. When the cannons stop, have your people ready to counterattack with archery and grenades. Kill as many as you can." He paused for emphasis. "But don't be overrun. When you have to, go to the second fort. Their cannons aren't supposed to shoot that far." *And the cannon balls—or whatever they were—weren't supposed to blow up like giant grenades, either,* he told himself.

He swung into his saddle then and headed for the ridge's second fort, his aides and orderly with him.

Waiting for the trumpet call, Ramuulo had been glad to be well back in the column. The *Maklannis* had a reputation as archers, and he felt somewhat protected by the mass of men ahead. Ordinarily he didn't like to wait, but he was in no hurry to maybe get killed.

Meanwhile, waiting, he'd had time to look at the rugged hills in front of him. He distrusted hills. In the lower Hasannu River country, where he was from, you could look in any direction and see no hills at all. Suppose the Maklaanis attacked from above. How could you fight with someone coming at you from uphill?

Somewhere well off to his left he heard a thunder weapon speak with a boom, and he looked at the fort to see what would happen. Dirt and rock geysered a little distance in front of it. After a minute the thunder weapon boomed again; this time he could hear the explosion on the ridge but couldn't see it.

Once more the weapon boomed, and this time rock erupted at the base of the wall. The officers said the thunder weapons were a gift from Hrum, to beat down the fort, and it looked now as if there might be something to that. If so, he was all for it.

The thunder weapon to his left was joined by another well off to his right. The first had the range now, and began to fire about twice a minute. He watched explosions against the face of the fort.

Trumpets interrupted his watching, pealing out the "ready" call; he took the target shield from his shoulder, slipped his left forearm under one strap and took hold of the grip. Again the trumpets called. The whole division began to mark time, then the lead ranks began marching briskly toward the canyon in front of them, opening intervals between ranks. Ramuulo marked time until the rank ahead of his had taken its first three steps, then his own rank began to walk, with him as one of its parts.

Although he'd been in the army for five years, with all the unit drills, weapons drills, and war practice that that entailed, Ramuulo had never been in combat heavier than drinking brawls, and now, suddenly, he discovered he was nervous. Extremely nervous. His gut felt knotted. *Shit,* he told himself, *just think of those poor shittin' Maklannis. They're the ones that's gotta be scared. We got the numbers, we got the balls, and we got the thunder weapons.*

Their brisk step brought them quickly to the toes of the long ridges, and they marched into the canyon, more than a hundred yards wide there. Ridges quickly rose to wall it; they made Ramuulo twitchy. In a place like this, numbers didn't mean as much. Rocks made the footing bad, especially in the shallow creek where they were wet. The canyon quickly narrowed. Boulders forced them to break ranks, men slipped and fell. The lines got ragged.

From ahead came shouts, and through the shouts a trumpet signalled first to draw swords, then to double time. They began to jog. Ramuulo heard screams, howls, roars of pain and rage. He stumbled on a rock, nearly fell, cursed.

Then, over the shouts and screaming, there were explosions as of little cannons, one, half a dozen, twenty! The column began to pack up, as if the foremost ranks had slowed to a walk again. The explosions ahead continued. Now Ramuulo could see a stone wall across the canyon, perhaps fifteen feet high, its parapet lined with bowmen. Arrows began to slice the air around him. He became totally alert, peering past his raised shield, walking onward, felt an arrow strike its thick, bullhide-covered disk, was surprised at the force of it, saw men fall wounded or dead.

He marched on past bodies with arrows protruding, bodies red with blood, bodies trying to crawl out of the way. And worse, there were beginning to be bodies torn open, bodies shredded. He stepped over them, hurrying. The explosions continued, some louder than others. One ripped a man open and cast him down, just ahead of Ramuulo; ugly warbling sounds passed his ears. Something hot and acid rose in his esophagus, and he swallowed it back. Dead men were everywhere, and he almost stopped. *When the fuck are they going to blow retreat?* he thought angrily.

The stone wall was just ahead now. He could hardly believe the bodies piled before it. The outer files were javelin men; these would stop, cast their spears at the bowmen, then sword still scabbarded, drop their shields to scrabble on all fours, slipping and swearing, up the ridge slope, trying to flank the wall. Arrows zipped and struck, men fell back sliding, sprawling, dying. And the explosions continued; Ramuulo had no idea what caused them. In the confusion at the foot of the wall, a sergeant had men throwing corpses to form a ramp against it. The sergeant exploded before his eyes, but the men continued their frenzied work.

In the midst of the noise, blood, and confusion, Ramuulo stopped, slung his shield over a shoulder, sheathed his sword. Then he clambered up the gruesome, yielding, slippery ramp, at the wall boosted a man up, heard him bellow and fall back. Then Ramuulo tried to climb it, fingers between dry-laid rocks, and saw what looked like a large, serrated iron egg bounce past him. It did nothing. Someone grasped one of his feet and boosted; Ramuulo got hold of the top of the parapet, swung a leg up. A sword hacked, got more rock than leg, and the swordsman fell backward with a javelin through him. And Ramuulo was somehow atop the wall with sword in hand, striking about him at the bowmen, felt his blade bite flesh, once, twice. Then a sword thrust him through. He felt someone pick him up and hurl him bodily back over the parapet past men who still came on.

Another iron egg arced over the parapet and fell toward him. He watched it and recognized death. It slowed, slowed, *slowed,* then inevitably struck the ground beside him. . . .

Sixty-Two

. . . Each nation on this world and no doubt elsewhere has constraints on its logic and on its willingness to contemplate or at least to act. These constraints can be rooted in painful national experience, and can explain otherwise perplexing failures. (They can also be an opening point in an analysis of cultural realities, something I may undertake in a future volume.)

Djez Gorrbul is a much more populous and powerful nation than Hrumma, and many of her kings have harbored the ambition to rule Hrumma. On a number of occasions, Gorrbul has invaded up the narrow and difficult isthmus which connects the two nations, only to be driven back with severe losses. It would seem that a seaborne invasion, or perhaps better yet a supplemental invasion by sea, would make more sense. Why did Gorrbul so long avoid this? The explanation seems to be as follows.

For very good geographical and economic reasons, Hrumma has a strong seafaring tradition, with many skilled mariners. In fact, Hrumma's seafaring tradition is older than her written history. By contrast, and also for good geographical and economic reasons, Djez Gorrbul has no strong seafaring tradition, and few of her vessels are larger than fishing boats. In fact, Gorrbul even imports some of its fish consumption from Hrumma.

However, about eighteen hundred years ago, a Gorrbian King, Grazonnu XIV, having been rebuffed in an attempted invasion up the Isthmus of Kam-

menak, decided to build a navy and conquer Hrumma by sea. Thus he built a large fleet, which en route to attack the then Hrummean capital of Serrnamo, met with a sudden storm that scattered the Gorrbian ships. Many were never seen again. Others were driven aground or ashore where they were broken up by the waves, and some found their way home. A few reached shelter in two of the Hrummean firths, *great inlets, where the ships were taken as booty and their crews and soldiers sent back on foot to Djez Gorrbul.*

The deity of both the Djezes and Hrumma is believed to be foremost a sea god, and on the basis of the above experience, the kings of Djez Gorrbul took the long-unexamined position that at sea, Hrum favors the seafaring Hrumma over the lubberly Djezes. It was as if to invade Hrumma by sea was to invite the wrath of Hrum. It was more than three hundred years after the loss of their fleet before a Gorrbian king invaded Hrumma again even by land. And in their rather numerous invasions since then, they had always restricted their campaigns to land. . . .

From: Memoirs of Midshipman
Erlin Werlingus

Ambassador Lord Vendel Kryger stood five feet tall, a bit less than average for an adult male Almite, and weighed less than a hundred pounds. Riding a small kaabor beside King Gamaliiu, he looked like a child, a balding preadolescent with a middle-aged face. Marshal Formaalu rode on the king's other side, and Midshipman Werlingus on Kryger's left. Two mounted squads of royal guards flanked them while another rode behind.

The weather had changed overnight. The humidity was lower and the midday breeze cool, with a flavor of coming autumn. The visitors had arrived the evening before, when it was too dark to see much. The country around Haipoor l'Djezzer was tiresomely flat, and it felt good to Kryger to view what the king had called mountains, though by Almaeic standards they were no more than high rugged hills.

Formaalu had updated them on the military situation, then given them a tour of the base before they'd ridden out of camp. Kryger had not been surprised at the order and discipline here. He'd recognized early that in some respects Djez Gorrbul was not greatly inferior to Almeon. Which made it even more attractive as a future imperial possession.

More interesting than the base had been the report on the war. Even though much they'd been told, they'd already known, for numerous kiruu carried miniature dispatches to the capital while an efficient system of mounted couriers rode a tight schedule. So he'd known that Gorrbian casualties had been heavy, particularly on the first day and on the day the dams were opened. And that the Maklanni (the Gorballis called Hrumma *Makklan*, "Hill Land," and its people *Maklanni*, both terms having a derogatory connotation) had a new weapon that looked like a stone and exploded when it hit. Usually. Some malfunctioned.

"Grenades. That has to be Brokols' work," Kryger had said to Werlingus when they'd first heard of it. "And Brokols is obviously responsible for spiking the howitzers. He's been more effective than I'd ever have thought."

As they rode, the king had been mentally reviewing their briefing. "How far did you say my army's advanced?" he asked the marshal.

"About twenty-five miles, Your Majesty. We're moving fairly rapidly now, but the Maklanni do a good job of bleeding us as we go. The isthmus is so damned narrow, our advantage in numbers won't really tell until we're clear of it. That's why I'm holding so many troops here at base camp: I can't really use them yet. I might as well not even have cavalry, as little good as they've been to me so far. But as soon as we break out of the isthmus, it'll be a different story."

Right, thought Kryger. "Your Majesty," he said, "it seems to me that this might be the time to set in motion—what we've prepared."

Gamaliiu smiled broadly. "Exactly what I was thinking. It should take some pressure off Marshal Formaalu's army, yet not leave our—other force susceptible to a major suppressive operation for too long."

SIXTY-THREE

It was night, but not as dark as it might have been. Great Liilia was rising two-thirds full, and Little Firtollio was about on the meridian, halfway through his swift transit. Ten boats in a loosely formed column of twos, rowed through an almost eerie silence broken only by the squeak of oars on tholepins. There was no breeze at all, and the swells, slow and easy, were unruffled, smooth as oil, reflecting the moonlight in two silvery trails.

Lieutenant Korvassu sat in the stern of the lead boat, a fishing boat, holding the steering oar, glancing up now and then at the lodestar which circled only three degrees off true north. On a sea like this, one of the steersmen could easily fall asleep, so most of Korvassu's attention was on the other boats of his flotilla. His was the "flagship," all twenty-five feet of her, and he the "commodore," responsible for seeing that no one got lost—that they all stayed together.

For a moment Korvassu removed his attention to look around as far as light allowed. Somewhere there were supposed to be forty more boats like these, in four separate flotillas. He'd probably never see them; they'd launched from other streams, and hadn't been intended to meet, or to land in the same area. Each flotilla had 250 troops, and the idea after landing was to destroy as much and kill as many, and generally disrupt as much, as they could.

What he hadn't been told, but could figure out for himself, was that the Hrummean army would react by sending a few regiments to hunt them down and kill them. Major Hamaalu was to have them stave their boats after they landed, stave them very thoroughly, supposedly so the Hrummeans couldn't use them. Of course, he couldn't use them either; that was the main and unspoken point. They were supposed to survive and keep fighting until the grand army took Hrumma over.

"Lieutenant!" called a voice from another boat. "My Hrum-bedamned hands are so sore I can hardly row. They're oozing, and sticking to the oar."

"Who's calling?" Korvassu asked.

"Private Nebbek, sir."

"Nebbek, any more bitching out of you and I'll have you thrown overboard. Now shut up and row!"

Their bit of the sea became very quiet again, except for the gentle rub and dip of oars. Korvassu was incensed. *What the fuck does Nebbek think this is? His mother probably didn't wean him till he was twelve*. He'd make sure to adequately punish the man for bypassing his boat sergeant. That would be Sergeant Serrak.

His thoughts went back to their mission in Hrumma. The first thing they had to do was get there. Korvassu had four experienced oarsmen in his own boat. Two were fishermen and one a sailor like himself; the fourth was the son of a river merchant, who'd taken a few minutes to get the hang of rowing in the swells. He'd assigned three of them to row the first hour, to get some progress made and show the lubbers how it was done. Now he was using one or two seasoned oarsmen at a time.

He wondered if he'd really throw Nebbek overboard. Ashore the man had seemed like a pretty good soldier.

Actually they weren't doing badly, probably making somewhat better than two knots. At that rate they'd get to Hrumma in a day or so more of steady rowing. Assuming the men held up, and they'd have to. He had men enough that no one needed to row more than one hour out of two or three.

Now if they'd just get a west wind. Or better yet a north wind, but that was too much to hope for this time of year. *Just be thankful there's no headwind,* he told himself.

Or storm. It was seventy miles or so across the Gulf of Storms, and being so shallow, a squall could build big waves quickly.

A sound pulled Korvassu out of his revery, a sound he couldn't place, and he looked in the direction he thought it had come from. A hiss. Then it repeated, but from the opposite direction, and a voice came across the water.

"Lieutenant! There's a serpent follow—he's gone now. It was a really big one, not ten feet off my . . ."

There was a sudden yelp from the same boat, maybe eighty feet away, then a half shout, half scream. Korvassu stared uncomprehendingly as an oar seemed to lift from the gunwale and fly through the air. A serpent head raised well above the water then, and a man jumped overboard on the other side. There was more yelling, another oar lifted in toothy jaws. His own men had stopped rowing to stare with him.

Abruptly a loud hiss sounded behind him, with a feel of warm, moist, fishy-smelling breath on his neck. Korvassu jerked around to face a large serpent at a distance of fifty inches, its open mouth rimmed with spiky teeth. He managed not to scream. The long neck curved then, the head swooping. It grabbed an oar, lifted and threw it to splash fifty feet away.

"Everyone ship your oars!" Korvassu yelled. Most of the men had never heard the term before, but almost everyone got the idea, and pulling their oars from between the pins, tried to put them on or under the seats. Then serpent necks lifted from both sides of his boat, jaws reached among the men, and more oars were slung away. Most of Korvassu's crew were screaming; two panicked and plunged over the side. Shouts and screams came from everywhere, serpent heads appeared by every boat, and some men threw their oars overboard.

After a wild minute, things went quiet again. Korvassu looked around in the moonlight and saw all ten boats still afloat. None had tipped over. No one was rowing.

"All right men!" he called. "Take a deep breath and relax. Nobody start rowing again, got that? Boat commanders, count the oars you have left, not counting the steering oar, and give me your oar counts starting with Boat Two. If you're missing any men, tell me."

He could hear them murmuring, then Boat Two gave its count. "Boat Two, four oars!" When the report was finished, one had seven oars, the most of any, and a couple had only two. Of the men who'd jumped overboard, all but two had been hauled back dripping. The two either couldn't swim, or the serpents had killed them. *Probably*, Korvassu thought, *the damn fools couldn't swim. If the serpents wanted to kill, none of us would be alive*.

They'd play hell rowing to Hrumma with the oars they had

left. It would be tough just getting back to their own shore. He looked at Private Kaldibbi. "Kaldibbi, you see that oar over there about twenty feet?"

"Yes, sir."

"You just volunteered to get it. Jump!"

"Yes, sir." The man got off his seat and jumped.

"Boat sergeants, if there are any oars floating near your boat, get 'em."

Kaldibbi swam back dragging the oar. "It doesn't look very good, sir. It's kind of slivered." Korvassu reached down and got it. *Holy Hrum!* he said silently. *Those fucking teeth! I'm glad he didn't grab me.*

"Lieutenant?" It was his own boat sergeant; the voice spoke quietly.

"Yeah?"

"Maybe Hrum sent them as Messengers, like in the first days. Maybe we aren't supposed . . ."

There was another yell, of pure terror, jerking their faces in that direction. "What the fuck now?" Korvassu said. There was wild splashing, high-pitched keening, and he saw someone being pulled back into Boat Four. "What happened?" he demanded.

"Anezzu was swimming back with an oar and a serpent grabbed it," a voice called back. "Anezzu didn't let go soon enough and got pulled under for a minute. He's okay."

Korvassu looked at his sergeant and nodded. It was time to stick his neck out. The major could counter-order if he wanted to, but at sea, Korvassu was in command. Or supposed to be; he'd soon know. He called to his little flotilla. "All right, everyone, listen up! And forget about recovering any oars. Here's what we're going to do. Remember what serpents are; they're the Messengers of Hrum. Well, we got his message! Turn your boats around. We're heading north for home!"

Cheers greeted the order.

"Stow the cheering!" Korvassu said. "Boats that don't have at least four oars, get more from Boats Four and Nine."

He waited then, for the exchange of oars, and possible trouble from Major Hamaalu. The exchange of oars took place, but if the major said anything, it was too soft to hear. Korvassu called once more: "All right, row." They started, and he pushed the steering oar in a long turn to starboard. When they were aimed at the lodestar, he straightened his course.

They hadn't rowed ten minutes when he felt the breeze on his neck and turned to face it. In a minute it was blowing at about ten knots.

"Boat sergeants, listen up! We've got a south wind now. Ship your oars and step your masts! Hrum's being good to us!"

They did, and quickly. The boats began to move faster than they had with ten oars driving them. *It won't be longer than maybe four hours at this rate,* Korvassu thought. *Now all I've got to worry about is what the hell the army's going to do to me when we get back.*

Sixty-Four

Lord Vendel Kryger watched the slave girl cut his breakfast sweetfruit into sections and remove the seed pith. He hadn't seen this one before; she was the loveliest yet. She caught his glance and smiled shyly.

Kryger's return smile was lupine; life had grown far more interesting since he'd had Werlingus transferred to quarters in the staff wing. Kryger'd never said anything to Gamaliiu, nor had the king said anything to him, but the train of girls could hardly be unintentional. Gamaliiu kept sending new ones—all small for droids, scarcely adolescent actually, but well schooled in pleasing. Kryger doubted there was anything like them in Almeon.

I'm going to have to break that pleasant habit, he told himself wryly. *It won't do to have even a hint of this around when the fleet arrives. Maybe later, after the military administration's been here awhile.*

There was, of course, a strong likelihood that he'd be called back to Almeon when the conquest was complete, unless he created a continuing place for himself here. There'd be no further need of an ambassador, and the emperor had said early on that Prince Kesler, his young half-brother, would rule here as his regent. Though the chance was that the indolent young man wouldn't come till everything was thoroughly secured and organized for him. *Perhaps I can interest Kesler in assigning me as his deputy or his military aide*, Kryger thought. *I'll work on it.*

He finished his custard and the girl served him his sweetfruit. "Thank you, my dear," Kryger said, and patted her hand.

His manservant entered. "Lord Ambassador," he said, "a page has brought a message from His Majesty, King Gamaliiu. His Majesty wishes to see you at your early convenience."

Early, not earliest. That meant he could finish breakfast at reasonable leisure. "Tell the boy I'll be there in fifteen minutes, if it pleases His Majesty."

The man bowed. "Thank you, Lord Ambassador," he said, and left.

Kryger finished the fruit, took another drink of satta, smiled again at the maidservant, and went to the bathroom, then left for his meeting with the king.

Kryger's apartment was on the second floor of the guest wing. The large corridor down which he walked was richly carpeted, and its roof was glass—different panes in different colors, the morning sun slanting through in corresponding hues. The corridor walls were painted white, but the west was varicolored by the transmitted sunlight. Entering the main building, he walked down marble stairs into a corridor built on a grander scale, but having less light. The aesthetics there were richer, its polished wood, tapestries, and paintings lost to proper appreciation in the subdued illumination.

At the king's office, a doorman informed His Majesty that the ambassador had arrived. A guard in formal uniform, silver breastplate polished like glass, accompanied Kryger into the king's presence.

Kryger bowed. "Your Majesty requested my attendance," he said in Djezian.

Gamaliiu nodded without his usual smile. He was a handsome man, even more than most male droids, middle-aged, and for a man given to sensuality, looked reasonably fit. Kryger was aware that he drilled frequently with both sword and knife. "Yes," the king said. "A new situation has developed. It seems that unforeseen difficulties keep arising."

Kryger knew of two. A few weeks earlier, the intended landing of Royal regulars on the north coast of Hrumma had failed, reportedly when the troop-filled boats had been turned back at sea by an assault of sea serpents. It had caused an altogether irrational amount of upset. Since then there'd been civil unrest, including riots, by crowds who took it to mean that Hrum disapproved the invasion of Makklan.

All this had reflected on himself. It was he who'd suggested the waterborne invasion.

"Indeed! What this time?"

"About an hour ago a kiruu arrived with a message from Koziida Manteeros in the southeast. It seems a large force of barbarians has entered the duchy, killed or routed much of the ducal defense force there, and has the rest holed up in the ducal fortress."

Kryger frowned. "Is this a problem for you, Your Majesty? Or is it simply the duke's problem? I understand the barbarians do raid the borderlands from time to time."

"Ah, my good Vendel, but this is not the normal raiding party. Or even the unusual large party of one or two hundred. The report has it that this is a veritable army, with thousands of warriors. Allowing for exaggeration, that probably means at least two thousand."

"Ah! That is more of a problem." Kryger pretended to consider the matter. "I suppose the barbarians are besieging the fortress?"

"At this point it seems probable. They'd just invested it when the message was written, day before yesterday. But they could bypass it and continue moving east."

Kryger nodded. "It doesn't make much difference to my suggestion. Being wildmen, they probably plan to live off the land. I suggest you order the surrounding duchies to drive their livestock west, so the barbarians can't use it for their own provision. Meanwhile— Meanwhile they seem to be enough of a problem to be worth sending a brigade or two from here to meet them and run them home."

Gamaliiu didn't answer at once. He'd retired behind a frown, fingers drumming on the arm of his chair. "I'd been thinking of sending a pair of brigades from Makklan. Now that we've broken out of the isthmus, the situation there is less demanding. We're in a position to settle for the status quo there till we've chased the barbarians back to their wilderness."

Kryger nodded. "True. But it would give the Maklanni time to organize and improve their defenses. And if I recall your maps correctly, the Throne District is closer to Koziida Manteeros; troops from here could arrive there more quickly." He paused, then went on diffidently, watchfully. "Or is there—a danger here from Djez Seechul?"

Gamaliiu's eyes narrowed. "Do not test my temper, ambassador," he said quietly. "Or the limits of my friendship. A king of Djez Gorrbul does not fear Seechul."

Time for some confusion, Kryger thought. "True, Your

Majesty. I did not doubt it for a moment. Forgive my imperfect use of your language; I sometimes fail to make myself clear.

"My point was that the vark might raid an unguarded border farm. But I get vark and kienno confused, the one deriving from the other. The king of Seechul is kienno, not vark, and your border districts are hardly unguarded. Removing one brigade here will leave three others, and anyway the barbarians seem to have more vark in them than the Sechuuli do. Meanwhile, by sending a force from here, you won't have to compromise your invasion of Makklan."

Gamaliiu's expression had gone blank. Kryger went on.

"Of course, my comments are always tentative. As yet, I don't know your continent and kingdom well enough to speak with full assurance on such matters."

He bowed then and stood waiting.

Again Gamaliiu retired behind a thoughtful frown. "You are somewhat right in this, nonetheless," he said. "I *will* send a brigade from the Throne District. The forces of the Vaski River dukes are enough to give Seechul pause. Certainly with a weakling like Labdallu on the throne there."

Kryger's nod was half a bow, and he waited a moment before speaking again, as if to be sure the king was through. Then he asked, "Which has the most formidable army, Seechul or Makklan?"

"Seechul, easily. Their numbers are much greater. The problem in Makklan is the difficult terrain. And the archery."

Kryger nodded. "I may have a solution to Seechul's army that will interest you," he said. "A weapon. A weapon much more difficult to make than cannons. It will take a lot longer to produce than cannons did, and you'd need far more of them, but I suspect your artificers can be taught to make them."

Gamaliiu's brows raised. "New weapon? What sort of new weapon?"

"We call it a rifle. It's like a very small cannon, small enough that a single soldier can carry one. It is accurate at longer ranges than a bow, and its projectiles will pass through shields almost as if they were cloth. I'd think that in a year or two you could have at least enough for a battalion. And a battalion of riflemen might well drive a full division from the field, I would think."

Gamaliiu's eyes were bright. "Draw me a picture of one of these 'rifles.' They sound very interesting!"

"Certainly, Your Majesty. If I may have paper and pencil . . ."

The king turned to his scribe. "Gossi, give the ambassador paper and pencil."

"Yes, Your Majesty."

Rifles, Kryger thought. *Before long you'll have thousands of rifles in Djez Gorrbul. Tens of thousands. Each in the hands of an Almaeic soldier.* "Thank you, Gossi," he said, taking the drawing materials handed him, and began to draw. *Meanwhile this one on paper will soothe your temper.*

SIXTY-FIVE

In an islet-sheltered cove at Hrumma's North Cape, the three east coast schooners had lain at anchor for eleven days, with submarine mines in their holds. They'd left Theedalit with seventy each, scarcely more than the project minimum of 200, not knowing when the Almaeic fleet would be reported. Two swift sloops had shuttled back and forth between Theedalit and North Cape, delivering more mines as they were built, till the three schooners had more than 100 each. Which meant they could lose one sloop and still have enough.

Each schooner had a captain, a mate, and a crew of eight, and for this mission ten marines. In addition, the "flagship" of the little flotilla carried Juliassa Brokols; her personal bodyguard, Jonkka Yelltis; and a smart and seasoned marine centurion, Varros Vemborros.

There was also a non-human contingent. Just aft of the bow, the flagship had two wooden tanks partly filled with seawater, the larger one for carrying three sullsi. The sullsi were vital to the mission. Off Haipoor l'Djezzer lay one of the longer of the sandy islands strung out along the Djezian shore. On its seaward side there waited more than two hundred sullsi and several serpents. Juliassa and her three sullsi, when they arrived, would brief and organize the sullsi mine-setting crews.

Sleekit's metamorphosis was complete. His arms had thickened, especially the left. It looked fearsomely powerful, ending in a huge hand like some clawed grapple, and he wore a thirty-inch, double-edged sword on his face, unsheathable, the outward half of it serrate and sharp enough to slice with.

His thickened and otherwise drastically altered facial skeleton made his air speech mostly unintelligible, but any sellsu, or any serpent, could understand his underwater speech without difficulty, picking it up with the rows of sonar organs along their sides.

The second tank was for an immature serpent, the bright and eager two-year-old, Tssissfu. He'd swum all the way from the Gulf of Seechul to serve as Juliassa's telepathic communicator, keeping her in touch with the sullsi/serpent force off Haipoor, with the serpent watch-pickets at sea, and with K'sthuump and Brokols at Theedalit.

It happened on the twelfth day.

Morale had sagged a bit from long waiting. The marines, Juliassa, and Jonkka had lived ashore in tents. The marine centurion had drilled his men a lot, and they gambled for low stakes in their spare time. Jonkka took the opportunity to work further on his sullsit.

Juliassa's morale had held up the best, though an edge of impatience and even anxiety lay not far from the surface. She'd spent considerable time, some of it with one of the sullsi, developing an alphabet and grammar for sullsit air speech. When the war was over, she'd told herself, she was going to collect sullsi sagas and write them down both in Hrummean and sullsit. And teach others. She'd already written down some of them in Hrummean.

On the west coast of Hrumma, early autumn differed from summer mainly in that it rained only occasionally, and the storms, instead of being brief squalls, could blow for several days. Thus, when a storm blew out of the east, with clouds and occasional assaults of wind-driven rain, they were concerned that the time to leave might come in weather unfit for sailing. Elver had been monitoring Almaeic fleet communications, and it seemed they must be drawing near the continent.

The twelfth day, however, dawned clear, and the near gale-force winds had slackened considerably, blowing now out of the south.

That was the day on which, finally, it happened.

Constantly at sea was a line of serpents, some thirty of them spaced a few miles apart, roughly two hundred miles off the Djezian coast. Their role was to watch and listen for the invasion fleet, while alert to other marine life that might notice ships.

Near midmorning, young Tssissfu "heard" from one of the pickets: It had sighted the Almaeic fleet.

Within half an hour the tents had been struck and loaded aboard the flagship. The sullsi and Tssissfu had been loaded into their travel tanks. The anchors were weighed and the schooners put to sea, driving fast before a moderate wind.

And Jonkka of course got seasick again, immediately and severely.

On the schooner, a lookout squatted on a crosstree. For hours he'd seen nothing but water. Wishing not to be noticed, the captain was sailing by the sun, out of sight of land, and when night fell he'd sail by the lodestar.

It was dusk when the lookout spotted something. "Small boat three points to port!" he shouted. "About two hundred yards! With someone in it!"

The steersman spun the wheel, peering through the dusk, seeing now what the lookout had seen. "Make ready to pick him up," the captain called, and men hopped to. The marines moved to the rail. Juliassa, napping in a tiny cabin below deck, didn't hear.

The wind had dropped to perhaps ten knots. Exhaustion had overcome hunger pangs, and the man in the small boat dozed, to waken with a start at the first shout.

He looked around, confused, then stood up, turning, and almost fell overboard. "Help!" he shouted. "Help!"

The ship was slowing but still had a lot of momentum, and for a moment he thought they'd run him down. As it slid past, no more than eight feet away, a sailor threw him a rope. In his exhausted state, the man was too slow-witted to loop it around a cleat. He simply grabbed it, and as the rope tightened, it jerked him from the boat. Desperately he hung on. The sailor and a marine hauled him alongside, hand over hand, like some ungainly fish, every pull jerking him under water. Finally he reached a ladder that someone had lowered, and desperately grabbed a rung.

The schooner had five feet of freeboard, but a sailor had come down the ladder to help him, grabbing his wrist. "You're all right, mate," the sailor said. "Here. Hang on with both hands and we'll pull you aboard." Then he climbed back over the rail, and a second later they pulled the ladder upward, with Tirros Hanorissio on it.

The moment his feet touched the deck, he collapsed, as much from relief as exhaustion and hunger, trembling as if he had the ague. As two men lifted him by the arms, he realized: They were speaking Hrummean, not Djezian!

"Here. Let's get you to a bench. Pravvo, bring him a cup of water and something to eat. A sweetfruit to start with."

They lowered him onto a bench. "You able to sit up?"

Tirros nodded.

"Here." A man pushed a cup of water at him. He took it and drank.

"He doesn't look too starved," someone said. "More like underfed."

"How're you doing?" someone else asked him.

Tirros feigned an inland dialect. "I ain't ate since early yesterday, nor slept since afore that. If I could have somethin' to eat . . ."

"Here." A sailor handed him a sweetfruit. He tore it open and ate it out of the rind, seed-pulp and all, juice dripping on his belly and pants, then looked around. "Can I have more?"

"Not too much. It might make you sick. Pravvo, get him another sweetfruit and a square of hardtack."

Tirros licked juice from his callused grimy hands. After a minute, someone handed him hardtack, dry, and he finished that almost as quickly as he had the sweetfruit, washing it down with another cup of water. The second sweetfruit he ate more slowly, then got shakily to his feet to spit seedpulp over the side.

Instead he almost swallowed it. He'd realized that some of the men wore Hrummean marine uniforms; there was even a centurion's helmet. Surely one of them would recognize him! He began to shake visibly, not from exhaustion.

The man who'd given orders earlier was the skipper. He took Tirros's arm. "Steady, lad! What's your name?"

"Barrkos, sir," Tirros answered, and told himself to remember it. "Barrkos Vendellto."

The skipper walked him forward as they talked. "All right, Barrkos. I've got no empty bunk for you. Matter of fact, I've given my own cabin to a guest, and I'm doubling up with my first mate. But we can give you better than that rowboat to sleep in, and you won't have a steering oar in your armpit." He gestured at a space between the forward hatch coaming and the anchor capstan. "Here. You won't be in anybody's way, you can't roll around, you'll have a pad to sleep on, and a blanket to keep you warm."

Tirros was almost too tired to nod. "Thank you, cap'n," he said. A sailor came forward with a rolled up sleeping pad and woolen blanket. He flopped the pad onto the deck and dropped the blanket on it. Tirros got down on his knees, laid the pad against the coaming, spread the blanket, and lay down. It took him about a minute to go to sleep, whispering his new name to himself: "Barrkos Vendellto, Barrkos Vendellto."

The skipper walked to the waist of the ship, leaned back against the rail, and looked shoreward. The marine centurion came over. "Well," said the marine, "that was an interesting change of pace. How do you suppose he got out here?"

The skipper shook his head. "Hrum knows. That accent of his is from so far back in the uplands, you'd wonder he'd even heard of the ocean."

"How long d'you think he'd been out here?"

"Not as long as he looks like. Probably blown to sea by that little storm we had. Probably from somewhere on the North Cape, the day before we left. He must be at least a bit of a sailor to have come through it.

"He's lean looking, but it's not the leanness that comes from starvation. More like the leanness that goes with a lot of hard work and barely enough to eat. Or not quite enough. I've seen men, more than once, that had been two or three weeks without food. They look different. This Barrkos Vendellto will look pretty decent with a good bath, a shave, and his hair cut." The skipper stopped for a moment. "You know, he didn't grow that beard in two or three days or a week. And his hair . . . it's not only long, it's stiff. Stiffer than sea water'd make it. I'll bet there's dirt enough in there to start a garden. Sticks out like a bush."

The centurion chuckled. "Not just his hair's dirty. When he gets out of the bath, you'll be able to bake bricks out of the water."

The skipper grunted. "I'll bet there's an interesting story there. I'll see if I can draw it out of him when I have time."

Tirros woke up with a little cry, from bad dreams of being adrift in a storm. There'd been a sellsu in the dream, and it had kept turning his boat over. He'd kept righting it, and the sellsu would turn it over again. Finally he just left the boat upside down and crawled onto the upturned bottom. Then he'd seen a fin coming—a sarrka. It paid no attention to the sellsu; it just circled the boat, looking at him. The sellsu had laughed and tipped the boat, dumping him into the water again, and the sarrka, with a ridiculously wide, toothy mouth, had started for Tirros. That's when he'd wakened.

Tirros lay there for a moment, panting. He knew what sellsu he'd dreamed about: his sister's. *I should have killed it when I had the chance*, he thought.

He had to urinate. Slowly he untangled himself from the blanket and got up. Ships generally had a urinal, a little trough, built into the bulwark aft, and he shuffled back to use it. When he'd finished, the wheelsman spoke.

"How ye doin', mate?"

"Better'n I was, that's sure." For the first time, vaguely in the night, he noticed another ship following—two others. Cautiously he asked: "Where's these ships a-goin'?"

"We're not supposed to talk about that. I don't suppose it'd hurt, seeing as how you're here now, but you'd best ask the skipper."

Tirros had no intention of asking the skipper. He nodded and started back for his pallet. When he got there, the two wooden tanks forward caught his eye, and he went to one of them to see what they were. There was no moon. All he could see were large oblong darknesses, three of them, partly in the water. One of them moved. Its head raised, turned toward him, a horrible head with a long swordlike snout. Black eyes stared, reflecting starlight, seeming to glare.

Tirros recoiled, stifling a scream that came out a squawk. Somehow it was like a continuation of his dream.

From the bow came a chuckle. "Took you by surprise, did it?" a man asked.

"Aye."

"They're sullsi. The one with the sword face is an oldtimer. You hardly ever see one like that."

Tirros looked again. He'd heard of sword-faced sullsi, but like many other people had thought them a myth. It had laid its head back down. "How come you've got sullsi aboard?" he asked.

"We ain't supposed to talk about that. They're friends of the lady on board; she talks to 'em. I guess I can tell you that much."

The lady on board. "Thanks," Tirros half mumbled, and started for his bed. There was only one person that could be:

his sister. He'd have to stay away from her; as different as he looked, she'd still know him.

Confusion hit him then, abruptly. He'd been sailing north; that he was almost sure of. Somewhere off the Djezian coast. Or— Had he gotten turned around somewhere? Were they in Hrummean waters headed south?

He looked past the jib at the sky. The lodestar was clearly visible, in the tip of the Spear. They *were* headed north.

Where could they be going, with her aboard? Could she be an envoy to Djez Gorrbul? If she was, there'd be an adept with her. He'd have to be careful, very careful, and draw no more attention to himself. He'd hole up in the cargo hold when dawn came.

SIXTY-SIX

Vendel Kryger looked the young midshipman up and down, then smiled and spoke in Almaeic. "Hmh! Add a few inches to your stature and you'd be a perfect example of the well-dressed Gorrbian profligate!" The ambassador stepped in front of the mirror then. "I'm afraid I look more like a jaded roue."

He turned to his Gorrbian houseboy. "You may go now, Fellik," he said in Djezian, and watched him out the door, then spoke again to Werlingus. "Let's go."

They left, followed by Kryger's two burly bodyguards, Almaeic marines. The bodyguards were short by Djezian standards, but they looked formidable nonetheless; dangerous. They were. They'd been assigned to Kryger from the Imperial Guard.

Midshipman Werlingus felt uncomfortable with his role in this. Lying was foreign to his character, and distasteful, even when the lie was only implied. Even when he saw the clear necessity of it.

Not to seem covert, the four Almites left the palace through the main entrance, as they usually did when invited to parties in aristocratic homes. And tomorrow was a Freeday—a convenient coincidence that made things considerably more comfortable. No one would wonder when they didn't return.

If they'd been followed, those earlier times, hopefully the practice had been abandoned as unnecessary. Although even being followed wouldn't necessarily prove dangerous.

Kryger had sent Werlingus that morning with his carefully packed Almaeic formal suit; he'd have it tomorrow when it was needed. Now they took nothing with them except the clothes they wore and what incidentals they carried in their purses. They must by all means look as if they expected to be back by morning. As before, instead of hiring a cabriolet, Kryger had kaabors waiting. They mounted and rode off down the unlit street, the hooves of their animals clopping on brick pavement.

A thirty-minute ride brought them to the city wall, where guards passed them through a narrow nighttime gate. This too was not unusual. Some of the city's wealthier merchant-aristocrats made their homes outside the walls—men wealthy enough to have and defend walls of their own.

Kryger had dropped his joviality. The eyes with which he looked about him now were calculating. Werlingus wondered what he was thinking. He also wondered what might happen to the two embassy staff they'd left at the palace. He could see why the ambassador couldn't take them all with him, but felt somehow guilty that he should escape while they wouldn't.

The road they took paralleled the beach at a distance of some two hundred yards, separated from it by fields and occasional private compounds, trees showing their crowns above stout encircling brick walls. After a mile or so, the compounds became rapidly fewer.

Finally, at one of the last, Kryger stopped. One of the bodyguards dismounted and, with a key, opened a heavy, ironfaced wooden gate. They rode inside and the man locked and barred it behind them. The place was the retreat of a merchant who'd been happy to lend it to Kryger for two days. He hoped to do a profitable business with Almeon, in what Kryger had portrayed as a coming export-import bonanza. He'd assumed, from a hint of Kryger's, that the ambassador planned a tryst with some noblewoman.

They dismounted behind the small two-story villa, and the Gorrbian groundskeeper/guard took their mounts to the shed, to feed and brush down. Normally the place had no house servants when the family was away, but for Kryger's convenience a housekeeper was waiting for them at the door. She asked if they cared for anything to eat or drink, then hurried off to prepare the spiced wine that Kryger requested for himself and Werlingus. The bodyguards would have satta; they were not to drink alcohol on duty.

Kryger was familiar with the house; he'd been a guest there before. The others followed him upstairs, where three balconied rooms faced the Inside Passage—the protected channel between the mainland and the intermittent chain of low offshore islands. He assigned the bodyguards to one room and Werlingus to another; then he and Werlingus sat on the balcony of the master's room which Kryger had taken. When the housekeeper had brought their wine, Kryger dismissed her for the night. She left wondering that they'd brought no pleasure girls or other women, wondering if perhaps the foreign lord preferred young men.

The two sat on the balcony in silence. Sleep would likely prove elusive. The fleet should arrive the next day, sometime before or around noon. It wouldn't do to be at the palace when it steamed into the roadstead and began leveling the waterfront district with naval gunnery. He'd informed the admiral of which villa they'd be at; a gig would be sent to pick up the four of them when the fleet had dropped anchor.

Sixty-Seven

After the midday meal, Tssissfu told Juliassa that the Almaeic fleet had entered the Inside Passage. The marines began hoisting mines out of the hold, and Tirros volunteered to help load the to-him-mysterious objects into the cargo net. Ordinarily he rejected even the thought of labor, but felt that working in the hold, he'd be less conspicuous, and less talked about, than lying around while others worked.

Also he'd hoped to pick up something on the purpose of the trip, and what these peculiar objects were that they were handling. The marine he worked with wasn't much for talking though, and questioning him seemed unwise. The important thing was to get ashore in Djez Gorrbul.

They didn't work hard. They'd load four of the things on the net, and with a light windlass, marines on deck would hoist the net up. Then marines unloaded it and apparently did something to the objects. It felt military to Tirros, and he discarded the notion that Juliassa was an amirrial envoy to King Gamaliiu.

Twice he saw her, on deck looking down at the loading. She paid no attention to him, and he began to feel more secure.

By supper, all the mines were on deck and their timers set. The captain kept a lookout on the foremast to watch. Meanwhile, he was counting inshore islands as the only way of knowing when he was approaching Haipoor l'Djezzer. It was dusk, and had clouded over, when he spotted the south passage into Haipoor Harbor, a mile ahead, and drew his sheets to cut speed; he wanted to enter by twilight.

* * *

A large number of sullsi were on or close off the island's seaward beach. They'd seen the huge invasion fleet arrive that morning, and knew fear. The serpents with them occasionally took a read on Tssissfu as a measure of how far away the schooners were. Now they were alert and somewhat tense; the little flotilla was getting close. A serpent, head high, called out in sullsit: "They are coming! I see them!" The sullsi began to pass through the entrance channel to join other sullsi already there.

The schooners entered one at a time and anchored less than 800 yards from the nearer Almaeic ships. Each lowered a platform with floats, tied it snug alongside, and sullsi soon filled the water around them. The humans could hear gunfire from the city, and in places, fire burned yellow and russet in the near-night dark.

Juliassa and a wan and wobbly Jonkka swung down onto the platform. Jonkka insisted on helping; now that they were in sheltered water, he said, he'd be all right.

The sullsi had been briefed by serpent communicators, and had organized themselves into working pairs, crews of twelve, squadrons of thirty-six. They'd scouted the harbor, seen the lay of the fleet, assigned sectors to squadrons and subsectors to crews.

But none had ever seen a mine or wrench or lagscrew. Sleekit's two packmates swam to the other two schooners to demonstrate methods. At the flagship, Juliassa and Sleekit worked together, Juliassa on the platform talking, Sleekit in the water observing and correcting technique. He couldn't speak effectively in air speech, but underwater had no difficulty making himself understood.

After a little bit, pairs of sullsi began taking mines into the water and disappearing with them.

From the rail of the Almaeic flagship, General Lord Vendel Kryger watched what little could be seen of the battle, listened to and interpreted its sounds. He kept to the fringe of the command group—the commander in chief, the fleet admiral, and the flagship's captain. There were sporadic light drizzles, and an awning had been erected to shelter them. Kryger was keeping his mouth shut. As a brigadier general he was heavily outranked, and when he'd made a suggestion earlier, the CIC had looked annoyed. Actually, no one was saying much.

Distant rifles and grenades popped, furiously at times, and now and then artillery thudded, the sounds dull in the heavy air. The Gorballis were resisting more obstinately than he'd expected, considering the new and frightening weapons they faced.

In parts of the city, fires had spread, ruddying the low-lying blanket of clouds, but construction was mostly brick, brick and stone, and thoroughfares were wide. A city-wide holocaust seemed unlikely.

Along the rail, seamen gawked too. *If anyone was on watch*, Kryger thought, *you couldn't tell it. Loose discipline!* Under the circumstances though, he realized, it hardly mattered; there was no hostile fleet to watch for. And these would be merchant seamen impressed into naval service. Even most of the ships' officers, even most of their captains, were merchant mariners.

Kryger took a match from his match safe and struck it with a thumbnail to look at his watch. After midnight, and he'd had little sleep the night before. He put watch and match-safe back in his pockets, excused himself, and went to Werlingus who'd been watching with two of the ship's junior officers. "I'm going to bed," he said. "Stand by the wireless room and have them tell you when there's any word about the king—his capture, his death, anything."

Then he went below, opened the porthole, and went to bed.

SIXTY-EIGHT

It was as warm as a summer evening. The front was a warm front, and the overcast held in the day's heat like a blanket.

Juliassa watched another mine disappear beneath the water, then straightened and looked around her. There were only four mines on the platform now, and there couldn't be many left on deck. A marine had one in his hands, waiting to pass it down; she and Jonkka, who'd been working with her, took it from him and set it down on the platform.

The drizzle had stopped; the moisture she wiped from her forehead was sweat. She knelt beside the tray of lagscrews and felt of how many were left. Not more than twenty. There couldn't be many mines left to set. If the other schooners had been keeping pace with this one, they'd sent out more already, by quite a margin, than there were Almaeic ships.

Or were there more than 200 ships? Perhaps even more than 300? More ships than mines to sink them with? In the night she couldn't tell.

Nor did she realize how organized the sullsi mining squadrons were. How did they know which ships they'd mined and which they hadn't? Sullsi were as intelligent as humans, but how were they at planning? At administration? Especially in an activity so utterly different than anything they'd done before. They had four fingers and two thumbs on each hand, and names for numbers to a hundred and forty-four, but how well did they deal with quantities?

(Had she been less rushed and anxious, she'd have known.

For the numbers they used reached the square of their finger count! At least they were able arithmetists.)

Would some ships be missed, and others have two or three mines attached? Supposing a half dozen ships survived, or even one. Might they, or it, steam south to the firth and shell Theedalit?

She didn't give worry much time, though. It was too late. The night was half over, and they'd done what they could. It was remarkable that they'd gotten this far without something going drastically wrong; Hrum seemed to be with them.

Straightening, she thanked Hrum for that. She told Jonkka to stand by, to hand out the next mines, then reached up, grasped a handhold, and pulled herself through the gangway onto the deck to see how many mines were left there. Not more than half a dozen, and there shouldn't be any down in . . .

"S-s-st! Miss!"

She turned. The man who stood there in the night was a stranger to her. He had to be the derelict fisherman she'd heard about, the one they'd picked up at sea.

"What is it?"

"Miss, there's one of them things still in the hold, makin' a funny noise. I'll show you."

He turned away before she could reply, and crossing the deck, disappeared down a hatchway. She hesitated, then followed. What he said seemed impossible, but best not ignore it.

It was darker below than topside, the blackness almost impenetrable. Her feet found the deck, and at the same moment an arm circled her neck from behind. A knife blade pricked sharply beneath her ribs, and a voice hissed in her ear.

"Take off your pants, or you're dead!"

She knew who it was, who it had to be, and a chill ran through her. In that instant she thought of Elver and all the things they'd talked about, planned. Without hesitation she reached down, unfastened her belt, pushed her trousers off her hips, felt them slide, got one foot free of them. *Oh Hrum!* she prayed silently, *just let me come through this alive*.

He forced her down on her knees then, dropping down with her. His pants had already been open; she could feel his hardness against her waist. Then he changed his grip to her hair, the knifepoint biting deeper to say "I mean it," and pushed her forward till she was on all fours. "Now," he hissed, and told her what to do.

He was like a frenzied animal, almost knocking her on her face, and it was over in less than half a minute. His movements slowed, stopped; she felt him grab her hair again and pull her head back. He was going to cut her throat, she realized, and screaming, twisted, trying to throw herself sideways.

Tirros was taken by surprise, but stabbed nonetheless, felt hot blood gush over his hand, and letting go the knife, he rose, jumped upward, grasped the coaming and swung himself onto the deck, scrambling at once to his feet.

He recognized the face staring at him through the gangway: Jonkka, the guardsman. Tirros turned, and with a single stride reached the far rail and vaulted into the water, plunging deep, stroked strongly to get distance between himself and the schooner before surfacing, sinewy arms sweeping in an underwater breaststroke until his lungs seemed near to bursting.

He surfaced, gasping air with as little sound as possible, and breathing deeply, turned to look back at the ship more than a hundred feet away. It was vaguely backlit by fire-reddened clouds, and he thought he could make out men silhouetted at the rail, as if looking for him. There were voices too, not angry but querying, overlying one another, but he could hear no sound of swimming. Quietly he took two more deep breaths, then submerged silently and stroked another fifty feet before coming back up.

Even looking over the rail toward him, it seemed to Tirros they wouldn't see him now. And this was the side away from the mainland; he'd swim to the long, scrub-grown island and trot to the far end, then take to the water again and swim the channel. They'd never find him.

He turned on one side and began swimming away, quietly, smoothly. The shouting had died. By the time they got a boat lowered, if they did, he'd be on the island and away.

As the man vaulted over the rail, Jonkka pulled himself through the gangway. The scream had to be Juliassa, and by the sound of it, she was in the hold. There was a moment of hesitation: Should he chase the man or see to Juliassa?

He decided, climbed down into the hold, stared unseeingly around, then stumbled on Juliassa's leg in the darkness. He knelt, found a naked hip, her shirt, her—*neck!* He recoiled at the thick hot blood, and roared, the sound of it bloodcurdling. Clamboring quickly from the hold, he howled like some nightbeast, then jumped through the gangway, landing crouched on the platform. Sleekit, in the water beside it, stared thunderstruck at him, realizing that something must have happened to Juliassa.

"What?" he demanded.

Words in Hrummean rushed from Jonkka.

"Again!" bellowed Sleekit, the demand barely recognizable even to another sellsu.

Jonkka stopped, not having caught the word but realizing what was wanted. He took a breath and repeated in sullsit, was aware that he'd been understood when the sellsu let go the platform and disappeared beneath the surface.

Sleekit dove under the schooner, flukes driving, his sonar sensing the hull shape, the long shallow keel. The guardsman's sullsit had hardly been intelligible, but there was no doubt of what he'd said: A man had killed Juliassa and jumped over the far rail.

He sensed the movement ahead, and closed on it. There, within reach! Great clawed hand open, his arm thrust straight.

Tirros was perhaps two hundred feet from the schooner and had seen no sign of pursuit. There'd been no splash of anyone jumping overboard, no sound of anyone lowering a boat. Inwardly he grinned, almost crowing out loud. A hundred yards more to the island. He'd done it, reached Djez Gorrbul and avenged himself.

Suddenly something terrible grabbed his calf, claws biting deeply, and without thought he screamed. What flashed into his mind was sarrka. In mid-scream he was jerked under, swallowing water, choking. The grip released, and arms flailing, he surfaced wild-eyed, strangling. A hand, rough and terrible, grasped his neck then, held his head up. The wet black sword was almost in his face. He tried to kick, to push free with his feet. They found slick, wet fur, smooth sides; the grip tightened. He grabbed the forearm with both hands, but the strength he struggled against was adequate to much greater enemies than he.

Two black eyes bore into him. Tirros stopped struggling, stared, found no mercy. Only, perhaps, recognition.

Suddenly the hand let go, and for just an instant he thought he'd been freed. But even as it released, the head disappeared beneath the water, and the sword thrust through his guts, driving out his back below the ribs. He was driven down into watery blackness, rushing backward, a hard, thick-boned forehead against his chest. He opened his mouth to scream again, spasming, and water rushed in.

Sixty-Nine

Shouts awakened Kryger. His first reaction was that men were cheering overhead; they must have gotten word that the fortress was taken, or the king. Whatever.

He rolled out of bed and was pulling on his drawers beneath his nightshirt when he heard the shouts again. They were not cheers. He had his nightshirt off and was putting on his shirt when he heard an enormous explosion, as if nearby some ship's powder store had blown.

Werlingus pounded on the cabin door. "Lord Kryger!" he shouted. "Lord Kryger! Something is happening!"

"Go! I'll be out in a minute!"

Kryger grimaced as he pulled on his trousers and buttoned them. "Fool! Of course something's happening," he muttered, then heard another explosion, this one small, and muffled as if under water, then another muffled but large, close, and the ship twitched beneath his feet. The shouting loudened, became urgent. Quickly he shrugged into his jacket, pulled on shoes, hurried into and along the passageway. Climbing the companionway, he was aware of commotion on deck, and what sounded like two more muffled explosions.

Emerging under the cloudy night sky, he paused. There was a deckhouse amidships; vaguely he saw sailors disappearing into it, down into the vacant troop hold. Nearby, to port, some debris was burning on the water. Kryger started aft toward the quarterdeck, concerned, confused. He couldn't imagine what was happening. Muffled explosions continued singly and by twos and threes, some seeming nearby, some at the edge of hearing.

The captain wasn't there, but the admiral and the commander-in-chief were. Neither was talking. Faces carven, eyes narrowed, they were staring shoreward, where now the guns were all but silent.

"What is it?" Kryger asked. "What's going on?"

It was the admiral who answered. "Something's causing explosions in the ships."

As if to punctuate his statement, demonstrating it, there was a string of the dull thudding explosions, half a dozen within two or three seconds.

"But— What could be causing them?"

"Shut up and look!" It was the CIC who spoke, his voice irritated, his arm pointing. Kryger looked. Slowly a nearby ship was heeling, her masts silhouetted against fire-ruddied cloud. They canted at ten degrees, twelve . . . elsewhere were two more dull explosions, another, another, but his eyes stayed fixed on the leaning ship. *Thud!* Then *thud!* again, louder, nearer, another farther off, two more almost simultaneous. The masts he watched leaned farther, farther. At about forty degrees they accelerated from their own weight, and he heard them snap. The vessel rolled slowly onto her side; water spilled into her broken stack, and her boilers exploded with a roar, blowing her stern apart.

As he watched her sink, there was another explosion in the flagship, almost under his feet. The deck beneath him had been tilting gradually forward. Now there was an abrupt lurch. Her captain came out of the midships deckhouse and shouted to abandon ship, then came over and ordered Kryger and the two ranking officers to a lifeboat.

While they moved to it, down the roadstead another ship blew apart as her powder stores exploded.

SEVENTY

Juliassa Hanorissia did not want to leave the stage. And she was more than strong-willed. Polarized though she was and sometimes headstrong, with all the consequent *can't know,* as a schoolgirl she'd been one of the best in her class in meditation, had even perceived, on occasion, her Kirsan and Nasrik, though they'd never merged or even touched.

The southern edge of the vast cloud blanket roofing Haipoor l'Djezzer lay a hundred miles north of Theedalit. Thus Panni and Tassi sat under visible stars in the cooling, early-autumn night. Their backs were straight, even Tassi's, but not at all rigid, and their open eyes were unfocused. Both were smiling, though not widely.

Both had felt the call for help, but they did not *effort* to change what had happened. It had happened, and that was all right. Nonetheless, at a subliminal level, they were touching the intelligent psyches over all the planet, psyches marine and terrestrial, getting approvals, weaving a fabric of agreement, very lightly and without the least insistence. And with a very few exceptions, mostly among the Vrronnkiess, none would remember, on this side of reality, any of it at all.

When they roused from their trances, the two sages wouldn't remember it clearly either. At least Panni wouldn't. But he'd remember vaguely, as in a dream dimly recalled.

The masters, the more advanced initiates, and a few others, at the monastery at Theedalit and every other monastery in Hrumma, had wakened independently and gone at once to the chamber of meditation. In its clean-scrubbed darkness their "Hrums" resonated in the night.

As the scene was finalized, the knife had sliced deeply across her neck muscles on the right side, glanced off her jaw and across cheek and nose. The captain, alarmed by her scream and oriented by Jonkka's roar, had dropped through the hatchway, found the body, and controlled the bleeding by the pressure of his thumbs. She was weak and in shock, and the cut would leave a deep scar, but the role and body of Juliassa Hanorissia would continue.

Seventy-One

A small pleasure barge rocked gently at the amirr's private dock on the Firth of Theed. Wavelets lapped and chuckled against her sides, while in the cabin, Elver Brokols dreamed unknowing. A large triangular head, a long muscular neck, rose smoothly from the water, and dripping, peered under the awning.

"Elver Brokols!"

A Vrronnkiess cannot whisper, can't even speak in undertones—not and form words. The sound jerked Brokols out of sleep, and he sat up, heart thudding. He'd been sleeping in the barge because tonight was to be the night of truth, and K'sthuump was his communicator.

"I have news for you."

He gaped, all traces of sleep blasted, and sucked air, wide eyes staring. "What?"

"The big ssips, your enemies, all are sunk! All of them! The sullsi did not miss one. And all our ssips are safe, coming home now."

Brokols felt suspended, as if he'd been away from his body and hadn't gotten back into it yet. As if in contact with it from outside. Mentally he stared at K'sthuump's words, examining them for meaning. *All sunk. Our ships are headed home.*

His mouth opened again, formed an *O*. The orderly assigned to him had wakened too, was staring from another couch, understanding none of it. K'sthuump continued.

"But the big-ssip people, a great number of them, have been fighting in the city. There are fires. [She used the

Hrummean word.] The noises of fighting have all but stopped. I think they possess the city now."

Brokols swung both good leg and bad off the bed. "Thank you, K'sthuump," he said in his own version of sullsit. He'd slept in his clothes. Now he found his left shoe and pulled it on. The orderly had his crutches ready.

K'sthuump withdrew her fearsome head, and the two men ducked out of the cabin. Brokols' shay was still tied to a piling, its kaabor looking at them, munching the last of the grain in her nosebag. The orderly went to her, removed the bag and fastened the bit in her mouth, then boosted Brokols into the shay.

"Thank you, K'sthuump," Brokols called back. "I'll see you in the morning. Love you!"

"Love you, Elver Brokols!" she answered.

Then Brokols told his orderly to start, and they set off up the street, going home, where he had things to do now.

K'sthuump hadn't told him all she'd learned from Tssissfu. It would be soon enough when the schooners arrived back at Theedalit.

Brokols went directly to his wireless room and jotted a message in Djezian, then sent an "on-the-air" signal to the wireless wagon at the Gorrbian headquarters in Kammnalit. In his mind's eye he visualized a Gorrbian officer on a cot, or maybe a noncom, wakening to the raucous buzzer, muttering, swearing perhaps, wiping sleep from his eyes and sitting down at the sender.

Brokols' receiver burped the man's acknowledgement. Tense and at the same time calm, Brokols waited, giving the Gorballi time to grab pencil and pad. Then he began to send.

"Imperial Almaeic Army has landed here in Haipoor from His Imperial Majesty's fleet, and has taken the city. Your king has been executed. His Majesty the Emperor now rules Djez Gorrbul. He orders you to leave Makklan, return to Haipoor, and surrender to me. Did you receive me? Acknowledge. Kryger."

There was a lag, as if the duty man at the wireless in Kammnalit was rereading the message, trying to grasp what had happened. Then Brokols' sounder began to tap.

ACKD AS FOLLOWS STOP IMPERIAL ALMAEIC ARMY HAS LANDED IN HAIPOOR STOP HAS CAPTURED CITY

STOP EMPEROR ORDERS US RETURN TO HAIPOOR AND SURRENDER STOP GRAND ARMY INTEL END COMM

Brokols leaned back sweating, and his hand trembled slightly. He wondered why. It seemed to him they'd surely pull out of Hrumma now, back across the isthmus, probably after requesting a cease-fire from the Hrummean field command. And probably they'd head for Haipoor. After that— Hopefully they'd fight the Almaeic army. It was hard to picture them turning themselves over to the Almites. And it had been the wireless man who'd ended communication, cutting "Kryger" off, so to speak.

The Almites! His people! He thought it to himself deliberately, alert for any feeling of guilt or dishonor. And found none at all.

Seventy-Two

As they walked up to it from the west, Kryger was impressed at the amount of damage to the fortress's wall. It looked as if two or three batteries had fired at it independently at first, not concentrating their fire. Seen from outside the walls, the palace towers, however, looked relatively undamaged.

Gate sentries in imperial green snapped to present arms as the commander-in-chief approached with his aides and the ex-ambassador. But the CIC, instead of entering through the open gate, elected to continue along the square to a breach his artillery had pounded through the wall a hundred feet beyond. It would have been easier to blast through the gate, but the officer in charge had decided to do it this way.

Good judgement, Kryger thought. *Get inside and open the gate, and you have a paved ingress not buried in rubble*.

Some civilians, dirty, haggard, and guarded by Almaeic troops, were throwing rubble out of the breach. One of the guards shouted at them in Almaeic to stop, and remarkably they did, as if reacting to the tone and situation. They stared at the richly uniformed officers. And at Kryger in mufty; they probably recognized him. The CIC led his party over the rubble and inside, in the process roughing his beautiful, glass-bright knee boots. ["Wellingtons" in another place and time.]

Seen from inside, the compound looked larger than from out. The palace stood near the west wall, and the appearance of its towers had been misleading. Parts of the magnificent building were heavily damaged. The wing where Kryger had been quartered had been gutted by fire.

The bodies had already been removed. Which was more than one could say for most of the city. Their enlisted driver had repeatedly steered his team around rubble and bodies. Then the CIC had gotten out, and they with him, to walk the last quarter mile, apparently to get a more intimate look at the aftermath of battle. Most of the bodies were droids of course, but corpses in imperial uniform were common enough. They'd poked around in a couple of buildings and seen the bodies of several women and girls who'd been raped and killed. Presumably in that order, Kryger thought wryly. He'd half expected the CIC to say something, tell an aide to see about identifying the troops who'd done it, but nothing was said. *Of course*, he thought. *They're droids. And the men who did it were commoners.*

He'd gotten so used to the Gorballis, he tended to think of them as people.

A colonel came hurrying up with his own aides, and saluted sharply before the CIC. "Colonel Gralbeg, sir, at your service! I'm in charge of the fortress!"

The CIC's eyes drilled through the man's forehead, and he imprinted the name for future reference. "Gralbeg. I am told the king here is dead."

"Yes, sir. We have not moved his body, sir. I assumed you'd want to see it where it fell."

"Take me to it."

"At once, Marshal Dersfolt!"

He led them to the palace and up the wide semicircular stairs to its grand entrance. In more than thirty years as a soldier, Kryger had never seen war before. It looked to him as if someone had poured buckets of blood on the stairs and on the landing at the top.

Inside, the great entrance hall was, if anything, worse. The splendid marble pillars were chipped and bullet-pocked, the marble floor gouged and pitted from grenades. Apparently the royal guard had tried to make a stand there and been slaughtered.

Considering they'd been engineered for pleasure, Kryger thought wryly, the droids were a hardnosed bunch of bastards.

The colonel led the command party down the central hall to the throne room. Remarkably there was little blood in the hall, as if Gamaliiu had insisted on making his personal stand alone. For whatever reasons. The body lay twenty feet inside the throne room door. The CIC went to it, his retinue following, and he knelt to examine what had been king there. Gamaliiu had been wearing ceremonial armor: gold cuirass and greaves and plumed gold helmet. The helmet lay several feet away, holed and bloody. His royal sword lay beside him.

"He was shot in the face," said the CIC, then looked up. "Between the eyes, and the bullet exited high in back."

He stood, and his eyes found the colonel. "Who was in charge of the unit that took the fortress?"

The colonel paled to near white. "I was, sir."

"Who was in direct charge of the unit that stormed the palace?"

Kryger looked at the colonel and felt a touch of pity for him. The CIC's tone said as plainly as words that someone's career was going to be destroyed.

"Captain Feelans, sir," the colonel answered. "Commanding Officer, Company Four."

"And who, personally, killed this king?"

"I don't know, sir."

The CIC looked long and hard at the regimental commander. "Colonel, all commanding officers down to company level were at my final briefing. Is that not correct?"

"Yes sir, to the best of my knowledge."

The cold eyes drilled him. "And did I not plainly stress the importance of taking the king alive if at all possible?"

"Yes sir, you did."

"I want you to identify the person who shot him. Probably someone vain of their marksmanship. The weapon was obviously fired from the waist, which suggests a sidearm. So does the exit hole. Only officers are issued sidearms."

Of course. Kryger thought. Gamaliiu had been tall, even by Gorrbian standards, more than six feet four. But even so, for the bullet to take the line it had . . .

"If he had to shoot him," the CIC continued, "he should have shot him in the leg. I want the killer arrested and charged with regicide. When you have him, I want his immediate superior arrested. And Captain . . ."

He turned to an aide. "What was the name?"

"Captain Feelans, sir."

"Captain Feelans. And when Captain Feelans has been arrested, I want you to turn yourself in for arrest. To Provost Marshal General Bronswo." He gestured with his head toward a burly, graying officer.

"Yes *sir!*" The colonel saluted, about faced, and left the throne room.

The CIC looked around, then turned on his heel and stalked out, the others following closely. They left the building, and the CIC ordered a sergeant to lead them onto a safe section of the west wall, then dismissed the man. He stood looking out across the city at the harbor. There wasn't a ship afloat, except for some small Djezian sloops and fishing boats tied to the wharf. All that was visible of the invasion fleet were masts protruding above the water at various angles.

"The Imperial Grand Fleet," he said drily, "and most of our munitions. We'll have to see what we can salvage. As it stands, we have enough ashore to last for perhaps two or three days of serious fighting."

He turned to Kryger. "How did this happen?"

Kryger's guts knotted. "Sir, I have no idea."

"No idea." The CIC's mouth twisted slightly, and his voice became ironic. "I know *I* didn't sink them, and I'm sure the admiral didn't. Or the seamen. Do you suppose it could have been the droids?"

Kryger's mouth opened slightly, but he could think of nothing to say.

Abruptly, loudly: "You were here! On the site! You were supposed to know what was going on! That debacle out there took a lot of preparation! And tons of explosives! How could they do that? How did they get the explosives? You should have gotten wind of it!"

Another thought struck him then. "You must have had a serious information leak! What kind of security did you have here? They couldn't have done something like this without knowing we were coming! Well in advance!"

Kryger began to see a glimmer. But it would make no difference.

For several seconds, Marshal Dersfolt, Commander-In-Chief of the Imperial Army of Invasion, glared at Kryger, the glare reducing to a look of grim disdain. He turned once more to regard the wreckage of the fleet, and when he spoke again, his voice was casual. "General Bronswo, arrest Lord Kryger for neglect of duty leading to gross disaster." He glanced back over his shoulder at Kryger. "Your court martial will be at noon today, your execution at sundown."

Seventy-Three

The manor house was built of stone and designed to be defended—almost a castle, but painted sky blue with yellow trim. Its nearly level grounds covered several acres, landscaped and tended. There were neat lawns; evergreens shaped by gardeners' shears. And broadleafed trees with massive boles, their crowns spreading vivid gold, flame, crimson, yellow-green, for here autumn's brush stroked weeks later than on the leeside of the mountains.

This baronial manor was the eighth the barbarians had taken, but only the first on the coastal plain, which extended from here for more than a hundred miles west. They'd crossed rugged mountains at the headwaters of the Hasannu River, and followed it; the mountain clans, awed at their numbers, let them pass without war. The mountain stream became a river, the mountains foothills. Then they'd passed through rolling piedmont that went on for more than a hundred miles—Gorrbian country, much of the land cleared of woods and in places badly gullied, used more for grazing than for crops. There'd been towns, rich manors, and they'd had skirmishes occasionally, but no real fight. The people said their regular forces had been called away to fight the Maklanni, leaving only a militia.

And finally, this manor had had no fighting men at all. The people said their militia had been called west to help fight a new enemy, had left only two days before.

Just now the manor's tended lawns were occupied by warriors of the Kinnli Innjakot, with their gear and cooking fires, absorbing the early sunshine after a chill night on the ground.

On the land around them were some five thousand more of various clans and tribes. Killed Many had told them they must sleep in the open, for they were warriors at war, not conquerors whose work was complete.

Killed Many too had slept on the ground. Now he squatted with the tribal chiefs by his cookfire, breakfasting on fresh roast. After weeks of sparse trail fare, his warriors had been eating well; gleebors were plentiful in this country, and no trouble to kill.

Killed Many's strong teeth wrenched off another mouthful. He chewed thoughtfully, his attention on something beyond the food, then glanced around at the chiefs who shared his fire.

"We will move on when we have finished eating," he said. "We have two armies to defeat, and if we stay here long, the warriors may become disobedient and ransack the buildings. They will take everything they like, and will not want to leave it behind. They will carry it with them, worry about it and fight over it, and cease to be warriors."

Spear Breaker, chief of the Tchook, grunted. "I have told my warriors that it is all theirs now," he said, "and to leave it here. I told them they need not take it with them to possess it."

At times like this, among the gathered chiefs, Eltrienn Cadriio listened and learned, seldom saying anything unless asked. He knew a great deal about the barbarians, but not yet enough to venture needless comments.

He hadn't foreseen some of the difficulties Killed Many had had. The barbarians had no tradition of a central chief, and their adjustment was not complete. Their first loyalty was to their clan chieftains, then to their tribal chiefs, and Killed Many held them only by the oaths those chiefs had sworn to him.

He'd had no defections, but twice it had been close. Once he'd had a clan chieftain executed by strangulation for refusing to obey an order. And when the chief of the entire Aazhmili tribe had called him a liar, he'd knocked the man down, then had drawn his sword and struck his head off. Both troubles had been with the Aazhmili, the most difficult of the tributary tribes.

Each incident, in its turn, could have begotten an intertribal war, but the Innjoka and Tchook had stood by him, while the northern tribes had kept aloof.

After having the chieftain executed, he'd outmaneuvered the clan warriors, telling them to name three men fit to command their clan. They'd have done this anyway—chosen candidates and discussed them. But now in choosing them, they were doing what Killed Many had ordered them to do. Then he'd stepped in and named their new chieftain from among the three; they could hardly reject the man they'd named first. Then Killed Many had taken the man's oath of loyalty and declared him chieftain, establishing a major precedent: The high chief can appoint clan chieftains.

Later, when he'd struck dead the tribal chief of the Aazhmili, he'd told the Aazhmili clan chieftains to name three of their number who they'd be willing to have as chief. "Swims in Winter" was the first named, and the one they'd agreed on most quickly, so Killed Many took his oath and declared him chief, praising him extravagantly.

Clever as it was, Eltrienn recognized, none of it would have worked if Killed Many hadn't been a rare and remarkable man. Few people, even Aazhmili warriors, could stand against his will. Apparently, even in his absence it wasn't easy to take a firm counter stance, and to stand against him in his presence was very difficult. The few who had, usually were in such an agitated state that they couldn't speak or act intelligently.

He wasn't sure how Ettsio Torillo had done it, or Sallvis Venettsio. Perhaps it was their foreignness.

Now Killed Many looked across the fire at Vessto. "Speaker With Hrum," he said, "why is it that these Djez so fear your people and this strange new army from the other side of the ocean, that they left this place undefended against us?"

"They do not fear us Hrummeans," Eltrienn answered. "They simply wish to take our land from us, and they know it will take a very strong army to do it. But the army from across the ocean they do fear. It is very big, has strange and powerful weapons, and they fear it will make their people slaves.

"While they know your people only as raiders. They have never seen you as an army. They believe that if they defeat the strangers from across the ocean, they can then easily drive you away."

Killed Many regarded Vessto almost broodingly. "And what do you think, Speaker With Hrum?"

Vessto replied calmly, almost blandly. "The strangers from

across the sea will be defeated. Because you will join with the Djez to beat them, despite their loud-barking stick weapons that shoot farther than the bow, and their fat iron logs that sound like thunder and destroy walls at a distance. You will fight them in the great Djez village, at night, where their iron logs and stick weapons are of less avail. Also, the strangers do not have swords. And while they can use their stick weapons as short spears, they are not skillful at it, easily losing heart. They much prefer to kill at a distance, which you will not let them do."

"How far away are these foreign soldiers?"

Vessto seemed to look inward a moment. "They are still at Haipoor, the great Djez Village, about a hard three-day march along this river. And what they are doing there will make them much more dangerous, unless they are stopped."

"Why should we not let the strangers and the Djez kill each other off? Then we can more easily beat the winner."

Vessto's gaze was steady on his own. "Because then the strangers would beat the Djezians. And later they would fight you in the countryside instead of in the village. The advantage would be theirs. But the great reason is that Hrum-In-Thee will make sure you fight them now."

Killed Many's face was impassive; it would be impossible to know his thoughts by his expression. "While you are prophesying," he said, "prophesy me this: Will I rule the Djez?"

"Not at this time. But you will go home with much booty, and kaabors to carry it. More important, you will take much knowledge home with you, and steelmakers, and many honors. It will have been the greatest raid of all time. And by then you may decide you do not wish to rule the Djez."

Killed Many took his eyes from the sage and stared off westward. Sometimes he believed this man's pronouncements and sometimes not. Before the others he professed to set great store by them; they helped him rule. But always he followed his own judgement; now he must decide.

After a few minutes during which none of them spoke, he brought his attention back, and standing, looked around. "We will make common cause with the Djez against this army from across the ocean," he told the chiefs. "Have your warriors form the marching order. We will not stop to cook till evening. A great army stands three days ahead; we will fight it and earn much honor. Speaker With Hrum will tell us more at the end of this day."

The chiefs dispersed then, and the Cadriio brothers drew apart. "The Almites are still at Haipoor?" Eltrienn asked. "Why is that?"

"I don't know." Vessto grinned then. "Hrum doesn't tell me everything."

"And the thing they're doing? That will make them much more dangerous?"

"Hrum didn't tell me that, either. But I got an impression of them working at their ships, which are sunken. Their fleet lies on the bottom of Haipoor Harbor."

Eltrienn stared at him, then shook his head and went over to pack his packsack. It had never before occurred to him to wonder: How could an adept, how could anyone, know the difference between whispers and pictures from Hrum and one's own imaginings?

Seventy-Four

All the way to North Cape, the breeze was out of the south, and the three schooners made slow progress tacking against it. Their sullsi, Sleekit among them, had gone northward to join their kin and tell a story such as none had heard before, and the serpents likewise.

At North Cape they spent a night and part of a day, and replenished their water, then continued toward Theedalit.

Juliassa's recovery was slow at first, and mostly she'd stayed in bed, eating what was brought to her, though the night at North Cape seemed to strengthen her. Often she stared long at her hand mirror and the deep and vivid scar creasing neck, jaw, and nose with purplish red.

As they sailed up the firth, Brokols, informed by royal courier of the sighting, and transported by hansom, was at the wharf on crutches. Leonessto was there too, and they stood together, Brokols grinning broadly as the ship approached. After a few moments he could see Juliassa at the rail, and waved wildly. She waved back, but without enthusiasm. *She's been sick*, he decided, *and it was a long hard mission*.

She was the first off the vessel though, except for the sailors who'd jumped down to set lines on the bollards. Brokols crutched rapidly along the wharf to meet her, while Leonessto walked more slowly to let them finish their greetings. Brokols had almost reached her before he noticed, and the grin slid off his face.

"Juliassa!" he said. "Hrum but it's good to see you again!" He embraced her with one arm; she held her body stiff. Then, "What happened?"

"We found Tirros," she answered, "or he found us. I don't know how he missed my throat. It's what he went for."

"Oh, darling!" Brokols said.

"Then he jumped overboard and Sleekit killed him. Sleekit's sword was full grown, and he ran him through." No tears welled; her eyes were dry, her words brittle. "He'd always done cruel things, from the time we were little. And now . . ." Her lips closed, tight and thin. Brokols didn't know what to do, so he hugged her again, and that was the right thing, for her rigidity lessened and she hugged him back, a brief stiff squeeze.

Leonessto had stopped some yards off and hadn't heard. Now Juliassa looked at him, and he started over. Then his eyes saw the scar, and shock flashed in them. "What happened?!" he asked.

"Tirros," she said. "He'd been driven to sea in a small boat, by a storm, and we came across him. It was night, or nearly, and the men who took him aboard didn't know who he was. He looked different—filthy, long-haired, half-starved. And somehow he learned I was on board. He hid himself away from me, in the hold I suppose, until he saw his chance.

"We were setting the mines, had set most of them, when he tried to kill me, but I screamed and he fled, jumped overboard. Sleekit caught him in the water." She gripped Leonessto's hand then. "He's dead, father."

Then, at last, she did begin to cry, a few silent tears. The amirr couldn't speak, just nodded, his own tears flowing, and Brokols' started too. The three of them stood weeping, others skirting them widely as they disembarked and left.

"Well," said Leonessto after a long minute, "shall we go to the palace? Your mother will want to welcome you."

Brokols and Juliassa had their noon meal with her parents, then went home. It was at home that she broke down, wept hard and loud, the violence of it shocking Brokols clear of empathy, though not of sympathy. He held her, patting her clumsily while she soaked his shirt with tears. Afterward they bathed, then made awkward love. After that, as they lay relaxed, she seemed—not entirely different from the girl he'd known. She commented on how active he was with his leg still splinted. "What does the healer say about you crutching around so freely?" she asked.

"I'm not sure. About the time you left, Panni came to see

me. Asked me questions. When he'd gone, my leg felt distinctly better."

She turned onto her stomach and raised up on an elbow. "What kind of questions?" There was an unexpected sharpness in her words. "Give me an example."

"Well, the last one he asked was what a broken leg might be used for." Brokols shrugged slightly where he lay. "And every time I answered, he asked it again. After awhile I was giving some very strange answers, and feeling better and better. And Panni was grinning! Finally I said a broken leg could be used for staying home, and I got chills from head to foot. He laughed out loud, bid me sleep well, and left."

Brokols paused, giving her a chance to react. She didn't, beyond turning pensive. He leaned toward her and kissed her. "Maybe we should send for Panni, if he's willing to come. Send a hansom; I'd almost bet he's never ridden in one. Perhaps he could heal the wound that Tirros gave you—not on your neck and face, but on your heart."

"Perhaps," she whispered. "But right now I want to be alone with you. And let you remind me that fucking can be an act of love."

Seventy-Five

Eltrienn stood looking at the Gorrbian camp a mile away in the hazy autumn sunshine. Farther, by about two miles, was the city. Killed Many called a break for eating; his signalman raised the curled horn he carried on a lanyard and blew a pattern of sonorous peals.

"You will speak with their commander for me then," Killed Many said to Eltrienn.

"Right. We'll go now; we've eaten on the road. We'll see what we can arrange with him."

The two Hrummeans shrugged out of their packstraps, and lightened, left, intermittently jogging. Eltrienn had kept his sword but left bow and arrows behind. Vessto had only the knife he used to cut his meat with. Nearing the Gorrbian encampment, they saw a party riding out in their direction. It came a hundred yards, then stopped and waited. Nearing, they could see a husky young captain in the lead, his hostility undisguised. He didn't wait for introductions.

"What army is that?" he demanded, pointing.

"They're barbarians from across the mountains, come to raid in your country," said Eltrienn. "Three days ago they heard about the foreigners from across the ocean. They want to join you in fighting them."

The captain's eyes searched them coldly. "You've an accent."

Eltrienn decided to ignore the question, and the hostility behind it. "We'd like to talk with the commander of your army," he said.

The eyes flashed anger. "You would, eh? To what purpose?"

"To plan a joint attack on the foreigners. We're envoys from the barbarian chief. He's prepared to . . ."

"We don't talk with barbarians," the man said coldly, "we kill them."

"I'd say you have enemies enough to the west of you," Eltrienn said mildly. "If you've got the good sense I hope you have, you don't want five thousand more to the east."

Without taking his scowl from the Hrummeans, the captain ordered his men: "Take these two spies out aways and dispose of them. Out far enough that the stink won't . . ."

A colonel had ridden out after the captain, and come near enough to hear the order.

"Hold on there," he said. "What's this about?"

The captain turned. "Renegade spies," he said. "I've just ordered them executed."

"Your name and unit, captain."

The captain's voice changed from hostile and deadly to military and obedient, and faintly resentful, as he answered. The senior officer looked him up and down. "Ah. A ducal defense unit from Koziida Monteeros. Captain, you're not back home riding patrol. We're army here, and you will damned well follow regulations. Stand by till I say you can leave, and hope I don't have you broken and flogged."

He turned to the Cadriio brothers. "Who are you, and what are you doing here?"

Eltrienn repeated what he'd told the captain, adding that he was Hrummean. It seemed safer than being taken for a renegade.

"And what are Hrummeans doing among the barbarians?"

"Just now, serving as envoys, as I said."

"You twist my question," the colonel replied, then paused. "Well, I'll take you to the general. We'll see what he makes of you. Captain, assign two of these men to escort the envoys."

His face dark with blood, the captain obeyed. The colonel walked his horse alongside the brothers, looking down at them. "I will put my question differently. How did you two come to be with the barbarians?"

"I am associated with a businessman on our east coast," Eltrienn answered. "He sent me to buy timber from them if I can."

"Umm. And your friend?"

"He's my brother, a man of Hrum, a holy man. He went with me hoping to teach among them there. The barbarians know rather little about Hrum beyond some ancient lore."

"You. Holy man. Do you speak our language?"

"Certainly, sir. They're not that different. And we're from Kammenak, where it's not unusual to know Djezian. More than a few have come to us there from across the border. When we were boys, our father sometimes hired one or two of them to work with my brother and me, herding vehatto."

The colonel grunted. "That explains your dialect. You must also speak the barbarian tongue."

"The dialect of the south coast," Eltrienn put in. "I was shipwrecked there a few years ago, on a fishing smack. My brother has learned it since, partly from me and partly since we came among the tribes."

The colonel's smile was dour. "I'd not like the job of sorting truth from lies in what you say. Well, what counts is whether you can be of any use to us."

There was no more talk then till they came to the cluster of broad tents that was army headquarters. The colonel dismounted—a lean man whose exceptional height became conspicuous when he stood—and took them in to the general.

"General," he said, "the large body of men reported east of us is the barbarian army, as you supposed. These men are Hrummeans they've sent to us as envoys."

The general tended toward paunchy, his hair gray tinged with yellow. He looked tired but strong, frustrated but functioning. "Hrummeans with the barbarians?"

He asked much the same questions then as the colonel had, and heard much the same answers, elaborated a bit.

"How does this Killed Many propose to help us fight the Almites?" he said to Eltrienn. "That's what they call themselves, Almites. We had some living among us before their army came."

"First we need to know more about them," Eltrienn answered. "How many of them are there?"

"We've heard estimates of thirty to fifty thousand, by several people, military, who watched them land their troops. They had 200 ships, huge things that gave off smoke without apparent fire. All three counted the ships the same, so that figure should be good. As for the number of men . . ." He shrugged. "Probably at least thirty thousand, which is somewhat more than we have until our other armies get here from the south and north. In addition they have strange and terrible weapons; the sound of them is bad enough, and they kill from a distance. Also, some of the ships carried kaabors of a sort, small and black. We don't know how many; they unloaded them at the dock, which made them hard to estimate. They took the city in a single afternoon and night."

The general's jaw jutted angrily. "I sent out a light probing attack. Their answer was to shoot their great weapons at us. Things we couldn't see burst overhead and killed scores of men in a minute. I tried it again by night and they shot torches into the air that lit the earth and sky, then shot their great weapons as in daylight. Hrum hasn't deigned to instruct me in how to deal with them.

"Yet they haven't attacked us. Which I suppose I should be grateful for, but it worries me. Certainly they'll have to, sooner or later. They have no way to leave Haipoor except through us, because after they took the city, all their ships sank overnight. Without storm. Perhaps Hrum took offense at them. Only their masts still stand above the water, leaning in every direction."

The story startled Eltrienn, despite what Vessto had said. "All 200 sunk? Overnight?"

"All. Unless some fled by darkness. It's said their masts look like a forest drowned by flood and falling over.

"Meanwhile their army seems content to simply hold the city. They haven't tried to break out. Which I assure you they could do, although we'd make them pay. They haven't even shot at us except when we attacked them."

He cocked an eye at Eltrienn. "Five thousand warriors, you say? What could 5,000 barbarian warriors do to an army like the Almites? Besides give them targets."

"General," Eltrienn said, "they are men who can stalk their enemy in the dark and not be seen or heard. They are men who use the knife skillfully. Let them pass through your army after nightfall and they will sift through the Almite camp like smoke. They will cut throats. And when the Almites realize they're there, they won't know where to shoot, or what to do. The barbarians will confuse and terrorize them.

"After your men have let the barbarians through, have your outposts listen carefully. The enemy should start to shoot their noisy weapons, and there will be war cries. Then I suggest you send forces of your own, quietly, not to probe but to strike and kill. Take prisoners if you can. Capture as many of their great weapons as you can."

Then a thought occurred to Eltrienn. "Did all the people flee Haipoor, or did many stay?"

The general frowned. "I have no numbers. Most fled, but also many stayed."

Eltrienn said nothing for a moment, thinking. "It would be best if you sent an officer back with us to talk with Killed Many—someone authorized to say yes or no. Killed Many should make the final agreement."

The general pursed his lips and looked at the man who'd brought them. "Colonel Kazirru, I want you to go with the Hrummeans and talk with this Killed Many. If, when you've talked with him, it seems the right thing to do, you are authorized to guarantee the barbarians free passage through our positions to attack the Almites."

The colonel saluted. "Thank you, sir. I'll be happy to do that."

The general watched them leave. *I'm grasping at straws,* he said to himself. *But then, straws is what I've got, if the Almites decide to break out before our reinforcements come. Or maybe even when they've gotten here.*

Grain stubble poked his body uncomfortably, but Eltrienn ignored it. Neither moon was up, and they'd crept to within fifty yards of the Almaeic outposts. Killed Many had made the call of a night darter, three times sharply, sending ten five-man squads, well separated, slipping forward to and through the Almaeic line. Now the rest of them waited for a sign.

From somewhere well off to their left came a bloodchilling scream, followed by a shot, then a flurry of shots, then a silence which wouldn't last long. Over there somewhere, waiting barbarians would be surging to their feet and running silently forward.

Killed Many and the other warriors nearby began creeping forward again, the Cadriio brothers keeping pace. In seconds, rifle fire flurried from the direction of the earlier disturbance, with screams and war cries. From well ahead came another scream, and shooting. Killed Many surged to his feet, running crouched in the darkness. The brothers followed, and a river of warriors. They came to a ridge of dirt, plunged up and over, then jumped the anticipated ditch behind it, plunging on. Some squads of warriors would be dropping into the ditch, swords chopping. If things got too intense for them there, they'd climb out and disperse in fives, killing through the camp. A hundred yards into the camp, Killed Many stopped and began directing traffic, left, right, straight ahead. The Cadriio brothers went straight ahead.

Behind them, firing still was scattered and less than heavy. Around them on both sides there were tents and confused shouting, but no gunfire yet. Squads of warriors peeled off the running column, these squads each with three swordsmen, and two spearmen who'd shortened their pikes to about six feet. A small man, shirtless and barefoot, gun in hands, ducked out of a tent and almost collided with Eltrienn, who cut him down.

The shooting became more intense; Eltrienn saw a barbarian fall just ahead of him, and heard the high-pitched keen of ricochets. Presumably the Gorballis would have started their charge now. He hoped the squads sent to kill the cannon crews had done their job.

They were beyond the bivouac then, and slowed to an easy lope. The warriors had been told to stop short of the city and circle back, savaging Almites. The idea had been for them to confuse the Almites and draw their attention while killing as many as possible, then return to their own camp. The Gorballis were to capture the Almite's forward artillery and drag it away. How much or little of all that would get accomplished, Eltrienn could hardly predict.

Then the brothers were through the Almaeic camp and into the fringe of Haipoor, small houses of adobe, some plastered over and some not. Presumably these would now house Almaeic soldiers too. The last of the warriors peeled off to investigate, and kill any Almites they found. The volume of rifle fire behind them was an unbroken racket now.

So far Eltrienn had no plan. He'd see what opportunity gave them. He knew the city and numerous of its people, from his time there as a spy, but the odds, or the value, of finding anyone he knew seemed slight. They slowed to a walk, hoping to pass in the dark for locals breaking curfew, and shortly stopped around the corner in an ink-black alleyway.

"What now?" asked Vessto.

"I have no idea."

"You need to take your sword off if we're going to pass for harmless," Vessto pointed out, then added, "I'd like to go to the harbor."

"The harbor? What for?"

He grinned. "I don't know. There's a reason, but I haven't found it yet. I should know when we get there."

Eltrienn stared at him for a moment, then removed his sword and laid it against a wall. It was harder to give it up than he'd have thought. Now Vessto led, walking briskly but never running.

Twice, before they reached the waterfront, they saw street patrols. Presumably the Almites had proclaimed a curfew. They ducked around a corner and the first patrol never saw them. The second did, and they ran furiously under chase, speeded by gunfire, dodging behind houses and up alleys till well after they'd lost any sign of pursuit. Occasionally they heard rifle fire that seemed to come from inside town. Eltrienn decided some of the barbarians had succumbed to the temptation of exploring the city.

After a bit they reached the waterfront district; the Almites had shelled it to discourage attacks on their landing troops, and fires had burned. Shortly afterward they saw water, the harbor, glass smooth and sparkling with star reflections. Without either saying anything, both men crouched low, slinking along the margins of rubble heaps, past broken walls. Finally, crouching, they could look along the nightbound wharf and make out a sentry walking his post on it, not far away. Presumably there were others.

There were big stacks of kegs and boxes here and there all along the wharf, as if waiting for work crews to clear a street of rubble and cart them off. Clearly they'd been piled there after the cannonading, which seemed to mean the Almites had put them there.

"S-s-st!"

Eltrienn turned to look at his brother. Vessto beckoned him back into the shadow of a standing bit of wall, then whispered softly. "We need to set fire to those kegs and boxes."

Eltrienn didn't ask why, just, "How do we do that?"

"We find a house or apartment with lamp oil and some matches. Then we come back and take care of the sentry."

Take care of the sentry? Eltrienn thought. *How?* He had no sword now, nothing but his knife.

They sneaked several blocks up a rubble-clogged minor street, to an apartment building that hadn't been burned. *Now,* thought Eltrienn, *is anyone at home?* It seemed doubtful. They tried a door. It opened and they slipped inside. The city had smelled increasingly of ashes and char as they'd hiked farther into it, but here it was the odor of old grease that led them through pitchy darkness to the kitchen.

They explored it with their hands. Vessto found a match

pot, the size of his palm and flat, recognizing it by the abrasive patch on the top. It was half full of matches, stout and waxy like those at home. He took one out and struck it against the patch; flame flared, then steadied, and by its light, Eltrienn found a large crockery jug with a whittled wooden stopper. He sloshed it; three-quarters full, he judged. Pulling the stopper, his nose identified the faintly fishy smell of lamp oil.

"Why are we doing this?" asked Eltrienn. "What's in those kegs and boxes?"

"Elver Brokols had thoughts of guns, cannons, and you've told me he was preparing to make a substance he called 'gun powder.' But he wasn't sure if the ingredients were available in Hrum. Gunpowder makes a loud noise, and seems to be what makes cannons function, and the smaller guns, the rifles.

"So I suppose the Almaeic army would bring their own. In large quantities."

Eltrienn thought he saw the rest of it now, but he let his brother continue.

"The Almites fought for the city through much of a day and night, and in the morning, their ships were all sunk. Do you suppose their gunpowder went down with the ships?"

"Ah-h!" Eltrienn took it from there. "And the reason they haven't tried to break out of the city, and the reason they haven't shot their cannons except when attacked, is that they are short of this 'gunpowder.' They're working to get it out of the sunken ships, and stacking it on the wharf temporarily."

"That's how it seems to me."

"Then let's go."

"Just a minute. We need to do something about the sentry. The sent*ries*. There are more than one of them. We need to consider means."

Eltrienn shook his head. "I should have kept my sword."

Vessto said nothing for a moment, seeming to concentrate, then gripped his brother's arm. "Never mind. I was wrong to be concerned. We'll have no trouble with the sentries."

Eltrienn blinked, puzzled, but Vessto had started out of the kitchen, so he shrugged and followed. As they reached the bottom of the stairs, they saw several men, barbarians, moving down the street, keeping close to the walls.

"Ho! Vinnta!" Vessto husked after them in their own language. *"Os innska o ha yollpos!"*

The five warriors wheeled, bowstrings half drawn, peering into the denser dark beside the building. The brothers came out, hands spread. These warriors had no doubt been spearmen, who seemed to have cast their spears. For each spearman had also carried a bow and a quiver of arrows. The swordsmen had carried only their swords and shields.

Vessto held a murmured conversation with them, then they all went quietly together toward the waterfront. There, at the corner of a wall, the leader of the bowmen drew back his bowstring and launched an arrow. The sentry fell without a cry. Vessto laid a hand on the warrior's arm and whispered.

"Killed Many said the spearmen should carry fire arrows. Do you have them?"

Nodding, the man patted the belt pouch where he carried his fire auger and punk. "Shall I make a flame to light them?"

"Not now. Do you see the big round wooden things piled on the bank?" Vessto asked, pointing. "And the square ones?"

"Yes."

"They hold a powerful magic the enemy uses. If we set them on fire, we will do him great harm. And also if we set fire to the big canoes tied at the bank. You two go that way along the shore, until there are no more of the piles. Then, with fire arrows, set fire to the last one, and to the others as you come back." He turned. "You three go to the other end and do the same thing.

"And when you shoot the piles, shoot them from a distance. That's important. Otherwise the magic may kill you. Also, be sure you kill any more sentries you see."

He took the match pot from his pouch. "I will give you some magic fire sticks. You can make fire quickly with them, like this."

Kneeling, Vessto struck a match on a piece of rubble; it flared. The warriors hissed, inhaling through their teeth; the squad leader put out his hand for some. Vessto gave him half; the warriors divided them and left.

After a moment's consultation, the Cadriio brothers followed the northbound three, keeping to cover as much as possible. Twice they paused while a warrior shot a sentry. When they'd reached what seemed to be the northernmost of the tied-up boats, the brothers stopped while the warriors went on. Vessto took a keg from the pile there, and squatting, dropped it into the nearest boat, a fishing boat. He did this to every boat for some two hundred yards along the wharf. Beyond that the boats were only a widely scattered few. Meanwhile Eltrienn trickled a train of lamp oil from pile to pile southward till he ran out. The warriors would have to take care of the piles farther south. He'd hoped to do the same from pile to boat, but ran out of oil more quickly than he'd expected.

They met where they'd started. "Is there any oil left?" Vessto asked.

"No. I used it all."

At that moment, someone shouted from a block or more up the street. Bullets cracked round them then, and they heard rifle shots. Both Cadriios sprinted off to their right. "Get as far from the wharf as you can!" Vessto shouted, and Eltrienn slanted for the next street.

Vessto didn't follow. Instead he darted out on the dock, knelt, scratched several matches in a bunch, flinching at the sharp burn they gave his fingers. By their sudden light he saw the oil train, and dropped the matches onto it. It flared at once, the flames beginning to crawl in both directions, quickening. Then he sprinted to the edge of the wharf and dove far out, surfaced swimming, and started toward mid-channel.

There was an enormous explosion, well off to the south, followed in a few seconds by one off to the north. The shock was almost stunning, far worse than he'd imagined, and those were the end piles, perhaps three hundred yards away!

Now he discovered how fast he could swim, which was remarkably fast for a man wearing pants and shirt. He'd lost his moccasins.

He'd had more time than he'd thought; when he was a hundred yards out, he looked back. Flames were licking over the tops of the first two piles. He turned and began to swim outward again, got perhaps twenty yards farther when the two piles exploded almost simultaneously. The sound shocked the breath out of him, seemed to drive him down, underwater. He came up and kept swimming. After fifteen seconds or so there was another explosion, less powerful, and he looked back again. One of the box piles, he thought. Fine debris burned all over that part of the wharf, and three boats had begun burning. Another stack of kegs went up then, a great towering pillar of fire topped by a red cloud, and another followed, a distance to the south.

He turned south then, swimming slowly now on his side, saving his strength. A boat blew up. Intermittent explosions rocked the waterfront for some minutes, and when he finally angled toward shore, southward well beyond the city wall, the only fires he could see were a couple of burning boats. They'd been shielded from the shattering blasts by the ruined wharf, and presumably set afire by debris.

Eltrienn had gone north through streets and narrow alleyways, picking his way over rubble, worried far more about pursuit than explosion. He'd gotten two blocks away when the first pile blew, well off to the south. Its violence shocked him, and he speeded to a trot, scrambling rather than climbing now over the rubble piles. He'd gotten more than another block away when the center piles blew, the sound beating him to his knees. After that his ears registered nothing for a bit, and it was several seconds before he got up and ran.

Five blocks from the waterfront, he turned north and worked his way parallel to the wharf, barely pausing now when another stack blew, jubilant at what they'd done. When the explosions seemed finally over, the silence was awesome. There was no longer even the sound of distant gunfire.

Finally the city's north wall showed ahead. He scouted it from a block away, saw a gate closed and guarded. He went back to the waterfront then and took to the river, bypassing the wall.

Great Liilia, early in her fourth quarter, was well up when Eltrienn found his way to the barbarian camp, to where his gear should lie near the road. The only warriors he saw awake were sentries who watched him into camp.

He sought around till he found his gear—his and Vessto's—but Vessto wasn't there. He wondered if his brother had been killed, then decided he hadn't. He was sure he'd know it somehow, if he had been. The world would feel different. Killed Many was there though, asleep; he wasn't sure what would become of the army if its great chief was killed.

After stripping off his wet things and spreading them to dry somewhat, he rolled up in his light blanket of yennsa pelts and went to sleep.

Dawn was paling the eastern sky when he awoke chilled. Vessto knelt naked nearby, spreading his clothes.

"Vessto," murmured Eltrienn, "where were you?"

His brother finished what he was doing, then squatted beside him.

"After I lit the oil," Vessto whispered, "I jumped in the water. Then I swam south awhile and came ashore. I got messed up in a terrible marsh there—the Hasannu River has a delta, you know—and right now I'm tired. How did the army do?"

"I don't know. They were sleeping when I got here."

Vessto grunted and rolled up in his blanket next to his brother.

"I'm going to suggest to Killed Many that he head back east," Eltrienn said. "Leave the Almites and Gorballis to fight it out. If he gets east far enough, he can pillage his way back to the mountains, and get home with enough loot and stories to please every warrior with him.

"But if he decides to stay around here, he'll be sitting between this army of Gorballis and the Gorrbian armies from the south and north. And if he does that, if he stays, you and I'll leave. Steal a boat along the river and ride her down to the ocean, coast southward, row at night and hide by day. Till we find something better, with a sail."

"Sounds doable," Vessto said, then lay quiet a minute. "But we won't have to. Killed Many'll have his army on its way home about two hours from now. That's the last thing he thought about before he went to sleep. It's going to be a long day's march for me, on so little rest."

Neither spoke for a minute, and Vessto was almost asleep when Eltrienn murmured: "You know, I've enjoyed this mission, including tonight. But I'll be glad to get back to Theedalit. I think I'll find a lady I like and get married. I sort of have one in mind."

Vessto said nothing.

"How about you?" Eltrienn asked.

"I'll stay with Killed Many and see what interesting changes I can start among the tribes."

Eltrienn didn't know how to answer that, and in another minute his brother was breathing in the slow, shallow cadence of sleep. He closed his own eyes and followed Vessto's example.

Seventy-Six

Interview with an Imperial clerical employee, published in the Shautler Province underground bulletin, The Objective Informer, *Issue 4.*

X: . . . . Yes, I'd say that characterizes the general situation rather well.

OI: *How did it start? We've heard all kinds of rumors of course, but you were on the inside, so to speak.*

X: Let's say I was on the outer edge of the inside. My familiarity with it began with a rumor. Supposedly word had leaked from the Imperial Security Bureau—the ISB of all things! And to be more specific, from the Department of Armed Forces. The entire fleet, every ship, was said to have been sunk in a droid harbor, and the report supposedly sent on a wireless taken ashore from the flagship before she sank.

Actually it was almost more than hearsay, in that I have a friend who swore he saw the message himself before it was taken down. You see, ISB headquarters has one of the new teletypes that print out messages as they come in through the ether. Supposedly someone smuggled the printed message out of the wireless center—on ISB paper—and posted it on an employee bulletin board, from which it soon disappeared. One story has it that it eventually was given to the underground in Larvis Royal.

Still, it *could* have been a rumor, a simple lie. I didn't see the teletype myself, so I can't vouch for it. In fact, at the time I really didn't believe my friend; the story was just too hard to accept.

OI: *But it's what started the disorders?*

X: Not directly, but ultimately yes. Initial credence was low. I mean . . . Every ship? Come now! But it didn't end there. It was the first in a supposed series of leaks, although that was the only message said to have been smuggled out in the original. Others were said to have been seen in the original by an army intelligence officer who had no chance to steal them. He's said to have memorized them as best he could and to have written them down later at home. Supposedly the someone was a Major Blenum, who'd then delivered the messages to the underground and gone into hiding.

These other messages, rumored or actual, carried the story further. One had it that most of the munitions for the expeditionary force had gone down with the fleet. Then supposedly men had dived down to the sunken ships—the harbor is shallow—gotten the hatches open, and set grapples onto powder barrels and shell and ammunition cases. The idea being to salvage all that they could. They'd made a fair start on the task when thousands of wild droids supposedly breached the army's defense lines around the droid capital by night and rampaged through the city setting fires.

So the story went. They set fire to the wharf and the entire waterfront—and the munitions stacked there blew sky high, destroying the salvage boats as well. The next to last message in this supposed series said that the army had driven the droids from the city, but that there still was fighting in the outskirts. The last said that a reinforced droid army had fought its way back into the city, that the imperial army was critically low on munitions, and that some units had mutinied in order to surrender.

Of course, anyone with a little basic understanding and a good imagination could have written those. And it would seem to me—there may be something

I am missing here—it seems to me that they could also have been wirelessed in not from the army across the ocean, but by some underground operation a mile away.

OI: *But the population of the capital was reading or hearing about all this?*

X: I don't know how many people actually read about it. In the underground reports, that is. Clearly though, enough people read about it to spread the stories widely, give them broad currency. I don't know what the stories may have been like after they'd been passed along orally enough times, but they could hardly have been much worse than I heard. Or than I read.

Naturally, the government tried ignoring the leaked reports, rumors, or what have you, for a week or more. But when it got to be the talk of the streets, they commented to the extent of denying it all. The whole thing was a hoax, they said, and this denial was in the paper and on the public boards. Their version was that the fleet was standing off the droid coast, monitoring the progress of the military campaign ashore by wireless. And that it all was going nicely, thank you. There'd been no messages of the type rumored, and there was no Major Blenum in the ISB.

Most people were predisposed to believe the government version, on the simple basis that the underground chronically spreads lies. As some underground organizations do, routinely, at least on the Island of the Emperor. Of course, so does the government. I think we all knew that. But it was more comfortable to believe the government than the underground.

Up to a point. The government's statement went beyond that point, because most people knew there was a Major Blenum in military intelligence, or there very recently had been, at any rate. He'd been publicly decorated less than a year earlier, by the emperor himself, for inventing the teletype; it had been played up very big in the paper. So the government reply gave these reports, or rumors—these stories—a certain odor of veracity, you see.

Then a man wearing the uniform and insignia of a captain in military intelligence stood up on the rim of a fountain in Emperors' Park at noon, when a lot of people were sitting about eating their lunches, and he began to shout that the rumors were true. That he personally had seen two of the teletypes. And then . . . then a policeman went up to him and cut him down with his saber where he stood.

It was a shocking thing to see, and scores or hundreds of people saw it. Including myself. It proved nothing, of course, but that one act probably quadrupled the percentage of people who believed the stories. And several people who'd seen it, including the friend I was eating with, claimed they knew the man personally, that he really was a captain in military intelligence, a Captain Margrin, or Margrun.

And of course, the subject matter was one of strong public concern. A great number of people, including, I'm sure, many here on Shautler, had relatives and friends in the expeditionary force. And beyond that, a lot of merchant seamen had been impressed to sail the fleet. Taxes had been raised sharply, as you very well know, taxes that already were quite severe.

So now there began to be impromptu gatherings in the streets, people listening to speakers against the chancellor and even, I'm told, against the emperor! Nothing all that big, you understand, but it seemed quite shocking that such things could happen right in the capital city, and the police were kept busy hurrying about breaking them up. And breaking heads in the bargain. Many people though, perhaps most, said good enough for them, that such lawlessness should be crushed in the bud.

OI: *So what caused things to escalate into large-scale rioting?*

X: When the police began cracking down on small public gatherings, the "trouble makers," as many people called them, turned to slinging rocks through government windows at night and ambushing policemen on patrol, that sort of thing. And after several policemen were killed, in a single night at that, martial law was proclaimed. Some people were accused and arrested, and a mass execution was held on a platform in Government Square. Your readers know about that, of course.

But it didn't work quite the way it was intended. Some of the crowd began shouting "down with the chancellor! Down with the chancellor!", and it spread. Mounted police rode in to break it up. But the day was chilly and rainy, and some people had come prepared with jointed javelins concealed in their raincapes and began spearing the police kaabors and the policemen themselves. So the police pulled out their repeating pistols and began to shoot, some perhaps into the air but some into the crowd. I know that's true because I was working extra-time and watched it all from my office window. The crowd panicked then, and a considerable number were trampled to death.

Next, of course, a curfew was invoked, and a Public Urgent Bulletin was distributed by the Postal Bureau that all businesses and government offices would be closed the next day. Except Security offices; that went without saying. And the curfew would be in force twenty five hours a day until otherwise officially indicated!

OI: *An around the clock curfew!*

X: That's right. But it didn't really happen that way, because "otherwise indicated" came the next morning, when the palace bells began to toll. And when Government Square had all the people it could hold, which is about three hundred thousand, the emperor spoke from a balcony. He said the chancellor had been set down, that the emperor himself would operate the government, and that there'd be an investigation.

There was a shot then, and the emperor fell. That started a genuine stampede, and apparently a lot of people were killed. Afterward it was rumored that the emperor was dead. Then the vice chancellor called the army in to clear the streets of all gatherings, and keep them clear. And a roundup was undertaken of everyone suspected of hostility to the government.

At least hundreds were arrested—thousands seems far likelier—taken from their homes and put into compounds. Afterward a dusk to dawn curfew was invoked, and nobody worked much. The waggoners stopped carting anything but food into the capital, and not much of that. There were ships set fire to in Larvis Harbor. Buildings were burned, whole neighborhoods. People seemed actually to have gone quite mad. And because I was known to my neighbors as an employee in the——— Bureau, it seemed well to take my vacation time and remove myself and my family from Larvis Royal. That's what it's come to.

Before going down to the carriage I'd hired, I looked out my living room window—I have an upper floor apartment—and saw the university burning. Guns were banging somewhere not too far off. And as for the last departmental rumor I'd heard—probably true, considering the source—Kelthos Province was in full revolt, some imperial police units there had been massacred, and the provincial constabulary was in mutiny and besieging the Kaitmar Military Compound.

I don't know how all this will end, but I fear it can never get back to the way it was.

Unless perhaps the fleet comes sailing back into Larvis Harbor. I most earnestly hope it does. But even if that happens . . . I don't know. I'm afraid that things may have gone too far.

Seventy-Seven

That day Tassi Vermaatio was more animated than he'd been for decades. Not only did he come down from the penthouse roof; he peered into the faces of disciples, peeked under the lid of the cookpot, dipped a finger into the bubbling contents with no sign of discomfort or damage, licked it to taste, smiled, nodded, smiled some more, went outside and squatted beside a planter to sniff, touch, examine. Then he went back up on the roof again, laughing.

He'd come back into the world, as if to refamiliarize himself with it.

But all of yesterday, he and Panni had continued unmoving on the penthouse roof. In midmorning a recent disciple, a boy in his mid-teens just back from an errand, climbed the ladder to see if there was anything he could do for the two sages. Neither showed any awareness of him.

The boy had lived in a monastery briefly, and had seen masters in trance; he was used to near totality of transcendence. But these two beweirded him this morning: Their eyes were not simply unfocused, unseeing. They looked as if there was nothing left behind them.

As for himself, he was beginning to feel drowsy. *They must be alive*, he insisted as he scrambled down the ladder. *They still sit upright*.

Sleepiness intensified abruptly as his feet found the surface below the lowest rung. Shuffling, he entered the penthouse. Everyone there was in trance, save one who was just arranging his mat by the wall as if to nap. The boy barely managed to roll out his own mat and lay down on it before he fell asleep.

In the monasteries that morning, no masters strolled the aisles with long batons. They all sat in trance. There were no resonant *Hrums*, no movement, no sounds at all. Throughout all Theedalit, everyone who could was in trance or asleep. Shopkeepers lay down in back rooms or amidst their merchandise and slept. Hansom drivers dozed on their seats as soon as they could unload their yawning fares. People who had no choice but to move about, did so unalertly. Fires dwindled in forges. Pottery wheels stood still. At his work table, Brokols sat with his head on his forearms, mouth open loosely, his breathing regular but slow.

To a lesser degree it was true in the Djezes too, and in Almeon. At sea, sullsi and serpents drowsed on the surface, and no sarrka molested them.

Brokols and Juliassa's servants, a middle-aged couple, normally went home after supper, and the newlyweds fended nicely for themselves in the evenings. Which came much sooner now than in early summer, and could be rather chilly for sitting in the garden, even as far south as Theedalit. So they sat at opposite sides of a table in their sitting room. Juliassa had returned to her project of writing down stories that Sleekit and K'sthuump had told her. Brokols was working on a project, diagramming and making lists.

The pull-bell jangled above their front door, and he got to his feet, crutching briskly off to answer.

Juliassa heard his near shout: "Eltrienn! My, it's good to see you! Come in! Come in! Juliassa, it's Eltrienn!"

She cleared her pen tip and capped her inkwell, then hurried to greet their guest. Eltrienn was grinning broadly. "So!" he said to Juliassa, and embraced her. "I turn my back and look what happens!"

He'd hardly blinked at her scar. It was far less conspicuous than it had been, though still plainly visible.

He turned to Brokols. "I got in late yesterday and had a good night's sleep. Then this morning I stopped at the Fortress to see if you were there. I wondered if you'd had anything to do with what happened to the Almaeic Fleet, and they told me all about it. Well, not all I'm sure, but the main features. I wasn't smart enough to ask if you were still at your old address. I had to go and find out for myself. Bostelli told me where you are, and that you two were married."

"Why don't we go in the parlor and sit," Brokols said. "You may know what we've been doing, but I'm afraid we know nothing about your activities. No one was talking about them. Perhaps no one knew."

"Would you like something?" Juliassa asked. "Wine? Cheese?"

Eltrienn was still grinning. "By all means. Both. And I promise not to say anything worth hearing till you're back."

She left for the pantry, and Eltrienn looked Brokols up and down. "So you did it! And she looks happy! That's good, that's good. I'll have to tell you, I was surprised. You were so, so un-Hrummean."

Brokols grinned back. "In your Hrummean idiom, I was something of a stick. Still am, I suppose, to a degree. But it's a condition that rather easily reduces, living in Hrumma. Especially with Juliassa."

Eltrienn laughed. "You must have shed quite a bit of it before she agreed to marry you. She's always been, or always was, a bit impulsive, but she's also *smart*. Wouldn't have agreed to marry someone she wouldn't be comfortable with. Or who couldn't have her the way she is.

"By the way. How is she? I saw a rather impressive scar."

"I'll let her tell you. We have a lot of talking to do, all of us."

They heard her feet in the uncarpeted hall, and turned to the door. She carried a cutting board with cheese and knife, and a bottle of wine. Then she got glasses from a cabinet and poured.

"So," said Brokols, "what did they tell you about our sink-the-fleet project?"

"Well, they said that after you and Reeno had developed a formula for gunpowder, and gotten grenade production underway, you'd come up with an idea to make what they referred to as 'mines,' like grenades as big as wine urns"—he gestured to indicate size—"that would blow a huge hole in a ship's bottom. That you took three schooners of them to Haipoor l'Djezzer and blew up the fleet at anchor there. That sullsi attached them to the hulls, underwater, and clockwork set them off after you were safely done."

He laughed again. "Simple enough to say, but how in Hrum's name did you ever pull it off?"

Brokols grinned. "Well, first of all, *I* didn't take them to Haipoor. When the time came, I was left here in Theedalit with my broken leg. Juliassa was in charge of actually destroying the fleet."

Juliassa told Eltrienn the whole story then, all but the rape, including Tirros's attempt to murder her, of Sleekit killing him, and of his burial at sea. Juliassa still trembled a bit, telling it, and when she'd finished, Eltrienn exhaled gustily through pursed lips.

"A person might be excused for wondering how Tirros got that way. Probably came into this life like that."

They'd almost neglected the wine, a dark and rather full-bodied vintage. Now Eltrienn refilled his glass. "I suppose it's my turn to tell." He chuckled. "It doesn't start out like much, but it had a considerable climax."

He described it all, from the landing at Agate Bay to his activities at Theedalit. "At about noon on the day we left the vicinity of Haipoor, Vessto told Killed Many we needed to speed up, that the southern army was getting close. That if we didn't move fast, they'd catch us between themselves and the army of the Haipoor District. Well, none of us wanted to find out what would happen if they did. The Haipoor forces might or might not consider us as friends; there'd already been some nasty little skirmishes when the tribesmen tried to go back through Gorrbian lines to their own camp. But to the southern army, beyond a doubt, we'd be a swarm of barbarian raiders.

"And Killed Many and his people had come to realize that an army of five thousand really wasn't very big after all, not in the open by daylight. So he never questioned Vessto, just had his signalman blow the signal, and the whole barbarian army began to jog. We jogged till midday, with a couple of short ten-minute breathers, staying on the north side of the Hasannu. The river.

"Finally Vessto said it was safe to slow down. I wondered at the time if his having had less than two hours rest had anything to do with that. But a little while later we could see a long train of dust, far off to the southeast, that had to be the southern army on the military road from Kammenak. It would hit the river behind us a ways. We seemed to be safe.

"At the next break, I said goodbye to Vessto and Killed Many. I'd decided I wanted to get home the quickest way possible, and that was through the isthmus to Kammnalit, where I'd be able to get a kaabor from the army. First I curled up by a haystack and slept till after dark. Then I started hiking, hard. I followed the military road most of the way, and made the two hundred-plus miles to the isthmus, on foot, in six nights on short rations. Comes from living with the Innjoka for all those weeks. During daylight I hid out and rested; got so I could doze instantly when I wanted.

"And I didn't have to hike all the way to Kammnalit. The army was already back at the north end of the isthmus, rebuilding the strong points, and I got a kaabor there. It took me six more days to get here, with a change of kaabors at Kammnalit."

He chuckled again. "The Gorballis left their cannons not far down the isthmus, where they'd been when we opened the dam. I knew what they were at first sight, even lying on their sides the way they were. I'm told they never fired them after the first two days, and they must have had a terrible time pulling them up the canyon as far as they had—rocky and rutted as it was. When they'd pulled out, they hadn't even righted them; just poured melted lead down their openings.

"I can't figure out why they made the wheels the way they did. They weren't much more than a foot in diameter, and ten inches wide. I'd have made wheels four feet high; they would have worked a lot better."

Brokols smiled. "Kryger no doubt designed them that way on purpose, and they must have followed his design exactly. With wheels like those, they'd never get them back to fight the Imperial Army. And I'll bet his design called for heavier barrels than they needed, too."

Brokols straightened. "So. What will you do next?"

"Enjoy three weeks leave. And then—I'm being posted as deputy commander of intelligence here! With the rank of major. An office job; it'll give me a chance to find some nice reckless young lady and court her.

"What about you?"

Brokols laughed. "I'm not really cut out to be a soldier. Of course, most people aren't."

He turned serious then. "The threat from Almeon isn't over, you know. What we won was time. Probably quite a lot of it, hopefully enough to prepare. I'll be working with Venreeno and a team he's assembling, to build a rifle, the shoulder gun you saw at Haipoor. We'll need them in large numbers. And cannons that can be set on the headlands to defend the firth, and small, mobile cannons for the army.

"I hate to say it, but things will have to change in Hrumma. And in the Djezes too, of course. I still have most of a small casket of the emperor's gold and jewels, and I'm going to start a college in Theedalit. To begin the teaching of Almaeic knowledge. If we stay as we are here, the emperor will have us yet, sooner or later."

Eltrienn nodded slowly. What Elver was saying made him uncomfortable, as if something dangerous was hidden there. Yet it seemed unarguably true, and he felt things stirring vaguely in his mind. To do with Gorrbul. And the barbarians.

"If you say so," he replied, and pulled his attention to Juliassa. "And you. What do you have planned?"

She smiled. "I'm still looking at a possibility; I haven't even talked with Elver about it yet. I want to be certain myself before I do."

When Eltrienn had gone, Juliassa refilled her husband's glass. "Dear," she said, "tomorrow I'd like us both to go and thank Panni for what he did for my face." Unasked, Panni had come to their home, laid his hand on the deep and vivid scar, and looked at her. Then both of them had seemed to disconnect from life for a long minute, standing blank and motionless, even to their eyes. When he took his hand away, the angry color was gone, and instead of a deep crease, all that was left was a white line of scar tissue.

It had awed Elver, and for the first time he began really seriously to think that there might be something to this belief in Hrum. Afterward though, he decided that the credit really belonged to Panni. Hrum or not, Panni was the one who'd done this thing.

"I thought you thanked him quite nicely at the time," Brokols said. "Especially after you'd looked in a mirror. But if you'd like, I'm quite willing."

"I would like. And I didn't know then that the nightmares would be gone too. Besides, I'd like to ask him something."

"Ah." About what she'd been so privately pondering, he supposed. "Very well. Right after breakfast?"

She nodded, then kneeling by his chair, embraced and kissed him.

After that she picked up the cheese and kitchen items and took them away. Meanwhile Elver crutched into his wireless room and did something he hadn't done before; he called Glembro Dixen at Haipoor n'Seechul. And told him what had happened to the fleet, not saying how or specifying his own role.

It wasn't new to Dixen, who it turned out had monitored wireless messages on the night of the sinking and intercepted others on ensuing days, from the fleet admiral and CIC across the ocean to the ISB in Larvis Royal.

He knew parts of the story that Brokols didn't, including the execution of Kryger and the imminent destruction of the invasion army; the last message had said it was a matter of hours at best before they were all dead or captured. That had been days ago.

Since then, Dixen had managed an appointment as advisor to King Labdallu, and been given two lovely wives. The ex-ambassadors agreed to stay in touch as long as their wireless equipment remained functional. It seemed to Brokols that Dixen and Djez Seechul might play an important part in what had to be done before another fleet arrived from Almeon.

Brokols and Juliassa went first to Tassi's penthouse, and learned that Panni had moved back to his cave, so they'd borrowed saddle kaabors at the palace and started out. Now, riding along the mildly upsloping ridge crest, Brokols and Juliassa could see far out over the ocean. The summer monsoon was well past, and the footfalls of their mounts raised puffs of dust. The sun stood at noon, not high as in early summer, but warm enough, even given the light seabreeze ruffling the empty seedheads of the thigh-deep grass.

They didn't find Panni at his cave. The man who met them said the sage was meditating somewhere along the ridge. He wasn't though. He was walking, looking out to sea, and when they spotted him, he turned as if he'd felt a touch, and waved. Brokols drew his crutch from the saddle boot, and they dismounted, leaving their kaabors to graze with reins trailing. Together they walked to meet Panni.

"We went to Tassi's to find you," Juliassa told him. "We hadn't known you'd moved."

"Yes. Tassi and I had finished what we were doing."

"What was it? That you were doing?"

"Two things. One, we were influencing the war."

Brokols eyebrows popped up. "Influencing the war?"

A grin wreathed the sunbrowned face. "Did not things go well? Very few mistakes? Luck remarkably good?"

"One can hardly argue with that. Things with that many factors impinging almost never go as planned." Still Brokols didn't let himself believe it then. "What was the second thing?"

The eyes grinned too. "Do you not remember?"

"Remember? What do you mean?"

"Was there a day you slept? The middle part of one? Recently?"

"Why, yes. Last Foursday. I couldn't stay awake, although I almost never nap. I've heard other people comment, too; they'd had the same sort of experience. It was as if something had blown in on the air. Some sleeping powder."

Panni laughed and looked at Juliassa expectantly. She nodded.

"I was practicing a dance for Harvest Festival," she said, "when suddenly the grass looked so inviting I had to lie down on it. I slept for about two hours. What was it?"

"Hrum called a great meeting. Everyone was there. You, me . . . all humans, the sullsi, the serpents . . ."

"Wait a minute," Brokols interrupted. "Where was this meeting?"

The clear old eyes twinkled at them. "On the other side of reality."

Brokols simply stared, nonplussed.

"And there were beings there I hadn't been aware of before, that run on two legs, with scales instead of skin or fur, great teeth like the sarrho, and hands with claws. They live in a land across the ocean, but not the one you came from. A vast land, I believe."

Brokols stared. "The sauroids. They hunt in packs. Close as it is, we've never settled on that continent, because of them. Them and the climate, and the harsh land itself."

He frowned. "But how could I have been there if I was sleeping at home?"

"Your body was at home. You left it behind."

"But . . ." He shook his head as if to clear fog away, then spoke more slowly. "If I left my body behind, how do you know I was there?"

"Hrum-In-Thee imaged a copy there. We all did. Why, I don't know; it wasn't necessary."

Brokols had no response to that, or nothing he could put into words.

"What were we doing there?" Juliassa asked curiously.

"Ah! Hrum had been considering discontinuing humankind in this playground. We are only his foster children, after all, here on condition. For too long, too many of us had been violating his purpose for the world—the reason most others had come here."

Brokols stared. "You mean he was going to kill us? With some epidemic or something?"

"No, not kill. Discontinue. We would cease to exist here. We and all our works. We'd have had to go elsewhere. Or be nowhere."

Brokols couldn't handle the concepts, and sidestepped. "I guess he decided in our favor then, eh? We're still here."

Panni nodded, chuckling. "We have been granted a charter, so to speak. You two are part of the reason."

Then, looking at Juliassa, Panni changed the subject. As if knowing he'd extended Brokols to his present limit. "There is something you wish to ask me."

She nodded. "But first I want to thank you again for what you did for my face. And my dreams! Tirros no longer—violates me and slashes my throat."

Panni's head bobbed. "And I wish to thank you, for what you did there in the harbor at Haipoor, and in the weeks leading up to it. Now, what is your question?"

"I—I wonder if I might study with you. Whether it's practical for a married woman. I'd like to become a master, but I can't live at a monastery."

"Yes, I will train you."

More tentatively then, she asked: "Do you think it will work?"

"I believe you have already seen your Kirsan and your Nasrik, yes?"

"More than once. Meditating when I was eleven and twelve. They didn't merge though."

"For one who sees them so young, the chances of Awakening are very good." He paused significantly. "Especially if one does not wish it intensely."

"Would she be expected to stay here?" Brokols asked worriedly. "At your cave?"

Panni smiled and shook his head. "You have a large yard

behind your house. If there was a small house there, of one room, where I could live, Juliassa could train at home."

She turned to her husband in delight. "May I, Elver?" Then, more soberly, "It's your home too."

Brokols remembered Master Jerrsio's wedding lines, remembered how right they'd seemed, and looked at Panni. "Will she change? Very much?"

"Oh, yes. But has she not already? And yourself! And you will continue to change, both of you.

"Why do you suppose disciples wish to live with Tassi? Or myself? Certainly it isn't the comforts that bring them, yet from time to time, we have to send some of them away. To cure them of dependence.

"To be much in the sphere of someone who has Awakened," Panni went on, "or who is progressing in that direction, is to change. In the direction of greater mastery of life. Unless, of course, one resists. Or strives too strongly."

"Well, then," Brokols said, suddenly businesslike, "how large shall I have it built?"

"Fifteen feet on a side will be abundantly large. The men who live with me here will not follow me when I move."

"Could you come to town and show us where you'd like it built? And what you'd like it to look like?"

Panni put a long brown hand on Brokols' shoulder. "Whatever you make it will be fine. And anywhere in your yard. It will be yours; I'll be but a visitor. It will be there still when I have gone.

"Now there is something else I must do." He knelt at Brokols' feet, and felt between the splints. "How long has it been since it was broken?"

"Um. Seven weeks I suppose, or eight. I've about as many more with this." He indicated the crutch.

"Have you tried to walk on it yet?"

"Oh, no. A broken shinbone takes fifteen weeks to heel enough for that. A dozen at the very least. I'd just undo what healing's taken place."

"Ah. Did I not touch it, not long after it was broken?"

Brokols frowned uncomfortably. He could see where this was leading. "Yes. And it reduced the discomfort considerably."

"Good. Do you suppose it had any healing effect?"

"Why—I suppose so. Some." He looked at Juliassa for help. She was smiling at him. Her fingers went to her face, reminding him of Panni's power.

"What," Panni said, "is a broken leg good for?"

Chills flowed over Brokols as he remembered. When they stilled, Panni thanked them for visiting him. They went to their kaabors, mounted, and turned back toward Theedalit. Brokols had still used his crutch, but as they rode, he was thinking that he might, just possibly, test the leg in a week or two. Very carefully of course.

"D'you suppose I could learn to meditate?" he asked.

"I don't see why not."

"Would I have to learn to sit with my legs folded together the way they do? I don't believe I ever could."

Juliassa laughed. "Don't be too sure. Think of all the things you've learned since you arrived."

He nodded thoughtfully. "I have, haven't I?"

and they lived quite happily
for a rather long time

Dramatis Personae

The characters listed here don't include those who appear or are mentioned in only one place, unless they have special significance. Names are listed alphabetically in the form usually mentioned. If commonly referred to by surname—for example, Brokols—the surname is given first and capitalized, thus: BROKOLS, Elver. If only one name is given in the story, for example Lardunno, the name is not capitalized, regardless of whether it is a surname or not.

Some readers feel more comfortable with names they can pronounce. In this story, most names are Hrummean, Djezian, barbarian, or sullsit. The convention is that the stressed syllable ends in a doubled letter, thus: ALLbarin VenjiANNi.

Allbarin Venjianni —counselor of the amirr of Hrumma
Always Fighting —youth name of the barbarian, Bloody Sword (see)
Amaadio Akrosstos—Hrummean herbalist
Argant—aide to Lord Kryger, Almaeic ambassador to Djez Gorrbul
BILLBIS—see Karrlis Billbis
Bloody Sword—Innjoka warrior, brother of chief
Borrsio—mythical Hrummean storm god; or, aspect of Hrum associated with storms
BOSTELLI, Arnello—landlord to Elver Brokols in Theedalit
BROKOLS, Elver—Almaeic ambassador to Hrumma
BRONT, Heskil—biologist on the warpship *Adanik Larvest*
CADRIIO, Eltrienn—see Eltrienn Cadriio
CADRIIO, Vessto—see Vessto Cadriio

Carrnos Frimattos—see Frimattos, Carrnos
Danntis Deltibbio—a centurion who accompanies the Cadriio brothers to Agate Bay
DISOTTO, Travvos—see Travvos Disotto
DIXEN, Glembro—Almaeic ambassador to Djez Seechul
Doziellos—Hrummean general at Kammenak
Eltrienn Cadriio—centurion, Hrummean intelligence officer, friend of Brokols
Ettsio Torillo—Hrummean ironmaker and timber merchant who opened trade with the barbarians; father of Sallvis Venettsio
Formaalu—see Grimmuh Formaalu
FRIMATTOS, Carrnos—handyman at Hidden Haven
Gamaliiu—king of Djez Gorrbul
Gerrla—widowed cook for the Bostellis; girlfriend of Stilfos
Gorrvis Vendorrci—Brokols' aide on the visit to Kammenak
Grimmuh Formaalu—commander of the Gorrbian invasion army
HANORISSIA, Juliassa—see Juliassa Hanorissia
HANORISSIA, Morrvia—the naamir (approximately queen) of Hrumma
HANORISSIA, Zeenia—see Zeenia Hanorissia
HANORISSIO, Leonessto—amirr (elective ruler) of Hrumma
HANORISSIO, Tirros—see Tirros Hanorissio
He Means It—youth name of Killed Many (see)
Heskil Brant—life support technician and last captain of warpship *Adanik Larvest*
Innjoka—the Agate River Tribe of barbarians
Jerrsio—master at the Theedalit Monastery
Jonkka Yelltis—Juliassa's (the namirrna's) bodyguard
Juliassa Hanorissia—namirrna (approximately princess) of Hrumma
Kaitmar III—("Great Kaitmar") the historical emperor of Almeon who completed the unification of the Almaeic Archipelago
Kaitmar IV—the historical emperor of Almeon who suppressed the Almaeic island province of Kelthos
Karrlis Billbis—a Hrummean adept, the criminal associate of Tirros Hanorissio
Killed Many—great chief of the barbarians
Kinnli Innjakot—the Agate Bay Clan of barbarians
Korvassu—Gorrbian lieutenant commanding a flotilla of raider boats

Krootar—a sellsu, packmate of Sleekit
KRYGER, Lord Vendel—Almaeic ambassador to Djez Gorrbul, and commander of Almaeic diplomatic mission to the droid states
s'Kthuump—an old female sea serpent
Labdallu—king of Djez Seechul
Lardunno—Hrummean government adept who goes with Eltrienn Cadriio on fact-finding mission to Gardozzi Bay
Lerrlia Vencurria—female associate of Tirros Hanorissio
LINFORRIO, Zivvas—a Hrummean adept employed by Mellvis Rantrelli
Lori Maloi—a biotech on the warpship *Adanik Larvest*
Lormallia—legendary "daughter of Hrum"; see Lori Maloi
Maatio—a Hrummean soldier in Vendunno's patrol
Marinnia Vencurria—female associate of Tirros Hanorissio
Panni Vempravvo—a sage, known as "the Lamp of Hrum"
Ramuulo—a Gorrbian soldier at Kammenak
RANTRELLI, Mellvis—a pious, politically active merchant of Hrumma
Reeno Venreeno—see Venreeno
Ressteto Istroovio—Ettsio Torillo's nephew, deputy factor at Agate Bay
Sallvis Venettsio—see Venettsio
Sellsu—singular of sullsi (see)
Sleekit—a sellsu, friend of Juliassa Hanorissia
Stedmer—captain of the Almaeic ship *Emperor Dard XII*
Stilfos—aide to Brokols
Sullsi—(singular, sellsu) "children of the waves"; intelligent marine mammals
Tarrni—young Hrummean fisherman who fights Tirros Hanorissio
Tassi Vermaatio—a sage, known as "the Is-ness of Hrum"
Terlenter—captain, warpship *Adanik Larvest*
Tirros Hanorissio—mirj (approximately prince) of Hrumma
TORILLO, Ettsio—see Ettsio Torillo
Torissia Korillias—Juliassa Hanorissia's young aunt and sometime chaperone
Travvos Disotto—Hrummean police inspector
Triivarum—a sellsu, packmate of Sleekit
Trinnia Akrosstas—wife of Amaadio Akrosstos
Tssissfu—a two-year-old sea serpent
VEMPRAVVO, Panni—see Panni Vempravvo

VENCURRIA sisters—see Lerrlia and Marinnia Vencurria
VENDORRCI—see Gorrvis Vendorrci
Vendunno—Hrummean lieutenant and patrol leader
VENETTSIO, Sallvis—factor at Agate Bay
VENJIANNI, Allbarin—see Allbarin Venjianni
VENREENO, Reeno—Hrummean adept and security agent
VERMAATIO, Tassi—see Tassi Vermaatio
Vessto Cadriio—a "country sage," known as "the Trumpet of Hrum"; brother of Eltrienn Cadriio
Vrronnkiess—sea serpent name for the sea serpents
WERLINGUS, Erlin—Almaeic midshipman, aide to Kryger
Zeenia Hanorissia—the amirr's sister, mistress at Sea Cliff

JOHN DALMAS

John Dalmas has just about done it all—parachute infantryman, army medic, stevedore, merchant seaman, logger, smokejumper, administrative forester, farm worker, creamery worker, technical writer, free-lance editor—and his experience is reflected in his writing. His marvelous sense of nature and wilderness combined with his high-tech world view involves the reader with his very real characters. For lovers of fast-paced action-adventures!

THE REGIMENT

The planet Kettle is so poor that it has only one resource: its fighting men. Each year three regiments are sent forth into the galaxy. And once a regiment is constituted, it never recruits again; as casualties mount the regiment becomes a battalion . . . a company . . . a platoon . . . a squad . . . and then there are none. But after the last man of *this* regiment has flung himself into battle, the Federation of Worlds will never be the same.

THE GENERAL'S PRESIDENT

The stock market crash of 1994 made the black Monday of 1929 look like a minor market adjustment . . . the rioters of the '90s made the Wobblies of the '30s look like country-club Republicans . . . Soon the fabric of society will be torn beyond repair. The Vice President resigns under a cloud of scandal— and when the military hints that they may let the lynch mobs through anyway, the President resigns as well. So the Generals get to pick a President. But the man they choose turns out to be more of a leader than they bargained for . . .

FANGLITH

Fanglith was a near-mythical world to which criminals and misfits had been exiled long ago. The planet becomes all too real to Larn and Deneen when they track their parents there, and find themselves in the middle of the Age of Chivalry on a world that will one day be known as Earth.

RETURN TO FANGLITH

The oppressive Empire of Human Worlds, temporarily foiled in *Fanglith*, has struck back and resubjugated its colony planets. Larn and Deneen must again flee their home. Their final object is to reach a rebel base—but first stop is Fanglith, the Empire's name for medieval Earth.

THE REALITY MATRIX

Is the existence we call life on Earth for real, or is it a game? Might Earth be an artificial construct designed by a group of higher beings—a group of which we are all members, and of which we are unaware, until death? Forget the crackpot theories, the psychics, the religions of the world—*everything* is an illusion, everything, that is, except the Reality Matrix! But self-appointed "Lords of Chaos" have placed a "chaos generator" in the matrix, and it is slowly destroying our world.

PLAYMASTERS (with Rod Martin)

The aliens want to use Earth as a playing field for their hobby and passion: war. But they are prohibited from using any technology not developed on the planet, and 20th-century armaments are too primitive for good sport. As a means of accelerating Earth to an appropriately sporting level, Cha, a galactic con artist, flimflams the Air Force Chief of Staff into founding a think-tank for the development of 22nd-century weapons.

*You can order all of John Dalmas's books with this order form. Check your choices below and send the combined cover price/s to: Baen Books, Dept. BA, 260 Fifth Avenue, New York, New York 10001.**

THE REGIMENT • 416 pp. • 65626-0 • $3.50 ______
THE GENERAL'S PRESIDENT • 384 pp. • 65384-9 • $3.50 ______
FANGLITH • 256 pp. • 55988-5 • $2.95 ______
RETURN TO FANGLITH • 288 pp. • 65343-1 • $2.95 ______
THE REALITY MATRIX • 352 pp. • 65583-3 • $2.95 ______
PLAYMASTERS • 384 pp. • 65610-4 • $3.50 ______

TIMOTHY ZAHN

CREATOR OF NEW WORLDS

"Timothy Zahn's specialty is technological intrigue-international and interstellar," says *The Christian Science Monitor*. Amen! For novels involving hard-edged conflict with alien races, world-building with a strong scientific basis, and storytelling excitement, turn to Hugo Award Winner Timothy Zahn!

Please send me the following books by Timothy Zahn:

____ COBRA, 352 pages, 65560-4, $3.50

____ COBRA STRIKE, 352 pages, 65551-5, $3.50

____ COBRA BARGAIN, 420 pages, 65383-0, $3.95

____ TRIPLET, 384 pages, 65341-5, $3.95

____ A COMING OF AGE, 320 pages, 65578-7, $3.50

____ SPINNERET, 352 pages, 65598-1, $3.50

____ CASCADE POINT, 416 pages, 65622-8, $3.50

Send the cover price to Baen Books, Dept. BA, 260 Fifth Ave., New York, NY 10001. Order soon, and as a bonus we'll also send you a copy of *THE WHOLE BAEN CATALOG*, which lists and describes all Baen titles currently available.
